Burning
Embers

HANNAH FIELDING

First published in the USA in 2012 by
Omnific Publishing

First published in the UK in 2014 by
London Wall Publishing Ltd (LWP)

This edition published in 2015 by
Andrews UK Limited
www.andrewsuk.com

Contents

The burning embers flicker,
Connection of two sights,
A touch of spark, wickers,
Forbidden its delight.
UNKNOWN

Burning
Embers

Chapter One

Coral Sinclair was twenty-five, and this should have been her wedding night. Instead, she watched a full moon sweep the Indian Ocean with silvery beams as a silent ship carried her through the night, its path untroubled by the rolling swell. It was misty, the air was fresh, and a soft breeze blew through her flowing blond hair. A solitary passenger on deck, outlined by a strapless, white-silk evening dress, she stood upright and still, her slender fingers clenching the rail, her voile scarf floating behind.

Coral could not sleep. She gazed into the tenebrous light, feeling helpless, lonely, and utterly wretched. Not a star interrupted that dense unity, not the smallest star, the tiniest speck of hope. The only sound was the thrumming of the ship's engines and the rhythmic echo of the waves smashing relentlessly against its hull.

After dinner she had paced up and down in her stuffy cabin, attempted to concentrate on a book, and flipped absentmindedly through a magazine. Unable to fix her attention, she had gone on deck to take some fresh air. It was deserted there except for rows of abandoned deck chairs. Their spectral shadows in the pale moonlight gave the place a desolate character that reflected her mood.

This had been a wonderful cruise, she told herself wistfully, attempting once again to snap out of her depression. She had not made the most of the trip, and she knew that she would regret it one day. After all, this was the kind of adventure Coral had dreamed of during the past years. She felt a lump in her throat. "No, not quite... " she whispered to herself. The circumstance that had induced her to make such a long journey was painful: she was going to take possession of her inheritance.

The ship was taking her back home — or at least the home she had known as a child in Kenya. *Mpingo*... Even the name warmed Coral's heart like the morning African sun. In Swahili, it meant *The Tree of Music*, named after the much sought-after dark heartwood used to make wind instruments. Like much of the white community in Kenya — an eclectic mix of landless aristocrats, big-game hunters, and ex-servicemen — Coral's family had originally been expatriate settlers. The desolate, treeless landscapes choked with dust and scorched with sun, which could have seemed menacing to some, had been perceived quite differently by Coral during those early years. For the imaginative child, every day had gleamed with tawny and emerald vistas to explore freely in the golden light of the African sun. She had imagined living there forever, and was unprepared when things abruptly changed.

Coral tried to recapture that clear morning in early April sixteen years ago when she had said farewell to the world she loved: to the sun, to Africa, and to her father. She had been nine years old, and although a lot of that period seemed blurry, certain memories remained vivid in her mind.

The constant quarrels of her parents had darkened an otherwise serene childhood. Often the memories came to haunt her nights, always dominated by the towering figure of her father, Walter Sinclair, a man whose debonair charm and reputation as an adventurer (not to mention his eye for other men's wives) had earned him the endearing nickname the *White Pirate* among the natives. Nevertheless, Coral had loved and admired her dashing father and had desperately missed him for a long time.

She remembered returning to England with her mother, Angela, in the spring of 1956, the divorce of her parents that followed, and being sent away to boarding school. That was the worst time. For a child who had known the wind-beaten spaces of the bush and the kaleidoscopic scenery of the tropical regions, this sudden confinement at an English school had been a restraint she found difficult to conform to, and never got used to. So she took refuge in the wonderful world of her nostalgic dreams throughout those seemingly never-ending years to womanhood, secretly vowing to return to her true home one day.

Then, when Coral was sixteen, her mother had married Sir Edward Ranleigh, a widowed barrister of great repute. The engagement had come as a shock to her despite his frequent visits to their flat in London. At first she had hated him and flatly refused to attend their wedding. Coral could not imagine someone taking her father's place in her mother's heart — or in her bed.

Uncle Edward, as she called him, was a jolly and gregarious man, a *bon viveur*, generous and unpretentious. Like her father, he had traveled the world, not so much to amass a fortune but mostly for his own pleasure. They had all moved to his luxurious flat overlooking St. James's Park in London and spent most of their holidays at his country home, Ranleigh Hall, in Derbyshire. With quiet patience, Edward had won her over. He had taught her how to ride and how to sail, and stimulated her imagination with stories of his adventures in foreign countries. Gradually, Coral got used to his presence around them, and her attitude toward him softened. Within a few months they were friends.

The year after had turned her world upside down again with the birth of twins to the newly wedded couple: Lavinia and Thomas, her half siblings. Coral had felt disturbed by the sudden, dramatic change to her life. She had carefully hidden her feelings and would have gladly moved back to Kenya, but it was made quite clear to her that relocating was not an option. Again, she resigned herself, and with time and the patient help of Uncle Edward, who considered Coral his daughter, she had warmed to the children and even learned to care for them. Then on Coral's eighteenth birthday, Uncle Edward held a ball in her honor and put a large sum of money in a trust for her. By then she had made peace with the new way of life that had been forced upon her. She loved the twins and was very fond of Uncle Edward, but he had never replaced her father in her heart, and she still longed for Kenya, the land of her happy childhood.

Lost in thought, Coral stood on tiptoe and bent over the rail to watch the seething white horses in the ship's wake. The salty mist blew about her, sending strands of hair across her eyes, and she pushed them away from a wide forehead to let the fine spray refresh her face. Coral never contemplated that circumstances such as these would take her home, and she returned to thoughts of where she had intended to be this evening, her wedding night. "A Fairytale Wedding" the gossip pages had declared unanimously. She had met Dale Halloway, a young American tycoon, at the 1968 opening of the Halloway African Exhibition in New York City. It had been her first professional journalism assignment abroad, a commission to cover the story and take pictures of the fabulous African sculptures and paintings, which offered a golden opportunity to further her career and one not often presented to young photographers, particularly women. Although things were changing fast and 1970 was heralding an exciting new decade, it was still hard to break into such a male-dominated world. Coral had wanted to be a photographer as long as she could remember, and while all her friends had grown up and followed the predictable path of marriage, Coral was pursuing her dream career.

When she'd met Dale at the exhibition, it had been love at first sight. He'd had the looks of an all-American hero and something of a *Great Gatsby* style about him. Always in the latest Halston or Ralph Lauren suit, he epitomized the powerful and successful American tycoon. That Dale and his family had connections with Africa contributed to the attraction. Dale's frequent travels round the African continent often took him to Kenya, and his stories helped to satisfy Coral's thirst for information about life back in the country she missed so dearly.

The couple had been inseparable for months, and although Coral had spent her late teens and early twenties watching the sexual revolution unfold around her, she herself had vowed to keep her virginity until her wedding night, and so the relationship had remained chaste. Dale had been equally smitten by Coral but was less enthusiastic about her traditional views on sex before marriage. Nevertheless, he had reassured her that he would wait until she was ready, and as they were living on opposite sides of the Atlantic, leading their own separate lives, the months seemed to fly by. After eighteen months, they had announced their engagement. The wedding was to take place three months later in New York, and they planned to go to Kenya for their honeymoon.

On a holiday weekend, she had flown to New York, unannounced, to surprise her fiancé. The nasty surprise had been all hers, since Dale showed little concern when she arrived at his office and caught him red-handed kissing his secretary. *The typical cliché*, she thought. Heartbroken, she had fled from the room and returned to England that same evening.

A month later, Coral had received a letter from a solicitor announcing that her father had died and she was the heiress to a substantial legacy in Kenya. The letter had been delayed — the post in Africa was not that reliable — and she had not been able to attend his funeral. In the space of a few months, her life, which until then had been quite uneventful and orderly, had become chaotic and uncertain.

Inertia had overwhelmed her. For some time, Coral had let herself drift from one day to the next, unable to think straight or make any decisions. Then, out of the blue, something cropped up. Her mother's friends, Dr. Thomas Atkinson, a member of the World Health Organization, and his wife were leaving for Somalia in the new year. They had been able to secure passenger berths on a cargo ship out of London calling at Kilindini, the new port of Mombasa in Kenya. Coral needed to return to Kenya to claim her inheritance and sort out her father's affairs, and this fortuitous offer had brought her to her senses.

"It will give you time to recover from the painful experience you've been through," her mother had stated, "and will be a chance to go on a leisurely cruise around the African ports, an opportunity you may never have again. Besides, things have changed in Kenya since Mboya's assassination. People say that President Kenyatta himself was behind it, but who knows. This tribal politics is getting out of hand. One day, you might not be able to go back to Africa, darling." As usual, her mother had been blunt.

Coral sighed. Although she was excited at the prospect of returning to her childhood home, Mpingo would not be the same without her father. She shivered.

"Are you cold?" A soft, deep voice emerged from the darkness behind her, disturbing her reverie.

Startled, Coral jumped and swung around.

"Here, this will keep you warm," said the stranger, slipping off his jacket and wrapping it around her bare shoulders.

She gazed at the man standing before her in the shadows. She tried to make out his features, and then recognized him as the new passenger who had joined the ship that morning when it had docked at the port of Mogadishu. She had been standing on deck, waving at Dr. Thomas and his wife who had just disembarked, and had noticed him coming up the gangplank. Again in the evening she had caught a glimpse of him at dinner, sitting at the captain's table.

He was tall, dark, and lean. In the moonlight, the eyes that viewed her with slow appraisal seemed black, but she guessed that in daylight they would have reflected other tones. His was not an outstandingly handsome face; it held something stronger, more powerful than conventional good looks: a blatant sensuality, a charismatic magnetism that drew her attention despite her desire to ignore him.

"These tropical nights are deceptive," he said. "The cold can take you by surprise." The stranger had a French accent, with a distinct lilt that was not unattractive.

Coral nodded in acknowledgment of his words and smiled demurely, revealing the small dimple at the corner of her mouth.

"We'll be arriving soon."

"What time is it?" she asked.

"It's four o'clock. In a few minutes, dawn will break over the horizon from there." She was disturbed by his close proximity, his shirt sleeve inadvertently brushing against her cheek as he pointed at some invisible spot. "Sunrise on the Indian Ocean is a breathtaking sight, especially when you're watching it from the deck of a ship." He spoke with a warmth that made the deep pitch of his voice quiver slightly.

Another day is starting. Sadness flooded her. Who knew how much more sorrow and loneliness it would bring? Hot tears welled up in Coral's eyes, clouding her view. Soon they would spill over uncontrollably, and the last thing she wanted was to make a spectacle of herself in front of this stranger. She clenched her teeth and swallowed hard.

"Is there anything I can do to help?"

Coral shook her head. Usually she would have resented this intrusion into her grief, but in an odd way she found his concern quite soothing.

She turned her face toward the stranger. He had edged away and was watching her, arms folded across his chest. His eyes crinkled into a smile. What did he want? Was he looking for an adventure? Surely not, Coral thought. He seemed unlike the young men she had so often met in her social circle. He was not even a young man, but simply a man: warm, compassionate, and tactful.

She relaxed. "You seem to know this part of the world," she ventured, now looking down at the dark ocean beneath them.

"I was born in Africa."

"In Kenya?"

"No, in French Guinea. I came to Kenya only eight years ago, but I've traveled around this continent quite a bit." There was a momentary lull, and the tone of his voice dropped a little. "Untamed Africa… " he whispered as though to himself.

Something in the way he uttered those words made Coral lift her head. The words of her mother echoed through her mind: *Things have changed in Kenya…* She turned toward him and met the dark gaze that was fixed on her face. He looked hard into her blue eyes and smiled in the semi-darkness. Suddenly she felt the urge to confide in this calm and reassuring man. "I was also born in Africa," she murmured, "but I left a long time ago, and so many things have changed since then that I'm dreading what awaits me there."

They stood close to each other, almost touching. His hand reached out and, with infinite tenderness, covered the slender fingers clenching the rail. A pleasant warmth flooded her. She was afraid to move in case she disturbed that initial, yet powerful, contact. For a fleeting moment, in this wan light and because he spoke gently, her wounded heart yielded to this stranger's soothing voice.

The sky was slowly clearing on the horizon. The black cloak of night began to lift, lazily giving way to a monochromatic dawn of decreasing hues, from indigo to steel blue. The first rays of the African sun broke through in the distance, a sallow slip of color outlining the eastern horizon. Coral felt the stranger looking at her, and heat suddenly rose in her cheeks.

Their eyes locked. She shuddered and pulled his jacket closer around her shoulders. As his gaze dropped to her soft, full lips, he flushed under his deep tan, then suddenly seemed to check himself and turned away. Coral, whose head and heart were throbbing, stood there silently, staring up at him with a mixture of curiosity and wonderment. The sensation she was experiencing was totally new to her. It was as if an unspoken affinity had been discovered and a connection established all in a single moment.

Variant tones of pink were gently spreading into the sky, struggling to seep through the symphony of blues. A few moments later the sun burst forth, dazzling in this multicolored canopy, and the dark outline of the landscape gradually loomed on the horizon, transforming first into the dark green, gray, and russet skirt of the jungle before revealing the bush, rising in layers toward the backcountry. Soon after, the port of Kilindini became visible, comfortably tucked away at the end of the estuary in the midst of vigorous vegetation. Coral could see it peeping out from behind serried ranks of coconut palms and wispy casuarinas trees, while its old lighthouse winked with steadfast tranquility in the half light. To complete the picture, the coastline of thin rolling sand dunes appeared, creating here and there immaculate white beaches.

Even with her mind awash with childhood memories, Coral found it difficult for her eyes, accustomed to the more sedate English countryside, to take in all at once the opulence of color, the sense of space, and the profusion of brilliant life. The burning sky seemed too blue, the rich soil too red, and the irrepressible vegetation too green.

Coral was overcome by emotion, remembering the last time she had seen this landscape. She thought of her father, who today would not be waiting for her. How empty her childhood home would seem without him. A lump formed in her throat, and she bit her lower lip while fighting to control the tears quivering on the edge of her eyelashes. Unable to restrain them for long, they spilled over and down her cheeks. She had forgotten her companion's presence while engrossed in her sadness, so she gave a faint start when he spoke.

"Please don't… " he whispered softly.

She did not answer; she did not even move. She simply stood there, limp and weary, tears continuing to mar her lovely features. He brushed her chin lightly with the tip of his forefinger and gently turned her drawn face toward him. With a white handkerchief he produced from his pocket, he carefully wiped away her tears.

"An African proverb says that sorrow is like rice in the pantry: it diminishes day by day." Despite his solemn tone, he looked at her with laughing eyes that the morning light had turned golden brown but remained almost as hypnotic as they had been in the moonlight.

"Forgive me," Coral murmured, smiling through her tears. "I didn't intend to make a spectacle of myself. It was rather childish, I suppose."

He gave a vague motion of his head and winked at her. "Even big boys cry sometimes, you know." There was a slightly hard edge to his words, and once again she caught herself thinking how appealing she found his husky voice.

In the light of this splendid dawn, the ship entered the port of Kilindini. All was still. The sea was smooth and glossy, the water so transparent that Coral could see where rainbow-colored fish dozed lazily among waving coral branches.

"We won't be disembarking before midday. You have time to rest for a while," the stranger said. "Come, I'll take you back to your cabin." Without being bossy, he came across as a self-assured man who was in the habit of making decisions and was unaccustomed to anybody resisting his will.

Coral acquiesced and gave him back his jacket. "My cabin is downstairs," she told him. As he took her elbow, she tried to ignore the tiny shockwave that pulsed through her body. She steadied herself and let him guide her to the floor below. "Just here," she whispered when they reached the door.

Coral stared up at him, meeting the brooding dark eyes that engaged her thoughtfully. He placed his large hands on her shoulders. Coral was petite, and he towered over her willowy figure. She became aware of how dangerously close she was to his hard, muscled body. His head was bent toward hers, his gaze fixed upon her parted lips. For a few seconds, she thought he would actually draw her to him and kiss her. Her pulse raced as she held her breath, but his jaw stiffened, his eyes clouded, and his grip tightened just a little on her bare shoulders.

"Now, young lady, you must force yourself to sleep." His tone was light, but his voice seemed deeper. "You'll feel much better for it." He relaxed his fingers, let his palms linger for a moment longer on her skin, then let his arms fall to his side. "Come now… sleep tight," he said before turning abruptly on his heels and striding away.

Confusion suddenly sprang up in Coral's mind. Was she disappointed or relieved that he had released her? She could not say; she was only conscious of the furious beat of her heart and the chaos of her thoughts. Never before had she felt such an immediate attraction. It was only when the cabin door closed behind her that she realized she did not even know the name of her kind Samaritan.

She lay on the bunk and closed her eyes, hoping to sweep away all thoughts of him, but it was to no avail — he had moved in there, large as life. Images of him crept into her mind: his powerful, tanned hands running over her body, those strong arms pressing her against him, his full mouth kissing her passionately. Was she going mad? She knew nothing of the man, neither his name nor where he came from. Nevertheless, a shiver ran up her spine as she recalled how he had touched her for a moment and she had felt the warmth of his palms against her skin. Her female senses told her that this would be a lover whose caresses, once experienced, would never be forgotten. Instinct urged her to run and hide, while logic told her she was acting like a silly teenager; he was probably married with half a dozen children, and their paths would never cross again.

***

Coral woke up with a start. Someone was knocking on the door — short, sharp, repeated raps. She must have dozed off, she realized as she wobbled to the door and opened it.

A young man with a dazzling smile gazed straight into her sleepy eyes. "Miss Coral Sinclair?"

"Yes, that's me," she said a little uncertainly.

"Splendid! Robin Danvers at your service. I'm the manager of Mpingo, come to welcome you and drive you to your home."

"What time is it?" Coral ran her fingers through her rumpled hair.

He grinned. "It's eleven o'clock."

"I must have fallen asleep," she mumbled. "Please forgive me; I'm not quite ready yet."

"There's no hurry. If you'd care to give me your passport, I'll see to your luggage."

The solicitor for her father's estate had mentioned in his letter that Robin Danvers, the manager of Mpingo, would be meeting her at the ship. Somehow, she had imagined an older man. Dressed in a white, short-sleeved safari shirt and dark trousers, he looked very clean-cut and not unattractive.

"Here you go," she said as she retrieved her passport from her bag and handed it to the young man. "I'll be ready when you come back."

"Are those your cases?" He pointed to two stacked trunks.

She smiled, slightly embarrassed. "I'm afraid they're rather large."

"Not to worry. I have brought the customs agent on board to clear your luggage. Then I will take them down with me and tend to any other formalities. Take your time. In Africa, we live at a slower pace," he added cheerfully. "The challenges of everyday life here have taught the Kenyans to take every day as it comes and live for the moment. You'll become accustomed to it in no time. It's a very wise and infectious philosophy — we call it going *pole-pole*, slowly slowly."

He took leave of her, and Coral was alone again with a moment to gather her thoughts. After saying goodbye to her knight-errant, she had stretched out on the couch, closed her eyes, and let her mind wander. The last thing she remembered was trying to imagine an alternative sequence of events, had circumstances been different — had he kissed her instead of leaving her so hastily at her cabin door. It was probably at that moment she had drifted into a deep, dreamless sleep. She actually felt much better for it: rested and enthusiastic. He had said she would, and the thought made her smile. Coral wondered whether she would see him again, deciding that she should be on the lookout for him, only to thank him for his kindness, of course.

Thankful that her fresh looks needed no artificial makeup, Coral applied just a tinge of transparent gloss on her lips and pinched her cheeks to add some color to them. Her mirror reflected eyes that were cornflower bright and shiny. Needing some practical traveling clothes for the journey, she had changed into hip-hugging, white cotton flared trousers that accentuated her long, shapely legs. The blue and white striped man's shirt, ends tied in a big knot at the waist, enhanced the golden tan she had acquired sunbathing on deck and set off the slenderness of her figure. She had just finished putting her hair in a French braid when Robin Danvers returned to fetch her.

Coral stood on the deck at the top of gangplank, dazzled by the reflection of the blazing light. The late morning sun spread its fan of fire over the shimmering sea. The baking heat was suddenly very familiar, and she did not dislike it. Here and there flying fish erupted from the water in a show of sparkles. The air was heavy with redolent scents. It was all coming back to her now: the blend of tar, sea, ropes, moldy timber, spices, and dry fish that haunts every port but which Coral mentally associated with Kenya and her childhood.

After the stillness of her cabin, the noisy clamor that filled the port had a physical impact. Blaring sirens of cargo boats carrying exotic merchandise alternated with the shrill whistles of panting tugboats towing their timber rafts. From time to time they would be drowned out by the din of heavy billets crashing down into the holds. But it was the continuous creak of the harbor's thick chain booms that grated on her already strained sensibilities.

Down on the quay, the colorful, mixed crowd of African natives, foreigners, animals, and cars was creating its own kind of chaos. Kenyan men and women chatted away, laughing, shouting, and jostling each other. Some hoisted sacks and crates onto trucks bound for Mombasa and the capital, Nairobi; others clustered round stalls of food, noisily bartering with vendors. Children darted through a sea of legs as horns beeped, goats bleated, and chickens flew up in all directions.

It had been too many years since Coral had been caught up in such a scene, and after the peaceful solitude of the ship, it was unexpectedly all too much. She hesitated a moment and looked behind her for Robin Danvers, hoping that he would lend her the courage to face this intimidating new world, but the young manager was nowhere to be seen. Struck by sudden panic, she was on the point of returning to the security of her cabin when a firm hand grasped her by the arm.

"Your companion is not far behind," said a deep, comforting voice she instantly recognized. "He's been held up. We're blocking the traffic. Come, let's go down together. He will meet you on the pier, no doubt." It was not a suggestion but an order. His grip was such that it gave her no option but to be marched down the wobbly gangplank and hustled through the crush toward a vaguely familiar looking dark-green Buick parked twenty yards away.

They had almost reached the car when Robin Danvers joined them, quite out of breath. "Forgive me, Miss Sinclair, if I've kept you waiting," he panted. "I was held up by some customs official."

"That's all right, Robin," she replied absentmindedly, still a little shaken up. "This gentleman very kindly looked after me. By the way," Coral added, turning to address her rescuer, "I don't even know — " But he had already disappeared among the motley crowd. "He was here a moment ago," she cried out, failing to conceal her irritation.

"I wouldn't worry," said the young manager sharply. "He must have been in a hurry to find his family."

Coral shrugged her shoulders dismissively but remained perplexed, feeling as if she was missing something. How did the stranger know where to guide her to go? They reached the car, and a Kenyan chauffeur smoothly appeared to hold the door open for her. "*Karibu*. Welcome, Miss Coral," he said with a smile. His inquisitive, friendly eyes reminded her how instinctively warm the Kenyans were, how much they delighted in hospitality.

"Moses is one of the drivers attached to Mpingo," explained Robin. "He is loyal and has been working with us for eight years. He also speaks good English."

"Hello, Moses." She returned the driver's radiant smile.

"I'm afraid I must ask you to wait another ten minutes," apologized the manager. "There are some formalities that still need to be dealt with. The bureaucracy here is quite overwhelming. I hope you'll be comfortable in the car. I suggest you pull down the blinds, which should make it a little cooler and protect you from prying eyes. Mr. Sinclair never got around to installing air-conditioning in this car. He didn't much care for it."

"You forget I was born here; I don't mind the heat," she reassured him. "Besides, I will enjoy watching the crowd. I am as curious about them as they are about me."

He laughed. "Very well, but if you feel the need for some privacy, don't hesitate to call Moses. He'll take care of you." Turning to the driver, he spoke to him in Kiswahili. It sounded somewhat familiar to Coral, even though she could not understand a word of it. Long ago, she had spoken Kiswahili, and now that her stay in Kenya could turn out to be a long one, she hoped that it would come back to her with practice.

Coral climbed into the back of the Buick and watched out the window as the manager headed off toward the gray buildings at the far end of the quay, next to which stood long warehouses stacked high with sacks and bales. At the doorway to the buildings, tall, slim, African women were making ropes.

Coral turned her attention to the gigantic cranes swiveling in the air. They reminded her of steel-fanged dragons on the lookout for their next victim as they lifted and lowered their strange cargoes bound for new shores. It was clear that the port was flourishing these days. Coral had kept up with the news in Kenya and knew that while the president, Jomo Kenyatta, was criticized by some for his increasingly autocratic governing of the country, Kenya was at least reaping the economic benefits of increased exports and aid from the West. A vision of a new Kenya seemed to be constructing itself in front of her eyes. And then, farther away to the right, where the marshy green belt of grassland sloped down gently toward the ocean, she saw an age-old scene. Magnificent, half-naked, ebony athletes went to and fro, some carrying on their shoulders and others on their heads, heavy loads brought in by rowing boats from larger vessels anchored off shore.

Coral's gaze wandered back to the stream of people bustling about frantically on the docks. She scrutinized this hodgepodge of form and color, searching for her stranger.

Suddenly she spotted him. He was striding energetically toward a luxurious, black Cadillac Fleetwood that had just glided into the port. For the first time, she took a good look at him from afar. A giant of a man, he was tall and elegant in his impeccably cut Yves Saint Laurent suit and dark glasses.

His overt magnetism, even projecting from this distance, went straight to Coral's stomach. The Cadillac pulled up to meet him, and the back door slid open before the uniformed chauffeur had time to step out. Intrigued, Coral strained her eyes so as not to miss any part of the goings-on, but her efforts were poorly rewarded. She only had time to glimpse the heavily bejeweled arm of a woman reaching out to draw him into the rolling palace, which immediately turned around to disappear into the dense traffic.

Robin Danvers was taking his time, and she was tired of watching the scenery around her. She laid her head back, closed her eyes, and concentrated on her own thoughts. No matter how hard she struggled to control them, they seemed to catapult themselves right back to her elusive stranger. Who was this man? His bearing, his commanding voice, everything about him spelled out self-confidence, power, and success.

"There, I've finished at last," declared the manager, jerking Coral from her meditation. "I hope you haven't found the wait too long."

"Actually, quite the reverse," she told him. "The bustle in your port provided great entertainment. So many things seem to be happening here."

"The port of Kilindini has become the largest and the most modern port in East Africa," he explained. "It serves the whole of Kenya and bordering countries. But the truly fascinating parts of Mombasa are the old harbor and the old Arab town that lie at the other end of the city near the Mombasa Shooting Club. We could have lunch there. On Saturdays they put on a special luncheon for ladies, who otherwise are not allowed in. After lunch, if you're not too tired, you could browse around the shops before we start back to Mpingo."

Coral welcomed the suggestion enthusiastically. She had missed breakfast and hardly touched dinner the night before. The heat and the humidity were making her feel slightly faint, and lunch in civilized surroundings seemed a very sensible idea.

They crossed the town, passing through the opulent district where the white settlers, the mzungus lived; here the roads were fringed with their colonial-style villas whose red-tiled roofs were buried under cascades of scarlet bougainvillea, purple wisteria, and yellow mimosa. Gray concrete office blocks and tourist shops occasionally interrupted this colorful sprawl, punctuated here and there by clumps of Arab-style houses, the last remnants of ancient harems. Soon the brooding bulk of Fort Jesus rose into view, guarding the old harbor. They drove past the pink walls before entering the port through high gates. By now, the sun was scorching. Some hundred dhows — graceful, lateen sailboats built to an age-old pattern — dozed, lying apathetically on their sides on the beach.

Moses parked the car in the square next to the Old Custom House, and emerging from the car, Coral felt as though she had entered a new world. Here the atmosphere was impregnated with an eastern ambience of magic, intrigue, and spice.

They walked through a warren of twisting, narrow, unpaved streets. On either side were clusters of tiny houses welded together like honeycomb cells and dark smoky shops where the tangy scent of incense lingered.

"This is where most of the trade takes place: the shopper's heaven," explained Robin as they passed vendors of exotic perfumes, dealers of second-hand Persian rugs, and merchants offering Zanzibar chests at discount prices. He led the way, carefully picking a path through the swarm of sly traffickers, smugglers, corrupt policemen, and provocative hookers who shared the space. "Hang on to your bag," he recommended as he took Coral's arm. "This neighborhood is pick pockets' heaven."

She shrugged her shoulders dispassionately. "That's all part of the atmosphere." She loved the unhurried way the people moved, wrapped in happy languor. They stopped from time to time to talk, haggle, or simply admire the variety of merchandise spread out in front of them. "I could spend days rummaging in these dark Ali Baba caves. Who knows, I may just stumble upon an old treasure."

"I hope you're not thinking of venturing around here alone. It would be very unwise," Robin declared. "This district is run by dangerous gangs. From time to time, European women have been attacked. In some cases they have disappeared, never to be found."

His quick speech and emphatic tone irritated Coral. "The people seem to be harmless enough."

"That's just where you're mistaken. Slave trafficking has not been completely eradicated from some parts of the Middle East, you know."

"I'll bear that in mind when on my next expedition," she retorted. The idea seemed rather far-fetched, but she decided to keep the peace and change the subject. She listened with only half an ear to Robin lecturing her about life in Kenya. She found him boring and patronizing. Pity, since he was so good-looking. What a waste! Unconsciously, she compared him to her elusive stranger, wishing she was having lunch with Sir Lancelot, as she had named him.

She concentrated on the exotic surroundings. In the midst of the clamorous hum of the crowd, she could single out the monotonous tapping of a craftsman's hammer. From time to time, it was covered by the full-throated cry of a seller, the lamenting wail of a beggar, the repeated trill of a bicycle bell, and very occasionally, by the panic-stricken horn of an automobile.

They turned onto a dark street bordered with small houses of coral rag. The space was so narrow that in some places the upstairs balconies touched those on the opposite side. She had read somewhere that a few of these tiny streets had been built only wide enough for a camel to pass, and that the houses owed their curious color to the large bricks carved out of soft coral which had been allowed to dry to a hard consistency before being used. She thought they probably looked much the same as they had in the early sixteenth century.

"We've arrived," announced Robin as the Mombasa Shooting Club came into view. It was very much what Coral had expected it to be: a little bit of England transplanted into Africa. They climbed a flight of marble stairs and found themselves in a wide hall with a floor of polished teak. A portrait of the queen had prominent place over the fireplace and regally dominated the room. The furniture was European and so were the pictures and carpets. The smell of beeswax lingered everywhere, reminding her of home, and the restaurant resounded with English voices.

They sat next to a window overlooking a sun-flooded garden and the sparkling sea beyond. "I'm afraid only sensible English cooking is served here," Robin told her. "You would need to try one of the local restaurants for anything more adventurous."

"The sole recollection I have of Kenyan food is *ugali*," she said with a little laugh. "It was a main part of my childhood. Aluna, my *yaha*, used to insist on serving me a bowl every morning. Actually, I quite liked it. It's very similar to porridge. By the way, how is old Aluna? I assume she still lives at Mpingo? After Mummy and I left, she didn't stay in touch, even though I wrote many letters to her, especially at the beginning."

"Aluna is still there," he said in an even tone of voice. He paused shortly, then added, rather guardedly perhaps, "She has been very affected by Mr. Sinclair's death, and — "

"And?" prompted Coral, sensing the young man's reluctance to continue.

The manager fidgeted in his seat. Uncomfortable seconds elapsed during which he seemed to be considering his thoughts and carefully picking his words before answering. "Since your father's death, poor Aluna hasn't been quite herself," he said finally. "During the two first weeks that followed his demise, she neither spoke nor ate. The news of your imminent arrival, though, has seemed to revive her. It's as if she's been given something new to live for. However, she's still silent for long periods, and when she does talk, she tells strange stories that come from old superstitions and her own hallucinations."

"It doesn't surprise me that Aluna has been so deeply affected. She's been with the family since the early years. She was in her twenties when she came to Mpingo. She was there when the new house was being built. Daddy taught her English."

She smiled ruefully. Looking back, she had mixed feelings about those times. As she recalled, Walter Sinclair and Aluna used to stay for hours in her father's study, a detached outbuilding at the bottom of the garden, while he taught her Shakespeare's language. She remembered her mother's resentment and understood it better now. Aluna was a handsome woman, in her prime in those days, and Coral now knew that Walter was known to have a roving eye. He had found in Aluna an intelligent pupil. He had given her classic books to read and even introduced her to opera, which she took to quite seriously, to the extent of wandering around the house warbling arias from *La Traviata* while getting on with her daily chores. He used to say that if she had been born in a different society, she would have gone far. "She has the brain of a scholar. Pity there's so much mumbo jumbo still lingering in there — a strange mixture," he had declared on one occasion. Coral wondered now if there had been an untoward relationship between her father and her yaha. That would explain why Angela Sinclair had decided so suddenly to leave Africa for good, taking her daughter with her.

They ate silently. "How did my father die?" she ventured eventually.

"One day, his heart simply stopped beating," Robin answered slowly.

"He was such a healthy man."

"Your father was seventy when he died. He was not a young man anymore, and during the last couple of years, he had been through a great deal of physical and mental stress."

"Daddy was always energetic and fit," Coral stated emphatically. "He never looked his age. I met someone a few years ago who had seen him and had been astonished to learn he was over sixty." She paused. "Daddy loved Africa and his life. What possible stress could he have had? I was not aware that he was sick. Hasn't the estate prospered?"

She heard Robin suck in his breath, but he recovered his composure almost immediately. "Mr. Sinclair had developed a serious drinking problem. If his heart hadn't given way, sclerosis of the liver would have definitely killed him within a few months. It grieves me to tell you this, Miss Sinclair, but most nights Aluna and Juma, the head servant, had to carry him up to his room in a stupor."

Her eyebrows knitted together in a puzzled frown. "Why was that? Did my father have problems? Was the estate not running properly? I wasn't aware that he was in financial difficulty."

The manager looked offended. "The estate is running perfectly well, I can assure you. I manage it myself. You can have a look at the accounts and see for yourself this afternoon when we get back if you would like. Everything is in order."

Coral repressed an irritated gesture. This was not about the estate manager, but about her father. "This afternoon will be fine," she said curtly. There was a lull in the conversation before she spoke again. "Did Daddy have a fall during one of his drunken sessions? Is that how he died?"

"No. Mr. Sinclair died in his bed, in his sleep. Mrs. Sinclair discovered him in the morning. She called the family doctor who, after a thorough examination, said that he had died a natural and peaceful death. He went to sleep and didn't wake up."

"Did you say Mrs. Sinclair?" Coral was taken aback. "I wasn't aware that my father had ever remarried!"

Robin Danvers coughed to clear his voice. He was obviously finding this conversation painful. "Your father remarried a few years ago to the present Mrs. Sinclair, Mrs. Cybil Sinclair."

"We knew nothing of this marriage. Surely Daddy would have written to us about it? Why would he keep this from us? Even after the divorce, my mother and father remained friends," Coral protested. "True, he seldom wrote, but what I mean is, their divorce was not acrimonious." A shadow passed over her eyes. "I suppose he felt really estranged from us after Mother's marriage to Uncle Edward — like he had lost us forever. Every year at Christmas, I sent him a recent photograph of myself, telling him about anything important that had happened in my life; he never commented, though he sent me a Christmas card." She remained thoughtful for a few seconds. "The lawyer's letter never mentioned a wife. Does this mean that I'm not the sole heiress to my father's property?" She disliked the way she sounded, grabbing and uncaring. Still, she sensed something was wrong, and she wanted to get to the bottom of it.

"Tim Locklear, the lawyer who has been in charge of your father's interests, is in a much better position than I am to explain to you the intricacies of it all. I'm sure he'll answer all your questions."

It was clear that the estate manager was uncomfortable discussing such family concerns with her, and despite the fact that she did not care much for him, she was sensitive to other people's feelings. "You're right," she agreed. "I quite understand your position. Please forgive me. I must sound terribly mercenary, but you've taken me by surprise. I shall do as you say and take the matter up with Mr. Locklear."

They talked about other things, but Coral was left puzzled and uneasy through the remainder of lunch. She would have a look at the accounts and would visit Mr. Locklear as soon as possible, she promised herself.

After coffee was served, Robin cleared his throat. "Miss Sinclair, I don't know if it is my place to give you this background, but now that you have returned to Kenya, you need to be aware of the general political situation here today."

Coral sat up straight. Knowing something of the political upheavals that had been going on in Kenya since independence in 1963, this was one issue she knew she had to come to terms with, but she had not realized that it would arise so soon after her arrival.

"Kenya is now set on a new course. The British are no longer in charge, and we have to recognize that we have a new government, hopefully a new *démocratie*. I am young, and so I can see that it is clearly the future." Robin shrugged. "Certainly I can see no point in raving against it."

Coral stirred her coffee pensively. "It seems that much has changed here since I was a child."

"Yes and no. Kenyatta came up with a slogan, *Harambee*: 'let's all pull together,' and in that spirit the government has tried to unite people. But one must also remember the old Swahili proverb: 'When two elephants jostle, what gets hurt is the grass!' With change comes conflict. Tribal unrest has begun to take its toll on communities. Added to that, many of the older white settlers are afraid of the new order, and certainly the assassination of the government minister Tom Mboya last July has made them feel insecure. Also, some Indian-owned small businesses have been under attack, with the owners leaving for Britain and the sub-continent." Robin paused and seemed to choose his words carefully. "Let me say this, Miss Sinclair… I believe in a bright and exciting future here, but it is a future for younger and more flexible people who can adjust to the new Kenya. The old ways of treating people are gone, and there is no reason why Mpingo should not continue to prosper — but we must tread carefully."

Coral digested this and nodded. "I hear you. So, Robin, are you saying I should sell Mpingo? Because I can tell you now that is not why I came here. On the contrary, I want to make it my home again."

Robin smiled with relief. "I'm delighted to hear it. Let's drink to that," he said, raising his glass as they finished their lunch and paid the bill.

Out in the sunshine, they had nearly reached the car when she collided with a man bursting out of a carpet shop. There had been no warning, no time to avoid him. The sensation that rushed through her body, sending tremors to every one of her limbs, should have warned her. She looked up and gave a start as her heart began to beat wildly. Subconsciously, he had occupied her thoughts all morning, and now he was here. A strange coincidence — or perhaps they were meant to meet again. Her lips parted to speak, but he brushed past without seeing her. Her head whirled madly. She stood there, paralyzed for a few seconds, her eyes following the lean, powerful silhouette that towered over the crowd, but he moved swiftly and in no time had merged with the ebb and flow of the human river.

Chapter Two

The green Buick turned onto the estate's drive through two great wrought iron gates. It glided slowly toward the house along the vaulted avenue of blossoming jacarandas. Here, patches of filtered sunshine and shifting violet-blue shadows mingled happily in the waning afternoon. And there, at the end of the bowered gallery, appearing in a luminous halo, stood Mpingo, the home of her childhood, set among vigorous and colorful vegetation. It looked romantically unreal, inviolate, as though set outside time and space.

For the second time that day, Coral found herself fighting against the onslaught of emotions. How many times throughout the years had she imagined this homecoming? Yet the setting was even more beautiful than what she had pictured in her fondest memories.

Her eyes fastened on Mpingo, Coral lay her slender hand on Moses's shoulder. "Please, would you stop the car," she said in a choked voice. "I shall walk up to the house."

She opened the car door. A vaguely familiar whiff of warm air, heavy with the fragrance of ripe fruit and sweet-smelling flowers, greeted her. Rising and standing there a moment more, Coral drank in the dazzling sight that met her eyes. A world of images, sensations, and conflicting feelings wrestled in her mind. Hesitantly at first, and then gradually quickening her steps, she went along the shaded alley toward Mpingo, a tiny figure among an ocean of flowers.

Mpingo! Was it a residence or an edifice, a challenge, an act of folly, or a dream — the materialization of Walter Sinclair's dream? Considered the black sheep of the family and rejected by his peers for refusing to conform to the rigid rules of a banking dynasty, Walter Sinclair had chosen to follow the example of so many European settlers in the thirties. After traveling around the world and accumulating a considerable personal fortune by trading in agricultural equipment and war surplus, he had elected to settle down in this far-off corner of the universe.

The property, called in those days Orchard Coast Estate, had belonged to an old English settler. In his late sixties, having neither heirs nor family, he had been happy to give his creation a new lease of life by selling it to the White Pirate and returning to England.

The old house was a simple, functional dwelling of eight rooms and had nothing of note in the way of architecture. The selling point for Walter Sinclair had been a twenty-kilometer stretch of pristine beach on its boundary and five hundred acres of orchard, one hundred of which were planted with the African Blackwood, the rare and rapidly disappearing *mpingo* tree.

With renovations planned and built with the help of an unknown architect, Walter Sinclair's new Mpingo was to become the zenith of the pioneer's ambitions. Not yet thirty, the young adventurer wanted solid foundations for establishing fresh roots and creating a legacy for future generations. All through the eight difficult years of the Mau Mau rebellion, those uncertain times that preceded Kenya's independence in 1963, he had fought with courage and determination to safeguard the estate for a new dynasty of Sinclairs. It had not always been easy, especially with a wife who hated Africa and a young child.

Built on a grand scale, the façade of the new building was of stone — a warm, rich color that evoked the coral reefs of the Indian Ocean, visible from each of the hand-blown, panoramic French windows on the north elevation of the house that gave the rooms a tinted, luminous air. All the windows had brown shutters that could be tightly closed during the monsoon months. The magnificent curved double staircase, the wall paneling, the large ceiling beams, and the floors had all been intricately crafted on site in imported cedar. Outside the rooms on the upper landing, a galleried veranda encircled the house, from where the extensive out-buildings could be seen. Coral remembered peeping through its lacy balustrade as a child of three to watch the gardeners at work, and later, spending lazy afternoons sipping cold lemonade there with her mother while listening to the birdsong and its accompaniment of rustling palms and whispering sea. Fond memories of playing hide and seek with her friends came rushing back, and she smiled in nostalgia. They could never find her, her favorite hiding place being the potting shed.

As she emerged from the shadow of the drive, Coral thought that Mpingo reflected an extraordinary blend of fantasy and reality. Yet it had been built with a concern for the practicalities of life in this challenging environment. Still, as she looked at it with adult eyes, she realized it had also provided a pretentious backdrop for her father's vanity.

As she approached the double front doors, they swung open, and a figure emerged on the threshold. Even though she was still far removed, Coral thought she recognized it. She quickened her pace and stared wide-eyed. Aluna! It was her! Coral began to run.

When they were only steps away from each other, the *yaha* smiled and stretched her arms out toward her former charge. Their hands joined in silence. The woman held Coral for a moment at arm's length, as though to examine her better. Then, drawing her forward, she clasped Coral tightly, shaking suddenly with unrelenting sobs.

"Oh, Missy Coral, dear Missy Coral," she said in between two gasps. "Aluna thought she'd die without ever seeing her little *malaika* again. Let me look at you." She stepped back and gazed at the young woman, her eyes filled with happy incredulity. "You left a child; you've come back a beautiful young lady." Aluna's voice resounded with infinite tenderness and pride.

Coral responded with a light, crystal clear laugh. "It's wonderful to be back. Just now, as I was coming up the drive, it was as though the years had stopped. Nothing seems to have changed." No sooner had she spoken those words than her eyes clouded over and a lump formed in her throat. "Obviously, everything is changed since Daddy's no longer here," she managed to say in a broken voice and turned back into Aluna's embrace.

"Don't cry, little one. You're here now, and that is the most important thing."

Coral pulled herself together. Aluna was right: she was back at Mpingo and that was all that counted now. Stepping into the hall, her heels clicked loudly on the highly polished floor, filling the room with discordant echoes. She glanced upward, and her eyes fell on the huge crystal chandelier, another of Walter's eccentric extravagances. She remembered fleetingly her childhood nightmare. It always ended in the same way: the diaphanous monster would come crashing down with such a resounding noise that she would always wake up with a start. The glass droplets moved slightly in the breeze from the open door and tinkled gently as though laughing at her disquieting thoughts.

Coral looked around her. On her right, the polished cedar doors to the library stood open, and she walked into a room she did not remotely recognize. The rich brown paneling, her father's heavy leather Chesterfield sofas, heirlooms which had been brought out to Kenya all the way from England, the worn Persian rugs, the light hanging curtains that blocked out the sun on hot afternoons — everything that had made it Walter Sinclair's den — had vanished. An obviously feminine hand had swept over the room with a magic wand, transforming it completely. The modern carpets that dressed its floor, the pastel paint that covered its walls, the soft-hued colors of the curtains and loose covers on the furniture — everything breathed a woman's exquisite taste. Coral hated it.

"Your father was a great man," said Aluna, "but like every human being, he had his weaknesses. His was called Eve, the temptress who was the ruin of Adam. It had always been that way for Bwana Walter. Among my people, wise men say that with ropes made from a woman's hair, one can easily tie an elephant. A wife must keep hold of her husband with smiles and love and good food. Otherwise he strays. Your mother was one of these modern women, and she couldn't keep a man like that. He never knew how to resist a woman, and because of the last one, he nearly damned his soul."

"What d'you mean, Aluna?" asked Coral, alarmed by the lugubrious tone her yaha had adopted.

The older woman's face became closed and reserved like a lump of clay. Only her eyes, peeping beneath heavy lids, were still lively. "Well," she mumbled, "it's a long story. I will tell it to you someday, but for now, you must forget all this and rest."

They returned to the big hall where Robin had just walked in, followed by Moses and two other servants dressed in long white robes who were bringing in Coral's luggage.

"Take Miss Sinclair's bags upstairs," ordered the manager. Then, turning toward the old nanny, he addressed her firmly while accompanying his words with his most disarming smile. "Aluna, would you show them up to your mistress's apartment? I must have a word with her."

"My missy is tired by her long journey," retorted the servant sullenly. "What you have to tell her can wait, I'm sure."

Robin Danvers ignored Aluna's bad temper. He gave her an affectionate but patronizing pat on the back. "I've no doubt you're in a great hurry to be alone with your missy, but there are some issues that I'm afraid can't wait. I promise not to keep her too long," he added slowly, as though he were handling an awkward child.

Turning to Coral, he urged her to follow him into what had once been her mother's sewing room. Like the other rooms, this one had been transformed beyond recognition. From a private living area, intimate and cozy, it had been turned into a functional room with steel filing cabinets and other modern business equipment, a cold and impersonal office.

Robin pulled up a chair for Coral. He sat down opposite her, behind the imposing mahogany desk that once had belonged to the White Pirate and now looked strangely discordant in its new surroundings. She gave a faint start that did not escape the manager's notice. He smiled apologetically.

"After your father's passing, Mrs. Sinclair thought it would be easier for the running of the estate if I was given access to the documents and files concerning the property as a whole, and we turned this room temporarily into an office. Together, your father and I had taken care of the economics and finances, while I alone had assumed the practical side of the administration. Now these tasks are entirely your responsibility, and it is for you to decide whether or not you would like me to go on with the management of the estate."

Coral nodded vaguely. Accounting, finance, administration — all these were terms with which she had no experience. Suddenly, she felt drained. She had but one desire: to be left alone so she could have a chance to assimilate this abrupt merging of her past with her present and most probably her future.

"Can't these business matters wait until tomorrow?" she asked wearily. "It's been a long day, and I'm rather tired. I would like to put off this conversation until the morning, if you don't mind."

"I'm sorry if I've inconvenienced you, but earlier on today you seemed eager to get stuck in as soon as possible. I'm off to Nairobi tomorrow at dawn and won't return before next week."

"I see." Coral suddenly wondered what the existence of a new Mrs. Sinclair might mean for the estate. "Is there anything important that needs attention and that you think I should know about before you return?"

"Not really. Everybody here knows their job. As I told you at lunch, I keep an eagle eye on matters, and the estate runs pretty much like clockwork."

"Super. I think we can resume this conversation on your return." She smiled.

"Before you go, I need to hand these over to you personally," he said as he left his chair and walked to the big, old-fashioned wooden safe. He opened the chest and took out a set of keys. "These belong to the basement rooms. I have no idea why your father was so insistent that you should have them. All I know is that on the eve of his death, Mr. Sinclair came to see me at the pavilion at the bottom of the garden which used to be my office, where I was working late that night. He looked ill, but at the time I wondered if perhaps he had been drinking. 'Take these keys, they are the basement keys,' he said to me. 'Keep them safely until my daughter, Coral, arrives.' When he left me, I had no idea I would never see him alive again. He died that night in his sleep... a heart attack."

They remained silent for a while. Coral examined the keys. Three were approximately the same size, and one was considerably larger. They were held together on a small key ring inlaid with little turquoise beads. "Which rooms do these keys belong to?" she eventually asked as she put them into her pocket.

"With the exception of the wine cellar and some other basement rooms of no great importance that Mrs. Sinclair has filled with a load of old junk, I can't think of any rooms these keys may open."

"I shall ask Aluna. She has been here since the early days and knows all the nooks and crannies of the house."

"You may prefer to wait for my return before exploring the basement. I'd be happy to accompany you."

Coral suppressed an impatient sigh. Danvers' over-officious manner was beginning to grate a little. She stood up and held out her hand to the manager, deciding to humor him. "Thank you, Robin, for your help. I may come and find you later."

"One other thing," he added as Coral was leaving the room. "Mrs. Sinclair is away for a couple of days. That'll give you time to settle down and acquaint yourself again with the house and with the neighborhood. I imagine it's changed quite dramatically since you left. Tourists have invaded the place these last years. Shall I accompany you upstairs?"

"No, I think I may be able to find my way alone, thank you."

"I hope you'll stay with us for a while," said the manager as she reached the stairs. "This house needs love. In many ways, it's been neglected for too long."

Coral turned around and met the young man's bright and laughing eyes. He had a devastating smile; pity he lacked that *je ne sais quoi* that would have given him the distinction he sorely needed.

She started up the free-hanging staircase, trailing her fingers along the polished acacia banister, and slowly, with an almost religious reverence, climbed the two stories that separated her from the nursery. Reaching the landing, she went along the corridor that ended with the three rooms she had occupied as a child, that is, when she was not gamboling on the beach. Coral stopped in front of her old bedroom, her hand poised on the handle, holding her breath.

"Aah… there you are, my princess!" Aluna had heard Coral's footsteps and opened the door suddenly, making the young woman jump. "What could he have had to say to you that was so important it couldn't have waited until the morning? Come quickly now. I've run you a hot bath. I've opened your suitcases and put away your clothes: the dresses here, the blouses and the trousers here. Your underwear and nightwear will have to go in another cupboard. You've more clothes than you used to... but, of course, you're a young lady now."

Aluna was bustling about and talking all at once like in the old days. The older woman's excitement was infectious, and Coral suddenly felt her spirits lifting. She grabbed hold of her yaha and carried her away in a crazy waltz around the room.

"Enough, enough, please, Miss Coral!" Aluna cried out. "I'm not as young as I used to be."

The young woman released her and went on twirling on her own until, tired and out of breath, she threw herself on the bed. "It's marvelous to be back," she said, elated as she stretched herself out, taking in the comfortable, familiar surroundings.

"The Lord be praised. I thought I'd never lay my eyes on my little *malaika* again."

"Dear Aluna. Did you really believe I would forget you, Mpingo, my childhood? Sooner or later I was bound to come back." She rose to her feet and planted two big kisses on the woman's wrinkled cheeks.

"I used to tell myself that again and again, so as not to lose hope," said her *yaha* in a dreamy voice. Her tone suddenly changed. "Here, we are talking while your bath is getting cold. Hurry up, my little one. Give me your clothes. I bet that out there they were never washed as white as when Aluna washed them."

Coral answered her with a crystalline laugh as she disappeared into the bathroom. There she lingered in her bath, enjoying the sensuous warmth of the water on her body, playing absentmindedly with the bubbles. She chattered away happily, relating to the old servant anecdotes of her teenage years, and Aluna put in a hoarse chuckle from time to time as she went about her work in the adjoining room.

"What sort of a woman is Cybil Sinclair?" Coral hopped out of the tub and slipped on a bathrobe of thick, blue cotton. "I'd never heard of her until today when Robin mentioned her. Daddy never wrote anything about — " She came into the bedroom and gave a start. Aluna was standing next to the bed, holding the set of keys and peering at them as though she was trying to work out what they were. Coral went up to the woman and took the keys firmly from her hands. "Thank you, Aluna," she said gently. "These are mine. They probably slipped from my pocket while I was stretching on the bed."

"Where did you get those keys?" said the *yaha* in a trembling voice. She looked angry.

"Come now, Aluna, what's come over you?" Coral answered, evading the question.

"Where did you get those keys?" Aluna repeated, her black eyes narrowing.

"Does it matter where I got them?" Coral asked, shoving the keys into her handbag. "Anyway, what is so extraordinary about these keys?"

"They are the accursed keys of a place that is taboo," whispered the African woman, staring up at Coral intensely. "Your father was under a spell from that devil and should not have kept his evil treasure locked away."

"Daddy's treasure? What do you mean, Aluna? What treasure?"

Aluna's eyes now had a faraway blank look about them, and she started to mutter to herself. "He should never have let him into this house and kept his cursed trophies here. Aluna should have stopped him. That devil betrayed him, and my poor master died because of his evil."

"My father died of a heart attack," answered Coral in an even voice, but Aluna had ceased to listen. Her arms dangled limply at her sides, and she hummed some sort of unintelligible litany, shaking her head from side to side. She went round the room twice, walking right past Coral, opened the door, and left the room. The young woman's eyes followed her as she disappeared around the corner at the end of the dark corridor, then Coral closed the door and sat on her bed, deep in thought. Aluna was forever talking about devils, curses, and sorcery. She had forgotten all the mumbo jumbo that was part of everyday life in this part of the world. It used to drive her mother crazy, especially that her father was a great believer in the occult. She had a sneaking suspicion that he dabbled in magic himself and had many acquaintances, if not friends, among the Africans who were in touch with witch doctors and other so-called sorcerers.

31

She recalled her earlier conversation with Robin, trying to remember what he had actually said about Aluna. Was the poor woman really going out of her mind, or were these simply the wild imaginings of a superstitious soul? The old servant, faced with the sudden and inexplicable death of her beloved master, must have drawn her own conclusions on the tragedy. Who was this devil — a witch doctor? Coral had heard that these witch doctors held great power over the people. Once again she remembered how her father had been a great believer in voodoo and witchcraft.

It was almost dusk; shadows had stealthily gathered in the room. Coral stood up at last. Troubled by dark imaginings, she had forgotten the time. Though it was not cold, she shivered. Wrapping her arms around her shoulders, she hugged herself and pulled up the collar of her bathrobe before walking onto the balcony. Leaning against the old banister, a memory of a little girl with sun-bleached plaits who used to stick her head through the rails to get a better view of the garden dispelled her gloomy thoughts. Aluna used to braid the young Coral's hair, and the little girl had asked her mother why her yaha sometimes wove so many different colorful beads and flowers into her own hair. "Many Kenyans love to decorate their hair, so Aluna makes you look pretty with ribbons instead, darling," Angela Sinclair had said.

A bird struck up his evening song. Others joined him, until the whole garden was alive with their twittering. She loved this hour. It filled her with a strange nostalgia, and as the light changed from amber to amethyst, she stood there gazing into the wilderness, watching the far-off landscape gradually slip into the night.

Coral thought of Dale, and a wave of bitterness swept over her. Her heart had been full of hope and romantic dreams. There was nothing she wouldn't have done for him. A cottage and a lot of love would have been sufficient to make her happy, but her dreams had been shattered by harsh reality. She thought of her father, and the ghost of her parents' old quarrels loomed in her memory. She remembered her mother's reproaches to him. "You'll go after anything in a skirt." *Were all men the same?*

Her stranger's face came unbidden to her mind. She could see his features quite distinctly: sparkling enigmatic eyes, well-defined lips, and determined jaw. She was seized by a curious desire to see him again, talk to him, get to know him better. They had only exchanged a few superficial words, but something unidentifiable in the attitude of that man had instinctively fascinated her. The black Cadillac and the woman's bejeweled arm came back to her. He was obviously attached. Reluctantly, she dismissed him from her mind.

Presently, the sun completely sank below the horizon. The great equatorial night had fallen. There, under the vigilant stars, lay the sleeping jungle, abandoned and mysterious, perhaps revealing its essence more in shadow than in daylight.

The noises Coral heard were all familiar to her and had been part of her childhood. For a fleeting moment, she closed her eyes, trying to identify each sound in the stillness of the night. It was as though she had never left. There was the sibilant whisper of mosquitoes, the plaintive song of frogs in neighboring ponds, the muffled squeaking of bats, while in the distance, the calling for prayer by unseen muezzins echoed out from the top of their mosques.

"I say, Miss Coral, you'll catch your death out here dressed in that bathrobe. The nights get cold, and you don't want the damp to get into your young bones." Aluna entered the room carrying a tray loaded with cold meats, salads, and various fruit. She set it down and hurried onto the balcony, shaking her head disapprovingly. "A young lady of your age should know how to take care of herself," she chided, "but, oh no, not you. You were always one to tempt the devil, as they say. You were climbing the highest trees, sliding down banisters, swimming out to sea without ever thinking of how to come back." Aluna returned to the bedroom to bring her mistress her night clothes. "Here, wear these," she ordered as she handed over a set of pajamas and a dressing gown.

Coral followed her into the room. The older woman was her normal self now. It was as if the episode of the keys had not occurred, as though Coral had imagined the whole thing.

"I thought you'd prefer to eat up here tonight, instead of in the dining room," she said. "You never did like that dining room. Stuffy, you used to say, stuffy and gloomy. You were right. It's stuffier and gloomier now."

"I'm not very hungry," Coral confessed. "We ate an enormous lunch, and I'm not in the habit of eating more than once a day."

"You'll soon lose those bad habits with our clean sea air, young lady. There's none of that nasty pollution you have in London."

Coral laughed. "Aluna, will you stop treating me like a child?"

They returned to the balcony. In companionable silence, Coral sat in the rocking chair, while Aluna settled down opposite her in one of the high-backed cane chairs. The heavy scent of magnolias filled the evening air. The young woman closed her eyes, leaned her head against the back of her seat, and rocked herself slowly. Meanwhile, Aluna peeled a mango that she sliced and arranged prettily on a plate of bone china before leaning across to hand it to her mistress. Coral thanked her with a faint smile, and still rocking herself lazily, savored the succulent fruit. This was bliss… Almost like old times.

Suddenly, Coral sat up with a start. The insistent, monotonous, and haunting rhythm of a solitary tom-tom sounded from faraway, making the night shudder. Coral sought to recall what could have occasioned the ceremony. Was it the Sabbath of young virgins? The preliminary ceremony to a funeral? Or… She shivered.

"It's only the celebration of the full moon," reassured Aluna.

Coral relaxed.

"It's getting cold and late. Your bedtime has long past. Come now, Aluna will tuck you in and will tell you a story — one of those strange tales of our land. You were so fond of them as a child, remember?"

"I remember," she said docilely. "I never tired of the wonderful African legends you told me while I lay cozy and safe in my bed." She smiled wistfully. "Good old Aluna." Coral went over to the old nanny and hugged her affectionately.

"Drink this while I talk. It will help you sleep."

"Ooh, one of your fragrant infusions. Which one is it? Have I tasted it before?" she asked as she slid between the sheets and took a sip of the steaming brew. "Mmm... very fruity and warming."

"It's made with stewed fruit and spices."

Coral snuggled down a little deeper under the eiderdown. "You've my undivided attention, Aluna," she announced, leaning back against the propped-up pillows.

The yaha took her place in the tattered armchair next to her young mistress's bed and began her tale, just as she used to long ago.

"At the beginning of all things, the sun married the moon. They traveled together for a long time, and the sun would go in front with the moon following behind. As they traveled, the moon would sometimes get tired, so the sun would carry her. One day the moon forgot to stay behind the sun and passed in front of him. The sun became angry, so the moon was beaten by the sun in just the same way women are beaten by their husbands when they forget their place." As she listened to the familiar story, Coral smiled to herself, remembering how Aluna had always been so old-fashioned about the duties of a wife; how shocked she would be if she knew what the feminist movement was up to in the West. She could feel herself drifting off to sleep already, lulled by Aluna's low and soothing voice.

"But the sun did not realize that he had married one of those women who fight their husbands. When the moon was beaten, she fought back, and wounded the sun on his forehead. The sun also fought, and scratched the moon's face and plucked out one of her eyes. When the sun saw that he was scarred, he was very embarrassed and said to himself, 'I am going to shine so brightly that people will not be able to look at me and see my scars.' And so he shone so hard that people could not look at him without squinting. That is why the sun shines so brightly. As for the moon, she felt no embarrassment, and so she did not have to shine any brighter. And even now, if you look closely at the moon, you will see the marks on her face that the sun gave her during their fight."

Aluna finished her story. While Coral was drifting off to sleep, she was aware of the older woman's movements: she took the cup from her hand as it rested delicately on the eiderdown, gently removed the extra pillows, smoothed out the covers a little, tucking them in at the side, and then stood there a while watching her. Coral opened her eyes one last time to see an expression of immense tenderness come over her yaha's ebony features. Aluna switched off the bedside lamp and tiptoed out of the room.

***

Coral awoke early the next day and decided she would go down to the beach for a quick swim. From the open window of her bedroom she could see the shimmering sea that appeared almost white in the slanting morning light. The sky was metallic blue; the glare was exceptional: clear, pure, and sharp as a razor. An absolutely unique landscape awaited her out there, and she was burning to be a part of it.

She wore a blue polka dot bikini and, to avoid getting any sand in her hair, swept up her golden mane in a top-knot held in place by two wide tortoise-shell combs. She shoved a towel, a book, and some dark glasses into an old beach bag that was lying in one of the corners next to her cupboard. Coral was ready. She was almost at the front door when Aluna called her back. "The sand is already hot at this time of day. You'd better take your sandals with you."

Her yaha was right; she had forgotten how scalding the sand could get. She climbed the stairs two by two. "What would I do without you, my dear Aluna," she said with a little laugh as she took the sandals from her yaha's hands and buried them in her bag. She blew the old woman a kiss and was off again in no time.

Coral crossed the garden at the back of the house that led down a narrow path to a gate. The three-mile-long beach greeted her in a sweep of dazzling dunes. She loved the freshness of these early morning hours, the unadulterated atmosphere, the daily rebirth of nature.

She walked along the wide, deserted shore, humming, digging her bare feet as deeply as she could into the soft, sugar-white sand, enjoying the warmth that soothed her toes and traveled up her legs, spreading heat through her body. A sense of anticipation, of almost reckless abandon, possessed her, and she ran down the last few slopes that lay between her and the calm aquamarine ocean before immersing herself in the cool, transparent shallows.

She could not have said how long she swam. When she finally emerged from the water, the sun was already high and hot. She stretched herself lazily on her towel and watched the seabirds whirling and squawking in the azure sky. Coral's eyes closed as an elemental sense of serenity swept over her.

Once more she let her thoughts roam back to those first hours of the previous morning and to the handsome stranger who, after being so chivalrous, had mysteriously disappeared into thin air. Was he from this part of the world, or was he only passing through? Would she ever see him again to thank him for his kindness? She supposed not and felt a faint pang of regret at that thought.

The seabirds fell quiet, leaving only the whispering sound of the sea. Determinedly pushing him out of her thoughts, she wiped her mind clear and relaxed.

All of a sudden there was a yap, and before Coral knew it she was startled by a dog hurling itself at her, licking her face with unbridled enthusiasm. She started with surprise and leapt up in one go. It was a beautiful Australian shepherd, remarkably well kempt. Startled too by Coral's reaction, the dog took off like the wind. Puzzled, the young woman launched herself after it, wondering where it had come from and to whom it belonged. In her mad dash, Coral forgot to put on her sandals, and she tripped, banging her foot against a sharp piece of coral. She cried out as she fell to the ground, a stabbing pain shooting through her heel. Coral groaned plaintively, eyes squeezed shut, holding her sore foot tightly in her joined hands. After a few moments, the pain began to subside, and she could see that blood was trickling from the cut. She grabbed her towel and wrapped it around her foot, hearing the Australian shepherd bark nearby.

"Shush, Buster," said a man's voice — one that she found slightly familiar.

Coral looked up. It was him — the kind stranger who had filled her thoughts since she had arrived — standing there, stroking the hound mechanically and watching her with raised eyebrows.

"What are you doing here?" she asked when she recovered from her surprise.

He chuckled. "I'm looking at you," he answered in a voice tinged with gentle irony.

"Why are you looking at me in that silly way?" she said, uncomfortable to find herself in this ridiculous position.

He laughed again, a low throaty sound. She noticed that his eyes this morning were the color of burnt sugar and they twinkled with contained mischievousness.

"Are you in pain?"

"What does it look like?" she snapped.

"Let me have a look."

"Are you a doctor?" Coral threw him an insolent look.

"Beggars can't be choosers," he said, still viewing her with amusement. He smiled good-humoredly, and then his whole face lit up with laughter. "To answer your question, yes, in a previous life I spent three years in medical school."

"I see," she said uncertainly. She raised her eyebrows. "Why did you give up?" She had forgotten the pain and was looking up at him curiously.

"Oh, I wanted something a little more energetic, more adventurous, I suppose."

"Mmm... " Coral felt self-conscious again.

"And now that we have established that I'm not a practicing physician, but that I have some degree of medical knowledge, do you think you can entrust me with your foot?" He had not abandoned his mischievous attitude, standing there, legs a little apart and arms folded, obviously entertained.

She nodded her consent reluctantly. He bent down to examine her foot, taking it in his hands. His palms were not smooth or soft. They were those of a man who was in the habit of using them — strong, masculine hands. Their warm, rugged touch subtly stirred her senses. Frowning, he inspected the sole of her foot, crouching on the sand, head bent. Coral watched him silently. The shock of black hair swept back from a wide forehead was strewn here and there with silver threads. The breeze had ruffled it a little, which gave him a boyish look that contrasted with the tiny lines at the corner of his eyes and slightly deeper ones etched in his brow.

"You must have stepped on a piece of coral. Such pretty feet should not be left unprotected against these nasty fragments scattered along our beaches. You've cut yourself, but the wound isn't deep. I will take you back home." Again, she noticed the smooth, lyrical purr of his accent, which was becoming unnervingly attractive.

"There is no need for that," she assured him hurriedly. "I'll manage on my own, thank you. Mpingo is not far off."

Suddenly she was anxious for him to go, eager to be left alone. She found his quiet and steady gaze disturbing and feared he might discover the inner turmoil he created in her, especially now when she felt at a disadvantage.

"Show me," he instructed.

She recognized the brisk tone of voice that had struck her the day before. Though perhaps a little arrogant, its sense of strength and security was not unpleasant. "Go away," she said faintly.

"Do you really think I could abandon you here when you're hurt?" he asked in earnest.

She did not answer but lifted herself up while he stood there in front of her, neither moving nor taking his gaze off her, seemingly mesmerized. Buster sat near him, growling quietly, his ears pointing toward the sky.

Coral was just about to stand when he bent down gently and, before she had time to protest, swiftly lifted her, one arm under her knees, the other around her waist. She sucked in her breath at this unexpected contact.

His arms were strong and muscular. She could feel the steely grip of his fingers against her ribs, just underneath her breast, as he held her tightly against his broad chest.

"This really isn't necessary; it's just a cut. I can walk perfectly well on my own if you'd give me a chance," she complained, trying to wrestle out of his firm grip.

"It'll be faster if I carry you. Now keep still," he murmured. Coral's lips were no more than an inch away from his clean-shaven cheek, and she could faintly detect the fragrance of the soap he had used that morning. Her indignation gave way to butterflies in her stomach.

His stride was smooth as he walked silently, staring ahead with a faraway look in his burnished pupils. In profile, his eyelashes seemed extra long and thick. She restrained her desire to lean her head against his shoulder, only turning her face slightly toward him. A lock of her hair brushed his temple. He lifted his chin a little, and she noticed his jaw tighten and felt the pressure of his fingers increase a bit on her bare skin, sending a tremor through her body. Was he aware of these strange new sensations that were flooding her?

He relaxed, and his palm slipped down to her waist, where it rested steadily as they approached the property.

It did not strike her at first that he was taking her to Mpingo without any directions on her part, so absorbed was she by the intensity and confusion of her emotions since she had set eyes on him the previous morning. Moreover, his touch and his proximity aroused her senses with an acuity that startled her, and some sort of instinct told her that the mute signals of her flesh had leapt from her body to his, blossoming into a desire similar to her own.

***

Presently they reached the rear of the property. Freeing one of his hands, he unlatched the gate and, looking down at Buster who was hovering around them restlessly, ordered him to sit and wait. The hound obeyed and, with his head tilted to one side, watched his master go.

"Thank you," Coral said, breaking the silence for the first time since they had started back. "You can let me down here, you know." She spoke in a low voice, rather demurely, and he smiled as if charmed.

"We're not quite there yet," he said softly. "You surely are an impatient young lady."

She had no time to reply for Aluna was hurrying toward them, obviously in a panic. "Missy Coral, my poor Missy Coral, what has happened to you?" she cried, rushing down the path to meet them. "I saw you coming from the nursery window. Are you hurt?" As she drew closer, her attention shifted abruptly from her young mistress to the man who was carrying her. Suddenly the fond concern turned into fury as she hurled herself toward him. "You?" she cried out, her eyes wild, her features distraught. "You? What are you doing here? How dare you! Haven't you brought enough pain and disaster to this house? Leave my missy alone. Leave her alone, I tell you! You were born under an evil star, and wherever you go you bring doom and catastrophe in your wake. My missy is taboo to you, do you understand? Taboo! If I catch you lurking around here or anywhere near her, I will kill you myself with these bare hands, and I swear to you that no witch doctor, however powerful, will be able to help you this time."

Chapter Three

Coral was seated comfortably in an armchair on the veranda with her leg resting on a pile of cushions that Aluna had fussily placed on a low stool in front of her. The cut on her foot now clean and bandaged, the pain had diminished, and by the evening there really would be little trace of her injury.

On her return, she had spent an hour trying to coax out of the sullen and silent nanny an explanation for her extraordinary behavior that morning but without success; the servant's lips remained tightly sealed.

"Who is this man?" Coral had asked. "How do you know him? What was all that about bringing sadness to this house?"

"What I would like to know," Aluna had retorted roundly, ignoring her mistress's questions, "is how he has managed to meet you already, when you only stepped off the boat yesterday? The man is the devil, I tell you. You listen to me, child, you stay away from him and the likes of him, or he will drag you down into a bottomless pit from where you may never return."

"Surely the poor man can't be as bad as you make him out! He's only been kind and courteous to me. He needn't have helped me back here. I'm sure he had better things to do. Who is he, anyway? What is his name? We never got down to that, thanks to your silly nonsense."

"You're not listening to me, child!" the native woman had cried, grabbing Coral by the shoulders and shaking her lightly. "This man will hurt you. Everything he touches turns to ashes. I have seen it happen, and that's why I'm warning you."

"Well then, tell me about him. Tell me all. I'm entitled to know what I should be guarding myself against."

"Birds are entangled by their feet and men by their tongues. There are things that are better kept buried. Time and chance reveal all secrets in due course."

They had left it at that, but thinking back on Robin Danvers' words and the yaha's irrational behavior on the previous evening, Coral was seriously starting to believe that the young manager had been right, and that fantasy and reality were inextricably intertwined in poor Aluna's mind. She promised herself to keep her ears and her eyes open in the future. Surely in no time she would stumble upon the truth.

Her gaze swept over the garden, which was exploding with color. In the sunny afternoon it had the dazzling brilliance of fireworks. To the left, the flower-surrounded lawn sloped gently to the jungle, a tangled mass of braided vines in varied shades of green. There bloomed the most magnificent orchids amid a noisy chorus of tree frogs, cicadas, and the myriad life of a tropical forest. To the right, twisted canopies of shrubs and huge flowering trees abounded — plumeria and African tulip and monkey pod bearing red, yellow, or feathery white blossoms — filling the place with color to rival the most daring Matisse. Behind this vivid screen, the rare *mpingo* trees stretched as far as the eye could see. Facing her, beyond the pond where dragonflies and lizards darted among the chalice lilies, the dramatic alley of jacarandas formed a startling ocean of purple-blue flowers.

A silver-gray TR6 Triumph convertible was now making its way up the driveway. It stopped in front of the house, and the driver, a slim young woman in her early twenties with long black hair and olive skin, nimbly hopped out. She walked up to the bottom of the veranda stairs and stood there, her hand resting on the marble banister.

"Hello there," she said with an engaging smile as Coral gingerly left her seat.

"Hello," answered Coral politely. "Are you looking for someone? I'm afraid there is no one at home except for me." She hesitated for a split second before adding, "Mrs. Sinclair is away and will be back in a couple of days. I am — "

"Coral, darling, you obviously don't recognize me." The young woman climbed the stairs hurriedly. "I'd have known you anywhere... you haven't changed that much."

Coral looked hard at the visitor, and in a flash, she remembered the rather chubby, brown-eyed little girl with long black plaits that Sandy Lawson had once been. With a cry of fond recognition, she forgot the discomfort of her foot and rushed toward her childhood friend.

"Of course, Sandy, Sandy Lawson!"

"How clever of you to remember." Sandy laughed. "I like to think that during all these long years I haven't been totally forgotten. After all, I lived more at Mpingo than at my own home."

"How could I forget, Sandy dear? We were inseparable!" They embraced with enthusiasm. "You have changed, though, I would say quite beyond recognition, except of course for your beautiful black hair. You were rather… well, chubby, if I remember rightly."

They both laughed. "You remember rightly," Sandy said. "It took loads of hard work and determination to shed that lot." Sandy still had voluptuous curves, but Coral noticed that her trouser suit belted at the waist showed off a substantially slimmer silhouette.

"Come, let's sit down. I'll ask Aluna to bring us some tea and cakes. You remember Aluna?"

"Of course I remember Aluna. But I'm afraid I must beetle off. I came by to invite you out for tomorrow night. A group of us are going to the Golden Fish nightclub, and it would be lovely if you could join our party. Kenya is a wonderful place if you have friends, but if not, it can be awfully lonely and depressing. You'd be packing your bags in no time. We can't have that!"

"I don't think I could ever become depressed in this country," murmured Coral dreamily. "All these years, I longed so much for this place."

"Once a romantic, always a romantic… We'll pick you up tomorrow at nine o'clock. They're a nice bunch. You'll like them."

"Thank you very much. By the way, how did you know I was here?"

"We're a small community with a strong grapevine. We all live more or less in each other's pockets. It can become a little worrying and rather stifling at times, but one gets used to it." Sandy sighed and gave Coral a sideways look. "Anyway, time and chance reveal all secrets, isn't that how the proverb goes?"

Coral gave a faint start. Was it her imagination or had Sandy's gaze suddenly become more intense, more scrutinizing?

"Remember, pick you up at nine o'clock," called her friend over her shoulder as she ran down the stairs, blew her a kiss, and sped off. The whispering breeze blew through the branches, scattering a handful of purple blossoms off the jacaranda trees as the silver convertible disappeared around the corner of the drive. Coral remained there, leaning against one of the cedar columns and staring into the distance, deep in thought. Was she really a romantic? Certainly it was her romantic notions that had carried her away in the case of Dale and blinded her to his true nature. She thought of her stranger again. Was she once more going to be the victim of her dreams and fanciful imagination?

"Who was that?" enquired Aluna as she joined her mistress on the veranda. "I thought I heard a car." She squinted suspiciously over the balcony.

"Sandy Lawson. You remember Sandy? We used to be quite inseparable."

"Oh, yes! I know Sandy Lawson… very odd that one," she mumbled under her breath.

Coral burst out laughing. "Aluna dear, you're quite the most amazing person I have ever met. Don't you ever have a nice word to say about anybody? Now why do you dislike poor Sandy?"

"I don't dislike Miss Sandy," retorted the *yaha* on the defensive. "I only said that she is odd."

"What does that mean?"

"It means that still waters run deep and that the wool cannot be pulled over Aluna's eyes."

"I still don't understand. I wish you'd stop this habit of speaking in riddles."

"Miss Sandy seems to be a very nice young lady, very sophisticated. She comes from a respectable family and works in her father's firm. But then she keeps strange company."

"What does that mean?"

"It means that she has some weird friends among the Africans, and for a lady of her position, I do not think it is good. She's also a friend of that Frenchman."

"What Frenchman?"

"Will you stop hectoring me, Missy Coral? I'm tired of all your questions. They make my poor brain ache."

"Forgive me, Aluna. I don't mean to be a nuisance, but you're so mysterious and there are so many things that I don't understand," Coral explained.

"Stay a little and news will find you. Shall I bring your supper out here or would you prefer to have it upstairs?"

"I'm not hungry, thank you. I'll have a tray of fruit upstairs later on."

It was almost seven o'clock. While Coral had been talking, night had fallen with tropical abruptness, the countryside sinking into a black-magic void. She wondered how she would occupy herself until her bedtime. In England, she had led an active life. This forced inactivity, even for so short a time, was beginning to weigh on her. She also felt out of place. Mpingo was her house, her home, but she was not mistress here. Almost everything inside it had been transformed or altered, and she would have liked to move things about but daren't in case that encroached on her stepmother's territory.

Her mind lingered for a while on Cybil Sinclair. A portrait of the woman was hanging in the living room. Coral had noticed it earlier on that day when, after her fall, Aluna had helped her into the sunny room. She had been surprised and faintly disturbed by her stepmother's youth and beauty. The redhead's portrait was strangely alive — the lithe and supple body seemed almost animated underneath the pleats of a black tunic, and the elongated green eyes smiled back at her enigmatically. She had tried to prompt Aluna to tell her about Cybil but had met with the same obstinate silence or cryptic nonsense that seemed to be the servant's mantra nowadays.

Coral suddenly remembered the keys that Robin had given her. Perhaps if she investigated those rooms in the basement she would find some answers to the list of questions that were rapidly accumulating in her mind. The keys were in her bag where she had left them, and so was the small, battery-powered torch she was in the habit of carrying around with her. She turned the key-ring over and over, examining the keys closely. They were old and rather ordinary, the sort you could have duplicated anywhere. Now why would anybody use that type of key to lock away something important? And why had Aluna discouraged her from going to the basement? She'd never know if she didn't have a look for herself and try to throw a little light on the matter, she thought as she made her way to the back of the house where she remembered the basement stairs to be.

Coral crossed the hall, past the kitchens. She managed to catch a glimpse of Aluna deeply engrossed in her cooking and the two servants who were busy laughing and chattering while drinking glasses of ink-black tea. The narrow corridor she traversed seemed shorter than she remembered. How many times as a child had she taken this route to go to the grounds, rather than the easier and more straightforward way that the front door offered? Eventually she reached the stone spiral staircase that ran into the garden and walked down its steps carefully. At the bottom, Coral hesitated for a moment, staring out into the opaque darkness of the great Kenyan night. Was she being reasonable? Straining her ears, she listened attentively for a sound, but could hear nothing else save the rapid beating of her own heart. Choosing to ignore her trepidation, she determinedly went round the stairway to a second door underneath the stairs, which led to the basement. Coral unbolted the door quietly, lifted the latch, and was relieved to find that it opened easily. As the vaulted ceiling was very low at the entrance, she had to bend her head to enter, and then gave a muffled cry as a moth-eaten, black cat slipped out of the darkness like a witch's familiar, meowing languorously as it rubbed itself against her bare legs before jumping onto the ledge of a window and slipping away into the wilderness.

Her torch only emitted a thin shaft of light, just enough for her to find her way. She crossed many vaulted rooms, some holding barrels and casks of wine. Others contained a salting tub, fruits and vegetables lined up to dry out on trestles covered with straw, and tanks of earth where the eggs had been kept fresh in the olden days. None of these rooms had doors to them, only small, barred windows.

Coral finally came to a storeroom on a lower landing that was covered with cobwebs. There were a few steps down, and then a great wooden door, gray with dust. *That must be it,* she thought as she felt her pulse accelerate again with excitement. At the bottom of the stairs, she took the keys from her pocket and inserted one of them into the keyhole, disappointed when nothing happened. Coral tried the second one, and this time there was a faint click, allowing her to push the door open with an eerie creak that resounded in the silence.

She entered a sort of gallery that was bathed in the moonlight filtering through the two encasements situated right at the top of the wall, almost at ceiling level. Coral ran her torch around the room. It was completely empty. Noticing a switch on the opposite side from where she stood, she went across to turn on the electricity but decided against it, lest someone outside noticed the light. Her foot involuntarily struck something hard jutting out on the flagstones. The ground shifted slightly underneath her and, jumping back, she could see there was some sort of trap door in the floor. Pulling on the heavy metal ring that lay on top, the creaking of the rusty hinges echoed through the basement as the door moved, uncovering a black gaping hole.

Coral bent down and aimed the light into the hole. Six steep steps led to another small room that seemed crammed with all sorts of junk, not easily discernible in the weak beam from her fading torch. She was of two minds whether to continue her search or come back another day at a more reasonable hour. After all, what was there to find? Finally she made up her mind and went down the stairs into the small room, which appeared to have no other exit. This time Coral had no scruples in turning on the light, blinking as the glare from a bare bulb hanging from the ceiling flooded the room.

There was some old furniture piled up in a corner, along with books, a stack of dusty crockery, and paintings... loads of paintings. As she took a closer look at them, Coral saw that most were paintings of her: in her childhood, as a teenager, and a few that were quite recent because they depicted her with a new hairstyle she had adopted only a year ago. She wondered: had her father been a painter? She picked up the one she thought to be the latest and scrutinized it. It was signed, but not by Walter Sinclair. In the right-hand corner, at the bottom of the portrait, clearly written in thick black ink was the name of the artist: "Raphael de Monfort."

Reading the name aloud, the sound of her own voice startled Coral in the silence. Another picture showed her at sixteen, at her first ball, in a beautiful pink organdie dress with satin ribbons that was still hanging up in her cupboard in London. Coral remembered sending her father a photograph of herself on that memorable day. She examined another painting, then another and another, until she had gone through the lot. Something about them was fascinating. They were so clear, so detailed, and most of all, so alive. It was as though the artist knew her, not just superficially, but deeply, intimately; he seemed to have captured the essence of her soul, and she found that thought altogether exciting and a little disturbing.

Coral looked at her watch. Time had jogged along: it was almost nine o'clock. Aluna would be looking for her and had probably worked herself up into a panic. She swept the room with a last glance, turned off the light, and started up the steep stairs. Then suddenly there was… a sort of a muffled noise above her, like the soft rush of feet. The beam of her torch chose to go out at that moment, and she tried to turn it on again but could not. The battery had died. Her blood ran cold as she realized that she was alone and defenseless. No one would hear her if she screamed. Holding her breath, she waited and listened attentively. Nothing. Gathering her courage, she went up the few steps that separated her from the moonlit room. Her eyes now accustomed to the dark, Coral stared in horror as she made out a tall, lean shadow standing in the doorway. A sudden shiver ran down her spine, making her hair stand on end.

"Shikamoo, Miss Coral," the shadow greeted her in a low but friendly voice as an oil lamp was lit.

Coral swallowed hard and tried to answer but only managed a faint squawk. She felt her legs would give way any moment now. The African man in his white caftan was already stooping in the low doorway, but he bowed politely to her. "I am Juma, head servant of Mpingo," he went on solemnly. "Welcome to your home. I am deeply sad that I was not here to greet you on your arrival, but I had to accompany *memsahib* on her travel. Please, let me now escort you back to the house."

"Thank you, Juma," Coral whispered, grateful that her fears had come to nothing and trying to recover her composure. "That will be very kind."

"Perhaps we should shut the trap door before going," he suggested as she walked to the door.

"Oh, yes, yes, of course, how careless of me," she answered quickly, sensing the disapproval in the servant's voice.

Coral locked the door behind her and replaced the keys in her pocket. As they silently made their way back, her fear dissipated, but she felt uneasy and nervous in the presence of the proud and quiet man who soundlessly walked in front of her.

"Has Mrs. Sinclair returned?" she asked as they went up the spiral staircase.

"Yes, Miss Coral, *memsahib* has returned. She is in the drawing room and is awaiting you."

"I see. Well, thank you, Juma, for bringing me back safely," she said, smiling awkwardly at him as they came into the big hall.

"*Karibu*. That is my duty," he replied with a bow. He took leave of her while Coral entered the drawing room. The room was brightly lit by the nineteenth-century crystal chandelier that hung from the ceiling, but it was empty. Closing the door, Coral lifted her head, and her eyes met those of the face in the portrait, smiling back at her in that puzzling way that had struck her earlier that day. On impulse, she crossed the room and approached the mantelpiece over which the painting was hanging, looking for the signature. The portrait was unsigned… or had the signature been removed?

"You must be Coral," said a rather melodious voice behind her.

Coral turned and once again met the smiling green eyes. The woman coming toward her though was slightly older than the lady in the portrait; the years did not diminish her beauty in any way — quite the reverse. Cybil Sinclair's appeared today as a more mature, a more languid and sensual beauty. Wearing a Givenchy dark blue dress, she was tall, slim, and elegant, with catlike features. The lush, tousled red hair that in the portrait fell over her shoulders was now pinned back into a sophisticated bun. Coral could understand why her father had been bewitched.

"I'm Cybil Sinclair. I see you're looking at my portrait. I don't care much for it myself, but poor Walter liked it, and I didn't think of removing it after… " Her voice faltered for a split second, but she continued. "Of course, now that you're here and the house belongs to you, surely you must have other plans… "

"No, no, not at all." Still recovering from her eventful day, Coral was taken aback by her stepmother's affability. "It's a beautiful portrait. I was actually admiring it. Who's the artist?" she asked on impulse.

Her stepmother shrugged, and her green eyes creased into a smile. "Oh, an old friend. It's a portrait that dates back to my early days in Tanganyika," she said casually. "Have you had dinner? We looked for you earlier, but Aluna didn't seem to know where you were." She paused, fishing perhaps for Coral to tell her where she had been, but the young woman did not volunteer any information. "Will you have something to drink?" Cybil went to a trolley at the far end of the room and, without waiting for Coral's answer, poured herself out two inches of neat scotch. She laughed. "Don't look so alarmed, my dear. After a journey such as the one I've just been on, I'm sure you'd also treat yourself to a little drink. The traffic in Nairobi can be absolutely hair-raising."

Cybil sat in one of the winged armchairs and signaled for Coral to do the same opposite her, facing the portrait. Her beauty and grace complemented the elegance of the room, which, like the others in the house, had been altered, but to a lesser extent. It had a classical, Georgian symmetry about it, dominated as it was by three large French windows opening onto the veranda. The gleaming brown floorboards, covered with old Persian rugs that she remembered from her childhood, gave it a familiar exuberance and warmth. Still, in this room, like everywhere else in the house except for the unchanged nursery, Coral felt uncomfortable and uneasy, as though she were an intruder.

"Yes," said Cybil, drawing Coral back down to earth, "coming back to that portrait. You can take it down anytime. I don't like it much, at least not anymore. You see, it was all part of another me. I was luckier in those days!" She laughed again, a little hollow chuckle that sounded false.

"I think it blends nicely with the rest of the room," Coral said softly. "If you have no objection, I will keep it there… for a while."

Cybil shrugged her shoulders and silently sipped her scotch. "When would you like me to move out?"

Once again Coral was caught off her guard. "Please don't feel in any way obliged to move out simply because I have arrived. After all, the house is much too vast for me to live in on my own," she mumbled quickly.

"Oh, I'm so grateful that there's no hurry for me to move just yet," exclaimed Cybil with an obvious sigh of relief. "You understand, the estate's old cottage is still full of poor Walter's belongings and is in a rather shabby condition. It needs complete renovation. I'll have to redecorate it entirely, you know… and everything takes so long here in Africa. You wait ages for materials and things to be sent over, and once they are here, workers are so slow and slack if not supervised carefully. Well, that does put my mind at rest for the time being."

By the time Cybil Sinclair started on her third scotch, the conversation, which for the past hour had been almost one-sided, was slipping into flippant trivia, and Coral was beginning to feel the repercussions of an adventurous day. Politely taking leave of her stepmother, she said good night and went up to her room. As Coral was closing the door behind her, she noticed Cybil Sinclair turn away, her fixed smile suddenly replaced with a hard, empty stare.

***

Coral woke up the next morning to glimpse, through the veil of the mosquito netting, a sulking Aluna bearing a tray of tea.

"Good morning, Aluna," she called out cheerfully.

Ignoring her mistress, the woman busied herself picking up the clothes Coral had shed the night before, still lying on the floor.

"You don't need to pick those up," said the young woman apologetically. "I was so tired last night, I could hardly keep my eyes open."

Aluna grunted and disappeared into the bathroom. Having run a bath, she was about to leave when Coral leapt out of bed and stood in front of the door, barring her passage.

"Don't go, Aluna," she cajoled, planting a kiss on her yaha's cheeks. "I would like to talk."

"Where did you disappear to yesterday evening?" asked the servant gruffly.

"Didn't Juma tell you?"

"No one tells me anything in this house. They all say Aluna's crazy." She shook her head sadly. "But Aluna isn't crazy. Aluna sees, hears, but doesn't speak," she added with a sudden burst of indignation.

"I wish you would speak, Aluna dear. Maybe if you explained yourself instead of using riddles, people would take you more seriously."

"You were meddling in those damned cellars, child, weren't you?" Aluna pointed an accusing finger at her mistress. "And don't you deny it."

"What if I did go down to the cellars?" retorted Coral impatiently. "I found nothing there that justifies your attitude. Really, I fail to see what all the fuss is about. The only discovery of any interest was a load of paintings — paintings of me! Imagine! I suppose Daddy had them commissioned. They're good too, but there are so many of them... Have you seen them?" Her eyes glittered with excitement.

"Evil! Evil, that is what they are. Listen to me, child, you must burn them. Tonight we will go together, you and I, and we will burn them."

"Burn them?" Coral cried out with undisguised horror. "Why on earth would I want to burn them? I love them. They're so real, so true. They don't only depict my features, can't you see? It's as if they're a reflection of my inner-self. This Raphael, or whatever his name is, is very gifted. He's a real find." She spoke vehemently, with a passion that surprised her.

It seemed to disconcert Aluna as well. The *yaha* moved to the chair in the corner of room and sank down into it, closing her eyes and sighing. When she opened them again, a sad and dismal look was on her face.

"Aluna, what is it?" Coral was becoming exasperated with her *yaha's* strange behavior. "Please will you tell me what on earth's going on!"

"Okay, my child, you want to know the truth? Then Aluna will tell you everything." The old woman sighed and began her story.

"It all began eight years ago, when the estate next to Mpingo was put up for sale. It is called Whispering Palms. Your father had been after it for a very long time, even before your mother left him to go back to England. He used to talk to me in those days. He would stand on the top veranda outside his bedroom in the evenings, before the sun went down, or sometimes in the mornings. From up there you could see Whispering Palms in the distance, you see. 'Aluna,' he'd say with that wild look in his eyes he used to get sometimes, 'this will all be mine one day. I will make it flourish and prosper for my little one. She will come back when she's grown up, and she will be the queen of the whole estate. She will reign on this land that I love and she loves, and then all will be as it should be.' He loved his little Coral and was content to wait for your return. That year was *mbaya* — unlucky — for Mpingo, a very bad year. There was no rain. Drought threatened our land with famine. The crops were bad, and on top of this there was a barn fire."

"A fire? What happened?"

"I do not know, Missy Coral. No one knew. Your father lost a lot of equipment too, but there was talk of it being started deliberately, and the insurance company refused to pay. It was also in the same year he met that witch of a redhead, the present Mrs. Sinclair."

Aluna's expression darkened. It was obvious she hated the widow with all her might. She cleared her throat before continuing with her narrative. "For two years *Bwana* Walter fought against bankruptcy, and yet Whispering Palms was still not sold, so he had hoped that it could still become his someday. Another two years passed, then, one morning, out of the blue, we learned that the estate was up for auction. By this time your father had recovered from his financial crisis, and he managed to get some sort of loan that would enable him to buy his dream, especially because rumors had it that the property was going cheap."

There was a lull while the servant reminisced silently, her eyes lost in memory. Coral dared not speak again in case the river of information she was finally getting ran dry. She quietly sat down on the edge of her bed.

Coming back down to earth, Aluna resumed her narration. "I shall always remember that sunny afternoon, the day of the auction. Your father was so excited. He reminded me of a child going on some sort of fairy tale expedition. He changed his tie three times before leaving for the auction an hour too early. 'Aluna,' he said before he got into the car, 'Aluna, I will come back the king of this universe.' Your mother always told him he had delusions of grandeur, and maybe she was right. But God creates dreams, says our African proverb — for what hope has a man in this life if he cannot dream? Still, I waited that afternoon, but I wasn't happy. Too many bats had been flying around the house the night before, and the sound of the tom-tom had kept me awake. The evil spirits were at work. Aluna had an ill feeling, a premonition that all would not go well.

"As the evening came, I grew more restless by the minute. Finally, when night had fallen and I could stand this waiting no longer, I heard chanting and wailing in the distance. I recognized that frightening sound: it announces disaster. It began to get nearer. There was a silence for a moment, and then they appeared at the bottom of the drive, all singing and making their way to the house, carrying the body of my master. In those days, Deif, the head boy, was still with us. Followed by two of the other servants, he went to greet the procession while I stood there frozen with fear and dread for my master. But your father was not badly hurt. It was only his ego that had taken a blow." Aluna wiped the tears that had filled her eyes at the sad memory.

"As it seems, the auction had been going in his favor. No one was showing much interest in the property, so it looked like he would get it at a very reasonable price. Then a young man appeared out of nowhere and began to bid against him. The outsider was a foreigner, and apparently he didn't care how much this foolishness would cost him as long as he laid his hands on it. My master had fought against his bids until *Bwana* Timothy, his solicitor, who had gone with him, forced him to stop. But your father was not going to renounce his dream without a last battle. He had challenged his competitor, who at first had refused to cross swords with my master. Unfortunately, my master would not give up. 'May the best man win,' your father had shouted and rolled up his sleeves, 'and what is more, may the victor buy Whispering Palms.' Though the foreigner was considerably younger than him, *Bwana* Walter had always been big, fit, and strong. They had fought each other hard with their bare fists, but finally the foreigner had knocked your father out."

"Poor Daddy," whispered Coral sadly, "that is just like him. He never was a good loser."

"A few days later," Aluna went on, "this young foreigner had the gall to turn up at Mpingo and ask to see my master. If it had been me he had spoken to, I would have given him a piece of my mind and sent him off with a flea in his ear. That would have saved a lot of grief, I dare say. But he was showed into your father's office by Deif."

"Daddy agreed to receive him?"

"Oh, yes, not only did he agree to receive him, but he listened patiently to the stranger's cock and bull story about his wife's death, after which my poor master was like putty in his hands. They became the best of friends, it pains me to say. From the very beginning, I realized that they were like king and courtier. For where would the sly fox go if the lion was not fond of praise? *Bwana* Walter did not only open his home, but poured his heart out to this stranger. His fondest topic of conversation was you, his baby, the apple of his eye, his ray of sunshine. I know he only wrote to you sometimes, but that just wasn't the master's way. He wasn't a man of letters. He was a dreamer. Still, he would talk to the Frenchman about you relentlessly, with stories of your childhood, showing him your pictures, sharing with him every one of your letters and your postcards, dreaming with him of the day when you would return. They used to sit down there on the veranda, hour after hour, drinking scotch until they were both quite merry. I did not like the way this foreigner spent so much time with *Bwana* Walter. I would lie awake in my room, listening to them joking and cheering until dawn. Then your father would stagger upstairs. I would put him to bed, and no sooner did his head touch the pillow than he would fall into a deep, heavy sleep, without a glance or a kind word to Aluna."

Coral thought how bitter her yaha sounded and how much she had aged. She could not be more than fifty, yet she already looked an old woman with her bulging tummy, frizzy gray hair, deeply furrowed face, and lifeless, haggard eyes. She could barely recognize the handsome woman with the shapely figure, the sparkling ebony eyes, and the bubbling disposition that she had once known. Coral remembered her mother saying that Aluna was a flirt: "She was born to be a courtesan, that one." At the time, Coral had not quite grasped the meaning of those words. Today, she could hardly describe Aluna as a courtesan.

"My master taught him everything," Aluna went on. There was no stopping her now. "Your father was the one who saved Whispering Palms from deterioration. Yeah, some will deny it, but I tell you that *Bwana* Walter helped him all the way up. I wouldn't be surprised if he had also lent him money. The man took and took without ever giving anything in return, except for those horrible paintings of you that the Frenchman used to produce from time to time to my poor Bwana's delight." Aluna shook her head.

"He would laugh at me sometimes, when I used to urge him to be cautious — not to give so much of his mind, his heart, and his money. I remember so clearly what he said to me. 'Aluna, if I were to listen to you, I would go nowhere, see no one, and do nothing. This boy is like a son to me — that is why I have asked him to paint those paintings of my little girl.' The Frenchman didn't get any money for them, it's true, but as far as I'm concerned they were poor payment for my master's friendship and hospitality. According to Bwana Walter, the Frenchman had suffered a great tragedy and it made my master feel good to lend him a hand." Aluna grunted. "Hmm, he lent him a hand, all right, and the dog turned round and bit it."

"What do you mean?"

"He hurt your father in his most private possessions: his pride, his honor, and his manhood." Aluna sighed. She was now leaning forward in the chair, her hands resting on her parted knees, pressing them down with her weight as she swayed her body backward and forward in a woeful, desperate fashion. Suddenly she stopped. She lowered her voice, casting a suspicious eye around the room, and signaled Coral to come closer, which the young woman did.

"That evil man was carrying on with her," she whispered, pointing her index finger toward Cybil Sinclair's room.

"That is a horrible accusation to make, Aluna," Coral reproached gently. "How can you make such a statement without any proof?"

"My master had proof, all right," retorted the servant bitterly. "That's why he went for them with his rifle. They had been lovers before, a long time ago. I have seen photographs of them in another country — that's where they had first met, and here they were just taking it up again, like in the olden days, under my poor master's roof. But he got wise to them. With all the whispering and shenanigans that occurred whenever he came into the room, he sensed that something fishy was in the air, and he caught them."

"What do you mean?" pressed Coral, horrified by these strange and unexpected revelations.

"Bwana Walter said he was going away, then he came back that same afternoon without warning. They were in the drawing room. She actually was in his arms. My master shot at them both. He missed her, but got him. In the ribs, he did… They were guilty, all right. Both of them, I tell you. Though the Frenchman took all the blame and said he was trying to kiss her by force. Ugh… let me laugh! That's why the snake never pressed charges. If the scandal had come out, he would have looked mighty bad. Everybody knew of his friendship with Bwana Walter. He left the country shortly after that, but bad pennies have a habit of always turning up again, and he — "

Aluna was interrupted by a knock at the door. Cybil appeared and, with what seemed to Coral a false smile, said, "Coral, dear, I'm going into town. Would you like to come?" She looked even lovelier than the previous night, dressed in a casual green Chanel suit that intensified the fire reflected in her hair and matched to perfection those catlike eyes now fixed on Coral intently.

Coral declined the offer politely, and Cybil swiftly disappeared downstairs again. After her strange talk with Aluna, she wished to avoid being alone with her stepmother in case she said or did anything that gave away her misgivings about the woman. Coral felt confused and was uncertain whether to believe Aluna's tale.

She wondered how long Cybil had been behind the door and whether she had overheard snatches of their conversation. She must stay clear of her father's widow until she had a better perspective on the situation, a more solid grasp on the facts. It struck her that she was too hasty in allowing Cybil to stay when her stepmother had asked the night before in the drawing room. But if her stepmother had intended to throw her, it certainly had had the desired effect. The next step for her to take tomorrow, she decided, would be to ring Timothy Locklear, her father's solicitor, and arrange for a meeting without delay.

***

Sandy arrived at Mpingo sharply at nine o'clock that evening to pick Coral up. She was accompanied by five friends, and Coral quickly invited them all in for a drink so introductions could be made. There was Bonnie Jenkins, a giggly red-haired girl with a turned up nose and great big eyes, and Fiona McCallum, a husky blonde who reminded Coral of Julie Christie and worked as a tour organizer in Mombasa. All of the three young women had come dressed for a glamorous night out: Bonnie in her Pucci-style evening dress which was a swirl of pinks, greens, and golds; Fiona elegant in a Christian Dior slim-fitting white evening dress cut bare over one shoulder, her hair adorned with a matching silk headscarf; and Sandy shimmering in her turquoise halter maxi dress that set off her shapely curves. Coral herself had chosen a scarlet-red Ossie Clark dress that she had fallen in love with in London, with fabulous balloon sleeves, smocked bodice with a plunging neck line, and full, flowing skirt. The three men were all smartly turned out in tuxedo jackets and shirts. Everyone in the group made themselves comfortable in the drawing room, and Coral set about fixing drinks, sensibly pouring a soda water for herself.

Of the three men, Coral took an instant dislike to Fiona's partner, Henry. Fiona's father employed him in his accountancy firm, and though he was attractive enough, Henry had an air about him that Coral found mean and competitive. His friend, Peter, a tall and rather jittery young man, was nice enough, and indeed had looked rather approvingly at Coral when vigorously shaking her hand. Sandy introduced Jack, the third man, as one of Fiona's work colleagues at the tour company. He kept himself quite aloof from the rest of the chatter, and for most of the time seemed almost bored, constantly smoking his Dunhills and peering round the room as they all downed their drinks and swapped pleasantries.

"Oh, is that the time? We'd better get a move on, especially as we haven't eaten yet," exclaimed Sandy, glancing at her watch and chivvying the rest of them to finish their drinks.

The party drove in two cars through the silent African countryside. Coral, Bonnie, and Peter went with Sandy in her car, while Henry, Jack, and Fiona followed in his gold Ford Capri. Coral shivered as she stared out into the black night, trying to make out some of the shadows silhouetted in the dark. Soon, they were following the coast, and the automobiles began their ascent to the top of the cliffs.

At an abrupt turning in the road, overhanging a precipice, the Golden Fish dominated the skyline, shedding light into the surrounding gloom. As they approached the beautiful nightclub, Coral saw that it was glass-sided and peak-roofed, with its feet in the ivory-colored sand, offering a view to the far-off old harbor.

The cars went through the bougainvillea-lined entrance gate and stopped in front of the wide porch. As the doors opened and they stepped out into the illuminated garden, they were given an exuberant welcome by ebony-skinned doormen in white caftans. The group was ushered into the foyer, where a retinue of young women received them. Coral thought they all looked like Scheherazade in their beaded waistcoats with bold-red sashes, their billowy trousers held in at the ankles, gliding rather than walking, attending silently to the needs of the new customers.

The actual nightclub was set atop a flight of stairs, the fronds of potted palms wafting in the sea breeze, creating an exotic and romantic mood. With its tall white arches, inlaid marble floors, and Moorish fountain warbling softly at the entrance, the atmosphere had all the flavor of Arabian Nights.

Coral felt like a guest in a mogul's palace as she followed her party into the softly lit room. Here again the Middle Eastern ambiance was enhanced by the tall, mosaic mirrors dressing the unusual five-sided columns and reflecting the flowers and candles of an elegant and festive scene. The audience was seated at small tables, all of them in evening dress, the women dripping with expensive jewelry. The room was hazy with cigarette smoke that curled up from the tables, and the whole place buzzed with laughter, chatter, and a frisson of excited anticipation.

The hostess led the group to an excellent table, very close to the bar, with a full view of the stage where a group of Kenyan dancers were finishing their routine, effortlessly leaping into the air to the sound of wild drumming and pipe music. Coral and her friends seated themselves on velvet-covered armchairs and a semi-circular divan as the audience applauded the end of the show. Coral joined in, sorry that she had missed their performance as she hadn't seen Masai dancers since she was a child and remembered how delighted she had been at their crazy acrobatics and mesmerizing energy. She turned her attention to the panoramic vista from the glass walls. The view was breathtaking: all palms and greenery in one direction and in another, the perfect sweep of beach and its midnight waters.

"What a stunning setting," Coral remarked. "I've never seen anything quite like it. I'd love to take some pictures for the articles I'm writing about Kenya."

"Yes, it is celebrated as a night club and draws *le tout de Mombasa*," Sandy declared.

"What are we all drinking? Sundowners, ladies?" Henry asked, leaning into his pocket for his cigarettes. The hostess then took their orders while the men settled for traditional White Cap Kenyan beers. Gentle strains of bossa nova music wafted through the room as Henry offered Coral a cigarette.

"No thanks."

"So, you're doing an article on Kenya, eh?" said Henry, squinting at her through his cigarette smoke.

"Yes, that's right, and doing some photography too." Coral noticed with irritation that Henry's smile was decidedly patronizing. "And the chances are it'll be the basis for a documentary," she added, trying to disguise the note of defensiveness in her voice.

"Well, my dear, anyone trying to cover what's going on in this country at the moment has their work cut out for them. I'm afraid to say Africa isn't the country it was."

"Kenyatta's certainly stirred things up, that's for sure," Fiona piped in, lighting up her own cigarette. "The tourists were flocking in. Last year, we'd never been so busy in the office."

"Bet that's all changed since the Mboya assassination, though, hasn't it?" said Peter, stubbing out his cigarette in the ashtray. Coral noticed that the twitchy young man had already smoked two cigarettes since they sat down. "Tribal politics has escalated. Kenyatta's not exactly running a democracy, and people are afraid."

"Well of course, the old settlers have the most to lose and are bound to be afraid of the new order," said Jack quietly, sipping his beer.

Bonnie chimed in: "My papa says we have a few more years at most. My grandparents had a dream of creating a little piece of England here. That's all finished now."

Coral added, "Just because that dream is finished doesn't mean that we cannot be part of the new dream, the new Kenya, where everyone has opportunities."

"Ha! The new Kenya?" Henry interjected. "The British should never have pulled out of Africa. Africa for the Africans? Look at the mess we're in now. The tribes are killing each other, and it won't be long before they start murdering us in our beds."

"Oh, pipe down, Henry." Sandy threw him an exasperated look. "The whole world is becoming more violent. It's a sign of the times."

Coral had to agree with her friend. The world did seem to be a more violent place. Only last year a fan had been stabbed to death by a Hells Angels gang at the Rolling Stones concert in California, and there was that grisly business with the Manson murders last summer. Young people were dying of drug overdoses; even Brian Jones had been found dead in his swimming pool. Was this the end of the Age of Aquarius?

As if reading her mind, Fiona tried to lighten the mood a little. "Perhaps Lennon and Yoko Ono need to climb back into bed again, in that case, and give peace another chance!" They all laughed, and Coral smiled, relieved as the conversation moved on to The Beatles and whether this would be the year they split up. Coral looked round the room again. The music had changed to Fausto Pappeti's seductive saxophone, and as she relaxed into her chair in appreciation, she felt Sandy nudge her arm.

"I love this place, don't you? When the owner took it over a few years ago, it was an ordinary night club with very mediocre décor and a rather ordinary show. He completely gutted it and rebuilt it. Such vision and imagination. He's really brought it to life and made it quite an extraordinary club."

"Who owns it?" Coral asked, her curiosity roused by her friend's words.

"A belated European settler, a Frenchman," volunteered Bonnie, who had been earwigging. She raised her eyebrows so that her eyes appeared even more saucer-like. "Some sort of a business-man-cum-artist, I think. He's really brought a French brio and sophistication to the place, don't you think? It looks like a real labor of love." Bonnie gazed around the room in admiration.

"It's cool, airy, and sparkling — a complete reflection of the woman that inspired it," remarked Jack with a smile. His words were greeted with general laughter.

"Ah, yes! The fascinating and sensual Morgana." Fiona cast a wry look at her partner.

"*Cherchez la femme*, no?" Henry added with a smirk. "Behind every successful man is a woman, d'you think?"

"You've all got sour grapes," said Sandy, who seemed annoyed at her friends' attitudes. "You can't fault his place, you can't criticize Morgana either, so you sneer… It's very easy to mock, much more difficult to build something from nothing."

"Don't get huffy, Sandy dear," Henry interjected. "We're only joking. Besides, we forgot that Mr. de Monfort is a good friend of yours."

De Monfort, thought Coral as she felt her pulse quickening. *Raphael de Monfort*? Could she be in the lion's den?

"Well, we may not be able to fault this place, and the beautiful Morgana may be beyond reproach, but that doesn't seem quite the case where our Knight of the Sorrowful Countenance is concerned."

"Oh, stop being facetious, Henry," Sandy said. "This is a childish discussion. Besides, at least at this nightclub, he doesn't tolerate people lolling around smoking themselves into a stupor with grass, or dropping LSD, like most other nightclubs round here."

Ignoring her, Henry went on. "Let's face it. The man has a dreadful reputation where women are concerned. Only a few months ago, he was shot at by the furious husband of one of his many mistresses. Served him right, too. Rumors have it that she was an old flame of his. He fled the country… that's why he hasn't been seen here lately."

"Well, he's here tonight," retorted Bonnie.

Coral had paled at Henry's words. "Where?" she managed to utter. She was burning more than ever to set eyes on the artist who had painted her with such emotion, intuition, and realism; the entrepreneur whose fantasy had created this magical place; the man who had caused her father so much grief.

"I noticed him at the bar when we came in. I can't see him now. He'll be back once Morgana comes on stage. He very rarely misses her show."

"I don't blame him," joked Peter. "She's rather ravishing."

"I've had quite enough of this conversation," said Sandy. She looked angry, Coral thought, but the others didn't seem to care.

"Isn't Raphael an archangel's name?" she asked.

"Archangel, my foot," Henry scoffed. "More like his nickname: 'Rafe.' Hardly anyone calls him Raphael now. Rafe has stuck, and it suits his rakish personality much better, don't you think?"

"I do wish you'd stop all this nasty gossiping," said Sandy as she eyed Coral uneasily. "Anyway, you don't know that all these stories about him are factual."

"Oh, yes, they are, trust me. At the time, the scandal was carefully hushed up; only snatches of the incident were leaked out. He ran away and has just come back. No doubt he hopes society has a short memory."

"Hopefully, this would have served him as a lesson," Fiona piped in.

"My dear, leopards don't change their spots." Henry was beginning to warm to his theme. "He'll be at it again in no time, if he's not already."

"I really don't care for your venomous tongue, Henry," Sandy snapped. "Rafe is a friend of mine, and I will not sit here and listen to you tearing him to bits."

"Oooh, touchy, aren't we? Holding a torch for the Frenchman?"

Bonnie nudged him. "That's enough, Henry. What will Coral think of us?"

Sandy suddenly forced some joviality. "Absolutely! Come on. We've had far too much talk. I'm starving. What does everyone want to eat?"

Coral barely touched her food. The lobster salad she had ordered looked and tasted delicious, but she had lost her appetite. She felt anxious and excited.

The lights in the room were now dimming, as those on stage became brighter. Members of the Tarabu Orchestra silently took their places at the far end of the dance floor. Soon after, hesitant notes, an insinuation of liquid melody, floated across the night club. With a sudden, dramatic rolling of drums, Morgana made her entrance.

At first, Coral had a vision of a shimmering comet that flashed across the stage. When she became accustomed to the woman's costume of glittering spangles, she saw that Morgana possessed the warm, dusky beauty of the women of the Middle East. So diaphanous was her skin, it appeared as if a golden light illuminated the design of her features, which were molded to the perfection of an ancient cameo. Her great, dark eyes flashed provocatively, and her thick, raven hair hung loosely to her waist, forming a dramatic black cloak around her shoulders.

The opening rhythms of the orchestra seemed to turn Morgana from a statue of marble into a living virago. The strips of voile that constituted her skirt alternately flared out then rolled themselves around her legs at every turn and twist, showing off and enhancing each curve of her beautiful figure. She was like a goddess and must have been conscious of her terrifying beauty; Coral had no doubt that the woman's movements ignited the senses of all the men in the audience.

As Coral detached her gaze from the dancer, she caught sight of her elusive stranger. She thought at first that she was hallucinating, but after closing her eyes for a brief moment, she had to face facts: Her stranger from the ship was there, sitting at the bar, sipping what she guessed was neat scotch.

Even before Fiona's husky voice had whispered in her ear, "There he is… de Monfort. The man in the white jacket, sitting at the bar," Coral had guessed the truth.

For a second, everything around her was turning: the dancer, the tables, the walls. What chaotic emotion the simple presence of that man aroused in her. He was looking at Coral, too, with a brooding but slightly dazed expression. Clearly he hadn't expected to see her there tonight.

Morgana had also noticed Rafe. She slowly danced her way toward him, but her professionalism ensured that her movements betrayed no emotion. Her face alone burned with passion, and her eyes, steadily fixed upon the man she apparently loved, were afire.

Morgana began quite obviously to dance for him alone. Coral remembered Dale telling her about this kind of thing happening in nightclubs in North Africa, where belly dancers chose a particular man for the evening and showered him with attention. She had wondered at the time if Dale himself had ever experienced one of these private dances. Coral watched as Morgana leaned over Rafe, brushing him with her black mane, jingling the silver bracelets on her wrists with her feline gestures. The Frenchman watched her, a slight smile on his face, but the look in his eyes remained detached and sad.

"It looks like the exotic Morgana is welcoming the boss back, tonight." Henry leaned back in his chair, smirking as he took a swig of his beer.

Coral couldn't stand it any longer. Henry's chippy comment was the last straw. "I need some fresh air," she whispered to Sandy. "I'm going for a short walk in the garden." As she made her way through the crowded room, she could feel Rafe's gaze following her, and that was enough to make her want to flee the place.

Outside, the night was balmy to perfection, with the heady scent of jasmine in the air. Coral walked along the path that skirted the edge of the cliffs. She could hear the lull of breaking waves directly below, while the sky above her twinkled with the light of a thousand stars.

She felt deeply disturbed. Everything seemed clear now. Rafe de Monfort's interest in her on board the ship, his elusiveness at the port fearing a confrontation with Robin, Aluna's fears and warnings, and even that day on the beach…

How foolish, how incredibly naïve she had been. Feeling disillusioned and angry, she suddenly hated the man who had made her feel so indescribably ridiculous.

"What can one dream of in front of the ocean? Of a departure or an arrival?" The voice that she knew she would never forget came from behind her. Damn it, he had followed her outside.

Coral turned to face the man who had hurt her father and who perhaps had the power to hurt her too, if she let him. She recoiled instinctively as she was confronted with the implacable gaze boring directly into her own eyes.

"Good evening, Monsieur de Monfort." Her icy voice belied the turmoil she felt.

"I see that I'm not an absolute stranger to you anymore."

"Yes, and your reputation has preceded you as well," she said.

"Ah… come now, don't be afraid of the devil. He isn't as devilish as people make out. Don't look so alarmed, young lady. I'm not a werewolf, even though in some mud huts parents threaten their children with me."

He gave a short, flippant laugh. She had the impression he was mocking her, and at that moment her temper got the better of her. At the sound of his laugh, all her suppressed feelings of shock and anger bubbled up to the surface — she had been deceived by this man who had seemed so kind and caring on the ship, by this man who had caused her father so much pain by betraying him with her stepmother, who Aluna tried to warn her about, of whose reputation she had heard plenty in the gossiping jibes of her companions tonight, leaving her feeling like an idiot. And then seeing Morgana dance so seductively for her lover — the man who had made Coral feel like no other man had done before… Before she could stop herself, her hand came up and slapped him across the face. "You're the most pathetic of parasites," she heard herself exclaim, "a leech that feeds on other people, and I despise you, Rafe de Monfort, for what you are and for what you've done in your mean little life." She was trembling not only with fury but also with amazement at her own behavior. *Where had that come from?* Coral always had a quick temper and a wounding tongue, but she also knew in her heart of hearts that there was more to her outburst than met the eye. Leaving him there, she turned on her heel and strode off.

***

Rafe's gaze followed Coral's slim figure until it had disappeared into the Golden Fish. He lit a cigarette and remained awhile on the cliffs, lost in thought watching the phosphorescence of the ocean beneath him and the familiar stars in the dark sky. The shadow of a rueful smile played around his lips as he rubbed his cheek, which was still hot from Coral's slap. So, Walter's little girl had grown up into an impulsive, passionate woman. He wasn't surprised; he had painted enough of Walter's photographs of her to guess at Coral's fiery nature: the flame was there in the shining blue eyes, the rebellion in the tilt of her chin, even in the earlier snapshots.

Before he had even set eyes on her, Rafe had found Coral's face intriguing to paint because of the mixture of strength and fragility he saw in her — the vulnerability and innocence as well as the passion that not only the artist in him sensed, but the man too. Walter had talked so much about his little girl, how engaging and unusual she was as a child, always running wild, looking for adventures with the local African children. Year after year, Rafe had followed the progress of Coral's character through her letters that Walter had shared with him, and those not so silent pictures, and gradually he had fallen for his muse.

And now she was here. He had immediately recognized her on board ship. When dawn broke and the two of them had been alone on deck, Rafe had watched as Coral's face emerged out of the shadows, revealing her delicately carved features. It had been a shock to see her in the flesh; her beauty and presence was even more striking in real life. Although everything about her spoke of gentle innocence, he was now struck by the seductive edge to her beauty and found her much lovelier than he had initially thought.

Translucent, fragile, and pure, her looks evoked the sylphs of northern legends — but most of all, he was conscious of her eyes. At first, he had only noticed their brightness, their dimension, and their infinite depths. Now, they told him more, so much more. And faced with this young woman, the man who, during his weathered, tarnished life had met an endless stream of women he could sum up at a glance, found himself confused and disconcerted.

A hand pinched Rafe's heart, and his eyes clouded. Could the idealistic, platonic love he had nurtured for her portraits turn into something deep and even more wonderful: the salvation to his jaded life? But how could a man with years of baggage behind him aspire to be with such innocence and purity? And how could Coral ever be interested in Rafe when general society condemned him for, among other things, disloyalty to a man who was adored and respected by everyone and who had lent him a helping hand? Her own father, no less. Coral had everything going for her: beauty, a promising career, money, and, by the looks of it, courage and character. Surely her heart was already engaged, and she wouldn't spare him a thought? Anyhow, as she'd said, his reputation had preceded him. And if he should try to defend himself to her... to what end? She would never believe him, and in any case, he had too much of a past for her to take on. No, it would be wrong to attempt to see her again or to entertain thoughts about things that could never be.

Rafe looked at his watch. It was getting late; he must return to the club. He sighed — a deep, heavy sigh — and threw away his cigarette butt, crushing it roughly with pent-up frustration.

Chapter Four

Two weeks had passed since the night at the Golden Fish — two long weeks during which Coral had attempted to forget Rafe de Monfort, Morgana, and all the nasty gossip. Most of all, she wanted to repress the memory of her irrational behavior toward the man they called the Frenchman. Now that she was able to stand back and be more objective, her intuition told her she had judged him too rashly, overreacting in the heat of the moment and allowing herself to be carried away by her emotions.

She had not seen Rafe again, and though she had attempted to drive him from her mind, her thoughts frequently drifted back to him. Despite what she had heard about Rafe, their few encounters had revealed him to be attractive, likeable, and even kind. Could he be that manipulative? Charming was the word. "Charming as the devil" went the saying, and Aluna had said he was the Devil with a capital D. And yet something in his attitude puzzled her. Was it his reserve or the sadness that, despite the charming smile, filtered through the fortress it seemed he had built around himself? Still, he had hurt her father badly, and by the sound of it, he was an unscrupulous philanderer; Walter Sinclair had not been his only victim. It was best to stay clear of him and of his dangerous games.

Robin had returned from his trip to Nairobi a few days before, and together they had visited Timothy Locklear, her father's solicitor. Locklear informed them that Walter Sinclair, while leaving his daughter the bulk of his estate, mainly the house and its property, had also made provisions for Cybil, giving her a handsome annual income and a home in Mpingo — a cottage on the grounds — for life. Would her father have been so magnanimous to his wife if he had thought she had been unfaithful? Coral thought it unlikely, but then again, Walter Sinclair always did have a generous heart.

She did not often see her stepmother who was almost always absent or, on the few occasions when she was around, stayed conveniently out of Coral's way. Coral had developed a busy social life. When she was not out on the town with Sandy and her gang, she would hop into her father's old Buick and explore the countryside, taking photographs that she would use for her articles on Kenya.

Sometimes, on a beautiful day, equipped with a straw hat, a snorkel, mask and flippers, sunglasses, and a towel, plus her camera in case she stumbled upon a particularly stunning scene, she would take a small rowing boat in search of a solitary bay. There she could peacefully retire, far from the masses that invaded most beaches.

Today was one of those particularly fine days — a sapphire sort of day, when the sky and the ocean blended. Coral ran down to the beach after a light breakfast. The sea was divinely calm and transparent, looking like cool liquid silk, and she spent most of the morning going in and out of the water to avoid the glaring sun. She could see the beaches of an island that had intrigued her since her childhood glittering across the smooth expanse in the distance. It did not look so far away, and Coral felt like this was the perfect time for an excursion. Fully armed with her usual paraphernalia, she set out in her rowing boat to the isolated reef.

Once at sea, the wind was refreshing. Wearing sunglasses to protect her eyes from the blinding glare, Coral rowed, filling her lungs with the clean air, enjoying the briny smell of seaweed and the taste of dry salt on her lips. Seagulls whirled around the boat, hoping to be fed, then swooped and dived, only to arch out of their fall to seize the small fish darting through the water.

It was not long before Coral reached her deserted island, which now appeared overgrown with a jungle greenery of tall palms and luscious shrubs. She pulled her boat onto the beach next to a heap of mossy rocks that appeared to mark the entrance to a cave. Pools of turquoise water dotted the stretch of tawny sand, creating curiously shaped coves and secluded creeks. This was a place to relax, she thought as she threw herself onto the shore, thrilled with her discovery.

Coral lolled about in the warm, clear shallows. Here and there the seabed sloped into cool, deep water, revealing a mysterious universe where she was surrounded by the gem-bright treasures of the sea. With amazement and wonder, she watched multicolored sea creatures nibble at the reefs, schools of brightly striped angelfish and others wildly spotted or recklessly patterned, swimming among vivid anemones and striking coral bouquets as if straight out of an artist's canvas.

The sun was still high when Coral decided to start back, but first she would quickly explore the rocky section of the shore where she had moored the boat. On closer inspection, the tall crags concealed a narrow entrance — they were the outer shell of an extraordinary cave. When Coral made her way inside, she found it was deserted. Scattered rays of sun filtering through the crevices reflected off shallow pools of water on the floor and gave it the eerie majesty of an empty cathedral.

Unexpectedly, this fragile illusion was shattered by the distant sound of voices. Startled, Coral stood still and listened. A woman's laughter floated toward her. *Could there be anyone else on this island? What was there on the other side of the rocks?* She heard the voices again, the words more distinct this time. She guessed they were speaking in English. The laughter chimed back to her through the rocks, a coquettish peal that sounded familiar.

Coral splashed through the puddles in the cave and climbed over the haphazard heap of stones, making her way toward the place she suspected the voices were coming from. Soon she reached an alternative way into the cave. It was another narrow passageway that opened up on a different stretch of golden beach. Coral craned her neck and peeped through a wide crevice just inside the entrance, almost losing her balance as she recognized Rafe on the sand in the company of her stepmother. Fate seemed determined to put him in her path again.

From her hiding place, Coral had a perfect view of him as he stood facing Cybil, leaning against a white dinghy. She had never before had the opportunity to look him over in detail; that day on the beach, when she had hurt her foot, he had been wearing a T-shirt. Now she could assess at leisure the hard, toned physique with its well-proportioned lines. The black swimming trunks that clung to him emphasized his masculinity. This sudden exposure of his tanned body came as a shock to her system, creating a strange, hollow feeling in her stomach.

The couple seemed to be in deep conversation. She strained her ears. "Eavesdroppers never hear good of themselves," her mother used to say. Nevertheless, she was curious to know what they were talking about and, from her position behind the crevice, could make out most of it.

"You had an open marriage," her stepmother was saying.

"That isn't true; she never played around."

"More fool her if she didn't, but don't give me that. Everybody talked about her, and you know it."

He sighed and let himself slide onto the ground in full view of Coral. She nearly lost her balance as she watched him stretch out his lean body on the sand. "What the hell, anyhow," he said, lying back with his arms behind his head. "I know she did, and I witnessed it on at least one occasion. Still… it's all in the past now."

"D'you still love her?"

His expression hardened. "Love? Love in my book is another name for sex. Women too often confound the two, which is very tedious, and from that stems all the problems."

Cybil laughed. "So you don't love me?" She sat down next to him and laid a caressing hand on his wide chest. The movement drew Coral's attention to the fine strands of hair curling on his torso and narrowing down to his navel in a silky, dark line.

"Oh, don't start all that again, Cybil. You've always known the score. I never once in word or in action gave you the slightest encouragement besides showing you how much I enjoyed our games. You're a very sexy woman, Cybil, a superlative mistress in between the sheets, but out of the bedroom… " Rafe pushed her hand away.

"You don't really mean that," she snapped. "What's the matter with you? Walter is out of the way now. You have no excuse."

"Just drop it, Cybil," he said firmly.

"I can guess what the matter is," she went on stubbornly. "It's that girl — she's got under your skin, hasn't she? I know you met her on the ship. She's not just a painting to you any more, is she?"

There was a pause while he played with the sand, letting it sift slowly in between his fingers.

"Well? Tell me, am I right?"

"I've told you to drop it, Cybil," he said quietly, still fiddling with the sand.

"Am I to understand that in his old age, the cold-blooded womanizer has turned into a romantic fool?" Cybil stretched herself out close to him — much too close — showing off the curves of her body that a skimpy bikini had difficulty concealing.

"No, Cybil," he answered in a smooth, husky drawl, "I'm not saying that." He shrugged. "I simply don't feel like talking about it." He sat up quickly, looking irritated and scanning the scenery. "What was it you wanted to talk to me about anyway, and why out here?"

Cybil carried on as if Rafe had not spoken. "It's those baby wide eyes, blushing schoolgirl's look, and not much else between her ears that you find appealing, I suppose. You'd soon become bored. Anyhow, she hates you now. That servant of hers made sure of that. Trust the old witch to make mischief. I heard part of their conversation one afternoon." She laughed. "Coral must hate me too, though I must admit she's very good. She hardly shows her emotions. Perhaps she doesn't have any, she's so damned aloof. For all I know, she's as cold and indifferent as she seems."

A shadow passed over Rafe's eyes. "You really don't like her, do you?" He picked up a bright pink shell on the sand. A sardonic smile flashed across his face. Muscles flickered under the golden skin of his lean thighs as he stretched out his legs and leaned back on his arms. "Do I detect signs of jealousy, Cybil?"

She laughed again, throwing her head back, a note of hysteria evident. "Jealous, darling! What... of that girl who wouldn't know what to do with a man if he were served up to her on a plate?" She pouted. "That's selling me short."

By this time, the light had finally dawned on Coral. It was her they were discussing so casually out there on a sunny afternoon. Anger rampaged through her, and it was only the fear of humiliating herself that kept her from storming out from her hiding place and showing them just how cold and aloof she was.

While they had been talking, a breeze had started up. Cybil shivered. "It's getting cold," she said sulkily as she jumped up from the sand. "I'd better be on my way. I'd hate to be caught up in a storm, as you don't seem in the mood to rescue me. We can talk another time when you're in a better mood."

He shrugged absentmindedly and watched with empty eyes as she put on her robe, stepped into a motor boat that was moored down the shore next to a coconut tree, and roared off in a cloud of foam.

I should get out of here too, Coral thought as she turned on her heel to make her way back through the cave. She nearly slipped, smothering a cry and grasping the rock with both hands to stop herself from falling. After that, she placed one foot in front of the other more deliberately, choosing her path with care. Coral had not gone far when steely fingers closed around her arm, pulling her back with a force that made her gasp.

"And where d'you think you're going, little damsel?" she heard Rafe's voice say. Coral pivoted and met curious, golden eyes watching her with contained amusement.

"Let me go!" she gasped, struggling to escape the iron grip.

"Not before you tell me what you were doing here. Eavesdropping, were we?"

"Take your hands off me!" she hissed, lifting her free arm and swinging it forward clumsily in an attempt to free herself. Rafe swiftly caught her wrist. His eyes had suddenly turned very dark, and they glittered dangerously.

"Oh, no, my girl, not this time you're not!" he rasped as he brought down her two wrists, immobilizing her. "Do you always go around hitting men, or is it just me who brings this nastiness out in you?"

"I was trying to get free, you idiot, I wasn't trying to hit you. And do you always go around creeping up on people from behind?"

He stared into her eyes, a disturbing gaze that stunned her. His body was so close that she could almost feel the rise and fall of his chest against her as his breathing quickened. His eyes traveled all over her face as if trying to find something. Suddenly his hands relaxed on her arms, but he did not move. Coral closed her eyes for a moment, her fury stumbling into something else. Warmth flooded her as his strong palms slid up to her shoulders, and she opened her eyes. She felt slightly dizzy; his mouth was so dangerously close, and she arched toward him a bit, instinctively wanting to increase their contact. *This is madness*, warned a distant part of her mind, but her body began to respond of its own accord, in spite of what she had learned about him. She was hovering on the edge of a ravine. She knew she should stop him, but his touch was inflaming her senses to the extent that she felt utterly powerless. She felt him stiffen and saw sadness creep into his eyes. Had he read her mind?

"Coral… Coral, I'm not who you think I am," he murmured. His words seemed to sober her up, to draw her back to reality. Who was he then? Why was she not running from him as fast as she could? Wasn't he a loathsome womanizer?

She pulled away from him abruptly, escaping the plea she could read in his dazed eyes as he still held onto her shoulders.

"No, I know who you are," she managed to say firmly, pushing him away with both hands, still trembling and panting for breath.

"But, Coral, you don't understand… You don't know everything about me," he whispered, his voice thick, his eyes searching hers urgently.

Oh, those eyes, those treacherous womanizer's eyes. She must not let them influence her. She must not succumb to their tantalizing spell.

"No," she said unsteadily. "No, Monsieur de Monfort." Her voice rang in her ears, sounding like a high-pitched caricature of her own. "You are quite mistaken. I know enough about you to know that you only care about your own gratification, and I want nothing else to do with you, not now, not ever." With that, she turned around and unsteadily started on her way back through the rocks.

Suddenly Coral stopped, petrified, as she recognized the long gray reptile with chevrons on its back, seemingly asleep, that was coiled on the rocks a couple of feet away. Her scream never materialized: it was choked in her throat while she watched with wide-eyed horror as the puff adder reared itself up, inflating its thick body, preparing to strike. She heard the famous hissing sound dart out, and then two strong arms snatched her up, throwing her to one side. Rafe was straddling the snake, gripping it about eighteen inches below the head. Coral watched him, her body shivering with fright as he fearlessly hit the flat head again and again, smashing it with a big rock. With a pang of remorse, she noticed that even though she had escaped unharmed from the venomous creature, its nasty pointed fangs had not spared her rescuer. Two deep scratches bleeding freely in Rafe's left thigh and two others on his right hand bore witness to his courage.

"You'd better go home," he said gruffly, without looking at her. "D'you have a boat?"

"Yes, thank you," she managed to say in a shaky voice. "How will you return?"

"Don't worry about me," he answered bitterly. "I'm a big boy. I can apparently take care of myself."

"But you're hurt," she whispered. "You can't row back in your present condition. Besides, that adder was venomous, and you must see a doctor immediately. Won't you come in my rowing boat?"

"Thank you for the kind concern. If you ask me, the quicker I'm shot of you, the better off I'll be. Serpents are not the only dangerous creatures around here."

"I'm sorry," she said in a toneless voice. "I've really made a mess of things, haven't I… ?"

"Just go now," he murmured. "I'll be all right."

She noticed he was very pale, and his features were drawn. He must be suffering. "Let me at least bring you my towel," she offered. "I could tear strips out of it and cover those wounds. They mustn't become infected."

He shook his head and wearily passed his hand over his forehead and through the shock of black hair. Suddenly he appeared vulnerable to her, and she attempted a step toward him, but he stopped her with a firm gesture of his hand.

"If you really want to help, Coral," he said with a weary sigh, "just go now." He managed the shadow of a smile. "Don't worry… I'll be fine."

As Coral rowed back to the mainland, she debated whether to send out help to him. She lingered anxiously on the beach, praying for him to return safely. Finally, she saw the white dinghy in the distance, a bright form moving across the ocean against the indigo sunset. She breathed a sigh of relief, and only then did she make her way home.

***

During the days that followed, Coral suppressed the urge to see Rafe again. She felt terribly guilty, and her mind would not rest until she was sure that nothing untoward had happened and he was not suffering some ill effect from the snake's scratches.

On her return to the house, she had looked up *snakes* and *snakebite* in her father's *Encyclopaedia Britannica*, and the information she found only reinforced her worry. Subsequently, she tried discreetly to find out the Frenchman's news from Sandy and her friends, but again without success. In a moment of panic, she considered asking Cybil whether she had seen Rafe lately, only to dismiss that alternative almost as soon as it crept into her confused mind. Finally, when she was at her wits' end, thinking that the worst had happened, it was Aluna who unwittingly brought her the information she was seeking.

Coral was dressing for a party. Aluna had brought in the clothes she had just ironed and was putting them away in the cupboard, chattering in her usual manner, when the faraway drumming of the tom-tom rolled out of the darkness.

"How I hate that sound," Coral whispered, clenching her teeth.

Aluna stopped hovering and concentrated, reading the rhythms like Morse code. "That's the tom-tom of the snake worshippers. They are preparing for the sacrifice."

"What snake? What sacrifice?" asked Coral, her eyes wide with surprise.

"The Frenchman, he killed their god, Koleo. Now he must die." Aluna's dark eyes flashed, and to mark the effect of her words, she was pointing toward the window with a long finger. "He has desecrated the spirits of the ancestors who take the sacred form of the snake in this world… The Frenchman is finally going to get his punishment," she gloated, still listening to the beating of the drums. "They could find no medicine to neutralize the poison. They even sent for the medicine man. They'll never be able to save him." She gave a satisfied laugh.

Coral felt her blood run cold. "I hate it when you talk in this way. I would have thought that with all the books Daddy gave you to read over the years, you would have realized this magic and wizard business is ignorant rubbish and not worthy of your intelligence."

"Your father, my child, believed in what you call rubbish as much as us Africans, so don't be fooled. He died because he believed."

Coral was not listening anymore. She rose and quickly slipped into the black one-shoulder goddess gown she had chosen for the evening. Her mind was made up. She would go to Rafe on her way to the party and see how she could help. After all, it was because of her that he was lying there, maybe fighting for his life.

While driving to Whispering Palms, she tried to make sense of her feelings. Since the trip to the desert island, her brain had been surging with a sea of contradictory thoughts about Rafe. Even though she could not help blushing at the memory of his body brushing against hers and the instinctive response that had ignited her own body before she had come to her senses, it was not the erotic images of the man that seemed to grip her the most. For it was not the slick, irresistible charmer who had touched a sensitive cord deep inside her, despite the warnings of her rational mind. It was the other side of him that was most attractive: the man she had met on board the ship; the one who had picked her up so caringly when she was hurt; who had leaped to her rescue without hesitation when she had been threatened by danger, putting his own life on the line; the man she could sense beyond the sexual predator.

Rafe was different from Dale, different from almost any man she knew. Sure, she had been strongly drawn to the American tycoon. At the time, she had even imagined that what she felt was love. How could she not have? Dale's personality had been so compelling. He was so sure of himself, so handsomely arrogant, that he had bulldozed a path into her life and swept her off her feet.

Coral was not a young woman of her time. She may have grown up in the "free love" of the sixties, but she didn't see herself as the typical modern woman who had been created by the Age of Aquarius. She had spent most of her formative years, both in Africa and at boarding school in England, sheltered in some way or another from the real world. At twenty-five, she was still a virgin — one of very few, as far as she knew, in her class at the photography school in London. Some of them were even taking the contraceptive pill, even though they weren't married. Dale had been surprised, even a little shocked, when Coral had insisted that they wait until after the wedding to make love. He'd found her inexperience rather frustrating. "We'll soon put that right, honey," he had said with a bored drawl. "There's nothing magical about sex — it's pure animal instinct. I've never understood what all the fuss is about!" Looking back, his comment seemed rather coarse and unromantic, but Coral had not dwelled on it at the time. He had certainly not awoken any part of her sensual nature, and while she admitted she was naïve in matters of the heart, she was definitely not frigid, as Dale had implied when she refused him. Again, images of Rafe's tanned and muscled body swam into her mind, and she struggled to dismiss them, concentrating on the road ahead.

She turned into Whispering Palms and started her zigzag up the steep, winding avenue of trees that gave the property its name. The house, perched high on stilts at the edge of a remote bluff overlooking a healthy sisal plantation, appeared positively eerie in the fitful moonlight. From what she could make out, it was a simple two-story block, completely surrounded by a gallery, with a makuti palm-leaf thatched roof and slender wooden posts supporting it at the eave line. Not a single light shone from its full-length windows. It looked deserted. Great — that was just what she needed.

She took an uncertain step out of the car into the smoky darkness. The night was still and warm. The threatening beat of drums had ceased, but the stillness of the countryside was just as unnerving. What was she doing here? He may not even be here. Or then again, he may be in the house, helpless while awaiting assistance. The idea of him lying there, weak and disabled, was enough to stifle any remaining misgivings about coming tonight.

Coral started up the wooden stairs. Almost immediately she heard barking, and within seconds, Buster was leaping out of the darkness.

"Quiet, quiet now, Buster," she cried out with grateful relief as she recognized the familiar Australian shepherd. The dog barked again twice — friendly little barks of recognition this time — accompanied by a great deal of tail wagging. "Good dog," she said as she patted him gently, "good dog. Now lead me to your master... Where's Rafe?"

The bright little fellow ran up the stairs, leading the way round the gallery and into a dimly lit room.

Rafe was stretched out on a divan in a far-off corner of the vast room, amid shadows and solitude. She tip-toed her way to him, holding her breath, afraid to violate his privacy. Silently standing over him, she watched him sleep — a lion in repose. For a fleeting second, she glimpsed something heartrending in the pained expression of his features. Was it her imagination? Still, for the time being, Coral would never forget the way he looked at that moment in the mellow light, exposed and unguarded. She found herself wanting nothing more than to be close to him, to protect him from the nightmares that seemed to haunt him.

Rafe opened his eyes, and she panicked, uncertain how he would react to her presence there. He closed his eyes and opened them again, running a hand through his thick black hair and over his face, unsure, as though in a dream. "What are you doing here?" he finally managed to say in a voice still thick with sleep.

"May I... sit down?"

When he signaled her to go ahead, she sat on the edge of an armchair, facing him. They were silent. Coral shifted awkwardly in her seat.

"I'm sorry," he said suddenly, staggering to his feet. "I haven't even offered you a drink."

"Thank you, I won't have anything." Her voice was almost inaudible.

"Come now, since you're here you'll keep me company, won't you?" He ambled over to a cabinet and turned on the light before taking out two small glasses and a bottle. "Crème de menthe... "

"I've never tasted it. I don't drink much apart from wine."

"You'll like this. It's a lady's drink."

She noticed he was now fully awake, relaxed, in total control of himself. He poured himself a double shot of scotch from a bottle that had obviously been his companion for the past few days. He took his place on the divan opposite her and sipped the amber liquid quietly, assessing her through his dark eyelashes.

"You look very elegant tonight. Going or coming from somewhere interesting?" he asked, the familiar playful smile floating on his lips. He glanced at his watch. "Ten thirty already… By the way, you haven't told me to what I owe the honor of your visit. What can I do for you?"

She coughed to clear her voice and swallowed hard before blurting out, "I… I… I've come because I was concerned about you, and also I want to apologize for causing you such trouble and for being so rude to you. I've said some horrible things to you. I feel guilty. I heard you were unwell… in danger, I mean, and… "

Rafe gave a sad, disenchanted laugh. "Of course, many of the things you said were true. I won't deny it. You see, Coral, guilt does not run with the flock, it chases after it like the shepherd's dog. I suppose I've done a few rotten things in my life. I must have taken more than my fair share. God says: 'Take what you want and pay!' Perhaps now I am paying." He leaned his head against the back of the divan and shut his eyes, appearing tired and worn.

She felt an impulse to put her arms around him and imagined smoothing out his brow, erasing with her lips every little crease and those dark rings she noticed under his eyes. But she sat there, glued to her seat by his presence and by the surprising power of her emotions.

"Don't feel sorry for me," he said, seeming to mistake the concern he read in her eyes for pity.

"I don't." Coral shook her head, feeling a little flustered. "But you look so weary. Have you recovered from those bites?"

"Yes, I'm okay now. It took a couple of days longer because I thought I'd been attacked by a puff adder, when all the time it had been a Kiko snake. I should have recognized it even though it's very similar to the adder, but darker. It's quite common in this part of the world. Its poison is much more potent than that of an adder, and that's where I went wrong. But luckily I have the antidote in my cupboard, and it's fine."

"I'm very relieved that you're safe." She smiled at him for the first time.

"You mustn't worry about me — you mustn't worry about anything. It's very kind of you to have come by. I'm deeply touched," he whispered.

She smiled again, more demurely this time, relieved that he bore her no grudge. "I think I ought to leave now." She rose to her feet a little uncertainly.

"I will accompany you."

He walked her to the car with Buster on his heels. She was just about to get into it when he placed a hand on her arm. She turned and raised her head a little, her lips parted. His mouth came down, tender and gentle, only lingering briefly on her cheek. She breathed in quickly. "Good night, Coral, and thank you," he said quietly, endearment in the tone of his voice.

For a long moment, they looked into each other's eyes. Her heart was beating very fast. Something inside her was beginning to quiver, a heated sensation that she now recognized immediately. He was beginning to have that effect on her. She knew she must leave without delay before she actually threw herself into his arms and made a fool of herself. "Good night, Rafe," she whispered, and climbing into the old Buick, she started for home.

Coral felt no desire to go clubbing tonight. She wanted to be alone; for some reason the idea of partying with her friends had lost its appeal. She wondered what it was about this man's company that confused her so. The fascination had been there from the first time she had set eyes on him, but it was the thought of him being in danger, seeing him lying there vulnerable, and most of all the fact that he bore no grudge for the grief she had caused him, that kindled a strange flame within her and made her look at him with newly awakened eyes. He was definitely a womanizer, but so had her dear father been, and that hadn't made him a bad person. And as far as she knew, at least Rafe wasn't committed to anyone. Everybody had a weakness, and Rafe's was clearly women. That made him a seducer, not the monster Aluna painted him to be, she told herself.

***

A few days later Coral was finishing a late lunch downstairs on the veranda, helping herself to a last cup of coffee before her usual siesta in a hammock tied among the shady branches of a frangipane tree. As she was alone, she had perched the radio on the table next to her, and Simon and Garfunkel's "Bridge Over Troubled Water" came on, giving her a pang of sad amusement at how it matched her mood. All morning she had been on one of her outings to the beach, secretly hoping to bump into Rafe, and now she allowed herself to feel a little disillusioned by her failure.

Juma appeared and handed her a note. The stamp on it was local, and the handwritten address indicated this was a personal missive, not a business one. Perplexed, Coral tore the envelope open. Her heart leapt as she read the bold signature at the bottom of the page before her eyes devoured the brief note.

> Enclosed are six tickets for a show by the Kankan Dancers, a French Guinea troupe that is touring Kenya and will be performing tomorrow at the Golden Fish for one night only. It would give me great pleasure if you and your friends would do me the honour of being my guests. I look forward to your acceptance.
>
> Yours sincerely, Rafe.

Coral tried to contain her excitement as she went to the phone and rang Sandy to tell her about the show. Unfortunately, Sandy was leaving the next day for Barbados, and the other members of their crowd were either out of town or involved in the annual charity ball at the Mombasa Yacht Club on Saturday night. As she put the phone down, Coral tried to suppress the growing disappointment and frustration she felt, gradually replacing the earlier thrill of anticipation. She couldn't ignore her desire to see Rafe again, and every time she had been on the beach she had listened for the Australian shepherd and his master. Rafe's note had been most opportune, and now she would have to decline his invitation.

Coral made her way to the front of the house and sat on the steps of the veranda. She encircled her legs with her arms and rested her forehead on her knees, deep in thought. Somehow she would find a way of attending the show, even if it meant going to the nightclub on her own. In the meantime, she decided to go to Whispering Palms and deliver the answer to Rafe's invitation herself.

She went up to her room to shower again, wash her hair, and change. A couple of hours later, clad in tight white jeans and a multicolored halter top that set off her golden tan, she skipped down the stairs, breezed through the front door into the garden, and flew straight to the car, trying to calm the excitement that radiated through her at the thought of meeting Rafe again.

It was nearly half past four when Coral arrived at Whispering Palms. The sun was still high, but the heat of the day had died down and the air was cooler. The house in daylight was quite different from the desolate impression she had gotten the night before. Built into the hillside, it looked down on the Indian Ocean in the distance across acres of sisal — the perfect place to enjoy panoramic views of stunning sunsets and dramatic storms with the incessant strumming of the cicadas in the background. Now she could see columns and repeated arched architectural details that dressed up the structural support for the roof, giving the property an elegant grandeur devoid of all ostentation, which fitted its owner's personality to perfection.

To Coral it was as though she had suddenly entered the forbidden Garden of Eden, lush with brilliant flashes of tropical flowers and tumultuous vegetation. Tropical wilderness had joined in, mixing and blending form and color with the artful genius of nature. She spotted Rafe ahead of her at the entrance to the house. Coral pulled up on the gravel drive, a little way from the building, and got out.

Rafe had his back to her, hands deeply thrust into his pockets. Broad shoulders and rippling muscles were outlined under his red T-shirt, with his narrow hips clad in the most revealing pair of jeans. He was totally absorbed in conversation with one of the plantation's workmen, so he did not hear Coral approaching until she was almost upon him. He turned abruptly, caught unaware, and she thought he flushed a bit under his nut-brown tan.

Rafe dismissed the worker with a few words in Swahili, all his attention now focused on his visitor. "Hello." He grinned, his eyes flickering appreciatively over the neckline of her revealing top.

Coral brought a self-conscious hand to her throat as the dark gaze drifted to her bare shoulders, silently appraising her. She raised her head slowly and looked directly at him. "I've come to apologize," she said, trying to steady her voice. "Unfortunately I'm forced to decline your kind invitation for tomorrow night. My friends are either away or taking part in the Mombasa Yacht Club charity ball."

Her face felt suddenly hot as the gold in his eyes intensified, burning into hers as though trying to read her most secret thoughts. "That settles it for your friends then," he said. "Shall we say that we'll first have a quiet, *al fresco* dinner here at seven, before I take you off to the Golden Fish for the show?"

"I didn't say I could come," she ventured, trying to sound casual.

The piercing gaze fixed her now with contained amusement. She was aware he was entertained by her little ruse. Coral glared at him. She was tempted to turn down his offer, but she refrained, realizing she would kick herself afterward for being too proud and over-sensitive. Wasn't his reaction what she had hoped for when deciding to come to Whispering Palms with her answer? Coral had been transparent, and Rafe had applied the same cunning, playing her at her own game. *Touché*, she thought and nodded her assent.

"Splendid," he said with unrestrained satisfaction. He smiled at her — a sweet, unassuming smile. "I'm about to do the rounds of the plantation. Would you care to accompany me? I'd like to show it to you." His tone was cajoling, his eyes secretly pleading.

She felt herself once more trapped in his charismatic aura; he did not need to plead. She was only too happy to stick around, visiting his plantation or otherwise. "Yes" — her reply was almost a whisper — "yes, I'd love to, thank you."

The sun was still warm on their faces as they walked down a well-kept path to the plantation, side by side, nearly touching. Rafe's fingers momentarily brushed against Coral's, and she thought he was about to seek her hand, but then he withdrew it.

Coral was already aware of the lean masculine body only inches away, and this fleeting contact sent her senses into a new spin. Scented flowers of jasmine, wisteria, and roses climbed around stone arches and pillars that formed the romantic walkway, casting delightful shade and light onto the paving. The stone, he told her, had been imported from the Burgundy region of France. There was a flowering cactus in bloom in a small crevice as they passed the rock garden. "That's beautiful," Coral exclaimed as she stretched out her hand to touch the fleshy surface of the thick leaves.

"Don't!" Rafe grasped her hand. "It's innocent looking, but *'il ne faut pas se fier aux apparences* — all that glitters is not gold,'" he said, tightening his grip, his face shining with hidden mischief. "There are thousands of invisible spikes on that apparently smooth surface. They're hell to take out, as they're very difficult to see." Finally, he released her hand, and Coral found herself immediately missing its warmth.

The plantation was an impressive sight. Neat parallel rows of sisal plants extended as far as the eye could see. The red of the loose, sandy soil and the green of the long, spiky leaves set under the azure-blue sky were like a vibrant painting. Workers were busy loading bundles of those leaves into light railway trucks, undoubtedly transporting them from the field to the processing factory.

"This land was derelict when I bought the estate eight years ago," Rafe said. "Today it is one of the leading sisal plantations in Kenya, I am proud to say. Most of the ropes and agricultural twine you find in this country are made from our plants, as well as insulation for houses and countless other things."

"I had no idea it was so big. It seems larger than our plantation at Mpingo."

"It is, even though in terms of acreage, yours is a bigger estate, but your land is divided into various crops. You've got the orchard, the sisal plantation, and the *mpingo* tree sanctuary. I have concentrated solely on sisal. We plant it, extract the fiber from it, and sort and prepare it for export."

"Isn't that maize I can see there, between those double rows of sisal?" Coral pointed to a plot on the right, brushing against his arm.

He started at her contact but regained his composure in a flash. "You're right, that is maize we've planted. In order for the soil to continue to grow sisal, we must grow other crops to give back to the soil the elements it needs to stay healthy. Also, as you know, with Kenya having one of the highest population growth rates in the world, we need as much agricultural land as possible, so growing additional crops like maize alongside the sisal makes sense to maximize our production. I like to think that we do our little bit here to help hold back the problem of deforestation in this country. Come, I will show you our factory," he said, a tanned hand firmly bracing her arm as he led her to one of the out-buildings.

Coral had experienced more than once the iron clutch of his fingers, and her heart fluttered like a trapped moth, her senses acutely aware of his presence beside her. She did not dare look up at him in case her thoughts were revealed in her eyes. Coral had the strange impression he could read her like a book.

"It takes about five years for the plant to come to maturity, with leaves ready to be cut and put through the decorticating machines," he told her. "Planters like myself must be prepared to wait. It needs determination and patience, and I've got both in ample quantities."

Coral sensed the smile in his voice. She had not missed the double entendre and had no doubt he was watching her now, assessing the effect his words had on her. Feeling her color rising, she caught herself up sharply. Had she no pride? She was reacting to him like an unsophisticated, gullible adolescent in the throes of her first love — or worse, if she was honest with herself and admitted to the wanton thoughts that crowded her mind.

"We're here," he said, stopping in front of one of the squat buildings she had noticed. He let go of her arm, and they entered the factory. It consisted of a series of large rooms where men were offloading the leaves onto a fixed table sloping toward the feed belts of the decorticator.

"The leaves of sisal are fed into the machine singly, by hand. The butt-end goes in first because of the need to thrust the thick end through the narrow gap. When the leaf has been pushed in for half of its length, it's withdrawn, and the exposed fibers are grasped so that the tip-end of the leaf can be stripped in a similar fashion. It's a very slow and inefficient method, but of course much cheaper." He spoke with excitement, his features animated, like a child showing off his toys. He was obviously very proud of his achievements and wanted to share them with her.

"It seems very complicated."

"It isn't at all, and it's by far the most reliable method for the production of high-quality, clean fiber. In some countries, they still use the primitive method where the fibers in the leaves are extracted by hand. The leaves are beaten to a pulp with a mallet before being scraped on a block of wood and the fibers are washed afterward."

"What comes next?" she asked with genuine interest. She could understand Rafe's pride in his estate. She felt privileged and moved that he should want to show off to her a creation that must have taken years of hard work. This was the farmer, the entrepreneur, the businessman who was talking to her and treating her like an equal, not the cynical womanizer who perhaps thought of her as just a pretty face.

He seemed delighted by her inquisitive attention. "If you are interested, there is still a lot I can show you. First comes the grading and sorting of the fiber, then it must be sun dried, brushed, packed, and baled before it can be transported to the various factories."

"Do all these processes take place at Whispering Palms?"

"Of course." His voice was matter-of-fact, as if it were ridiculous to assume otherwise. "The fiber comes from the decorticator in bundles for sorting and grading. I have just bought an automatic grader that makes the job relatively easy. It should arrive in the next few days."

From there they went back out into the sunshine. Again, Coral was amazed at the number of workers that were spreading the fiber thinly over lines to dry in the sunshine.

"You've provided work to a great number of people," she said.

"Yes. I've always dreamed of providing jobs, of building a dynastic empire," he added, dropping his voice a little as though he were talking to himself. Once more she was aware of a sadness in his tone as he spoke, but it was there and gone in a flash, and perhaps had only been a figment of her imagination. "Shall we continue our round? Or maybe you're tired and would like to rest?"

"No, no, please let's go on. I'm finding it fascinating. I haven't really taken an interest in the sisal plantation part of Mpingo. I've left it to Robin, who seems to know what he's doing."

"That's a shame. Employees never look after one's interests in the same way, but I can see the difficulty you have. If I can be of any help, let me know."

That would set the cat among the pigeons, Coral thought. She could just imagine the reaction that sort of decision would have on the people at Mpingo. "Thank you," she said, smiling sweetly at him. Amusement had returned in the golden eyes that surveyed her through dark lashes. She sought to keep her expression neutral. "What comes next, then?" She wanted to get him back on a safe subject.

He complied and took her step-by-step through the next stages of the operation.

"Where did you learn all this?"

She felt him stiffen. He shrugged. "Oh," he said rather dismissively, "I worked for a while on a sisal plantation in Tanganyika." Maybe she was mistaking the sudden distant note in his voice as he moved away from her a little.

They strolled along to the next building. Rafe paused, clearing his voice. "Here ends our tour. The packing and the baling that are the last stages of the preparation for export take place in this hall." He smiled at her with that charm that made her stomach leap. "Once the bales are ready, we transport them to Mombasa Harbor by road."

There was a brief silence, vibrating with curious undercurrents, as they locked gazes. Then they meandered back to the house, Coral feeling strangely contented with their afternoon together. In the garden, the masses of flowers were folding their petals for the night. A nightingale sang in a bush of blossom, but when it heard the couple's footsteps up the path, it stopped suddenly.

"Will you come up for a drink?" Rafe asked her as they reached the house.

"Thank you, but I'd better be going. I've had such an enjoyable and interesting afternoon." Without thinking, she laid her hand over his, then, realizing what she had done, pulled it away self-consciously.

"Why?" he whispered, as he searched her eyes intently. Taking her hand, Rafe turned it over and tenderly kissed the center of her palm with his warm lips. It was a small and innocent gesture, but this most sensual display of his feelings made her heart surge.

Coral was trembling inside. He was still holding onto her hand, as if mesmerized by the moment. She did not know whether she wanted him to let go of it or not. The physical chemistry between them was again at work, and she was confused as always by his presence. He must have read the panic in her eyes, as he quickly let go of her hand. "I'll walk you back to your car," he said softly, "and I look forward to seeing you tomorrow, seven o'clock. Wear an evening gown. Time will seem long until then, rosebud."

Chapter Five

Coral sat on her bed, staring at the three long dresses she thought would be suitable for her evening out with Rafe. It was already past five o'clock, and she still hesitated. She should soon be making a start if she wanted to be ready on time. Aluna had been of no help. "You'll look beautiful in whichever dress you choose to wear," she had said dotingly. Coral had thought it wiser to tell her *yaha* as little as possible about the rendezvous, so Aluna was taking it for granted that she was going to the Yacht Club charity ball like most Mombasa young ladies of her group.

Coral glanced at her watch — time was marching. She must make up her mind between pink, black, and sapphire blue. Pink was nice, but she thought it a little bit too "coming out ball." Her beloved black Radley dress, sophisticated and chic with its delicate satin straps, nipped in waist, and long column skirt, was so *Breakfast at Tiffany's* but maybe too formal for this occasion. Finally, her eyes shifted to her third option. Coral ran her fingers thoughtfully over the layers of diaphanous fabric. It had been especially created for her to match the deep blue color of her eyes. The memory of the one time she had tried it on brought a rueful smile to Coral's face. There had been no wedding and no ball afterward, so it had remained neglected in her wardrobe. She would wear it this evening for Rafe. That decided, Coral finished getting ready, and as she spent time getting her hair and makeup right, she was aware that the prospect of spending a whole evening with Rafe was making her pulse race a little.

"You'll be the belle of the ball," Aluna proudly told her as she helped Coral slide into the silky georgette gown. The Grecian-inspired garment with its cascading draping, plunging neckline, and low back was figure-enhancing. Coral slipped on delicate, high-heeled sandals, giving height to her slender silhouette. She hesitated before adding a gold Roman arm cuff studded with sapphires and a pair of matching dangling earrings that were specifically designed to complement the outfit. Deciding it would be too much, she laid aside the coordinating necklace.

Coral surveyed herself critically in the mirror. Her hair was piled up in a mass of tendrils that looked artlessly sophisticated but at the same time retained a youthful vulnerability. She was glad she hadn't gotten the fashionable Sassoon sleek crop a few years back when it was all the rage. As far as she could remember, she had never taken so much trouble dressing up, not even for her coming-out party. What was it about this man that had so gotten under her skin? Was she playing with fire? But then again, her friends were always telling her to loosen up and have fun. What harm was there in having a flirtatious evening? She smiled at her reflection.

Coral was on time, arriving at Whispering Palms when the shadows were beginning to lengthen among the giant palms dotting the grounds. As she was turning off the ignition, Rafe appeared from behind the house and began making his way toward the car with that lazy grace that so personified him. He must have been waiting for her in the garden. He wore with casual elegance a white dinner jacket, white shirt, black dress trousers, and a bow tie that hung unfastened around his neck. He was as overpowering as ever, and Coral's pulse beat a little faster as he helped her out of the Buick.

"How dazzling you look," he murmured, his eyes sweeping over her plunging neckline. She colored faintly and looked away so as not to betray how much his inspection affected her. "I thought we'd have dinner on the patio in my secret garden." He gave her an enchanting smile and took her arm. Unlike his usual iron grip, Rafe's warm hand barely touched her, as if he was determined to handle her with extra care this evening.

"That sounds marvelous," she said in a small voice, smiling up at him, certain he could see the admiration in her eyes. There was a little pause. Coral sensed that Rafe was reading her: her longing to give, and also the pride that held her back.

His hand had moved to the small of her exposed back as he escorted her along the garden to the secluded spot behind the house. Pleasurable shivers trailed up and down Coral's spine, making her skin tingle with a delicious sensation. Still she was relieved when they reached their destination and Rafe fell a pace back to allow her onto the patio first.

Coral saw a temple covered with entwined roses, wisteria, and begonia dwelling heavily on a cedar trellis that sagged in the middle under their weight. The evening air was balmy, heavy with a symphony of scents from dwarf citrus trees in huge, clay planters. A murmuring old fountain with circular seats cut into the stone provided a perfect complement to the surroundings. In a corner, under an elderly fig tree, two rustic chairs and a stone table covered with an ivory-colored linen tablecloth had been set with unaffected elegance. The music of the flowing water and contrast of light and shade evoked a sense of mystery, creating an enthralling scene.

"This is my haven… " he said while assisting her to sit facing the fountain. "My very private place."

How many women had he brought here to dine in this very romantic, very private place of his? The thought gave Coral's heart a nasty little pinch. "It is truly enchanting," she said, accepting a glass of champagne. She closed her eyes and breathed in the rich aromas as she savored the fine wine.

Rafe walked behind her, to the other side of the patio where a service trolley stood. "I'm afraid it'll be a cold dinner tonight. I thought it would be refreshing and more practical. We'll start with avocado and smoked venison in a chive dressing." Coral smiled to herself; his obvious care over the food was so very French.

"It sounds delicious. I don't think you would ever hear an Englishman talking so knowledgeably about food!" Coral laughed. The champagne was already having a beneficial effect on her nerves, and she relaxed a bit.

Rafe returned with the first course which he laid in front of her before taking his place at the table. As she lifted her head to thank him, her eyes fell on the calligraphy engraved at the top of the fountain. *"We chase dreams and embrace shadows* — Anatole France," she read out loud, raising her eyebrows and looking at Rafe enquiringly. "Is that your motto?" She smiled with mischievous intent.

"No," he replied, regarding her with an indulgent smile, "it is there as a reminder."

"A reminder of what?"

He looked at her steadily, his eyes grave and dark now. "It's a warning against mistaking one's hopes for realities. Do you speak Spanish?"

"No, not really, just a little."

"Have you read *Don Quixote*?"

She shook her head. "I have very little knowledge of foreign literature."

He nodded. "You should read it sometime. It's very enlightening." He smiled lazily, watching her intently.

She shifted a little uncomfortably under his stare and tried to concentrate on her starter. "This is delicious. Did you make it?"

"Yes, I made it. There's not much to it, you know." He laughed deep in his throat.

"Do you enjoy cooking?"

"I do. I find it relaxing, but I don't have the time to do it as often as I would like. I'm seldom in one place for long, as I'm called away on business most weeks."

"Where do you go?"

"Mostly around Africa, sometimes to Europe, and occasionally to the United States."

"Why is that?"

"To find new markets for my sisal, apart from cordage and textile manufacturers. Do you cook, Coral?" he asked, abruptly changing the subject.

"Yes, sometimes, but I'm not very good at it. I like eating, though." She smiled modestly. "The food at your nightclub is of very high quality."

"I like to think that everything I deliver is of high quality." His eyes were twinkling, making her feel uncomfortable at his flirtatious subtext.

"I really enjoyed that, thank you," she said, laying down her knife and fork, trying to ignore his steady gaze.

"My pleasure." He stood up and took her plate.

"Can I help?"

"No, no, please. It's all under control."

Yes, everything seemed perfectly under control; he was very well organized by the looks of it. Practice makes perfect. A league of women must have sampled this cool efficiency, including her stepmother. Again, she noted that nasty little squeeze in her heart. "Is it a coincidence?"

"What?" he asked as he busied himself with preparing the main course.

"The phrase engraved at the top of the fountain."

"I hope you are fond of monkfish," he said, returning with a plate that was altogether colorful and simply arranged. "It's been marinated in a citrus dressing. That is a mousse of scallop roe with fresh tomatoes picked today in my greenhouse, and it is resting on a bed of julienne root vegetables."

"It sounds absolutely marvelous. I'm impressed." She paused as he regained his place opposite her. "Now, to come back to what we were saying…"

"Yes, food."

"No, Anatole France's saying."

"Umm?"

"The phrase engraved at the top of the fountain," she repeated a little impatiently, knowing he couldn't have forgotten already.

"Oh yes… " He started on his monkfish.

"Well? What's it all about?"

"You'll have to read *Don Quixote,* won't you?" He was eyeing her again with amusement.

"I will, but I'm just a little curious. Won't you give me a taster?"

He laughed loudly now, a warm, spontaneous laugh. "Oh, Coral, Coral," he said, pouring them both another glass of champagne. He nodded before taking a sip out of his glass. "All right. It's about chasing unrealistic dreams."

"And why do you need a reminder? Have you been chasing unrealistic dreams?"

"Maybe," he said, his voice now guarded.

Coral gave him a sharp look. "But isn't there also a saying that goes: *He who dreams, dines*? That was the White Pirate's motto."

"And it was also the motto that brought down Walter Sinclair, the man," he said.

"If it hadn't been for his dreams, Daddy would have never left the family business back in England, wouldn't have come to Africa, and certainly would not have risked all his savings in a place which, let's face it, was still an unknown prospect."

"Many people were investing in Africa at the time and made large amounts of money. It was a no-brainer."

"Is that what you did?"

"To some extent," he whispered.

"So where does your quotation fit in where Daddy's concerned?"

"Having chased his dreams, was your father happy?" His tone seemed to have hardened somewhat.

"I presume so, for most of the time I spent with him, at least."

Dark eyebrows lifted.

"Do you doubt it? I'm told you were very close to him." Coral hadn't forgotten that there was much that still disturbed her about this man, and she was challenging him to answer her.

Rafe did not answer but rose to his feet, a brooding expression on his face while clearing the table for the next course. Coral decided to push him further, hoping to ruffle his feathers.

"You mean he can't have been happy because in his search for true love he married a woman much younger than himself?" Coral said. "There's nothing wrong with that, provided it's the right woman." There she went again — her tongue getting the best of her even with threatening undercurrents in the air. *It must be the champagne.*

"True love is the most cruel and dangerous fallacy of them all." He was standing behind her at the trolley, but his tone was harsh, and she sensed that she had struck a raw nerve.

"Surely you don't mean that?" She looked at him over her shoulder to see him coming back to the table.

"Terrine of tropical fruit in jellied Sauterne," he announced.

Coral had the distinct impression that he was fighting some inner battle. Rafe clearly did not care to answer. Fair enough, she thought, leaving it at that. Anyway, having heard his opinion on love once before, she did not care for a repetition.

Taking her time, Coral savored the richly scented cold dessert. She wondered why he was being so evasive about the phrase engraved on the fountain. What prompted such cynical beliefs in a man who seemed to have such a sensitive nature? She would return to the subject another time.

"Here, taste this." Rafe stretched out his hand, picked a ripe fig from the tree above their heads, and gave it to her. "It's a delicious experience."

"Thank you." The fruit was still warm from the day's sun. It was fragrant and luscious as she bit into the rich, juicy flesh. Rafe had sat back in his chair so his face was in the shadow, but she knew he was watching her through half-closed eyes. When he leaned forward, the fire from the candles flickered, throwing shadows on the planes of his face. She could see his eyes clearly now, and their steady focus was causing her insides to stir. There was romance in the still air; the rhythm of dripping water from the fountain behind him, the velvet sky studded with stars, the balmy perfumes of the night, all combined to accompany the endless song that had begun in her heart again as she watched him, enthralled.

He stretched out his hand again, this time to wipe away a minute drop of fig juice that lingered at the side of her mouth. So filled with emotion, overwhelmed, Coral's eyes welled up with tears. He pulled back immediately, mistaking her reaction. "I'm sorry," he whispered in a husky voice. "I couldn't help myself — you're so beautiful... irresistible."

She wanted to tell him it was all right for him to touch her, that his attention was welcome, and he was just as irresistible. But she could not find the words, and even if she were the uninhibited type, she still feared he would think her forward.

The moment passed. Rafe seemed to regain his composure. "Coffee?" he asked, once again the perfect host.

She was trembling a bit with the cold. "Yes, please." Perhaps the hot brew would warm her up.

They drank their coffee in silence, until Rafe glanced at his watch. "Ten o'clock — we must be going, or the show will start without us." He smiled and helped her out of her chair. "Or maybe you'd like to refresh yourself upstairs first?"

Coral decided it would be better to wait until they got to the Golden Fish, so they made their way to Rafe's black Alpha Romeo, and soon the car was speeding through the night in the direction of the nightclub.

For this occasion, the stage at the Golden Fish was set outside, perched on top of the cliff, the sea as its backdrop and a full stage with tables tucked around it in a crescent. Whenever there was a lull in the talk and laughter, the silence was filled by the singing of palm trees as the breeze blew through them and the breaking of waves against the rocks. The fierce landscape provided both ambiance and drama. Rafe, the artist, had done it again; he had let nature speak and, with a bit of lighting, had brought it all together, a triumph of natural artifice. Contradicting words, Coral thought as she formulated them in her mind, but there was no other way to describe the subtle yet powerful scene that took her breath away.

Rafe walked her to their table. His palm skimmed lightly over her bare back, sensuous and questing, holding her close. They brushed against each other as they moved, and Coral noticed the tensing of his muscles every time their bodies came into contact. She had vacillated between a feeling of excitement and vulnerability for a fair part of the evening, and now his closeness was torture, a delicious sort of aching torture, but torture nevertheless.

Rafe smiled. "What d'you think?" he asked as they reached the table.

"It's fabulous, breathtaking, awesome." Coral's eyes were shining. The scenery seemed to fit the amazing aura of her escort. Was she falling for this man? At no cost must she betray her feelings. But how could she allow herself to fall for a man who, by all accounts, had taken advantage of her father for his own ends — and possibly wanted to do the same to her? She was sure he wanted to take her to bed — it was written all over him — but one-night stands were not her style. Stupid girl! He was rich, successful, intelligent, and charismatic. What more did she want? Some women would kill for the attention of half the man he was. And besides, there was something that didn't add up about his so-called scandalous reputation. Still, Coral concluded, it would be emotional suicide to get involved with him.

"Not bad, eh? Not bad at all." His grin contained a bit of self-congratulation. "What will you drink? Champagne? You may prefer something else. Cointreau? Grand Marnier? Crème de menthe?" He fell into the role of perfect host once again.

Already floating from the alcohol served at dinner, Coral knew she should avoid more spirits but nevertheless heard herself say, "Oh, a sundowner, thank you!" She really needed it to help her remain sane. All her senses were acutely attuned to Rafe's presence. He was sitting so close that she caught faint whiffs of that delicious aftershave that was becoming familiar.

Rafe signaled to a waiter and ordered their drinks. "The show will be starting soon. I'll have them bring the drinks now so we won't be disturbed."

"I think I might use the cloakroom," she said. "Tidy myself up a little."

"I'll show you the way."

So off they went again. This time he took her arm in a swift movement, and in doing so, the back of his hand pressed against the curve of her breast. Startled, they looked at one another, brown velvet gazing into deep blue. For an instant, they were the only two people in the world. But this was neither the time nor the place for such displays, even though her heart raced — or was it his she could feel pounding so wildly? Rafe was the first to pull back. For a moment, he looked confused; then he seemed to regain his composure and swept her through the tables that were now filled with guests.

By contrast, the cloakroom was empty save for the African assistant whose polite offer of help was declined. The only help Coral needed at the moment was a cold shower to sober her up and get her through the evening without making a spectacle of herself. She refreshed her face with tap water and took a minute to touch up her makeup; her eyes seemed over-bright, her cheeks a little flushed. The cocktail had left her throat feeling parched, though, so before returning to the table, she slipped over to the bar and asked for a glass of cold water. While waiting to be served, she heard a familiar voice, but she couldn't see where it came from.

"You've never been privy to my personal life."

"And in the seven years I've known you, you've never acted as you have lately." The woman sounded defensive.

100

"Where I go, what I do, who I see is no concern of yours — and I'd be grateful if in the future you didn't pry," he retorted.

"I've noticed the way you look at her — she's just a girl, for heaven's sake."

"Get a grip on your imagination, woman."

"And you get a grip on your hormones," the woman spat.

A curtain next to the bar suddenly parted, and Rafe stormed past Coral without seeing her, towering over tables and guests as he darted toward the back of the club where the double doors led back out onto the terrace and the open-air stage. Wondering what that was all about, and feeling indignant that yet again she was being discussed by one of Rafe's mistresses, Coral drank her glass of water. On top of that, she resented being branded a girl; she was a woman, and recalling the way Rafe's eyes gazed at her when she was around, he definitely made her feel every bit a woman. That thought induced Coral to hurry back to their table.

Rafe was talking to some guests a little farther away from their table on the terrace. Coral sat down, glad of the cool air on her face after the smoky atmosphere of the room inside, and looked out at the ocean glistening under a full moon. Tonight the waves whipping against the distant rocks seemed savage and relentless. Coral shivered. She much preferred the sea when it was in a benevolent frame of mind. Rafe's hard voice from earlier on drifted into her mind, and she wondered at the man coming toward her now, all smiles and charm. Who was he really? And what did he want with her? Did she care about his motives? It felt so wonderful when she was around him.

The lights were dimming. Rafe took his place next to Coral. "This show is quite something; they have just started to tour outside French Guinea," he whispered, his eyes twinkling. "I saw them once, some time ago when I was there. I hope you enjoy it."

Silence descended. Coral's attention shifted, and the spectacle began.

The overture was dramatic, evoking the crack of thunder and torrential rain; stage lighting gradually turned from red to gold, conjuring the breaking of daylight. Two sculptural figures became outlined against flashes of lightning: a man and a woman, naked except for a most exiguous loincloth, like the first humans at the dawn of time — alive but not yet awake.

The music built to a crescendo together with the humming of the chorus, and the dance opened. As the sun began to rise, the man reached out to the woman, and they clasped hands. He cradled her, and languidly they lifted themselves up to their feet, their bodies brushing, their eyes lost in each other's. Sensuously, deliberately, they danced, moving as though they were one, their body language smooth as their limbs carefully unfolded. They twirled and rocked, intertwined and separated, nearly leaning onto one another but barely touching, their movements sometimes tender, sometimes almost violent. The man's erotic movements against his partner were at first tentatively inviting, then inciting, before becoming more and more demanding and forceful. The woman was hesitant and shy to start off with, then increasingly yielding as his caresses seemed to excite her. As she watched, Coral felt contrasting emotions ignite in her as the furious energy of the dance alternated with sudden scenes of silence.

Finally, clasped together, making full contact for the first time, the couple swayed and spun around the stage in a flowing wave motion to the provocative rhythm of the music. As the frenzy reached its paroxysm, the orchestra's fury intensified and stopped. Moments passed while the dancers held tight to each other, as though their bodies were melting together. The expression on their features as they lifted their faces to the sky was one of unimaginable joy. The show had come to an end. The dancers, still panting, their bodies glistening with sweat, took their final bow from an audience who were stamping, shouting, and throwing flowers at them in appreciation of such masterful art.

As the lights came on, Coral was still feeling goose bumps rise on her skin. It had been a captivating story of man and woman — the eternal combat between the two sexes — an unflinching tale of lust and love vibrating with uninhibited passion and primitive eroticism. With talent and finesse, the dancers had transformed what could have been sleazy into a masterpiece of art and sensuality.

Coral had thoroughly enjoyed herself and been deeply moved. She turned to Rafe. His eyes, watching her, were more intense and compelling than ever. During the show, she had felt his stare fixed on her, but she had guessed what he was thinking and had deliberately kept her own attention focused on the stage. Why had he asked her to this show? Was it just because he sincerely thought she would appreciate the magic and the beauty of such a *chef d'oeuvre?* Or was there an ulterior motive behind his invitation?

Rafe smiled at her. "How did you like it? What did you think of it?"

He was very close, helping her get out from behind the table with his arm encircling her waist — such a normal and chivalrous gesture but one that nevertheless made her skin prickle. Not for the first time she asked herself why Rafe had such an effect on her. Why was she now longing for him to tighten his hold around her so she could feel his powerful frame against her? It was becoming embarrassing, not only because she felt at a disadvantage, but because she was sure that he was aware of her confusion.

"I loved it, thank you." Coral lifted her head, meeting his ardent gaze. "It was very… "

"Provocative?" he asked as they walked toward the car-park.

"Yes, yes, that's a good word," she said, laughing at his attempts to tease her.

"A dance of seduction and pleasure, no?"

"No," she answered quietly, "I would call it a dance of desire and love."

After Rafe ensured she was comfortably seated in the Alpha-Romeo, he walked around the car. Although she could not see his face, somehow Coral knew that he was brooding. He drove in focused silence, his jaw tight and a minute vein throbbing at his temple. Yes indeed, he was brooding.

She looked at his powerful hands on the steering wheel. They were beautiful hands, with elongated fingers and wide palms — those same palms that had held her only a few minutes ago had also expertly fondled and caressed numerous women. The image of Cybil, on the beach, lying next to him in her skimpy bikini, and of Morgana, dancing for him at the nightclub and probably in more intimate settings too, came unbidden to her mind. No doubt he had made love to them, and for a split second she envied her stepmother and the oriental dancer.

Coral was jerked out of her reverie as the car drew to a halt in the drive of Whispering Palms. She turned to him, laying a hand on his arm. "Thank you, Rafe. It's been a fabulous evening."

"My pleasure. I'm glad you enjoyed it," he said quietly. When he took her hand to help her from the car, his fingers were trembling. There was a heart-stopping pause while they looked at each other silently. Is he going to kiss me? Rafe didn't budge, still watching her, his dark eyes full of innuendo. Surely he did not think that she would make the first move? Coral was on the verge of taking her leave when he gave her one of his enigmatic smiles. "Would you like to come up for a quick nightcap?"

Was she so transparent? Why had Rafe asked her to that show? Had he known that on that evening Sandy and her friends would be unavailable? There were a thousand questions, all shouting that it would be madness to accept this new invitation, that the whole thing had been part of a planned scenario: the cozy intimate dinner, the show afterward, and now... Now she could see. Yes, it was clear as daylight: all along he had had his own agenda. Unfortunately, she had drunk a lot, and her senses had been in turmoil all evening. The electricity she felt in the air between them was no figment of her imagination, but a red flag urged her to run to her car and get out of there as fast as she could.

The palm trees sang with the breeze — such a beautiful sound. The surf was up tonight; its pounding in the distance echoed the thumping of her heart.

"Yes, that would be nice." Her answer resonated in her ears, and for a moment she was surprised by her own reaction. What was she doing? Well, there was no time for her to get into Rafe's ulterior motives now. She would worry about that later. After all, she was young and should be living her life. Here was a chance, in this most romantic of settings, with a man who was not only attractive but who also made her feel alive and wanted. She was going to enjoy every moment of it. Anyway, what harm was there in one drink? Heart searching and character analysis would have to wait.

The sky was immense above them with polka-dot stars that winked away at her as Rafe steered her toward the stairs and passed in front of her to lead the way up to the house. Coral felt vaguely uneasy, trembling inside. This behavior was so uncharacteristic of her. She had meant to turn down this unexpected extension to the evening. It wasn't too late to change her mind, she was still on the shore, but as they reached the top of the stairs, the voice of reason whispered that soon it would be too late. No, there could be no retreat now; otherwise, he might lose interest and she would never see him again.

"We're here," Rafe said as he turned on the lights. Buster appeared in the doorway, wagging his tail in welcome.

The last time she had been inside Whispering Palms, the house had been in semi-darkness, and worry had distracted her from taking notice of the interior. Now, as Rafe guided her through the hall to a big living room, Coral saw that his furniture was luxurious, but like everything else about him, it was in perfect taste. The walls were a warm yellow with accents of pale gold and olive green, lending the room a pleasant and sophisticated feel. Wall sconces and table lamps provided dim lighting. Spears and shields patterned with the black, red, and white zigzags of some African tribe adorned one wall while the opposite one was laced from top to bottom with book-filled shelves. There was a bowl of orchids on a side table, and the wooden tray in the center of the coffee table was loaded with a mouth-watering pyramid of exotic fruit. The floor and sofas were dressed with fine leopard and cheetah skins. Expansive windows opened onto a large veranda shielded from the garden by trellises and a jungle of scented creepers. A couple of bamboo chairs and loungers provided a comfortable place to relax and dream away the days.

Rafe reached for a bottle and two glasses from a cabinet. "A small cognac? Or maybe you would prefer some coffee; either will warm you up." Once again he surprised her with his attentiveness; he had noticed that she was trembling. The shivers could not have resulted from the beautiful, balmy night, and she wondered if that had also crossed his mind.

Coral decided to be sensible for a change. "I'll have some coffee, please."

He gave that devastating smile that made her melt inside. "Make yourself comfortable. I'll be back in a flash."

She stepped out onto the terrace. It faced south, giving it full sun all day. The fragrance of the plants and creepers here was bewitching, making her head feel lighter. The voices of the countless insects seemed to make the air vibrate with a continuous faint pulse. For a second, she had a disconcerting feeling that her mere presence here was an intrusion, that she was treading the edges of another human being's private moonlit universe: Rafe's world. She momentarily found herself wishing to be part of that dream forever.

Coral sensed his presence behind her and turned. Rafe was standing very still, just looking at her. His dinner jacket had been removed, his bow tie hanging loosely around his unbuttoned shirt collar, and his rolled-up sleeves revealed strong, tanned forearms. Approaching a tall raffia basket that served as a table, he set down a cup of steaming coffee, a glass, and a bottle of cognac, then took a blanket from over his arm and wrapped it around Coral's shoulders, letting his palms linger a little over them as he had done on the boat not so long ago. Her heart turned right over in her breast, and perhaps she started a bit, as he drew away from her instantly. Her shivering only seemed to increase.

"That should keep you warm," Rafe whispered as he handed her the cup of coffee. "Sip it slowly." His voice was caressing and silky. "These coffee beans come from the plantation of friends of mine that live in the plains of Southern Kenya along the border with Tanganyika. The aroma is stronger than the brands you find on the market."

The hot brew warmed her up: it was soothing and comforting. Rafe took a pace or two away from her and savored his cognac with the air of a connoisseur. He leaned on the bannister of the terrace and gazed out over his domain to the sea in the distance. A light breeze flicked at his dark hair, and he pushed it away from his eyes.

"A shooting star, Rafe. Make a wish," Coral exclaimed, trying to draw him back to reality. He stared fixedly at her, perhaps wondering what her wish had been, then gave her one of his enigmatic smiles. His hand slid along the top of the balustrade and touched her elbow. It was a momentary contact, but he drew away quickly as if suddenly afraid of touching her. Coral could see him staring at her lips, and her breathing quickened. He met her eyes, and still he did not move, his steady gaze delving into her soul, as if searching intensely for something in Coral.

And then all at once, she was melting in his arms, trembling against his powerful body as his mouth moved tenderly over her eyes, her cheeks, her neck, whispering his desire and his need softly in her ear. This must be what paradise is like, Coral thought crazily as she strained toward him.

When he finally kissed her lips, his mouth was sensual, persuasive. The kiss went on and on, slowly, deeply, as his hands slid gently down her back and pulled her harder against him so that she gasped slightly. She felt the magnetic power pulsate between them so strongly she was unable to stop her body from responding to his. Her breathing quickened; her ears were buzzing, warmth was flooding every part of her body, and she could already feel the wave building, threatening to engulf her.

Abruptly, he drew away from her. "No. No, this is not right. I'm sorry… " He bent his head and ran a hand through his hair again. "You mustn't fall in love with me, Coral." He looked up at her and scanned her face with an aching intensity, but then his eyes clouded over. "It's just a physical attraction that draws you toward me. Don't fool yourself. You know nothing of me, and what you already know can only push you away from my life." Rafe's voice was flat as he spoke. He gulped down the liquid left in his discarded glass and poured himself another drink. His lids flickered as he breathed raggedly.

"That's not so. I feel good when I'm with you. I don't know what it is about you… your voice, your eyes… It's as though I've always missed them," Coral whispered. She could feel his desire for her wrestling with something else. What was it that tormented him so much?

Rafe drew her toward him in a protective surge, and she rested her cheek on his chest. "Yes, I know," he said, so softly she could barely hear his caressing words. "I've known from the first moment that we were attracted to each other in a wondrous, frightening way, isn't that so? It's as though we have been created

107

with the same piece of clay, come out of one mold. I know that — I felt it as soon as you looked at me. It was like we were alone in the world, you and me. I sensed it before I even met you, when I looked into your photographs, and you became real to me. But then I hadn't yet acknowledged the extent of the miracle… "

"Don't stop talking. I love your voice. I love what you say to me. Don't stop talking, please." Coral hugged him and felt him take a deep breath.

"Coral, my love, you are too pure, too innocent, too alive for me," he said slowly, almost carefully. "My world is like a drawing in black and white on a gray canvas, without a single note of color to bring it to life. And now, on this pale and melancholic picture, a red flower has fallen, a warm and scented flower." He sighed. "It's a wonderful contrast, but too vivid… "

Coral shut her eyes, lulled by the sound of his voice, refusing to accept such a sad and desolate image. "If that's true, what is this strange and wonderful feeling filling my heart?" she murmured.

He did not answer, but closed his arms around her, holding her tightly against him. There was nothing erotic in his embrace now, only tenderness.

"Rafe," she breathed.

"Shush, my love, my sweet, my innocent love. Let's stay like this a while, just silently savoring this fleeting moment borrowed from time, from life… so foreign to each other and yet so close, as if we had always belonged together."

They remained thus, clasped in each other's arms, under stars twinkling like golden pinpricks in the floor of heaven, listening to their hearts throbbing in unison in the deep silence of night.

***

Rafe stood alone on the terrace, watching Coral's car speed off into the night. He turned away, slumped down into a chair, and lit a cigarette. What on earth had possessed him to ask Coral up to the house? He had no right to look at her, want her, touch her the way he had all evening. He was fully aware of the effect he had on her; far from feeling smug, he was ashamed. His chin took a determined slant. Why should he be ashamed? Morgana's words hit him like a slap in the face: *"She's just a girl."* Was Coral too young? Even when they stood apart from each other, her feelings reached him, touched him, and excited him. She was not a girl. She was a ravishing, warm-hearted woman.

The memory of the way she had felt in his hands that day on the rocks, her lips so tantalizingly close, made him dizzy. Since then, he had not been able to drive her from his mind. And he had to admit, even though he had known countless women, none of them, as far as he could remember, had affected him like this; the power she had over him was frightening. He gave a self-derisory inward laugh. *Who had seduced whom?*

How eagerly she had looked at him tonight, right here where he was sitting now. He had managed to draw away at first, afraid to give way to his weakness. Then he met her eyes, seemingly bluer from the questions they held. Her beauty was so intoxicating that it made him ache. He had never dreamed such a creature existed. He was spellbound. He had glimpsed the swollen curve of her breasts as they rose and fell a little faster than normal, her soft lips slightly parted, making him want to blend his exhausted breath with the sweetness and the freshness of hers. He had looked into those eyes, searching for an answer, a sign... And then it had happened... he remembered her trembling against his body as he found himself kissing her face and the delicate vein pulsating in the middle of her throat, his fingers tracing with deliberation her arching back and yearning to explore further those lush curves that trembled under his touch. He could not believe how wonderful she had been as she instinctively moved to mold herself to his body. She was soft and yielding against him — a dream from which he never wanted to wake. The urge to take her there and then had been overwhelming. The memory made his senses start to ache with arousal once more.

Again, he shook himself back to reality. What was he doing? Even fantasizing about Coral was not right. He had desperately fought against the power of his passion and succeeded in pushing her away. But now the desire that burned his body was sidetracked and channeled toward a feeling just as powerful: guilt. If only she knew the darkness that enveloped his past, she would not want him anymore. Besides, what she felt for him was schoolgirl infatuation.

"That's not so... your voice, your eyes... It's as though I've always missed them." Her words came back to him, so beautiful they warmed his lonely heart, awakening all sorts of feelings that had lain dormant for a long time in a tiny corner of his mind. Rafe could feel himself softening, yielding, and losing the battle. A great sadness flooded him. He remembered the scent of her hair and the feel of its silkiness brushing against his neck. At that moment, Rafe knew that he wanted Coral more than he had ever wanted anything in his life. She was everything he had ever dreamed of, everything he had always wished for.

Rafe was experienced enough to realize that Coral wanted him too; despite her attempts to fight this growing attraction, everything in her body language told him so. He could see that whenever they were close the chemistry between them flared up. In those blinded moments, his mind clouded, his resolve not to touch her evaporated, and his desire for her was almost overwhelming. At twenty-five, Coral had a unique innocence that combined with a generous and passionate spirit, and Rafe knew that he was awakening the dormant sensuous woman in her. Soon her body would make its claims on her, and they would both be lost to their desire. No, he was not the one to initiate this.

Dear God, what was happening to him? Why was he giving in to his feelings, indulging in sentimentality? And why on earth had he bared his soul to her, divulging things he had difficulty admitting even to himself? He could not remember when he had last been so soft, so weak, in front of anything or anyone, least of all a woman. It must be his French blood taking over — another new experience. A freezing wave of fear gripped his heart. He would never forgive himself if harm came to her, especially at his own hand. The only way to protect her from him was to run.

***

Coral awoke the next day with the immediate realization that there was something different in her life — something new and overwhelming. As the golden light of early afternoon filtered

110

through the shutters, she lay between the silky sheets, her mind and body still numb with sleep, remembering, basking in the sweetness of her freshly found love. "Rafe," she whispered softly into her pillow as she recalled the proud, lean profile of the artist. Her heart filled with tenderness, and her body flooded with yearning for him.

Coral threw back the covers and leapt out of bed. The clock showed it was almost two in the afternoon. She had slept for ten uninterrupted hours. After running herself a bath, she slid her flimsy nightdress off and stood naked in front of the full-sized mirror, regarding herself critically, as though it were his eyes moving over her nudity. It had never occurred to her before, but she was proud of her body — young and slim, with curves in all the right places. She was proud of her virginity too. Suddenly it ceased to be a harassing obstacle and became a wonderful gift. Her nakedness had never been exposed to a man's eyes. No one had explored the mysteries of her body, and when the time came, she wanted to finally become a woman at Rafe's hands.

Coral washed and dressed hurriedly, impatient to see him, talk to him, and touch him. As she was preparing to leave the room, Aluna walked in bearing a tray of fruit.

"Good afternoon, young lady," she said, laying the tray on the table. "You were late at the ball last night." She gave Coral a slanting look. "I see you're off again today."

"Oh yes, yes, Aluna, dear, darling Aluna." The young woman's face radiated with uncontained happiness as she planted a resounding kiss on the *yaha's* cheek.

"I hope you're not up to any mischief. You look a little flushed." The old servant's tone was laced with suspicion.

Coral was not listening, still basking in yesterday's euphoria. "I've climbed to the top of the highest mountain, and life up there is wonderful."

"Uhahhh," the older woman grunted. "Hasty climbers have sudden falls."

Coral ignored the glum response as she flew out of the room, down the staircase, and into her car, impatient to get to Whispering Palms again.

She parked her car in the shade of the courtyard and started on her way up to the house.

"Looking for someone?" demanded a woman's voice behind her.

Turning around, she found Morgana, swinging in a hammock strung between two coconut trees. "If it is Rafe you've come to see," she continued, sliding off the hammock and onto the grass with the languid grace of a panther, "you're out of luck — he's already gone."

"Then I'll come back some other time," Coral answered pertly and turned back to the car.

"I'd save myself the trouble if I were you."

"But you're not me," retorted the young woman.

"I don't think I'd like to be you at the moment." The dancer ambled toward her rival.

Now that they were both standing next to the car, Coral fiddling unsteadily with the lock, while Morgana, her bearing proud, viewed the younger woman through lavish eyelashes.

"And why is that?" asked Coral without glancing up.

"I don't think you'd like what I have to say."

"Try me," Coral retorted, tossing her head up to meet the kohl-darkened eyes that regarded her with a steady expression.

"Come then — let's sit inside. It's cooler, and we'll be more comfortable."

"I'm fine here."

"Suit yourself." The dancer shrugged. "If you don't mind, I'll sit down." Morgana lowered herself to the ground and leaned her back against the trunk of a palm tree. Even in repose, her body was the personification of grace. The tight black kanga dress she wore accentuated her beautiful curves, and Coral felt a nasty pang pierce her heart as visions of Rafe making love to the dusky, oriental goddess flashed painfully through her mind.

"Why are you here, my friend?" asked Morgana.

"That's none of your business, and you're not my friend," snapped Coral. Her head was swirling furiously now with memories from the night before. *This woman was his mistress.*

"He's left Mombasa. He's running away from you."

Coral turned away, preparing to leave.

"Let him alone. He can never be yours."

"I think I've heard enough," Coral said as she opened the car door.

"Wait," Morgana cried out as she leapt up and caught Coral's arm. "Don't go. Hear me out and then decide." There was something compelling in the urgency of the dancer's voice, or was it the hypnotic gaze of those dark eyes that stared at her now with such insistence?

Coral leaned against the car and folded her arms. "All right," she conceded with a sigh, "I'll listen to what you have to say, but make it quick."

"You may think that what I will tell you is prompted by jealousy. It isn't."

Sure, thought Coral, *and I'm the Queen of England*. "I'll be the judge of that. Go on, I'm listening."

"Certainly I love Rafe. For him I would do almost anything without ever asking for something in return, and he knows it. He's my man, my master; I am the *bint el lail*, the devoted mistress who fills his nights, who soothes and caresses until nightmares have vanished, who replaces pain with rapture."

"I haven't come here to hear about the games that you and Rafe get up to in the bedroom," Coral cut in.

"Perhaps, but you will still listen, because you are proud, intelligent, and sensitive."

Flattery will get you nowhere, thought Coral. "Well, then, since I'm all that, why should Rafe run away from me?"

"Because to him you represent a dream — the illusion of what his life could have been if he had made different choices and if fate had not already interfered so cruelly in his world. It is too late for people like him, like me… "

"Don't you think it's rather presumptuous of you to compare yourself to Rafe?" Coral interrupted.

Morgana lifted a peremptory hand. "Please," she said, her eyes grave, "let me finish."

Coral sighed. "Fine, get on with it then."

"I compare myself to Rafe because in many ways we are similar. There are certain events one never forgets, wounds that never heal or, if they do, the scar remains as a vivid reminder. Life has made nomads of us, and our only hope is to keep on the run. He will spend his life looking for something to keep him in one place, yet he will never find it. Do you know why?"

Coral was losing patience. "No, but I'm sure you're burning to tell me."

"Yes, I will tell you why he will never stop searching for happiness, yet why he will never seize it. That is because, though he will always hope to find it, the effort to hold the dream would be too great, too overwhelming. It would exhaust him."

"If what you're saying were true, three quarters of the world would be roaming aimless on this earth."

"Believe me, young lady, when I tell you that there is no place for you in his world of ghosts and nightmares — no place for your fresh beauty or your unmarred dreams, no place for your wonderful hope. He can bring you nothing, because he has lost everything. Don't try to keep him, to tie him down, because if you succeed, if he weakens, he will hate you for it. Let him be. He is not unhappy; he is resigned. He has surrendered and acquired at a high cost a deep understanding of life."

Coral was shaking now with anger and fear. Something inside warned her that her love was being threatened by a perilous shadow beyond her comprehension. The way Morgana spoke about Rafe, he might as well be dead. Oh, where was he? Why wasn't he here? Why didn't he appear suddenly and prove to this woman that she was wrong?

"How can you say you love him when you use such cruel and horrible words to describe him? I will neither believe nor accept what you say. This might be true where you're concerned, but I can assure you that Rafe isn't like that. I know he isn't. One can't talk, touch, love in the way he did with me last night if one's soul is dead. The stranger you're telling me about has no heart, no senses, nothing… "

Morgana's eyes were now glittering, revealing her fight to remain calm and collected. "These hours he spent with you, they are but brief, transient moments out of life that he steals from time to time when the temptation to pursue the dream becomes overwhelming. They only last for as long as he can fool himself, only so far as he can shut away reality."

"You talk of him as though he was old, an invalid, or… " She drew a deep breath, afraid to formulate what was on her mind "… or dead."

"Inside he is all of those things," the dancer insisted.

"No!" Coral tried to suppress the sob that died in her throat. "Rafe is a healthy, charismatic, and talented man with a soul who can love passionately and bring alive all his dreams and all hopes. Look around you."

"If he is as you say, my friend, why is he not here today?" Morgana asked, her voice caressing, though she fixed her young adversary with burning eyes. "Why is he not waiting for you? He knew you would come. Still, he went and left me to deal with reality."

Chapter Six

As she dressed for dinner, Coral went over the events of the last few weeks in her mind. Almost a month had elapsed since her stormy conversation with Morgana. At first, she had not given much credit to the dancer's words, putting them down to jealousy. She had thought that Rafe had gone off on one of those business trips he had mentioned to her over dinner. But as time went by and he did not reappear, Coral was forced to face up to reality: she had read too much into what seemed to have been only a passing fancy on his part. He had seemed so sincere; his wonderful words had made her dream of the future. Now she knew differently. Sharp knives cut at her heart as she recalled every moment of the last evening she'd spent with Rafe at Whispering Palms.

How could she have been so dim? She had always thought of herself as reasonable, poised, and self-confident. She was rapidly discovering that she was impulsive and emotional, and her self-confidence was being sapped away at a rate of knots. Her engagement to Dale had been a huge mistake — and he had betrayed her — and no sooner had she emerged from that painful experience than she had thrown herself headlong into the next disaster. Why was she always attracted to womanizers? And to think she had wanted to trust Rafe and even thought she might be falling in love with him. Would she never learn? There was definitely something wrong with her, especially where men were concerned. Either her judgment of them was poor, or else she had not the faintest idea how to handle them. Why could she not be more relaxed, more detached? Other women of her age flipped from one casual affair to another quite happily, taking in their stride the good with the bad and putting it all down to healthy experience. It was time she pulled herself together and got on with her life.

Coral had spent days trying to ignore her misery, throwing herself into work, taking more pictures for the documentary and making more notes for her articles. She often went down to the beach with her camera to capture a beautiful sunrise or sunset, but still found herself looking out for Rafe on the wide stretch of sand, scanning the ocean for the white dinghy. A part of her still longed to see him again, unable to forget the way he made her feel, while the other part rebelled and fought and hated him. None of it made any sense.

"I don't like the looks of you, my child," Aluna had remarked again and again. "You don't tell Aluna much these days, but your old yaha is not blind. You can't fool me — there's a man behind all this, there's always a man. Uach! Men, all the same… hunters! Women are their game."

Then the invitation to Narok had come. Friends of her father's whom she vaguely remembered had written to say how delighted they would be if she and "dear Cybil" would visit them for a couple of weeks at their coffee plantation. She had never been to the Rift Valley and the Masai Mara; it would give her the opportunity to see a different part of Kenya and to take some interesting photographs. It also meant she could get away from the coast and leave behind everything that reminded her of Rafe. Maybe then she would be able to forget.

She had welcomed the invitation even with the unpleasant prospect of spending so much time in her stepmother's company. She was happy Aluna was also invited. Lady Langley had expressly mentioned her, writing:… *and I do hope that your lovely yaha, who looked after us so well when we stayed with poor Walter, will be able to accompany you.*

"I suppose they need an extra pair of hands in the kitchen," Aluna had grumbled, but Coral knew that even though Aluna understood what her role would be on the trip, deep down the old servant was tickled to have been remembered.

Lady Langley's Kongoni plantation lay splendidly perched on a ridge in the foothills, midway between Nairobi and Narok, at the end of a sandy road running through a belt of cocoa palms. All around it were open plains, rolling bush country, with a lake reflecting sky and hills just below. The house was a 1940s villa entirely built in old stone, with olive green shutters and multicolored creepers hugging its walls. From a very wide veranda, low steps led down to a large expanse of emerald lawn dipping toward a small private lake where pink pelicans basked in the sun.

The Kongoni estate consisted of five hundred acres devoted mainly to coffee growing and, like Mpingo and Whispering Palms, was one of a few working estates still belonging to settlers. In the last six years, after her husband's death, Lady Langley had built a few bungalows in the grounds and quietly taken on a handful of paying guests she selected with care after discreet inquiries had been floated about. Despite Kenyatta's assurances that everything was fine, much of the British expat community was becoming increasingly worried about the political situation in Kenya, and many of them were selling their farms and returning to England. Lady Langley had resolutely refused to do the same. She loved her life in Africa and had spent time creating her perfect home there with her late husband, and then building it up on her own. Like every Englishwoman, her garden was her pride and joy, and she had taken great pains to recreate a little corner of England in the exotic African landscape. Of the five hundred acres that made up the estate, the three of them that surrounded the house grew the most wonderful beds of English flowers, their nostalgic scent filling the dry African air.

Coral had immediately been taken with it and had been happy during the first few days to laze in a hammock while reading, listening to the chirp of birds and far away noises of the Kenyan bush. Sometimes she would borrow one of the many plantation Jeeps and stray down to the local market at the foot of the hill to rummage through rows of ramshackle stalls displaying pyramids of fruit and corn-cobs, baskets of fish and cassava, gourds of palm wine, and other exotica and oddities. Often Aluna would accompany her to this dusty vortex. Those times were the most enjoyable because she found herself drawn into the heart of a riotous circle by the bartering, colorful exchanges, and wayside gossip in which the old servant engaged. Coral had almost forgotten how hugely gregarious Kenyan society was, and it amused her to think how alien the Western idea of "personal space" was to these people as she watched the cheerfully packed groups chatting away, occasionally with someone interestedly peering over her shoulder to see what she was buying and asking where she was from.

Today, though, Coral had not ventured from the house after learning what was to come. "Quite a few interesting guests will be joining us for our annual dance tonight," Lady Langley had announced that morning at breakfast, "among them one of the best hunters in this part of the world, an old friend of my husband and I who comes to stay from time to time when he has business nearby. You may be able to persuade him to act as a guide on one of those exciting private safaris. He can never resist the request of a beautiful woman."

Coral put the final touches to her toilette, anointing her temples, throat, and wrists with her favorite scent while reflecting on her hostess's words. She had always wanted to go on a safari. It would be so exciting; besides, she had her documentary to think of and was eager to make more progress with it in a different direction. What better way to gather material than on a safari? She remembered the irritation she had felt as a child when denied the pleasure of accompanying "grown-ups" on such exciting expeditions. Old-fashioned safaris were rarely conducted these days because of the lack of foot treks and the great cost, but from time to time one heard of fully-rigged safaris, operated by ex-hunters, with a camel train carrying everything from the morning coffee to the evening bath, just like in the early days. There was much else about the settlers' old way of life that would now fade into the past, she reflected. With the coming of the new regime, the older generation would soon have to lose other things like their armies of servants, which they were going to find rather difficult. But still, a new and more realistic Kenya was a far more exciting prospect for the new generation. However, in terms of today's safari, she did not think old-style expedition was the sort of extravaganza Lady Langley had been alluding to, but even a modest venture, Coral reflected, would suit her needs.

While looking through her wardrobe to pick a dress for the evening, her eyes had fallen on the sapphire gown she had worn for Rafe. Coral had quickly quelled an impulse to indulge in thoughts about what had happened, telling herself there was no point in mulling it over again. Rafe's memory would have to join the rapidly mounting pile of dead flowers she had set in a recess of her mind.

The attire she chose instead was a black mini-dress. It was fairly risqué — sleeveless, with a plunging neckline and a hemline high enough to expose the greater part of her legs to advantage. In an adventurous mood, Coral had bought it in New York's Upper East Side, from "youthquake" designer Betsey Johnson's new boutique, thinking that Dale would approve. Covered in minute sequins, the fabric shimmered with every one of her movements. Black became her, enhancing the sun-warmed tone of her skin and the golden glints of her hair that on this occasion she left hanging loose.

Coral normally shied away from eye-catching outfits and kept to the more conventional look that suited her personality and desire for comfort. But tonight she felt ready to put the naïve little girl behind and reinvent herself a little. Even her makeup was different: a rich burgundy lipstick gave her mouth an enticing gloss, and the tawny blush on her cheekbones made her face seem even slimmer, intensifying the blue of her eyes. Her mirror reflected the image of a confident and seductive woman, much to her surprise.

Coral panicked for one moment before leaving the room, assessing her image, wondering whether she may have overdone it. Her mother certainly would not have approved nor would Aluna for that matter, and she was thankful that her *yaha* had not appeared, probably too busy lending a helping hand in the kitchen. Coral gave the mirror a last glance, then, shrugging off any qualms, went to join the party.

Walking down the corridor toward the hall, she almost froze as she spotted Dale, standing at the foot of the main staircase, apparently engrossed in conversation with his hostess. What on earth was he doing here? Coral's step faltered as she tried to conceal her shock. Dressed in a perfectly tailored dinner jacket, a glass of champagne in one hand while the other rested casually on the banister, he exuded wealth and power. She could fully recognize the attractive aura that had swept her off her feet once but that tonight left her cool. He was still extremely handsome, but there was something loud and vulgar about him that she had never noticed before.

Coral had often wondered what it would be like to see Dale again and how she would feel. Now she knew. As he lifted his head and she met the calculating, gray eyes assessing her with obvious approval, Coral felt nothing but indifference for the man she had once agreed to marry. Strange how one's feelings could change so quickly; after all, it had been less than six months.

Dale's gaze softened as she reached him. "Hi, Coral! What a surprise to see you — you look ravishing." The broad American accent that had once set her pulse racing had not changed, but it failed to move her in any way.

"Hello, Dale," she said in a casual voice as she held out her hand and smiled coolly at him.

Meeting her ex-fiancé like this was about the last thing Coral would have expected or wished for, but the obvious admiration she could read in the young man's eyes and the fact that he no longer roiled her emotions made her wonder if this encounter could turn out to be rather exciting. Since the morning, she had sensed a sort of enchantment in the air, as though something important was about to happen, and instinct had made her dress up for the occasion accordingly. Tonight she felt reckless. It would certainly be flattering and fun to enjoy Dale's attentions once more when he was powerless to hurt her.

Their hostess had tactfully joined another group of guests, and the couple was now facing each other in silence. Coral moved to let someone pass, and without warning, Dale slipped a possessive arm around her waist and walked her to the living room. Why was she surprised that his closeness did not affect her in any way? On reflection, it had never done so, at least not in the way Rafe's touch did. Rafe... Her heart gave a little painful squeeze. Where was he now? That thought lasted but seconds. *No, forget and move on.* Dale was here, she knew him well enough, and this was her opportunity to innocently have fun and show him what he was missing.

"Let's get out of here," he suggested after a few minutes of conversation, laying his glass down on a table close by. "This room is too bright, too hot, and too crowded."

Outside the air was crisp and cool. But for the multicolored bulbs that hung in the shrubberies and the gleam of the water below the sloping lawn, the African night was black, with the branches of great trees looming over the pathways. Ahead of them, over the far-off hills, the enigmatic half-moon seemed to be watching them. They walked down the cobbled footpath. Dale had tucked her arm through his, slowly guiding her toward the lake.

"I have a confession to make," he said, suddenly breaking the silence and stopping abruptly.

Coral frowned and kept her response detached. "Do I want to hear it?"

He beamed. "It wasn't really a surprise seeing you here."

Coral gave an insouciant shrug. Strangely enough, it had crossed her mind that it wasn't this small a world. She knew that Dale and his family had traveled to Kenya often and had many friends here, hence the fabulous collection of African paintings and bronzes that made up the exhibition where she had met him, but she wondered how he had wangled this meeting. No doubt he was burning to tell her.

"I rang your house in England, and your mother told me you had gone to Kenya. I then remembered that you had spoken of your father being a keen hunter. Josh Langley also loved to hunt, and he was a very good friend of my father's. So I got in touch with Lady Langley on the off chance that she had known your father. I was in luck. I told her we had been engaged and that I had made a mess of it and wanted to make amends. I asked if she could help me by inviting us both to one of her house parties. She needed a little persuasion, but I got there at the end."

He looked very pleased with himself, and Coral felt a fool. She did not like being manipulated, and the situation had obviously been managed shrewdly. Perhaps others would have been flattered, but she felt trapped. She clapped her hands. "Bravo," she said her tone icy. "But why am I surprised. It sounds just like you."

"I'm a go-getter, I've always been so, and that is why I always get what I want." He leaned closer to her as they walked.

"This time you won't," she said, trying not to betray the tension she felt inside.

"Oh, Coral, I've been so stupid." He pulled her to him, burying his face in the warmth of her neck. "Tell me it isn't too late for us, baby," he whispered, searching for her lips urgently.

Alarmed at such an unusual and unwarranted display of passion from him, Coral felt her body stiffen. "No, Dale," she said firmly, pushing him away. "Stop, please stop… "

"I'm sorry," apologized her partner, checking himself immediately. "You look so beautiful and desirable tonight — but you're right, forgive me. I must tread gently."

"That won't make any difference. Even if I'd had any doubt before, which I hadn't, what you've just told me makes it perfectly clear that we aren't suited for each other. Let's just enjoy the evening, shall we?"

"Give me a second chance, Coral. I know I've acted like an idiot. Let me redeem myself. For a start, I will fetch us both a drink while you wait for me on that bench." He pointed to the wooden seat that stood a few feet away under a flamboyant tree. "Will champagne suit you?"

Coral nodded her assent and made her way down toward the edge of the lake. She would not create a scene, resolving to even be friendly with Dale tonight. After all, it was quite fun to be courted. During the last year, her ego had taken a cruel blow, but if Dale was going to be another of Lady Langley's houseguests, she might decide to cut short her stay in Narok.

The night was filled with the sweet scent of shrubs and flowers wafting on the cool breeze. Watching the ripples break out on the lake's murky surface, a shiver went through her at the thought of how deep those waters were. Coral was starting back toward the bench when the hurried beat of her heart warned her of the presence of a dark figure standing motionless beside the seat. She would recognize that silhouette anywhere, but still had to stifle a cry of surprise and suck in her breath.

All of Coral's inner promises to remain calm should they ever meet again fled as she blurted, "What are you doing here?"

"Presumably the same thing as you — tasting the cool of a peaceful night."

"How long have you been standing there?"

Rafe laughed shortly. "Oh… I'd say long enough to have witnessed the effect you had on your partner and your own very predictable reaction." There was an edge to his calm voice.

"What d'you mean?"

"I mean that when one chooses to wear such a minimal outfit as that, one shouldn't be surprised at the reaction of young studs showing their appreciation. If you play with fire, one day you'll burn yourself."

The tone was sarcastic and pompous; though Coral could not see his eyes, she guessed at the look that filled them. He had the effrontery to think he could swan into her life, take her by storm, and drift out just as casually, without the slightest consideration for her feelings. And now he seemed to be judging her behavior. She battled to master her anger.

"What business is it of yours anyway?" She managed to recover her composure, but her voice was quavering. "I'm old enough to take care of myself."

"Sure… Still, I just meant it as a warning." Rafe stepped out of the shadows and offered an uneven smile. Here he was, appearing out of nowhere after all this time, expecting her to fall under his power instantly. Who the hell did he think he was?

"Do you know something, Monsieur de Monfort?" she burst out, clenching her fingers so tightly that she could feel the imprint of her nails cutting into her palms, "you've got a cheek… you've got one hell of a cheek."

"I have? And do you know, Miss Sinclair, what I'd most enjoy doing right now?" he countered, a mischievous gleam in his dark eyes.

"No, and I really couldn't care less!" she snapped back, cutting him off before he had the satisfaction of telling her.

Coral took several deep breaths to calm herself down. She was trembling so much her limbs seemed totally out of control. Damn the man. He had a way of looking at her that made her feel limp with… No, it was best not to dwell on that. Through the corner of her eye, she saw Dale emerge from the house. It would be an effort to walk past Rafe in her bottom-hugging skimpy outfit about which he had been so disparaging. She felt naked, and she was sure he would notice her embarrassment. However, calling on all her willpower, she managed to toss him a haughty look and went to meet Dale. With quivering fingers, she took the drink from his hands, spilling a few drops of champagne in the process.

"What's wrong?" asked the young man. "You seem upset."

"Oh, nothing… I thought I heard an animal in the shadows," she replied, saying the first thing that popped into her head. "Let's go in. I find it rather chilly out here."

They went back into the house and made it through the crush across the dining room where a group of guests were already milling around an attractive buffet. "Shall we get something to eat? The smell of food is making me hungry. You?" asked Dale.

"Ah, there you are, Coral dear!" exclaimed Cybil, threading herself through the throng.

She looked aloof and sophisticated in her loose-fitting, green silk, flapper-inspired outfit. The low-slung bodice was held up by thin shoulder straps while the skirt fell to knee length. The decorated hemline ended in handkerchief points, accentuating her shapely calves. The fuchsia sash double-knotted around her hips emphasized the swing of her body as she walked. Everything from the perfect kiss-curl in the middle of her forehead to the strappy shoes contrived to create a slick and sexy image that Coral was sure was meant to attract Rafe, which pinched Coral's heart with a jealous twinge.

"Hello, Cybil," she said as her stepmother came up to them, twiddling the beaded ends of a rope necklace hanging loose to beneath her waist. "Cybil, meet Dale, Dale Halloway, an old friend. Dale, this is Cybil Sinclair, my stepmother."

"Oh, yes, Dale Halloway, I know… I recognized you from your photographs." Cybil's glance slid over him with amusement as she emphasized the words, alluding to the society photos that had announced their former engagement. "How extraordinary for you both to meet like this again, so unexpectedly and in such a romantic place too. What a small world this is!"

"Yes, it's lovely to see Coral again," agreed Dale, putting a possessive arm around his companion's shoulders.

"Umm…" Cybil took a deep puff from her cigarette that glowed at the end of an elegant amber cigarette holder. Ignoring her stepdaughter's presence, she continued, stressing her words to make her point sink in, "Coral has been feeling rather down lately. Perhaps the rekindling of an old flame will do her some good. I'm counting on you, young man." Cybil smiled at Dale and gave his arm a knowing squeeze before drifting off toward a group of friends who, judging by their effusive greeting, were delighted to see her.

"I'll fetch us something to eat. D'you have a preference for anything?" Dale asked.

Coral felt wretched and no longer in a mood to socialize. It was bad enough having to put up with Dale all evening, but having to suffer and contend with Rafe's presence and his sarcastic remarks on top of that was more than she could bear. "No, I'm not very hungry."

"Nothing like some warm food to boost one up."

Coral sighed. If she'd had any appetite at all, that last interlude with Cybil had destroyed it. The evening was unexpectedly turning into a nightmare, and she was tempted to end it there and then on the pretext of a headache and get back to the solitude of her room. Had she been honest with herself, she would have realized it was Rafe's appearance that made her uneasy and was causing the sick feeling that gnawed at the pit of her stomach; she would have recognized the nagging little stab that caused her to glance at the door every time someone walked into the room. Coral did not know what she would do if he appeared again, or what she should say. Still, even though he threatened her emotional equilibrium, she perversely craved his presence and... perhaps more.

Dale came back, carrying two plates heaped with appetizing fare. Coral accepted hers graciously, wondering how she would get through it all. While her companion tucked in merrily, she picked unhappily at the small mounds of meat, rice, and vegetables.

"Aren't you hungry?"

"I seem to have developed a headache." Coral was aware that she was probably dampening the atmosphere and spoiling his fun.

"I'll tell you what… this will fix it," answered the young American as he signaled to one of the servants milling around and topping champagne glasses.

Until this trip to Kenya, Coral had never really been fond of alcohol, but of late had certainly developed a taste for it. She emptied this second glass of bubbly in one gulp. Despite her partner's assurance that this would "fix it," as he put it, common sense warned her that on an empty stomach, guzzling down several glasses of champagne was hardly the answer.

Dale liked to talk. He talked all the time: about his business, which was flourishing; about the economic and political state of the world, that by the sound of it would have been in a better shape had the people in charge taken his advice; about Concorde's first supersonic flight and, of course, how he had flown on the jet plane himself; about men landing on the moon in July of the previous year, and how he always kept up with the latest news about the space program; and about his parents, and of how disappointed they had been at the way things had turned out between the two of them. Actually, Coral did not mind him talking — quite the reverse — it took no effort on her part to keep the conversation alive. She could let her mind wander, and wander it did, with unacknowledged anxiety at Rafe's whereabouts as dinner was ending and there was still no sign of him. Maybe he was not hungry, or perhaps he had been kept in conversation by some other loquacious person. For all she knew, he may not have been invited to the party at all… but then what had he been doing in the garden earlier? Was the European social circle in Kenya now so small that this sort of coincidence was common? Come to think of it, Rafe had mentioned he had close friends who owned a coffee plantation in the southern plains of Kenya, even serving their coffee on that last evening at Whispering Palms.

The guests were now moving to a neighboring room where a jazz band played. "Care for a dance?" Dale asked as he relieved her of her plate.

"Er — yes, that'll be lovely." Coral attempted to sound enthusiastic. There was nothing worse than being a wet blanket; she was determined not to let Rafe ruin her evening.

The room had been cleared of furniture for the occasion, and flashing bright lights were strategically placed to give a nightclub atmosphere. The band sat on a raised platform set up between two French windows that opened onto a terrace. Drinks were being served at a bar in one corner, and the dance floor took up the remainder of the room.

Dale danced well; he was light on his feet and had an excellent sense of rhythm. They alternated between dancing and drinking, bringing Coral back into a party mood.

With midnight approaching, the lights were dimmed and the music slowed. The sultry voice of a female vocalist breathed across the shadows, filling the atmosphere with a romantic tune. Couples drew together. Likewise, Dale pulled Coral gently toward him, holding her firmly against his tall frame as he glided slowly around the dance floor. Light-headed from the champagne, Coral did not find this masculine contact unpleasant. She relaxed, moving a little closer to him, and closed her eyes. As they danced in silence, her partner's palms slid lightly up and down her back, over her shoulders, and onto her bare arms. Coral let herself imagine being held this way by Rafe… but she knew only too well how it would feel. She was comfortable in Dale's arms, but there were no butterflies in the pit of her stomach; the blood did not rush through her veins furiously. Her heart continued beating at a normal pace, and the warm ache that flooded her when Rafe had touched her was missing. Lately she had hoped she was getting over him, even though thoughts of him always lurked somewhere at the back of her mind. Meeting him unexpectedly this evening seemed to set her back again, and the bittersweet pain of her feelings toward him were threatening to resurface.

The warm voice of Frank Sinatra filled the room as the music changed to "Strangers in the Night."

"Having a nice time, Miss Sinclair?"

Jerked from her reverie, Coral pulled herself back from Dale's arms like a guilty teenager. The sardonic inflection in Rafe's voice had not escaped her. She felt the color rise to her burning cheeks. She whirled round sharply, unconcerned that, to onlookers, the vehemence of her reaction would seem peculiar. But the flow of biting words that was about to tumble out stopped right there as she realized Rafe held his own dancing partner too closely to his chest: Coral's glamorous stepmother.

He grinned back candidly at her glare as though to say, *Come, then, Miss Sinclair, where's our sense of humor?* And she knew beyond a doubt that the silent message *I've none tonight, Mr. de Monfort*, conveyed in her own glowering eyes, was similarly unambiguous to him.

"Is anything the matter, dear?" enquired Dale as she snuggled back into his arms. She shook her head and smiled up at him, her eyes riveted on his face, determined not to let them stray and betray her secret. Still, it wasn't easy avoiding Rafe on the dance floor. Although the area extended the length of the room, she sensed rather than saw that he was never more than a few paces away. It made her feel awkward and uneasy, despite the fact that his presence had definitely added spark to the evening. Would he ask her to dance? Any unacknowledged hopes she may have harbored were rapidly quashed as she caught sight of the couple out of the corner of her eye. The picture presented confirmed her wildest fears: her ravishing stepmother was clinging to Rafe like a boa, running crimson-tipped fingers through the thick dark hair that flirted with the edge of his collar. Pangs gnawed at Coral's chest while her throat went tight.

Suddenly, all the grief and anger she'd felt during the first few weeks following her father's death were alive again. It was quite plain to her now: they had been and still were lovers. As the couple came into focus once more, Coral bit her lip sharply, trying to control the tears that were welling up in her eyes. She turned her head, incapable of looking at them.

"You're trembling," remarked Dale as he took the opportunity to draw her closer to him. "Are you cold?"

"No, no," she whispered weakly, "only a little tired."

"Let's sit down at the bar."

"I think I ought to go to bed. I've already had too much to drink."

"One more for the road," he coaxed. "It needn't be potent. I'm sure Lady Langley's ingenious barman will be only too happy to concoct one of his non-alcoholic specialties for you."

Too tired to argue, Coral followed him limply through the elegant crowd and perched herself on one of the high stools. Dale ordered the drinks and soon found an audience for his latest ideas on African economic strategies.

Coral was growing wearier by the second. Her head was swimming, and despite the cooling drink, she was flushed and her mouth felt dry. She was pondering whether to discreetly call it a night when a deep-timbered voice interrupted her thoughts and sent her heart racing.

"Are you going to dance with me, Coral?"

She looked around to find that Rafe stood behind her, his charred-brown eyes regarding her with an almost hypnotic gaze. Frank and Nancy Sinatra's "Something Stupid" was now playing.

Of all the damned cheek, she thought angrily, this man really did have a nerve. "I don't think so," she said in a definitive tone, raising an unsmiling face as she brushed past him to leave the room.

"Suit yourself. Perhaps you prefer the company of your American millionaire."

She felt a pang of disappointment that he had called her bluff, but as she walked out the door, she didn't look back.

***

Coral spent hours tossing and turning in the old-fashioned double bed. Jumbled images of Rafe, Cybil, and her father spun through her mind in an uncontrollable merry-go-round, intermingled with snatches of reprocessed conversations that had occupied her thoughts ever since she had arrived in Kenya.

Waking with a start, Coral bolted upright in the bed, her chest rising and falling as though she had run to catch the last train to paradise. Her ears pounded with the thumping of her riotous heartbeats. Under her nightdress, her skin felt hot and clammy, and her hair was damp and clung to her scalp. The room was claustrophobic, so she pushed aside the heap of covers and tumbled out of the bed. Pushing back the shutters, she filled her lungs with cool air.

Coral staggered toward the bathroom, switched on the light, and flicked it off again with a groan, finding the sudden glare unbearable. Anyway, the room was bathed in starlight from the open window. With trembling fingers, she poured herself a glass of water and gulped it down, and then did the same again. She was already beginning to feel better, though her body was still stiff and numb. Nothing like a shower to freshen you up, she thought as she turned on the tap and stepped under the icy drizzle, shivering and shuddering while energetically washing her goose-fleshed limbs. Five minutes later, she emerged from the bathroom, clad in a pink robe, her skin feeling clean and smooth.

She turned on the bedside lamp and glanced at the clock. It had just turned two o'clock. Her bed looked as if a thousand cats had been fighting on it. Though her headache had subsided, sleep seemed far away now. She turned off her lamp, remembering that in Africa light attracted all sorts of unwanted creepy-crawlies.

Like most of the guest bedrooms, the one Coral had been allotted was on the ground floor of a courtyard at the back of the house. Dorian columns supported the awning overhanging the arcade. Two windows looked out on clumps of spindly, exotic pawpaw trees that dotted the courtyard and bordered a cobbled pathway leading out to the coffee plantation in the distance.

She walked to the open window. Crisp air gusted into the room. Africa slept in enigmatic darkness beyond the door…

Withdrawing into the room, Coral pulled on a clean nightshirt of blue silk trimmed with lace and stepped out into the cool stillness. The moon, unnaturally close and still bright, hung suspended in a sky thick with stars over the vague outline of the treetops. She stood a while at the edge of the tiled patio, leaning against one of the columns and listening to the even breathing of the bush.

"Can't sleep?" Rafe's voice emerged from the night, making Coral jump. A stifled gasp escaped as she spun around, her hands flying to her throat. Surveying the surrounding emptiness, the shadows stared back at her — there was no one there.

"Unfortunately, I too suffer from insomnia from time to time," he said, and Coral could hear the smile in his voice as he moved from outside the guest room that faced hers, across the courtyard, and drifted toward her. He stopped only a few paces away, and she instinctively stepped back, not quite knowing what to expect next.

At this distance, she could detect the faint scent of his cologne. "Do you make a habit of creeping up on women in the dark?" she hissed, ignoring the effect his proximity was having on her senses.

"I'm sorry, but I do have a habit of prowling around at night when I can't sleep. Besides, the garden is for all the guests, isn't it?"

"One should be able to feel secure at this unearthly hour," she mumbled.

He moved closer and lifting her chin up with his thumb and forefinger, he looked intently into her eyes. "Remember this, Coral," he whispered huskily, "in the treacherous jungle of life, the safest way is never to feel secure."

Coral tensed at his touch but managed to tear herself away. "No doubt that is true in your kind of world."

He gave a deep laugh that was edged with a note of sadness. "According to you, what might be my kind of world?" he asked quietly as he stepped back and leaned against the bark of a nearby tree.

"A primitive sort of world," she said. "Barbaric, lawless, and promiscuous, like yourself."

Rafe laughed shortly, but he shifted uneasily. "Those statements are unfounded. Your case, Miss Sinclair, would never hold up in a serious court of law. Come now; be more specific. I'm sure you can do better than that."

The challenge in his voice was unmistakable. Common sense cautioned her to ignore it and change the subject or, better yet, bid Rafe goodnight and return to the safety of her room. But suddenly Coral was feeling vicious and vindictive; she hated this man with his quiet self-confidence; she hated the way he looked her up and down as though he was admiring his latest possession; she hated his ability to get away with anything. Yet if she were honest, most of all she hated the impact Rafe had on her emotions, what he did to her own self-confidence… the passions he stirred inside her.

"Do you really want to know what I think of you?" She moved toward him, her eyes glittering defiance.

"I'm most interested to hear your views, dear lady."

"I think you are a disloyal friend and a womanizer."

Rafe nodded thoughtfully. "I see. Those are rather unpleasant accusations you have just made, you know?"

"Maybe." Coral shrugged a bare shoulder. "But they are quite justifiable."

"Some may care to disagree with you."

"I don't think so. Everybody believes my father was a good friend to you. It is general knowledge that when you arrived here, you were a human wreck, and he saved you. He let you into his home, set you back on your feet, and you repaid his kindness and hospitality by stealing his wife and breaking his heart."

"Cybil and I are old friends. We knew each other long before either of us met your father," he said.

"Oh, I know all about that." Coral's eyes flashed with a belligerent light, and she moved toward him — the mention of Cybil's name alone was enough to spur her anger on. "You've always been lovers." She thought she would choke on the word. "And poor Daddy's heart couldn't take it, so now you should have his death on your conscience," she ended, having successfully fired her vitriolic missile, regretting it as soon as it had been delivered. She did not know what to believe but felt deep down that her words were unjustified.

Rafe remained cool and detached, his eyes studying her intently, though she could see his jaw harden. Suddenly she became aware of how close she was to him, her cheeks glowing with anger, and she wished for more clothing than the clinging fabric of her nightshirt.

"Yes, Cybil and I had a brief fling in a previous life — " Rafe ran a frustrated hand through his hair " — but that was all before I knew your father and became his friend. Your father worshipped Cybil… But there was a misunderstanding. You have to take my word for it. I would never have betrayed your father or hurt him in any way."

Damn the man! He made it sound so believable, but she sensed that there was more to this than he was admitting. Why did she have to take his word for it?

"And is it because of your father that you refused to dance with me tonight?" Rafe added, not giving her time to respond.

"Yes, among other things," she replied, knowing he could see her anger.

"Such as?"

She arched a brow. "Well, for one thing, you think you can waltz back into my life after all this time, with no explanation, expecting me to swoon at your feet."

Rafe smiled at her as his eyes searched her face and his voice became lower. "I'm back now, Coral. That's all you need to know, isn't it?"

"Oh, is it? There's a lot I need to know, but you seem to think yourself above all explanations." Her defiant gaze held his. "In fact, I find your behavior quite repulsive." She was aware of the charged atmosphere between them. Coral saw the thunderous look on his face too late. She would have moved away had she sensed the warning undertones of his deceptively soft voice and recognized the danger signals in his narrowing eyes, but she was too deeply immersed in her little battle, too busy scoring points and letting out some of the nervous tension that had been building up inside her.

"All right, young lady, so you think I'm repulsive?" he rasped as fire flashed in his eyes. He grabbed hold of her shoulder, whirling her round and pinning her against the tree. She was rooted to the spot, a prisoner of his iron grip. Rafe paused, staring at her. Stunned, she saw that the anger in his eyes had turned to passion; she was mesmerized by his mouth so close to hers. Coral parted her lips to protest, but no sound came out of her throat. Fighting her own desire, she tried to wriggle out of his grip, but Rafe pressed himself against her, his warm masculine body dominating and demanding. His lips claimed her mouth, igniting her with hungry kisses. She shivered as his chest pressed against her breasts, which were straining against the fragile barrier of silk. She felt her body come to life.

As he slid one arm around her waist, the other hand moved farther down, teasing the soft curves of her body. He pushed his legs between her thighs, pressing his arousal against her. Coral arched toward him, sensing his need and unconsciously urging him to fulfill it. Suddenly he groaned, pulled back, and turned away, muttering something incomprehensible under his breath.

Her eyes flew open. "What's wrong?" she gasped, her senses still aching, her mind awhirl.

Shaking his head, he released her and leaned one trembling hand against the smooth brown bark of the tree, his eyes fixed to the ground. "Damn you, Coral, you could drive a saint to drink," he said, his voice thick and trembling with emotion. "I don't know what came over me. I'm sorry. I shouldn't have let that happen. I swore I wouldn't. Go to bed. Go and sleep."

"I can't sleep now," she protested, trying to catch her breath. "I'm too hot!"

"Then take another shower," he suggested as he stormed off into the night.

Chapter Seven

It was only pride that enabled Coral to face Rafe at breakfast. At first, she was tempted to spend the morning in bed on the pretext of a hangover, but it would have been tantamount to admitting that she had taken his sudden sobering up as a rebuff and that she cared. She blushed at the memory of her own wanton response as his hands had slid over her body, stroking and exploring her slender curves through the thin fabric of her nightshirt. She had never felt wanted in this way before. Yet he had been the one to pull away, to call them back to reality. What would be his reaction this morning? Would he bring up their tête à tête of the night before? She had used some pretty harsh words to his face, and then she had responded to his furious desire with equal fire. Would he chastise her? Ignore her? Mock her? To hell with the man! Coral's mind flashed with resentment and anger, but underneath she recognized Rafe's hold on her. Nevertheless, she would not hide away like a sensitive flower. She put on a determined air and forced herself to go downstairs.

When Coral walked into the dining room, she noticed too late that Rafe was on his own, making his way to the sideboard. "Ah, Miss Sinclair," he exclaimed jovially as she appeared in the doorway, "did you sleep well?" Coral's first instinct was to rush from the room, but she stayed. Without looking at him, she knew that he was watching her, and she was damned if she was going to give him the satisfaction of an undignified retreat.

"Can I help you to some eggs and bacon? Absolutely delicious! Or maybe you would prefer a cup of coffee to start off with? Nothing like a cup of the hot brown brew to sober one up."

Coral met the devilish, tawny-brown gaze. She would have gladly wiped that Cheshire cat grin off his arrogant face, but she restrained herself. "Thank you, Mr. de Monfort," she said coolly, even managing a brave smile, "but I think that I'll pour myself a glass of orange juice."

Walking toward him, she couldn't help but notice how Rafe's faded jeans molded to his hips and muscled thighs, and she tried to ignore the way the sight of his neck through the unbuttoned top of his shirt affected her, hinting at the broad chest below. As he stepped back to let her pass, a whiff of cologne that mingled with the clean, manly scent of his skin tickled her nostrils, sending unwelcome tremors through her body. This was not turning out to be such a good idea after all. "The house seems awfully quiet. Where are the others?" Coral asked lightly, hoping her tone did not sound too rattled as she sat down at the large dining table.

"Most of them have had breakfast. I fear we're lumbered with each other for the remainder of the meal." He beamed, taking a seat opposite her. "Can I pass you the toast?" Rafe stretched out the long, lean hands that had stroked her so effectively a few hours before, reaching out for the silver toast rack.

"No, thanks," Coral said without looking at him, strangely stirred by his amused attention. She wouldn't have minded a refreshing pawpaw or a mango. The artfully arranged basket piled high with clusters of exotic fruit looked tempting enough, but it was placed on the far side of him, and the steady pupils unnerved her to such a degree it made her tongue-tied and gauche.

"You should eat something — you look a little pale. Maybe some fruit?" Rafe suggested sympathetically as he lifted the colorful basket across and laid it in front of her. Damn the man. Was he a mind reader?

"Thank you," she said, reluctantly glancing at him and settling for the first fruit that came within her reach.

"Funny girl," he murmured as if to himself.

"What's so funny?" she snapped, seizing the opportunity to have a go at him. Tension was in the air.

"You are. You're suddenly acting like an awkward schoolgirl," he said huskily, his voice openly teasing but still caressing, "when every inch of you loudly proclaims that you are anything but." Rafe raised an eyebrow and leaned closer to her, mischief sparkling in his eyes. "More like this ripe fruit here, succulent and ready to be savored… "

"That's enough!" Coral rasped, interrupting him, as she fought the familiar heat that raged through her veins. She did not know how to deal with Rafe's disarming directness, and once again he had managed to push all of her buttons. How could he be so flippant after she had made herself so vulnerable in front of him last night? Pushing her chair back, she stormed out of the room, more embarrassed than angry, and almost collided with Cybil who had just appeared in the doorway.

"What's the matter with her?" her stepmother asked in a mocking voice.

Rafe shrugged. "Not a morning person, I guess."

It was mid-morning, the house was stifling, and Coral had to get some air. Needing to walk, to get away, she rushed out into the garden, down the drive, and toward the front gates. She had barely reached the end of the dirt road that ran along the boundary fence when she heard a car coming up fast behind her. It was Rafe's Land Rover. The car swept passed her and screeched to a sudden stop a little farther on, obstructing her way. The driver rolled down the window. "And where do you think you're going, rosebud?" said the all too familiar, all too irritating voice. She swore under her breath. Was there no getting away from this man?

Ignoring him, she managed to squeeze past the vehicle and continued on her way. She heard the door of the car slam shut. In a couple of strides he had caught up with her, grabbing hold of her arm.

"Let me go," she said sharply. "Let me be." She lashed out at him, but he wouldn't listen and maintained his grip. "I'll have you arrested for assault," she threatened, kicking and struggling frantically, all claws out.

Rafe's eyes glittered dangerously in the sunlight. "Steady, little tigress," he muttered, "I'm stronger than you are, even though you do put up a good fight. I'm just trying to stop you running off. Don't you realize you're walking straight toward the jungle?"

"I'm either a rosebud or a tigress." She was still wrestling to free herself from the powerful clasp of his fingers around her wrists. "I can't be both, so make up your mind. What do you want with me anyhow? You're not my keeper. He's dead, remember?"

Her words obviously stunned him. The clamp loosened, and she wrenched herself away.

"Get into the car," he ordered, glowering at her.

"No, I won't," she declared plainly, her face flushed, as she glared back at him steadily.

"Come now, Coral, get into the car. I'll give you a lift to wherever you'd like to go."

"I don't think so," she retorted hotly. "I just want to have a walk, and you're the last person I'd choose for company."

"Going for a walk in this part of the world can be dangerous," he said. "For one thing, the sun is already hot. Soon it will be unbearable, and it will scorch your delicate rosebud skin. We wouldn't want that to happen, would we now?" He was smiling at her indulgently, his voice softer, almost tender. "For another, you may have been away from Kenya since you were a girl, but you must remember that white people never go walking alone here, not even the local expats. Besides, we're in the middle of the bush, on the edge of the jungle; you could have some very unpleasant encounters with creatures much more dangerous than I am. Whatever you think of me, Coral, try to bear in mind that I only have your best interests at heart." Rafe's anger had been replaced by concern. He had a point there, she thought; it probably wasn't such a clever idea to go wondering off on a hike in this outlandish place.

"So, what do you suggest, clever clogs?" Coral looked up at him, arms folded. "I'm not used to being imprisoned; besides, I've got work to do. I may have a year's unpaid leave, but I have promised to get together photographs and material soon for an article next year on Africa. I'm not in the habit of letting people down."

"I never suggested that you should let anyone down," Rafe said, "but there are other means to go about it."

"Such as?"

A smile touched Rafe's lips. "More than one way comes to mind," he said pensively. For a few seconds his attention seemed to drift away; then he pinched her chin affectionately between his thumb and forefinger. "Come along, rosebud." Rafe smiled mischievously as he pulled open the door of the Land Rover to let her in. "It's already too hot out here. Let's continue this conversation in the car. I'll take you for a drive and show you some countryside." Coral stopped arguing and followed him to the car.

The narrow road climbed and descended along the edges of gaping ravines and precipices, winding its way across the foothills. The views were unexpected and magnificent. Orchids sprouted from emerald green grass between banks of compact, glossy thorn bushes and flame-colored reeds. Along the road, acacias, tamarind, frangipani, and purple jacarandas thrust their flowering branches into the never-ending, azure sky. On all sides everything was colossal; the space surrounding them made them seem reduced to Lilliputian size.

They drove in silence, each absorbed in their own thoughts. Rafe was a steady driver, and Coral watched through the window as the scenery rolled by. She felt an urge to ask more about him but did not know quite how to go about it. Clearly Rafe's knowledge of her was much greater than hers of him; the oils he had painted were alone proof enough. Walter Sinclair must have spoken to Rafe about his daughter, but to Coral, the man sitting next to her was a total stranger. Although she recognized herself to be a private person, somehow there was something more evasive about him, something studiously vague. She thought back to their first two encounters. Rafe had deliberately not introduced himself. Maybe he had felt awkward because of the gossip surrounding him, Cybil, and her father. Yet he must have realized that sooner or later they would meet socially and that she would find out his identity. Kenya's social circles were not that wide after all; everybody knew everybody, and everyone gossiped about everyone. Maybe this was part of his style, to make himself seem more attractive; she had known a few people like that. Still, his Sphinx-like attitude made her feel uneasy.

Rafe, who had been watching Coral for some time, suddenly stopped the car, jerking her back to reality. Totally absorbed by her thoughts, she had not noticed their arrival at a clearing. There, in the middle of the depression, entirely enclosed by flowering shrubs, lay a phosphorescent expanse of water, shimmering like a sheet of silk in the rays of the midday sun. High above, a solid mass of white foam thundered from a narrow gulley; it leaped down, rolling over part of a sheer wall of mountain that stood like an impassive sentinel, its head in the clouds. Farther up, exotic trees stooped over the crystalline lake.

Coral got out of the car, her senses reveling in the magnificent scenery, submerged in this world of color. Apart from the light roar of the falls and the singing of birds, it was a tranquil haven of beauty. "It's so peaceful here," she murmured.

Rafe came round and stood next to her. They watched silently for a while as the sunlight caught the cascades, making them dazzle like diamonds. "Am I forgiven, then, for teasing you at breakfast?" Rafe's voice was soft, the inflection a seductive caress. Coral looked up at him and met his amused expression. Laughter bubbled up in her throat, a spontaneous answer to his question.

"Fancy a swim?" he asked, his eyes sparkling almost as fiercely as the water.

"My swimsuit is at the house," she said in a low voice as she stared at a spot in the distance, very much aware of his attentive look.

He chuckled. "That's a very lame excuse, rosebud. You'll have to do better than that. Who needs a swimsuit anyway?"

She felt her cheeks color. "I do," she uttered, still determinedly focusing on the scenery opposite.

"Is that a blush I see?" he asked with a light chuckle. "How inhibited you English are. Don't you know that it's the most delicious sensation to feel water against one's naked skin? Nakedness is a perfectly natural and beautiful state. We were all born that way, and if we are happy to be naked as babies, why not as adults?" His tone was matter of fact as he continued to stare at her steadily.

"That's not the same." Her blush increased as she recalled the events of the previous night. A confusion of emotions tore through her: a mixture of embarrassment and excitement, of modesty and anticipation. Red lights flashed in her mind, a warning against the turn this conversation was taking. She should put a stop to it immediately before it skidded down to a level of no return, but she was spellbound.

"Why the inhibitions? Why the hang-ups? You have the most ravishing body, enough to drive men crazy. You should be proud of it, revel in its beauty, indulge it, please it." Rafe's voice was a teasing provocation, and yet it was smoldering, charged with all sorts of sensuous intonations.

Coral forced herself to face him, but she was unable to cope with those indiscreet, burnished eyes boring into the very depths of her soul, and she had to turn away. Despite being fully dressed, she felt stripped bare, exposed to the core, more so because she was aware of Rafe's body so close to hers. He had awakened a physical sensibility in her that no man had even got close to generating, and she knew that he was aware of it.

Suddenly, there was a rush of air above them as a white-headed, full-winged eagle dropped out of the sky. It swooped down upon the lake, large talons clawing forward, and snatched a fish from the water, its strong muscular legs dragging it across the surface to the shore without pausing. Startled out of her meditation, Coral sucked in her breath.

"That's the African Fish Eagle," Rafe whispered, "one of fifty species of eagles that inhabit various parts of Africa. He is the king of all birds of prey in this dark continent." In silence they watched the formidable predator rise back up high into the air, its broad, powerful black wings completely extended as he glided majestically back to his perch, carrying his prey.

"I wish I had my camera with me," Coral said wistfully.

"We can come back another day. His nest must be quite close. These creatures never venture far from their territory. There," he said, pointing at one of the more distant trees stooping over the lake. "Look, there he is." Indeed, there it was, upright, perched on a branch, lordly and sublime, its keen, bright eyes surveying the terrain as though it owned the whole land. Then, in a burst of fluttering wings, it abruptly flew off into the sky, patches of snow-feathers shining in the vibrant light.

"Let's sit in the shade for a while," Rafe said, taking Coral's hand and steering her toward a flame tree in riotous flower. He stretched himself out fully on the soft grass and put his hands behind his head, totally relaxed. Coral hesitated before seating herself next to him. Drawing her knees up, she encircled them with her arms and rested her chin on top of them. "Don't you want to lie down?" Rafe asked. Coral felt self-conscious as he regarded her with undisguised anticipation.

"No," she said, making sure her tone was final. "I am very comfortable right here, thank you."

He laughed deep in his throat. "I promise to be a good boy." She shrugged and turned hastily away from him, trying to hide how flustered she felt. "All right, you win," he said with a conciliatorily grin.

"What an unusual looking bush," Coral said, pointing at a sprawling shrub where masses of mauve, deep purple, and white flowers bloomed.

"It's known as the morning, afternoon, and evening tree. Its heady scent can sometimes make you drowsy. Tropical plants flourish in this spot with a special luxuriance, probably because of the high rocks around the lake. It's a sun trap, and the space is confined and sheltered from the wind. I don't even think many wild animals come tramping around here. At least, I've never seen any. It's strange, though, I would have thought that they'd use it as a drinking spot."

"You seem to know the place well. Do you often come here?" Coral was relaxing now, as she steadily watched him. Rafe looked back at her, and there was a pause before he spoke.

"Do you have any hobbies? I mean, apart from photography and writing, which I presume are not only a job to you."

Coral smiled. "Back home I ride. I also like to swim, but I'm not very fond of swimming pools, and the weather in England is not too conducive to water sports. Consequently, I only swim when I go abroad."

"Do you travel often?"

"Sometimes, for my job and usually when I'm on holiday, but nothing like the amount I would like to be doing. Have you done a lot of traveling?"

"Yep." His brief answer suggested that he did not want to be quizzed on that subject. However, the only effect it had was to sharpen Coral's curiosity.

"Where?" Rafe had closed his eyes, his long, dark lashes deliberately excluding her. She repeated her question. "Whereabouts have you traveled?"

"Oh, here and there, too much, too often," he said, his face unrevealing.

"Is that why you came to Kenya? And is that why you bought Whispering Palms, to settle down here?" she pushed, feeling that for once she had the advantage.

"Aren't we inquisitive?" he said, not annoyed but with an edge of irritation. He jumped to his feet and brushed off the grass from his jeans. "It's getting late, and they'll be wondering where we are. Lunch is usually at one thirty here, and we mustn't keep our hosts waiting."

"Oooh!" She was disappointed, her lips taking on a pouting mien. "Is it really time to go?" The small dimple in her check appeared. "I was enjoying our little conversation," she teased.

His head lifted, and his black pupils fixed her with an intense stare. His brow furrowed as he seemed to debate his response. He strode back to her and crossed his arms. Coral met his frown with bold defiance.

"If you like stories, let me tell you the African legend of the Curious Monkey," he said, towering over her. His voice was low and calm, but behind the words and the cool composure she could discern a hint of agitation. "Once upon a time, a dog was comfortably asleep in the jungle next to a fire. He was the first dog to ever be born into the world, and he was a happy dog. All he ever did was sleep, until a monkey happened upon him." Rafe leaned against the flame tree, his arms still folded, and shot Coral a wry look as he started to relax into his story.

"The monkey was, of course, curious, as monkeys are, and he scampered down from his tree to examine this strange new creature. He looked at the dog from every possible angle and flew off to tell all the other monkeys about his strange encounter. Soon all the animals of the jungle heard about the creature, and along with the monkey, they came to where it was sleeping, debating amongst each other what kind of creature it was. The monkey asked all the animals if they knew what it was, until only the tortoise was left. The wise old tortoise knew what the creature was, as she had been around since the beginning of all creation. 'That's a dog,' said the tortoise, and when he heard his name, the dog suddenly awoke.

"He sprang to his feet, looking with bewilderment at all of the animals around him. The dog was furious that he'd been woken

144

up, and he charged at the other animals, barking and scowling and snapping his jaws. The only animal that didn't run was the tortoise — she didn't have to. 'You won't catch me, dog,' she said and withdrew into her shell, 'but from this day on, you are condemned to chase any creature you look at.'"

Rafe walked over to Coral and squatted down next to her, his forearms resting on his knees as he looked straight at her. "And that, my dear Coral, is how the saying came to be: 'Better to let sleeping dogs lie.'"

In the car on the way back, Rafe was silent for such a long time that Coral sneaked a glance at him. His face was set, a small vein pulsing at his right temple just visible. Apparently sensing her scrutiny, his eyes crinkled into a smile, which she found rather sad. "Hey, rosebud," he said in his usual amused tone. "Don't look so alarmed. I'm not a mad dog, even if I do growl from time to time." They laughed, and she assumed she had imagined the sadness.

***

The pattern of the next week followed a simple routine. Coral would wake up early, before the heat, and swim a few lengths of the pool. The air at that time of day was a little chilly but invigorating. The rest of each morning was set aside for exploring the area round the Kongoni estate, the afternoons for dozing and reading.

She had taken some colorful photographs of local foodstuffs in the market and some rather interesting ones of the indigenes. Natives enjoyed posing for the camera, which made her task much easier, though she was always careful to ask their permission. In some places in Kenya, especially the rural areas, superstition still suggested that the camera was a stealer of souls. But most often the locals would beam as they held up a paw-paw or happily sat playing dominos over an upturned barrel as she snapped away around them. Coral always made sure she took some extra money with her to show polite appreciation with the customary token payment afterward, plus sweets for the children who kicked a ball around in the streets.

Still, she had not as yet been able to take any pictures of the flora and fauna of the bush. One day as she was driving to town, she had nearly run over an antelope that was crossing the road. It was a truly magnificent animal, crowned by curved, smooth horns and bearing a coat of grayish-blue with a bright white strip down the back. She had been driving slowly so she was able to brake in time, but with a mighty bound the beautiful creature had fled into the bush before she had time to get out her camera.

Coral had not seen Rafe again after the morning at the lake. She had gathered by the conversation of the other guests at the plantation that he had gone off on some special errand or jaunt — no one was quite sure where, as he had been very mysterious about it. Once, she had tried to go back to the magical spot where they had last been together, but she was unable to find it. Did she miss him, she asked herself? Of course she did, despite her determined efforts to blot out his image every time it careered into her brain. Rafe was not for her. She had let him take her to the lake that day and of course felt that familiar thrill she experienced whenever he was near, but that was merely lust, she told herself, and she had already allowed herself to be too vulnerable to his attentions. His reputation was that of a compulsive womanizer, but she did not need other people's opinions to know what she was up against. Rafe was a hunter; he liked women, and they drifted to him like butterflies to a lavender bush. He reveled in the courting, the teasing, and the mutual seduction, and she knew full well that all he wanted was to coax her into an affair. But she could never be his mistress, one of the many Morganas and Cybils that hopped in and out of his bed at the mere snap of his fingers. The thought of that alone made her feel ashamed; it would be too degrading. Aluna's words came back loud and strong: "My missy is taboo to you," the old *yaha* had screamed at him that morning not so long ago, and she was right. He was wrong for her, and that must be the end of it.

It was early afternoon, and Coral was sitting in a rocking chair on Lady Langley's veranda, engrossed in a book. The weather was cooler; a fresh breeze was blowing from the north.

"Hello, kiddo." Dale had just strolled onto the terrace, his face lighting up as he saw her. "Care for a drive? It's a beautiful

146

afternoon, not too hot. Maybe we can wander a little into the bush or visit one of the reserves?"

The offer was tempting. Coral did not particularly relish the idea of spending a whole afternoon with the American tycoon, but if Dale drove, at least it would give her the chance to take some good photographs and enable her to get on with her articles. Inspiration had dried up, and she was very behind with her work. In a couple of weeks she would have to return to Malindi, and this fine opportunity might never present itself again. Although the specific goal of her trip to Kenya had been to assume her inheritance, she had now committed to bringing back some good material for the forthcoming documentary, and she knew her firm was counting on her to deliver.

"Thank you, Dale," she said, lightly jumping up from her chair. "I think that's a marvelous idea. Give me five minutes to gather up my camera and bits and pieces. I'll be straight back."

They drove for miles in brilliant sunshine. Dale's monotonous voice talking about his many successes as a businessman provided a steady background of chatter, leaving her to concentrate on the task at hand. The man certainly liked the sound of his own voice, and that suited her fine. Coral's camera clicked away as they passed giraffes, wildebeest mixing complacently with zebras, and a group of native women in single file, every one of them with some object poised on her head, hips swaying in rhythm with her chanting as she walked along. They even came across a rare black-maned lion, stretched out majestically on the grass as he sunned himself sleepily, watching the world go by. Coral urged Dale to stop the car so she could get a better view of him. The huge beast stared at them for a second, then the yellow eyes closed, the jaws opened in a wide yawn, and he turned his beautiful head disdainfully, drumming the ground with his long, powerful tail.

"What a wonderful sight!" said Coral, her cheeks flushed with excitement.

"Umm. We caught one of those a couple of years back. Come to think of it now, it was quite easy," Dale mused as though lost in happy memories.

Coral frowned. "What do you mean you caught one of those?"

"My father and I went on a hunting expedition some time ago with a few friends. Our guide was a brilliant hunter. We used some sort of wheel trap. The way it works — "

"I don't want to know," she interrupted him briskly and glared at him. "It sounds horrible. How could you be so cruel?"

"Oh, don't be such a baby," he said with a snort. "It's the law of the jungle."

"It certainly is not," she retorted hotly. "More like slaughter. It's cruel and unsporting. There is no excuse that could stand against such exploitation. It's people like you that give a bad reputation to hunters."

"Yeah, yeah, sentimental twaddle," he drawled, his lips curling upward into a derisive smirk. "It's like these parks," he went on. "They're useless — just zoos in reverse. It's us who are caged in our cars and not the animals. How more ridiculous can one get? Who wants to just look at animals, eh?"

"I've had enough," she snapped. "Let's go back."

Coral was fuming. The more time she spent with Dale here in Kenya, the more she wondered how she could have considered linking her life to his. She didn't remember thinking he was a pompous lightweight when she was dating him. Had he changed — or had she? Perhaps he was feeling insecure and was trying to woo her back in his own clumsy fashion. Either way, it had been a close miss. Some guardian angel must have been looking after her. Actually, the more she thought about it, the more she realized that Dale had never really meant anything to her. Had she ever had the chance to really get to know him? The glitz of New York had dazzled her, sweeping her away in the whirlwind that had engulfed them both during the two exciting weeks of the exhibition, and somehow the long-distance nature of their relationship had kept the illusion going for a year and a half afterward. How very naïve of her! Still, she had been a little over-protected in England. Dale had been her first proper boyfriend; before him, she had barely had a few dates. The embarrassing fact was that at the ripe old age of twenty-five, she was inexperienced — green, some would say. The word rosebud came to mind, and Coral smiled wistfully, wondering what Rafe was up to. Probably in bed with some woman, she thought, and immediately willed him out of her mind.

It was late; night was falling. They had reached the main road, and Dale was burning up miles, driving faster and faster. "Slow down, Dale, for heaven's sake, you're going to get us killed!" Coral firmly clutched the edge of her seat as the young man accelerated, rocking the Land Rover from side to side.

"Don't worry, baby, I'm an excellent driver. I've traveled all around the States and tackled roads much more dangerous than this, I can assure you." He forced the pace further as he turned on his headlights.

He was showing off, and she couldn't bear it. "Slow down, Dale, I nearly ran over an antelope the other day not far from here, at the crossroads, I think," she warned, but Dale was not listening.

Coral had barely finished speaking when a shadow shot past the lights at an extraordinary speed. There was a bang and then a thump as the car was thrown out of control from one side of the road to the other. It bounced once, twice, somersaulted again, and landed on its roof, wheels in the air.

A few minutes elapsed before Coral managed to shift uncomfortably, her head spinning and aching. Apart from the shooting pain across her eyes, she did not think she was hurt. The last thing she remembered was telling Dale to slow down. *Dale...* Where was he? Coral was lying on her back and tried to move to rid herself of the seatbelt that was pinning her chest against the ceiling. After several attempts she managed to free herself, turn on her side, and wriggle out through the open window. That task proved easier than she had imagined. Her slender frame slid smoothly through the gap, and soon Coral found herself lying on the ground. Getting up was more difficult. Her legs wobbled, and there was a strange buzzing in her ears. Dale was lying a few meters away, one headlight throwing a weak beam across his face.

Coral was shivering, and drops of a gluey substance were now trickling from her forehead. Still a little unsteady on her legs and feeling slightly queasy, she managed to make her way slowly toward his immobile figure and painfully drop to her knees beside him. He was breathing regularly. "Dale," she called slowly, her voice trembling, "Dale, can you hear me?"

There was a groan as he tried to move. He opened his eyes. "What happened? Where am I?" he asked, his speech low and indistinct.

"We've had an accident. Don't move — you may be hurt. I'll try to get some help." Coral staggered back onto her feet and paused, wondering which way to turn. Apart from the car's single headlight, the night was black and silent. As her eyes adjusted to the darkness, she was able to assess the extent of the damage. The windscreen was broken and one of the back doors on the driver's side was completely bashed in. Dale's door was open; she assumed that was how he had been propelled out of the car. The Land Rover was probably a write-off, but at least they were both alive. What could have caused such a disaster? Coral turned her painful head just as a wan moon swam out from behind a cloud, and then she saw the outline of an enormous bulk lying on the opposite side of the road. It was obviously an animal, but she couldn't deal with that now. There was no time to waste: Dale was lying there practically unconscious, and she had to find help.

Coral had just started on her way toward a familiar market village when a car rumbled up. There was the grinding sound of breaks, doors opened and shut, then the bright shaft of torchlight shining in her face and dazzling her. "Over here," shouted an authoritative voice she recognized. "Over here! Bring out the stretcher for the man — I'll take care of her." A wave of dizziness and nausea swept through Coral, and she faltered before her legs folded beneath her. Strong arms lifted her up swiftly. "Hang on in there, rosebud. I'm here now; I'm in charge," she heard Rafe say, and then came the black hole of oblivion.

***

When Coral came to, she was lying on a narrow bed in an unfamiliar room. It was dark save for a weak shaft of moonlight filtering through the opened window. Her head ached, just across her temple, and she still felt a little squeamish. She struggled to lift herself up, but fell back limply onto the pillows.

"Hey, don't you dare move!" Rafe's command was sharp and concise. In a flash, he was by her side, feeling her pulse.

"Playing doctor, again?" she asked, regretting her words as soon as they were out. She should be grateful instead of being sarcastic, and Rafe's grim face told her that he was not amused. "Where am I?" she asked, attempting a brave smile.

"In the lion's den."

"I'm sorry," she said as tears blurred her view. "I've been a real nuisance, haven't I?"

"Shush, stop talking and go to sleep." Rafe's face was set, his features closed as he crept away.

"Rafe?" Her voice was weak, almost inaudible. He stopped dead in his shoes and turned, drifting back to stand next to the bed. Coral gazed up at him, regarding him anxiously. "How did you know where to find us?"

"When you did not turn up for dinner, Lady Langley was worried. I had just arrived from Nairobi where I'd been on business. She told me that you had gone off with Dale to take some pictures of animals at one of the nearby game reserves. I was worried that something might have happened, so I took a search party along the most likely road to the closest reserve, and would have gone further until I'd found you. But you weren't so far away from the plantation after all, just a few miles, and when I saw the headlight shining up toward the trees, I knew I'd been fortunate."

"What did we hit?"

"An antelope." Rafe smiled, his face holding a mixture of amusement and concern. "Don't worry, rosebud, you're in good hands. We transported you both to this clinic. It belongs to Dr. Frank Giles, a friend of mine and a reliable doctor. The hospital was too far. You're in a flat attached to the main clinic."

"And Dale?" Coral saw a twinge of irritation flicker across Rafe's face.

"Dale is all right. You were both very lucky to get away with concussion and a few minor scratches and bruises. You've banged your head — nothing serious, though, just a nasty graze. Frank has given you a sedative to ease the pain, so that's probably why you feel drowsy. You'll be better after a good night's sleep." Rafe's tone was warm and soothing as he tried to dispel her fears. "We'll keep you here under observation for twenty-four hours, just to make sure everything's all right. We sent word to the plantation so they wouldn't worry. There, now, does that answer all your questions and set your mind at rest?"

Coral parted her lips to speak, but his fingers brushed her cheek in a soft caress. "Shush, rosebud. Sleep now. Tomorrow we shall talk."

She nodded and shut her eyes, filled with a sense of safety and of peace.

That night was a turbulent one for Coral, with nightmares of wild monsters chasing after her up and down ravines, around dense forests, and into deep oceans, where Rafe could not reach her. She heard herself cry out his name a few times as she drifted in and out of sleep; often she felt his presence beside her, mopping her damp brow, handing her a glass of water, his voice soothing and reassuring.

Coral woke up the following afternoon. The shutters were pulled together, but bright sunlight seeped through its narrow vents. The easy chair next to the bed was empty. She had a vague recollection of Rafe's presence during the night as she had swum in and out of consciousness. Coral lifted herself and managed to sit up. Her head was a little painful; still, she lowered her feet to the ground and tried to stand. Black spots danced in her vision, and she fell back pathetically onto the pillows with a small groan.

"What the devil do you think you're doing?" Rafe had shot into the room and was glowering down at her. Coral glared back, her frustration beginning to rise. "You can look at me with that stormy expression all you like; I'm not letting you out of bed," he said gruffly.

"I feel better. I want to get up. Besides, I need to get out of these clothes. I feel dirty," she said, embarrassed and annoyed at her own helplessness. Rafe looked tired, his features drawn, a day's stubble throwing a blue shadow over the sculptured jaw. He obviously hadn't slept since yesterday.

"You're still weak. You should have called out."

"Where's the nurse? I need some clean clothes. Where's the doctor?" Coral hated having him standing there, and pride and vanity got the better of her, making her snap at him.

Dark eyebrows went up. "There is no nurse and there is no doctor at the moment." Rafe regarded her with amusement.

"I thought — "

He interrupted her impatiently. "Aluna came by this morning and brought you a clean set of clothes."

Coral's face brightened up with relief. "Where is Aluna?" she asked.

"The poor woman was really beside herself with worry. You know how agitated she can become. But she was making an exhibition of herself, and there's no need for that sort of outburst around here. She was told to leave the clothes and was sent back to the plantation."

"Who sent her back?" Coral suddenly felt a desperate need for her old yaha.

"I did," he confirmed rather tersely.

Coral nodded. "Where's Dr. What's-his-name?"

"Dr. Giles has gone off for his afternoon calls; he'll be back later. But I'm here to keep an eye on you." Rafe grinned.

"Where are my clothes?" Coral asked. "I need to shower."

"They're right here." Rafe opened a cupboard and took out the things Aluna had dropped off together with some other belongings. "At the risk of disappointing you, I must tell you that there is no shower, even though this is a clinic. You're not in England now. In case you've forgotten, we're in the boondocks here. We're lucky to have running water today," he added curtly.

Coral gritted her teeth and lifted her chin. "I'm getting dressed," she said determinately.

Dark brows flickered. He gave a short, derisory laugh and folded his arms, watching her. "Suit yourself."

"Where's the bathroom?"

"It's at the other end of the flat. I'll help you wash and dress, if you like, rosebud," he suggested, shooting her a playful look.

"Never!" she exclaimed, a little too forcefully.

His eyebrows flew up. "You keep forgetting that I have studied medicine."

"That doesn't make you a doctor, and anyhow — " she threw him a sarcastic look " — I'm perfectly capable of dressing myself, thank you very much. Nice try."

"You needn't worry, rosebud. I don't set my cap at the weak and helpless."

"I'm not weak and helpless; I'm just a little shaken. You would be if you were in my place," she retorted sharply. She picked up her clothes, thrust back the sheet, and stood up. Two steps and her head was reeling again; she faltered, gave a little groan, and would have crashed to the floor had Rafe not moved swiftly and caught her.

"Are you convinced now that you're in no condition to move?" He laid her down gently on the bed and pulled the sheet over her. "I'll bring you something to eat and some hot tea. We'll take it from there," he said in an even voice, then looked at her solemnly and walked out, leaving her alone in the room.

Coral choked back a sob. She felt guilty about the way she was behaving, but Rafe's provocative attitude infuriated her, making it impossible for her to act normally around him. Of course she was obligated to Rafe. He needn't have stayed by her side at night; after all, they were virtually strangers, even if there was obviously a strong attraction between them. And despite the fact that she always felt so unnerved around him, she remembered the relief that had swept over her as she heard his voice at the scene of the accident, and then again later that night when he had tried to calm her fears. Strangely enough she felt safe in his company. His whole being reverberated authority and confidence, and even though she hated to admit to it, a part of her melted at the thought of that commanding strength.

Rafe was away for some time, leaving her to her somber thoughts. Coral could hear him whistling somewhere in the flat and wondered what was taking him so long.

"There you are, my untouchable *princesse lointaine*," he said as he came back into the room, rolling in a hospital tray that he positioned over the bed in front of her. "I hope you enjoy the breakfast that I have so lovingly prepared."

Indeed, she had to admit it was a most inviting and appetizing sight. Coral surveyed the home-made fruit salad — exotic morsels glittering like small jewels in the center of a bowl — the slice of warm toast spread with a thin layer of marmalade, the glass of freshly squeezed orange juice, and the cup of steaming hot tea. Everything had been arranged on a white cloth. At the far side of the tray, a tumbler with a single pink rosebud gave it the final special touch.

Coral smiled sheepishly. "Thank you," she said, "it looks really tempting. I love fruit."

"Well, rosebud, stop being just tempted and tuck in, for heaven's sake," he said cheerfully as he sank into the easy chair next to her bed. "*L'appétit vient en mangeant*, goes an old French proverb. 'Appetite comes with eating.' I'm not used to playing housewife, but if it'll bring a smile to your pretty lips, there's nothing I wouldn't do."

Coral ate slowly, sampling the food at first, feeling a little awkward under Rafe's steady look. "Wouldn't you like some?" she offered, holding out her plate. "The fruit is really delicious."

"Watching your enjoyment suffices to make me a happy man." She was annoyed that he was teasing her again.

"Where's Dale?"

Rafe scoffed. "I wondered when you'd get around to asking about him." He gave a dismissive grunt. "He was propelled out of the car, probably before it turned over, so he didn't receive the same battering to the head that you got. I'd cheerfully have killed the son of a bitch, but Frank is averse to blood and guts. Anyway, don't worry; your irresponsible boyfriend is actually in better shape than you are. Frank released him at noon, and he went home."

"He's not my boyfriend," Coral snapped.

Rafe's look stabbed her with disbelief. "No?" The word carried an almost imperceptible quaver.

"No." Her voice was firm.

He regarded her steadily, his expression slightly skeptical, probing for an explanation.

Coral shifted uncomfortably on the bed and busied herself with the cup of tea, averting his keen scrutiny and gulping down a mouthful. "Though it's no business of yours, I will indulge your

155

curiosity," she said shortly. "Dale and I were once engaged. It didn't work out, and that's the end of it."

"And that's why he followed you to Kenya?"

"Probably, but I'm not Dale's keeper, so I had no knowledge of it. Anyhow, there's no need to read more into it than there is. Dale and I are just friends now."

"I see." He gave a dismissive shrug. "Well, as you've told me several times, it's no concern of mine. I'm not *your* keeper, and you're old enough to look out for yourself. After all, you proved that yesterday." He had punched beneath the belt, but Coral took the blow without a word. Was he jealous? It didn't matter. She was tired, and this wasn't the time for an argument. Wrenching herself from the accusing eyes, she pushed the tray away gently. "Thank you for the breakfast," she said evenly. "I feel so much better now."

Rafe took the table away and rolled it out of the room, his features an impassive mask. She knew that look; it had appeared only a couple of times, but enough for her to recognize it. He was brooding. Why couldn't she and this man get along without incessantly leaping at each other's throats? Was this what was known as a love-hate relationship? *More like a hate-your-guts battle.*

Rafe had been right to force her to eat something; it had given her some energy. She got out of bed and ventured through the door into a sort of reception and waiting room with a large window looking over the rolling countryside. By now the sun had dropped behind the hills, which were flushed with the clusters of red-hot pokers peeping through banks of aloes. The views of pink, purple, and blue-gray over the valley were breathtaking.

"What are you doing here?" Rafe's stern voice broke her reverie.

"I was looking for the bathroom and stopped to admire the view. The scenery here is so striking, so impressive," she said, hugging the set of clothes a little too tightly against her chest.

"Yeah," he agreed. He seemed far away, his mind on other things.

Coral looked up at him. He had washed, shaved, and changed into a pair of beige chinos and a Nile-blue polo shirt.

The color suited his gold-tanned skin, and the cotton molded him to perfection. Invisible fingers pinched her heart as she acknowledged once more the undeniable charisma that emanated from this man. His features were not those of an Adonis in the strict classical meaning of the word, but every pore of his lithe body exuded virility and sex. Coral cleared her throat.

"Where's the bathroom?"

"Right behind you." He signaled with a toss of his head. "There's running hot water, soap, and a set of clean towels, but no shampoo. Such luxuries are scarce around here. I'm afraid you'll have to make do with what's available for now." His mouth was set into a thin line, his face devoid of all expression. He had become remote, speaking to her as though they were strangers, his aloofness setting a barrier between them more effective than any wall.

It chilled her heart. A huge lump of unreleased emotion constricted her throat as Coral tried to fight back the tears that threatened to spill out at any moment. She swallowed hard. "That sounds perfect, thank you," she said flatly as she scurried off to wash and get dressed.

Once in the bathroom, she looked at herself in the mirror and grimaced. The graze on her forehead had been cleaned and was starting to heal, forming an ugly crust. Washing and drying it would not be an easy task. It was awkward washing her hair and face over the sink, but once she had managed it, she dried her head with a towel and pulled her hair back into a tight knot at the nape of her neck. She could not disguise the scar. Well, it could not be helped; this would have to do for now. Coral took her time, running the soap smoothly on her neck, around her breasts, on her stomach, between her thighs. The warm water on her skin was bliss, washing away the tension of the past twenty-four hours. For a few moments, she forgot about Rafe and the bitter chilliness that had frozen up her heart. She welcomed the clean underwear and clothes that Aluna had brought down. Bless her, everything was there: toothbrush, comb, the little bag of makeup, and even a bottle of her favorite scent.

When she came back out of the bathroom half an hour later, Rafe was not alone. "Ah, there you are," he said with a polite smile that appeared alien on him. "This is Dr. Giles, my old friend."

Frank Giles was tall, lean, and blond; he was attractive without being particularly handsome. His forbearers must have been Scandinavian, Coral thought. Pale blue eyes surveyed her kindly as she looked up at the man standing beside Rafe. "I hope you're feeling better," he said, his face breaking into a warm smile, putting her immediately at ease.

"Yes, I am." She returned his smile. "Thank you for putting me up and looking after me so well."

"I'm afraid this place is not very modern. We keep things to a bare minimum, but it's effective. We do our best." He sounded apologetic, and Coral felt obliged to reassure him.

"Really, I've been very comfortable, and Rafe has been most attentive." Coral glanced at Rafe, and for a split second she thought the chill in his expression had vanished — or was that her fancy playing tricks?

"The bump on your head seems to have gone down, and the graze, I see, is healing nicely. I will need to look at it once again, just to make sure that it doesn't get infected. I assume your vaccinations are up to date?"

"Oh, yes, yes. I travel a lot so I need to be careful. I may get myself into scrapes from time to time, but I'm very reasonable when it comes to keeping those things in order." She smiled weakly, and they laughed.

"Frank will drive you back to the plantation," Rafe broke in. "I had a previous engagement and regretfully will not have that pleasure." For a moment, she had the impression the old Rafe was back, but when she turned to face him, he had his back to her and was busy closing his briefcase.

The three of them went down together. As they reached the door of the building, Rafe fell back a few paces, letting them take the lead. Coral had no time to wonder why. Walking out onto the pavement, she stood rigid, frozen to the spot, as waves of ambivalent emotions hit her. The luxurious black Cadillac that appeared the first day at the port was parked on the other side of the narrow road, facing them. The street lamp threw a shaft

158

of light onto the open window. The arrogant black eyes of the dancer met the blue stormy ones that held their stare.

"Is anything the matter? Are you not feeling well?" Frank Giles enquired, apparently alarmed at Coral's sudden reaction. "My car is not too far, just there behind the black Cadillac."

Having recovered her composure, Coral smiled up at him. "I'm fine, absolutely fine. It was only the shock of fresh air after confinement."

Rafe had now come out of the building. He strolled across the road, making his way to the Cadillac. This time, the uniformed chauffeur was prompt enough and had opened the back door. Rafe disappeared into the car, but not before Coral had noted the broad smile on his face.

"We'll let them go first, shall we?" Frank told her.

She nodded her assent and smiled wryly.

A sense of loss swept over her as she watched the black beast roar into life and move off into the night.

Chapter Eight

The days that followed were difficult. As she recuperated, Coral had to contend with Dale's unwelcome advances, as he seemed to think that the accident had somehow "brought them closer together," Cybil's inquisitiveness about her time at Dr. Giles' clinic with Rafe, and Aluna's over-protective fussing. Most of the time, not quite recovered enough to get out and about, Coral skulked about the house, feeling annoyed and smothered. Besides, Rafe was still away, and she missed him. Lady Langley had told her over lunch one day that Rafe was a paying guest and he used the Kongoni estate as a base whenever he was called on business in the neighborhood, which was the case at the moment, and it was an arrangement that suited them both very well.

Coral was lucid enough to realize that her feelings toward Rafe had taken a new turn. However much she inwardly kicked and screamed against the lunacy of it, however much she had tried to ignore her terror at getting hurt again, her heart could not deny it now. She was beginning to fall in love with him. The more Coral had gotten to know Rafe, the more she had caught glimpses of the man behind the infamous reputation, and the less she could find to justify Aluna's hostile words about him or the disparaging hearsay echoed by her friends. Rafe was naturally charming and compassionate; people were drawn to him. Coral had noticed the courteous and friendly way he always treated the servants at the estate, and they in turn all seemed to respect him and genuinely like him — hardly the devil he was painted. Apart from his teasing, which she often found outrageous, he had never been anything but kind to her. Added to that, Rafe was certainly cultured and knew so much. Coral recalled the evening she had spent with him at his plantation. It had been wonderful; he had thought out every detail to make the occasion a complete pleasure for her.

Even though it was painful to admit, she knew this feeling Rafe aroused in her was more than sexual desire. Yes, he was a born womanizer and a flirt, but the only reason this needled Coral so much was because he stirred her emotions to the very core. Of course women like Cybil and Morgana were drawn to him like to a magnet, and Coral knew that the jealousy that cut through her whenever she imagined Rafe with one of them left a telling mark.

Still, Rafe's caginess bothered her. Why was he so evasive if he had nothing to hide? Sometimes when he looked at her, Coral glimpsed sadness in his eyes that betrayed the aching loneliness of his soul. Was that because he felt guilty about having an affair with his best friend's wife? She recalled Cybil's words on the beach: *Walter is out of the way now. You have no excuse.* It was ambiguous — could it mean that he had not engaged in any relationship with her stepmother while her father was alive? Despite his reputation, it didn't seem to fit Rafe's personality to be underhanded; he was too direct.

Rafe flirted with Cybil like he would with any woman. But Coral had watched them together, and even then, he seemed to keep her stepmother at arm's length; it was always Cybil that sought out his company. Thinking back, at Lady Langley's party, when Coral had gotten upset seeing them dancing together, it had been Cybil who was clinging to Rafe, but she did not remember seeing Rafe returning her stepmother's ardent attention.

Coral could see that Rafe never looked at Cybil in the way he looked at her. That night at Whispering Palms, his tender words had made her think that he was falling in love with her, that his attraction was not only to her body. Did his feelings for her run deeper too? But then he had left without a word, letting Morgana confront Coral.

From the very beginning, Rafe had blown hot and cold: one minute he was passionate, sensitive, and tender; the next, the shutters came down, he was elusive, and he became Rafe the womanizing charmer again, leaving her plagued with doubts. Coral would never find out the truth once and for all unless she risked telling him how she felt and challenged him about the rumors and gossip. What was he was hiding from her? If this was what love was like, did she have a strong enough stomach for it?

On the way back from the clinic, in the doctor's battered old Jeep, Coral at least had found out a little more. As they'd talked, she'd learned that Rafe and Dr. Giles's friendship dated back a long time. Frank's parents were missionaries in Tanzania. He had studied medicine in England on a scholarship and then had gone back to Tanzania to open a clinic. It was there he had met Rafe and become close friends with him. Frank had come out to Kenya only a couple of years ago to help set up one of the new hospitals.

"So, do you have a family out here?" Coral had asked.

"No. No family. Unfortunately, I became married to my work instead, and time just seemed to fly by. I've always felt so dedicated to my patients that I never seem to have the chance to meet anyone," he had explained a little sadly. She had tried to quiz him about Rafe but met with a brick wall, apart from his obvious dislike of Cybil.

"I'm afraid that Cybil is the sort of woman who likes to get her own way, particularly where men are concerned. She has an uncanny way of finding their weakness and exploiting them for her own ends. Luckily, I've always been immune to her charms." Frank had given a short laugh. "And perhaps that's why she's never liked me very much either." Coral had spent the rest of the drive back to the Kongoni estate in quiet contemplation.

Now she spent her days going for long drives, wandering around the markets taking pictures, talking to people, and writing scripts. Coral always kept to well-known roads and tracks, generally making sure that someone at the plantation knew of her whereabouts. She had made friends among the natives; they liked her sweet and quiet nature and seemed charmed by her delicate, elfin looks. Down at the markets, Coral found it great fun to barter with the traders, who were loath to set prices for their wares. "What do you want to give me for this?" they would demand cheerfully. She had learned from Aluna to ask for their best price, walk away, and wait to see if the seller would let her go or call her back for further bargaining.

Coral wanted to return to the falls to capture its dramatic scenery on film, but was met with blank expressions whenever she enquired about them; no one had heard of the lake, so nobody was able to give her directions. Rafe's little haven was obviously a well-kept secret.

One mid-afternoon as Coral was driving around, she came to a junction. The scenery seemed vaguely familiar, but she had explored so many places and most parts of the jungle looked alike. She drove up a small lane haphazardly. It was muddy and rather awkward to tackle as there were bushes blocking part of the track. Was this the way she had come with Rafe? At the time, she had been distracted, so maybe that was why it all looked so unfamiliar. Suddenly she saw the eagle. The king of the air was performing his undulating flight as he rose and fell over the countryside. Rafe's voice resonated clearly in her ears: *These creatures never venture far from their territory.*

Excited, she got out of the Jeep. The lake must be close by; it might be better to continue her investigation on foot. It was still quite hot, but dressed in shorts and a light skimpy top, she did not feel the heat. The eagle had disappeared, and Coral scanned the cloudless sky for the bird, a hand across her forehead shielding her eyes from the blinding sun. A few seconds more and the sound of the crashing water became audible; Coral turned a corner, and the hidden falls appeared at once in front of her.

She had come in from a different side, but this was the place, and her heart leaped with joy. At last she had found it. Hurrying back to the Jeep, she retrieved her camera and notebook.

She sat in the flickering shade of the flame tree where Rafe had stretched out a couple of weeks before, admiring the lake and the jagged peaks that reared up behind it into the heavy air. The radiance of the sun glowed on the water, transforming it into a great mirror of gold. In the heat of the afternoon, nature was out, blooming and contented. The air was trembling with the hum of insects, the fluttering of vivid butterflies, and the faint rustling of leaves. There was trilling and cooing in the foliage around her, while the steady roar of the waterfalls resounded in the background. From her vantage point, she had a full view of the black rocks, like mysterious giants, fringed by splendid trees. Coral spent a few minutes taking some photographs and then lay there gazing at the wild beauty of the crystalline cascade.

The eagle was back, perched grandly on a tree quite nearby. It puffed out its feathers, and Coral picked up her camera again. Looking through the viewfinder, she was able to appreciate in much more detail the contrast between the white upper body and tail, the chestnut belly, and the magnificent black wings. She took more photographs, moving as stealthily as possible so as not to disturb him, until the bird swooped off again. Coral watched an electric blue and fire-red lizard scurry down the bark of a tree to steal up on some wasps; it paused and looked back at her, examining her without moving, as though he knew she was staring at him. The sun made his brightly tinted scales look as if an artist had daubed him with big blobs of color. A few seconds later, he raced away and disappeared into the undergrowth.

Coral felt relaxed and happy as she bit into the apple she had brought and took a sip from the Thermos flask of cold water she always carried with her on her treks. After writing a few lines in her scrapbook, she felt a little drowsy and lay down on the green moss, drifting off to sleep.

When she woke up, the sun was setting rapidly, casting its reflection on the treetops, the rocks, and the water, painting them with the most beautiful shades of orange, purple, and crimson. The vague recollection of a dream played on the edge of her mind in which Rafe whispered her name tenderly and brushed her lips with a kiss. Coral dragged herself up on her elbows, her eyes still filled with sleep, her body still numb with a pleasurable indolence. She blinked, and then her eyes widened. Was she still dreaming?

He emerged out of the lake, the declining sun drenching him with aureate light, the droplets on his body iridescent in their beams. He walked confidently toward her, almost every inch of his sculptured body exposed in his black swimsuit. Each sharp contour of muscle glistened, each limb unfolded with lithe grace as he approached, his eyes riveted on her. Coral watched spellbound, a yearning surging up within her, eager and expectant. The air around them trembled with infinite anticipation.

He was taking his time, and Coral felt that he was deliberately delaying, tormenting them both with the ache of unsatisfied desire until it was so overwhelming that neither of them could bear it any longer.

A few paces from her, Rafe stilled. Coral stared up at him, her lips slightly parted, and their eyes met and held. He reached out a hand, his face intent. His evident arousal sent waves of excitement rippling through her. Instinctively her head went back, she licked her dry lips with the tip of her tongue and then, holding his gaze, arched her back, every nerve ending of her body inviting.

In a sudden, decisive movement, he pulled her up to him, and she shuddered, feeling the strength of his virility as their bodies touched. He ran his hands down her curves, lingering on her hips; he lifted her a little, welding her to him, creating a frenzied urge in her body. A deep savage groan was torn from his throat as her nipples hardened, pressing against the wall of his chest, and she knew that he craved her as passionately as she hungered for him. He cupped her chin and tipped her head back a little, his burnished eyes boring deep into hers with a new fever and intensity. Pleasure surged through her as his warm lips moved tenderly over her face, showering butterfly kisses that sent tiny electric shocks through her limbs, making her melt in his arms.

Then he claimed her lips. His kiss was soft to begin with, tasting her slowly, and then he became more and more demanding, almost savage. He thrust his tongue deeper, exploring, teasing the inside of her mouth. His hand at the small of her back was binding her slender frame to him, letting her feel the extent of his arousal. The more she felt him dominating her, the more she desired to submit. She felt a moist warmth pulsate between her thighs. Tremors of pleasure surged through her, and at that moment she knew beyond a doubt that she wanted to give herself to him more than anything in the world.

With a sudden boldness she would not have suspected herself capable of, Coral slid her hand downward, and Rafe tensed as her fingers probed the hardness of his masculinity. He groaned as she stroked him, responding with a shudder that told her the extent of the pleasure she was giving him. His kiss deepened, and the ache down below intensified, the wave of passion for him escalating so that the only thing that mattered was the two of them.

"I want you. Make love to me," she breathed, her heart and senses trembling for him in anticipation. "Make love to me, Rafe." Rafe's eyes turned to soft amber, his breathing quickened, and his strong hands moved over her back, his arm encircled her waist as he gently slid her down onto the grass.

Suddenly a terrifying sound, between an explosive cry and a barking cough, startled them out of their embrace, making them spring to their feet. Rafe looked up sharply. At the top of the rocks loomed an enormous creature, half crouching, half standing, his long muscular arms akimbo, his jet-black sunken eyes staring fiercely down at them through the thick foliage of the trees.

"*Mon Dieu!*" Rafe sucked in his breath, smothering a cry of awe. "A silverback gorilla!" Coral had recoiled into his arms, clinging at his chest, tremors of terror replacing the pleasure that had shaken her body earlier. "They are quite unusual around here, but no need to be alarmed," Rafe murmured reassuringly, stroking her head. "He's too far away to get to us; besides, these gentle giants are quite shy and don't attack unless they feel threatened."

Rafe's confident, low voice dispelled Coral's apprehensions. She looked up hesitantly, realizing there may never be a similar opportunity. The shock had acted like a cold shower, making her attentive and alert. Suddenly her wits were about her, and the reporter and the photographer in her took over. "Can I use my camera?"

"No, definitely not," he cautioned. "Gorillas don't like to be stared at — to them, because the whites of our eyes are more visible, eye contact makes them nervous."

The enormous animal abruptly shifted his posture, rising to his full height, a majestic figure in his shining black coat as he continued to glower fixedly down at the young couple. The bellow erupted again like thunder, its echo making the mountains and the bush shudder around them.

Coral jumped in fright. "Let's go," she said in a muffled voice. "It's getting dark, and this place is really eerie." They both looked up again. The great silverback was thumping his chest furiously with his large black hands, stomping and growling. Rafe and Coral moved off slowly.

"I came in a different way than the one you showed me last time," Coral told him.

"I know. When I arrived earlier and found you here, I realized that, so I moved my car. It's now parked next to yours." He beamed at her.

The sun had set, turning the bluish shadow of the trees to violet. The bush was now hushed, but soon the couple would be faced with the sounds that split the jet black curtain of African nights.

Rafe had swiftly pulled on a pair of trousers and a shirt that he took from the Land Rover. "I'll drive," he said, sliding into his shoes as Coral got into the Jeep.

"Why? What about your Land Rover? Or don't you think I'm capable of driving? I did get myself here."

"Get into the Jeep, you irritating creature, and stop arguing." He grinned down at her as he took the keys from her hands. "I'm not letting you drive at night around here in an open Jeep, especially not after what happened to you last week."

"May I remind you that I was not the one driving that night?" She looked at him askance. "You really do think I'm incapable, don't you?"

"No, I don't think you're incapable, but I do think that these roads have no lights, that we're not in London, and that I would be devastated if that pretty little face of yours was mangled in any way."

"You don't mince your words either, do you?"

"I've told you before, rosebud, I only have your interests at heart." He ushered her into the Jeep.

"What about your Land Rover?"

"That can wait. I'll come back for it tomorrow. Anyhow, it's locked and out of the way. No one knows about this place, so it'll be safe here."

"You're probably right. I tried asking many people for directions to the lake during the past week, but nobody could give me an answer. I came by it quite by accident this afternoon. It was the eagle that guided my steps, really. I wasn't too far when I saw it and remembered what you said about it not straying far from its territory. How did you know I was there anyway?"

"I didn't. When I got back to the plantation this afternoon, I saw you weren't there. Someone mentioned that you'd been asking about a lake, so I assumed you'd gone looking. And not underestimating your determination, I thought you'd probably find it, so I took my chance."

"You must have seen me. Why didn't you wake me?"

"I must admit that it was tempting. I did actually call you, but you looked so angelic lying there, your body completely relaxed, that I couldn't bring myself to disturb such a beautiful picture and was content just to gently kiss your lips while you were asleep." Rafe glanced at her with a smile.

"Funny, yes, I think I felt it, but thought I was dreaming." There was a brief pause, then she asked abruptly, "Why did you go away last week?"

"I do have engagements, work, duties, you know?" Rafe answered evenly.

"You mean you have a mistress," she retorted, remembering Morgana's face looking out at her so defiantly from the black Cadillac that had taken Rafe away.

"Yes, I suppose, that too." His tone was quiet, his gaze now fixed straight ahead.

"A mere dancer, if I'm not mistaken."

"Dancing is a job like any other, which in fact demands a lot of skill."

"Not quite," Coral scoffed. "Nightclub women use their bodies to tantalize and excite male clients so they become regulars and spend on drink, drugs, and whatever else is on offer."

Rafe looked at her with serious eyes. "Morgana is a very kind, warm, and beautiful woman."

"She may be kind, warm, and beautiful, but that doesn't make her any less loud or vulgar."

"There's no need for you to be so disparaging," he retorted. "You don't even know the woman."

Coral turned to him, her posture rigid and her eyes stormy. Now that her jealousy had taken hold of her again, it burned with even greater cruelty. "I can't believe you're defending her," she said, her voice tipped with a slight trill. "These women use men's sex drives to take advantage of them," she went on, deliberately goading him. "They're calculating and wanton." Coral didn't try to hide her contempt now, or her jealousy. Burning with hurt and anger, all she wanted was to know the thoughts that hid behind his closed features and find out how deep his feelings went for Morgana.

"And you're not capable of being wanton, Coral?" he bit back in an insulting tone.

Blood rushed to her face, making her ears and cheeks burn. Rafe was right, she thought, remembering those moments earlier that afternoon when her whole body had pulsated with unrestrained desire in his arms. She had bared herself to him, her body begging for more, and she had not bothered to conceal her delight in his touch. She had lost all self-respect, and now he was contemptuous of her. Oh God, what had she done? Her mother had warned her about that sort of reaction in men, and she had ignored it. But this was not her; she did not recognize herself. She had never been one to indulge in those sorts of carnal pleasures. What had he done to her? What was she turning into? Was this what people called love? If so, she wanted none of it; it was too painful. Hot tears burned her eyes as she tried to restrain them.

Conscious of her distress, Rafe put out a hand and stroked her wet cheek softly. He pulled out a handkerchief from his top pocket and gave it to her. "Here, I'm sorry, rosebud. Wipe your tears and don't take this silly banter too seriously. If it's any consolation to you, there is really no need to be worried or jealous of Morgana or anybody else for that matter. You've bewitched me, and nothing seems to be able to quench the yearning I feel for you."

"Still, that didn't stop you from leaving the clinic with her when I needed you," she argued reproachfully, knowing full well that she was being irrational and unfair.

He gave a bitter laugh. "You could have fooled me! A more rebellious and belligerent woman I have never seen. Anyhow, even if I did go, I couldn't stay away very long. I'm back, isn't that proof enough?"

"Yes, you're back, but for how long?" Why could she not stop her jealousy and insecurity taking over?

"Oh, I don't know." Rafe gave a tired sigh.

"I'll tell you," she said, eyes blazing. "You're back for as long as it takes you to get me into your bed. I've known men just like you. Here today, gone tomorrow.'"

Rafe's brows meshed. "Why are you always so quick to condemn me? What do you know about me, Coral?"

"Then tell me about yourself. I only know what you have shown me. I want to know everything. I think I'm falling in love you." The words had come blurting out — she would have taken them back as soon as she had said them.

Rafe smiled sadly, but it was dark, his face was in shadow, and Coral couldn't see his eyes. "You don't love me, rosebud." His voice was low and wistful. "You're just discovering the needs of your beautiful body; it's demanding, and you respond to it with infinite generosity."

"How do you know that?" she went on. "What do you know about love anyhow? For you it's just a sexual exercise, and you think that everybody is like you." Coral knew her behavior was churlish, yet the violence of her emotions made her act foolishly, and her wiser self could only look on.

"Come on, rosebud, don't spoil the wonderful afternoon we've had. Stop tormenting me and hurting yourself. It must be obvious to you by now how much I want you, even though it kills me. Didn't every part of my body give you enough proof this afternoon? *Mon Dieu*, Coral, no woman has made my senses come alive the way you have; no woman has ever made me obsessed the way you have. You must realize that by now."

"I'm sorry, Rafe," she whispered. "But I can't bear the idea of you with another woman, doing to her the things you've done with me, and more. It hurts too much that you escape to her to fulfill your needs."

"That's the problem," he murmured as though to himself. "Nothing is able to blot you out of my mind. No one else can relieve the need you talk about, absolutely no one."

He was doing it again, his words almost a palpable caress, stroking her, inflaming her. "Stop it," she cried out, "I can't bear it any more. You're driving me crazy!" She was trembling, her senses raw with the need for him without any immediate hope of release.

"Join the club," he muttered with an almost inaudible self-deprecating grunt.

"I don't want to join the club of women that hanker after you," she replied hotly. "I have no desire to be your puppet. I won't let you play with me, take me up, and then put me down whenever the fancy takes you… "

He drew in a harsh breath. "You've misunderstood my words," he interrupted, trying to explain. "I didn't mean it in that way." But Coral wasn't listening. Calmly, Rafe parked the car on the side of the road.

"Don't you dare try to talk to me in those alluring tones you use so well," she continued, anger burning her cheeks as Rafe watched with a bewildered expression on his face. "Don't try to seduce me, Rafe de Monfort." Coral felt completely out of control, lashing out at him as wounding words indiscriminately rolled off her tongue.

"You'd better do something about this temper of yours," he murmured as he started the car engine again. "It doesn't become you."

They rolled along in silence. When they got to the plantation Coral went straight to her room without dinner. Aluna was waiting for her. The old *yaha* did not need to be told she was upset. Coral could see the observant black eyes taking in her swollen lids, flushed face, and her tense stance.

"You were with that Frenchman again," she said, eying Coral disapprovingly.

"That's none of your business," Coral answered tersely. She recognized she was being brusque, but her *yaha* had cared for her during the first ten years of her life, so Coral found it easy to fall back into the ways of a temperamental little girl prone to her stormy moods.

"I have told you before and I will never tire of telling you that this man is poison for you. You must believe me, my little one, or he will destroy you."

Coral sighed. "Not tonight, Aluna, please, no lectures tonight."

"You have fallen for him, haven't you?"

Coral didn't answer, not only because she was tired, but because she had no answer. Rafe confounded her. She had never met anyone like him, neither man nor woman. She could not understand what was happening to her. Jealousy was not a natural trait with her; she had never thought herself capable of such a lowly emotion. Was this really love that made her flood with such jealousy every time she thought of Morgana? The stabbing pain that gripped her heart told her that this could not be anything other than love.

Coral showered and climbed into bed. Aluna came back into the room, bearing a tray of fruit that she placed on the bedside table. "Where have you been all afternoon?" the older woman asked, still prying in the face of Coral's taciturn muteness.

"I was at the lake."

"So, you found the lake you've been looking for?"

"Yes, Aluna." Coral was becoming irritated.

"Aluna knows there's something wrong. You are normally so full of stories when you come back from your wanderings. Talk to me, my little *malaika*."

"What do you want me to tell you?"

The older woman came and sat on the edge of the bed. "I want you to tell me what you were doing again with the Frenchman. He has upset you, I can see. He has troubled your mind and your body." She sighed. "I was afraid of that. I knew he would get to you as he has gotten to every woman around here."

"Since you know it all, Aluna, why do you ask?" Coral snapped.

"There is no reasoning with you tonight. I will let you sleep." Aluna got up, turned off the light, and left the room.

Coral twisted and turned in bed for an hour. Sleep was evading her, and all sorts of thoughts were clamoring in her brain. She couldn't remember half the things she had said to Rafe, but she knew that she had been rude and wounding, which of course had been her intention in the heat of the moment. She regretted it now. Rafe really brought out the worst in her, but he had also brought out dormant physical desires that she never knew could be so overwhelming. If only she could reach over the barriers between them. But then again, to what end? Rafe was a hunter; he collected women like others around here accumulated animal trophies. Did he love her, or merely lust after her? Lust, however potent, was ephemeral. She wished she could be sure of him.

Coral got up and pushed back the shutters. Her heart felt like lead in her chest. The night was a dense black. The sky was full of unusually large and clear stars flickering so brightly they seemed like crackling embers trying to convey their eloquent message in a twinkling language.

Coral walked out into the garden. The temperature was hot and heavy, the air without breeze. It took a moment to become accustomed to the darkness. The trees stood motionless, eerie shadows standing like dark sentinels on a summer night. Silence was king save for the persistent singing of crickets and bull-frogs.

"Still prowling around like an angry wild cat?" Rafe's laugh scorched Coral's skin, and she turned abruptly, her heart beating a little more rapidly. Rafe drew on his cigarette, the minute bead of fire winking defiantly at her, exposing his location. He was leaning nonchalantly against a tree a few yards away, a hand in his pocket, legs crossed, his dark, exotic features hidden.

Coral went to him slowly. Although she managed to control the biting answer that instinctively rose to her lips, she gave him a slow and determined look. "You do know how to hurt someone, don't you?" It was more of a statement than a question. She was close enough now to see his eyes. They were not hooded in anger; they were staring at her with a devilish smile.

"Then we truly deserve each other," he said, his grin broadening. In a frantic outburst of relief, they laughed — a cheerful, healthy laugh that went on for a few moments. Tension melted; the ice was broken. They were friends again.

They wandered through the garden together and spoke for a long time, touching on many subjects but keeping stealthily off those of a personal nature. Rafe asked her about her work, and Coral spoke freely about the job and the assignment she had been given, the fears she had of not meeting with the firm's standards and expectations, her ambitions, and the places she had traveled to.

"You needn't worry about collecting material for your commission. I've been keeping very quiet about a surprise that has been my preoccupation for the past week," Rafe said with a smug smile. Coral looked at him quizzically. "Have you ever been for a ride in a balloon?" She shook her head, her eyes widening expectantly. "Ballooning has been my hobby for some time. I touched on it slightly when I was in Tanganyika, but it's only during the past few years that I have taken it up seriously. I do it quite often."

"Is it safe?"

"Yes, when the rules are followed, just as in flying an airplane. Basically, a hot-air balloon is literally that: a large bag, filled with hot air, attached to a basket that holds the passengers and the equipment. The burner, which is the engine of the balloon, propels the heat up inside it and is placed in the bow, between the basket and the balloon."

"To be honest, it sounds downright dangerous," she said, eyebrows pulling together in a worried frown.

"If I can say so myself, ballooning is an art, not a science. You need to know what you're doing, and the only way of learning is from personal experience. I've done a lot of balloon flying."

"It must be rather scary," Coral said, still not convinced.

"Maybe for the ten first minutes, but once you're up in the sky, there is nothing that compares with the sense of freedom you get as you glide through cloudland. The silence and the peace while the balloon drifts over the unfolding countryside are unparalleled."

Seeing the sparkle in his eyes and the glow of happiness on his face couldn't help but make Coral feel his exhilaration. "Will you take me up there one day?"

"Lady Langley has asked me to put together a morning's ballooning over the Rift Valley and the Masai Mara. I have arranged it for the end of the week. The balloon in question can carry up to six passengers. We'll lift off just before sunrise, when the air is still cold. You'll be able to take the most wonderful photographs and see breath-taking scenery. This is an experience not to be missed. I promise you will not be disappointed." Rafe smiled into her eyes and then gazed off into the distance, his features relaxed.

"Who will be coming with us? You said that the balloon carried six passengers. I can only think of five."

"Frank will be coming along. We often balloon together. He started in Tanganyika and was the one who introduced me to the sport in the first place."

"I like Dr. Giles. He seems a very kind person."

"He is," Rafe said thoughtfully. "A kind person and a very good friend. The natives like him too; they don't distrust him as they do most bwanas."

"Do they really distrust us?"

"Oh, yes, very much so." He threw his cigarette to the ground and stubbed it out with his foot. "One of our workers was injured on the estate. His leg was crushed by a tractor. I wanted to fly him over to Frank's clinic, but he insisted he wanted to go back to his village. I told him there would be no doctor to care for him in his village and that the wound could get infected — that he could lose his leg or even die. He grinned back at me, looking me straight in the eye, almost insolently. 'I would rather die in my village, *bwana*, than take the remedy of the white doctor.' Luckily Frank was staying with me at the time. I called him over, and within an hour, he had convinced our reluctant friend to be transported to his clinic."

"Frank told me that he never married because he never had the time to meet the right person. I do think that's terribly sad, don't you?"

"He's a dedicated medicine man, a good Samaritan who loves Africa and deeply cares for its people."

"You, too, love Africa."

"I used to. I don't that much anymore," Rafe said, almost in a whisper.

Coral looked up at him, sensing his tension and the change in his voice. She knew better than to probe; for once, they were having a civilized conversation. To her surprise, Rafe went on, unprompted. "Africa has been much romanticized. Nostalgia and the clouded memories of the old hunter-cum-writer have created myths that have nothing to do with reality. There is poverty, illness, savagery, and death around every corner in Africa. Rebellion, war, and misery are simmering at its heart. My only hope is that you don't stumble into the same pitfall, and that your articles and photographs are not an account seen through rosy spectacles."

Coral looked up at him a little puzzled. "Meaning?"

Rafe lit another cigarette, inhaled, and watched the smoke curl up into the night. Whatever emotion had seized him earlier was now gone, and he was looking at her gravely. "Do you really want to hear what I've to say on this matter?" he asked.

"Of course I do. My recent experience of Africa is so slim; I need any help I can get."

Rafe shifted his position and hesitated a few seconds more. "I meant that, when you come to deliver your account, I hope you will illustrate both sides of the coin. More often than not, writers only describe one aspect of a situation, usually completely out of context. The tribes' men and women become people who are staggeringly handsome, having a most idyllic life. There is no mention of the ignorance, poverty, and disease that plague them. Seas, lakes, and rivers have a powerful and mysterious beauty, but the sharks, crocodiles, pythons, and other monsters that inhabit them are conveniently forgotten or barely hinted at. Elephants, lions, and panthers become those fabulous peace-loving animals that lazily trumpet or bask harmlessly in the sun. Basically, perfection reigns in an ideal world." Rafe raised his hand as if he was going to touch Coral's cheek but checked himself.

"And now, Miss Sinclair," his voice held a tenderness as he smiled at her ruefully. "I think it's long past your bedtime. We'll not put the world right tonight."

***

When Aluna brought a cup of tea to Coral's room before dawn on the morning of the balloon excursion, she found the young woman already dressed and ready to go. The old yaha looked gloomy to say the least and shook her head disapprovingly. "Most people would be content to go for a drive on solid ground, but you've got to go haring off in some flying machine."

"Oh, Aluna, don't spoil my fun. I'm so happy," Coral said, excitement surging through her at the prospect of the adventurous expedition. Rafe had been away during the past few days since their last conversation, and her heart leaped at the thought of seeing him again. After her childish outburst in the car, she was relieved to find that he did not bear a grudge against her.

She glanced in the mirror for a final check, debating whether to wear makeup and deciding to simply dab on a little lip gloss. Her eyes sparkled with expectation, and the little dimple appeared at the corner of her mouth as a secret smile touched her lips. Rafe had strongly recommended sensible footwear, so the form-fitting beige jumpsuit she wore was tucked into a pair of sturdy tan safari boots.

Aluna gave her a long, silent look. "You're like a moth attracted to fire. Your wings will get burned. He is an afiriti, a devil. He has cast a *dua* over you, and you will need a kizee to free you. Believe me, my little one, there are stories about him, many stories going about among the people."

"Yes, there are stories, and I'm sure they're only stories. I don't need a magician to free me from anything, so please stop your mumbo jumbo, Aluna. I'm not in the mood," Coral retorted, still surveying herself critically in the mirror. "Should I wear a belt? Umm, I think I will," she said, grabbing a tan-colored belt with a large copper elephant head buckle, trying to ignore her yaha's cryptic words.

Aluna made her feel uneasy. Many native Africans seemed to have this uncanny sixth sense; it was all part of their culture. Coral had been born in Africa and spent the first ten years of her life there, and secretly a part of her could not dismiss their superstitions. Her *yaha's* words had struck a chord. Deep down, she realized just how little she knew about Rafe. A small voice at the back of her mind told her there was something about him — something primitive and dangerous — warning her to retreat while there was still time.

Still, today Coral did not want to think of that or of any other unpleasantness. She was elated and wished to enjoy that to the full. "I'm going now, Aluna." She slung over her shoulder the canvas bag that contained her camera, films, and other bits and pieces necessary for her work, giving the older woman's cheek a featherlight kiss in farewell. "Try not to spend the whole day brooding; you'll make yourself ill." Downstairs, Coral was surprised and a little disappointed to find that Rafe, along with Cybil, had already headed off before the rest of the party, and that Frank Giles would be driving Lady Langley, Dale, and herself to the location for the balloon launch.

"How come Rafe didn't wait for the rest of us?" she asked Frank as they walked to the car, keeping her voice low so she would not be overheard by Dale and Lady Langley. Frank piled all their bags into the back of his Jeep and put a kind hand on Coral's shoulder.

"As the pilot, Rafe has to be on site earlier than everybody else to check the equipment and the wind direction. He also needs to supervise the layout and, finally, brief the crew." That didn't explain why her stepmother had to be with him, Coral thought irritably as she climbed into the Jeep after Lady Langley.

The sun had not yet risen. Along the horizon, there was a vibrant layer of color, a mixture of bright green and purple, the blue sky coming up immediately behind it. She saw them the instant the Jeep glided onto the field. They stood together examining a map, their forearms touching, the slant of their bodies making a most eloquent picture. As the vehicle approached, Rafe's head shot up, and Cybil's long fingers claimed his arm. Why was Rafe letting her stepmother grasp at him so obviously? Coral took a deep breath and tried to control her irritation as she got out of the Jeep.

Untangling himself from the other woman's grip, Rafe strode toward the newcomers, a lazy smile revealing his even, white teeth. He was dressed head to foot in black, and somehow it emphasized his predatory charms.

"Good morning," Rafe said as he went across to the other side of the four-wheel drive where Lady Langley was standing. "Sorry to bring you out at such an unearthly hour, but we must lift off before sunrise while the breeze on the plains is still cold. Hello, Dale, Frank." Rafe turned his attention to Coral, his mouth widening into a rakish smile, golden eyes flicking over her appreciatively. "All ready?"

Coral stiffened slightly as the masculine body moved closer to her, and she merely nodded, her eyes avoiding his gaze.

"Splendid." Rafe leaned over to take the canvas bag from her shoulder, and his hand brushed against her neck. Coral instinctively drew in a sharp breath and turned so that he could not see how the mere contact with his skin had disturbed her. He seemed to sense her reaction, and still looking away, Coral was aware of him scrutinizing her profile for a few moments before he walked away. With legs of lead, she followed him to where a large envelope of brightly colored textile was sprawled over the grass.

"It's a grand day," he went on cheerfully, "perfect for ballooning. This is the balloon," Rafe said, scanning Coral's face as they drew closer. He looked a little smug, as if he had presented a child with a surprise present.

Stretched out in a big heap on the ground, the uninflated balloon was bigger than Coral had imagined, and a little scary too, with half a dozen men scurrying around it. A large rectangular wicker basket with a metal surround holding a steel tube was placed a little farther away. Sandbags were hanging over its edge, and it contained a number of ropes, wires, and two cylinders. Rafe came and stood next to Coral, looking at her as if searching for a sign of approval. Coral had so looked forward to this, but her stepmother's presence and obvious territorial attitude with respect to Rafe had taken some of the spark out of the day. Still, looking forward to the adventure ahead, she managed enough enthusiasm for a smile.

The group watched the preparations for take-off. Cybil had moved closer to Rafe again so that he stood between the two women, at ease, arms folded over his chest, legs apart. Still, he was near, too near for Coral to be entirely comfortable as she recalled how passionately they had been entangled a few days earlier at the lake. Whiffs of his aftershave mingling with the familiar very personal scent of his masculine body were finding their way to her. An avalanche of chaotic sensations, sharp and intoxicating, ran through her veins. This was neither the time nor the place, she reprimanded herself, and stepped a little away from him. Rafe turned, a puzzled look sweeping his face. She could feel him willing her to face him. For a few seconds, tension sprang in the air between them, a silent battle of wills, while Coral determinately refused to submit to the fiery gaze. Duty called, and his attention shifted.

Six men had picked up the hem of the balloon and were lifting it high above their heads, then flapping it down toward the grass. This exercise went on for a few seconds. "They're trying to waft cold air into the balloon," Rafe explained to his small audience. He had assumed the efficient and authoritative air that had struck

Coral at their first encounter on board the ship, leaving no doubt in anybody's mind that he was in control of the situation and there was nothing to fear on this expedition.

When the balloon was completely inflated and had reached its full shape, Dale was the first to get on board, while Frank helped Lady Langley and Cybil. Before Coral knew it, Rafe had picked her up and was placing her safely into the basket, climbing in behind her. He glanced at his watch. One of the African men on the ground indicated to him that the balloon was ready to take off and shouted for the other helpers to stand aside. "Here we go. It's just about the right time," said Rafe as the craft glided smoothly into the air, almost at the same moment the red dawn came flashing up through the mist hanging over the surface of the savannah.

It took more than a few minutes for Coral to recover from her discomposure after Rafe had literally swept her off her feet. Waves of heat flooded her from top to toe. She could still feel the powerful forearms sliding under her armpits, his strong hands pressing against the side of her breasts as he lifted her off the ground. Rafe had made a deliberate appeal to her senses, knowing the erotic effect his touch had on her, and he had not been mistaken. The devastating truth flashed through her mind as she acknowledged that her entire being would always instinctively respond to him. She gave him a sideways look; he was busy pumping fire into the balloon.

A few minutes later, they flew over a crash of rhinos. "Look, those are the black rhinos," Rafe called out. "In Kenya, there are two types: the black and the white. The white rhino is slightly different and has a broad mouth adapted for grazing. The black rhinos you see below have a more pointed upper lip and a sharp sense of smell and hearing but poor eyesight. They are the more dangerous of the two. Believe me, you would never want to get close to one of those beasts."

Gradually the mist had lifted, and the sun burst forth, a ball of fire radiating the sky with unnaturally incandescent hues. Coral was reminded of the strident brushwork and wild colors of the Fauvist paintings that filled her mother's gallery, which Coral had always loved. The scene was now set for the show to begin: the drama in which the broad, breath-taking landscapes of Africa were the stage and the animals the actors.

The balloon was still rising, its direction fixed by the whim of the wind. The air was crisp, a whispering light breeze hitting them in the face as the aircraft ascended. The passengers watched silently as the thrilling spectacle of nature's daily life unfolded. They caught sight of a herd of elephants rushing toward a lake in the distance: massive, magnificent animals led by the female, their large ears flapping in the morning air.

"Where is your camera?" Lady Langley was the first to break the silence as she addressed Coral.

Coral started, still a little disturbed by Rafe's presence and her own exasperated senses. She had the impression that Rafe was gently toying with her, wanting her to join in, but she felt ill-equipped to take part in the sport.

Before Coral could utter a word, Rafe answered for her. "It must be in here," he said, handing her over the canvas bag, mischief pouring out of the devilish eyes. "I'm the culprit. I've been hogging your bag, keeping a vigilant eye on it. You should have asked for it." He searched her face as she turned to him, still playing the earlier game of "I'm here, look at me." She stared back at him reluctantly.

"Thank you," she said, controlling her voice but wondering if the look in her eyes had given her away. She felt so inexperienced and unworldly, and it made her feel a little vulnerable.

Coral tried to shrug off her disquiet and began to rummage in her bag, gathering together the various parts of her single-lens reflex camera. She adjusted the aperture, put in place color filters to cut out the glare, and affixed a telephoto lens that would zoom in the picture, giving her a more favorable outlook to make her photographs do justice to the stunning scenery. She quickly settled to the task at hand, shuffling skillfully between a telephoto lens that allowed her to record in more detail a particular creature and a wide-angle lens that could capture the entire panorama. In an instant, Coral snapped into professional mode, completely absorbed in her work and only vaguely aware of the rest of her entourage. She was spellbound, fascinated by the incredible lushness of color, the brilliance and grandeur of the views, and the magnificent wildlife below. She was good at her work, flexing her body in various ways to take advantage of animals and sceneries that presented themselves at different angles.

Coral noticed that Rafe watched her steadily, as if he was trying to read her mind, to anticipate her next move. Was it admiration she detected in his eyes? A quiet navigator, he moved the balloon farther up into the sky or down, sometimes almost brushing against the surface of a canopy of trees, or floating in and out of white puffs of clouds so she could get a better view of an elephant, an antelope, or some other exotic being that took her fancy, doing his utmost to facilitate her work.

They flew over the smooth and silky expanse of Lake Baringo. The distant spread of water seemed to shine with an inward light, an awe-inspiring landscape at this time of day, scattered here and there with dark islands that looked like little black dots on the silver scales of a giant fish. The vegetation around the lake sheltered innumerable colonies of birds, and Coral got excellent shots of cormorants and the beautiful flamingos that were stalking for food or basking in the sunlight on the shores.

Coming across a flock of ducks, Dale took the opportunity to tell everybody how he and his father had once shot one hundred wild duck and geese in a single day during the season there, and a better game meat he had never tasted. "The tribesmen couldn't make out what we were playing at." He gave a derisive laugh. "They kept saying to us 'Too much, *bwana*, too much.' They didn't understand our sport," he ended with an air of self-importance. Coral thought to herself how much more obnoxious Dale had become since they had broken up. Dale moved closer and winked at her, but she hastily turned away and carried on with her work.

"Tribesmen in Africa seldom kill wild game for the sake of killing," Rafe pointed out coldly. "They kill if they're threatened by some mortal danger, or if a superstition or a tribal rite requires it, but mainly they kill for food. When they've got enough to eat, they don't need to kill any more. That's also the law of the jungle among the predatory animals themselves." Dale merely ignored Rafe's comment and suddenly became engrossed in the view.

They saw impalas and antelopes, delighting in mighty leaps into the air, and witnessed large numbers of hippos playing in a big pool close to the surface of the water, while others dozed lazily on the rocks surrounding it, their great pink mouths yawning in the bright gold sun that was now high in the sky.

All the while, Coral worked passionately and without a break. Moving swiftly, she dexterously changed film, setting the aperture and the focus with expert precision. From time to time she would stop to make notes, writing down her impressions, drawing a few sketches. It was all nicely coming together, just as she had planned, and it excited her.

They glided over a herd of black buffalo, their mighty hooves dredging up clouds of gray dust as they thundered away at full speed. Coral wondered what could have sent the most dangerous beast of the bush into such a panic. They saw zebras, their skin of black and silver stripes glistening in the sun. There were also bucks, rhinos, and undulating towers of giraffes in clusters of six or more — a paradise for a photographer. Still, the monarch of the wild remained elusive.

Rafe looked at his watch. "It's time to descend," he announced. "Ten minutes to landing. Everybody, please tidy away binoculars, cameras, and whatever bits and pieces you've been using. Don't forget that the only place you are allowed to hold on to is the edge of the basket. Please be alert and don't take any risks," he cautioned. "If you hold on to any lines, they could become slack, and as they tighten again, someone could get snatched out of the basket." His voice was calm with only a light inflection that spelled danger.

Dale unexpectedly objected. "We haven't yet seen any lions or leopards. Let's continue for a little longer."

"It is too early for the lions." Rafe's words cracked like a whip. "They don't appear until later on in the day." It was obvious to Coral that Dale irritated him, and she was amused to see that he was definitely not about to take orders from her ex-fiancé. "After breakfast, we will be riding back to the house, and we'll go through the park," Rafe continued. "We're sure to come across some lions and other wild beasts." His explanation seemed more for the benefit of Coral, and they exchanged a brief look.

Rafe smiled at her; his eyes held no arrogance or teasing. There was something different in Rafe, Coral noted, an unassuming expression that made him seem vulnerable and went straight to her heart. She could read his disappointment that he had not been able to show her any big cats for her camera to take advantage of. Coral gave him a slow, reassuring smile.

Piloting the balloon lower, Rafe was now starting to level it off. Coral watched him gazing down with his head tipped to the side as if debating the risks and precautions for several possible courses, his features set in keen concentration. A few minutes elapsed, and he switched off the burner. As the basket touched the grass, Rafe maneuvered a bit, and the balloon sank gently to the ground, safely upright.

A magnificent spread awaited them, laid out on a long trestle table under a white marquee. As they scrambled out of the basket, Cybil managed to get herself entangled in one of the wires, and Rafe stayed back to help her. Coral went with the others to the breakfast table, where she watched her stepmother and Rafe, who appeared to be having an argument. Maybe her stepmother was objecting to his lack of attention during the journey. Anyhow, it couldn't have been too bad, she thought, because soon Rafe was jovial and Cybil, her head thrown back, was laughing and swaying provocatively toward him. Cybil swayed again and stumbled, holding on to him to stabilize herself. Then huddling a little too close to Rafe for Coral's liking, she walked with him toward the others. Why did he always allow her stepmother to flirt so outrageously with him? Coral wondered whether if she had more experience in love, she might have been more philosophical about the games that people play in relationships, but instead the familiar pangs of jealousy began to rear up, and she found herself lost in confusion once more.

"Are you going to join us for a spot of breakfast, Coral? It does look rather tempting, I must say." Frank Giles had appeared quietly at her side and, glancing only briefly toward the advancing figures of Rafe and Cybil, gave Coral a kind, reassuring look.

"Yes, of course," said Coral, smiling with gratitude at the distraction, and they both went to join the rest of the group around the table.

Plates were piled high with guavas, pineapple, passion fruit, paw-paw, grapes, and star fruit as Lady Langley's servants bustled around the party, carrying steaming bowls of *ugali* porridge that other staff were busy heating on portable gas stoves. Glasses were filled with chilled mineral water and fruit juice, Kongoni coffee and *chai*, and stacks of warm *chapatis* and *mandazis*, the local African pastries, were served up with cheerful efficiency. Breakfast was lively, everybody giving their impressions about the morning's excursion. Dale was, as usual, effusive about his own exploits, telling whoever would listen about his participation in hunting parties after great herds of elephants. "We set off from Baringo, over the hills of Kamasia into Turkana and Samburu country. But the best place for hunting elephants is, of course, the Tsavo Park. Unfortunately, the hunters from the Wakamba and the Waliangulu tribes seem to have the monopoly there. It's such a shame, really. They use some sort of poison that they find in the bush. Rather primitive but quite clever, I suppose."

"Yes, they use poisoned arrows that they make themselves with vulture feathers and giraffe intestines," Rafe volunteered. "The poison is taken from a local tree called the *acokanthera frisiorum*. There is nothing quite as venomous as that bush, and there is no antidote for its poison. The fruit looks much like an olive." Rafe shifted in his seat, and his eyes narrowed dangerously. "These people you're talking about are called poachers not hunters, and their trade is illegal."

"Oh, illegal stuff and nonsense. There is no such thing as the word 'illegal' in Africa," Dale sneered. "Rhino horns are exported, the crocodile's skin fetches a fortune, giraffes are killed because their tails provide some sort of twine used for making arrows. Everybody's out there making a quick buck. It's an organized business, I tell you, and long may it last, I say. Let's not be, *plus royalistes que le roi*, as your French proverb goes." He eyed Rafe pointedly. "The customs officials on the coast know all about these practices and turn a blind eye."

"All you have said is true, but that doesn't make it legal or right," Rafe said quietly. Though his eyes were shielded from her, Coral could feel the tension underneath his calm exterior.

"We should be going," said Frank. "I have to get back to the clinic — patients are waiting." He smiled in the nicest possible way but seemed anxious to get going. "Sorry if you feel that I'm breaking the party up."

"Not at all," said Lady Langley, jumping up from her chair. "If you don't mind, I'll come with you. I hope that it's not too much out of your way. I'm not used to these early mornings and feel rather tired. I'll be glad to put my feet up."

Rafe turned to Coral. "Would you care for a ride in the park? We didn't get a chance this morning, but we may get lucky and come upon some lions. Not surprising we haven't seen any yet, though. Lions prefer to come out in the late morning, and they usually hunt at dusk." He was smiling at her, the burnished eyes intent on her face.

She smiled at his efforts to be friendly. "I'd love that. I don't have many more days here, and even though this morning was extraordinary, it would be nice to get some shots of lions. People do seem to love those creatures, and somehow an article on Kenya wouldn't be complete without them."

They rode in the Land Rover, Rafe and Dale at the front and Coral and Cybil in the back. The sun hung high in a cloudless sky. They drove through groves of giant acacias with wide boughs in some places, flat tops of green filigree through which the sunlight filtered. In other places, trailing branches leaned over and brushed along the side of the vehicle as they passed. On each side of the road was a world of flickering shade and light teeming with insects and little furred creatures of the bush.

Suddenly, on the edge of a bank fringing a marshy depression, they saw a leopard. It was a colossus of an animal in a fearful rage, his hind leg caught in the powerful jaws of a snare fastened to a tree by a long chain. Rafe pulled the vehicle to an abrupt stop and seized the stun gun. Before anyone could stop him, Dale had also grabbed Rafe's rifle and was out of the Land Rover.

"This pile is for me," he said as he advanced toward the beast. The feline at first retreated, growling fiercely.

"Watch out!" Rafe shouted as Dale lifted the rifle to aim and tripped over a small tree trunk. As Dale fell to the ground, the rifle flew out of his hands and went off with a bang, wounding the animal. The leopard snarled and sprang out in a mighty rage. He caught Dale's arm just as Rafe, who was not far behind with the stunning pistol, shot the cat on the bridge of the nose, getting him right between the eyes. The magnificent creature dropped like a rock.

"Stay where you are, both of you, and don't move!" Rafe sharply roared to his two petrified passengers. Dale was sprawled on the ground, unconscious. First reclaiming his rifle, Rafe picked up the young American and brought him back to the Land Rover. He examined the mauled arm. "Not too bad," he grunted, "a very small price to pay for such rash and reckless behavior. Stupid man! He's obviously got a death wish!" Rafe muttered to himself as he took out the first aid box from the boot and started to attend to the wound.

"The animal only grazed him," he told Coral and Cybil who were both trembling as they went about helping Rafe place Dale comfortably into the vehicle. Coral took out a small bandage from Rafe's pharmacy kit, and both she and Cybil addressed the wound.

"He'll be fine in a couple of days. I'll get Frank to look at this, just to be on the safe side. Coral, come and sit in the front. Cybil, you look after Dale. He'll soon wake up and will need reassurance; it must have given him a massive shock." Rafe gave a devilish grin. "Maybe this will teach him not to be so cocky in the future." Coral noticed Cybil's face fall; she seemed on the verge of protesting the seating arrangement but did as she was told.

The leopard was still out cold on the ground, and Coral had never seen such a beautiful animal. His fur was very pale in color, almost silver; his throat was spotted with a circular band of black patches that hung like a necklace around the base of his collar. Rafe hesitated, then, to Coral and Cybil's horror, he calmly approached the wild beast. He examined the leopard carefully and slowly proceeded to free the creature from the steel trap and undo the chain that held him captive. Ambling back to the Land Rover, he got in without a word, slammed the door shut, and turned on the engine.

Underneath the calm exterior, Rafe was seething. "Snaring is an indiscriminately cruel and cowardly method of killing," he said. "Thankfully, it looked like this leopard hadn't been caught long, and he'll recover to roam again freely. And now, I think we've had enough excitement for one day. Let's go home." Turning to Coral, he smiled again. "I'm sorry we haven't been able to provide you with a lion, but I promise to make it up to you. I still have a few ideas up my sleeve." His eyes twinkled with infinite mischief.

***

That night Rafe couldn't sleep. He sat in the dark in an armchair in his room, leaned his head back, and closed his eyes as images of the day flooded his brain. Coral had been full of surprises. It was difficult not to watch her as she went about her work, so masterful with her camera, and he found himself wanting to share in her experience even if it was just showing her where to get the best pictures. He had never seen this side of her before, so professionally immersed in her craft. She was dazzling. Her energy had radiated through, making her complexion luminous and her eyes glittery. He had kept his gaze fastened onto her, taking in her beauty.

Rafe had always found her body irresistible, and now he had discovered another part of her that was even more compelling. He checked himself; he must not dream the impossible dream. She could never be his, entirely his forever. It was not fair; it was not right. A great portion of his life was behind him while all of hers was still in the future.

He must keep repeating this in order to stop himself from straying. But he was aware of the potency of feelings between them and how suddenly their emotions were developing. In his mind's eye, he replayed the way she had watched him as he came toward her out of the lake, the silent passion in her eyes, the way she had trembled in his arms when he had pulled her up against him, and the warmth of her as she returned his kisses.

The temptation to give in to their mutual attraction was so strong that he feared his fiery French blood would rule and he would surrender to the passion that burned in his gut. He couldn't… He mustn't… Though he was used to having his own way with women and might seem to others an incorrigible womanizer, he could never live with himself if that happened.

It wouldn't be fair to Coral. He suspected it before, but now he had no doubt that this had gone way beyond a physical craving for her. He had never been a jealous man, even with his wife, but he couldn't bear Dale's attention to Coral. The insufferable young man irritated him; at times, he would have gladly made mincemeat of his smug face. Rafe had to admit that, for the first time in his life, he was experiencing the bitter pangs of jealousy.

And then there was poor, loyal Morgana to think of. For so long, her kindness and loving nature had been the tonic he needed to obscure his pain. Whenever he had been troubled by the nightmares of his past, he had always been able to forget them momentarily in Morgana's arms. But of late it had been impossible. Rafe found himself avoiding the dancer and, since he met Coral, rebuffing her advances. He couldn't stomach the thought of being with any other woman than Coral, and this new and painful feeling stunned him. His life was ruled now by a tyranny of mood swings when he was around Coral: from exhilaration and teasing playfulness to melancholy when the darker side of him took over and he couldn't help being a little gruff. No wonder the poor girl couldn't make out what was happening. He loved Coral with an intensity he never thought possible. For the jaded cynic in him, the obstacles to their love seemed insurmountable unless he could let go of the past. For the romantic dreamer in him, a tiny portion of his heart still believed in rainbows.

Chapter Nine

Two days later, Coral and Cybil were sharing an uncomfortable breakfast alone together. The other guests had gone out for the day, and Lady Langley had gone off to the local market. Neither of them was speaking much, and the atmosphere was decidedly cool. Cybil was clearly still bristling from the attention Rafe had paid to Coral during the balloon ride and furious that he had lumbered her with Dale in the back of the Land Rover on the way home. The young woman in turn was puzzled. It was clear that Rafe had some kind of feelings for her, so why did he still allow her stepmother to flirt with him? Rafe certainly seemed to show a keen interest in her work, and the atmosphere between them was constantly charged with undercurrents of passion. At times, she had almost felt he loved her. As she was lost in thought, Rafe walked into the dining room looking very pleased with himself. He had just returned from taking Dale to Nairobi to catch a plane back to the United States.

"What's up, Rafe? You can't stand the man," Cybil had said when he had announced his intention to accompany the American to the airport.

"I want to make damn sure he's on that plane," he had replied. "Dale's a show-off, the most dangerous kind of daredevil, the type who doesn't have an ounce of common sense in his handsome, thick head. He had a close miss with that animal the other day, but I doubt it'll have taught him a lesson. Who knows what he may dream up next, and I don't want to be around when that happens."

Now free from the Dale's presence, he addressed Coral with a dazzling smile. "Care for a plane ride around the jungle this afternoon? We may find that lion that has been eluding us so cleverly."

Before Coral had a chance to answer, Cybil butted in, "I'd love to! It's been ages since you've taken me on one of your airplane jaunts." She crinkled up her nose, smiling at him in a teasing, intimate way.

"You were not asked," he replied, ignoring Cybil's obvious dismay at such a brutal answer. "Besides, it's a two-seater." Turning to Coral, he smiled again. "Shall we go?"

"What should I wear?"

"Your favorite scent and a smile." His dark brows jerked upward.

Coral shot him a mocking look. "I'll see what I can do to oblige."

Cybil cleared her throat noisily. "Well, actually, I've just remembered that there's something I really must get in Nairobi today, so I couldn't join you anyway," she spat, and turning on an elegant heel, she stalked out of the room.

Coral went up to her room to collect her camera equipment. Rafe was treating her like the queen bee of his harem this week. Well, if it amused him to think so. She had to admit he had been bending over backward to help her gather material for this documentary. Of course, she suspected he had an ulterior motive, but it was up to her not to fall into his trap. After all, her mother had always said that no man could take from a woman what she didn't willingly want to give.

They set out an hour before lunch. The small two-seater was already waiting for them, gleaming in the field. After Rafe had chatted to a couple of officials on the tarmac, he helped Coral up and clambered after her into the plane. Coral had never flown in a light aircraft before, but her job had made her acutely aware of the many incidents in which these sorts of machines had gone down in the jungle. This was not a reassuring thought. Still, the great distances and the bad roads in Africa did not lend themselves to quick and easy travel, so a number of people used airplanes instead of cars. This did little to calm the butterflies in her stomach.

"A little nervous?" Rafe viewed her with concern as he leaned over to check that she was properly strapped in.

Coral shrugged. "I've never done this before."

"There's always a first time." He chuckled.

It seemed to Coral that Rafe's eyes, his smile, even his voice were full of innuendo today. It would be a difficult task to keep this wild animal at bay. But did she really want to? Coral stole another glance at him. He wore a beige bush shirt and tight-fitting jeans, and his hair had been cut, which gave him a boyish air that was rather touching. "Here, wear these." He handed her a set of headphones with a microphone. "So we can have a friendly conversation," he added, grinning when he noticed her raised eyebrows.

They took off straight into the sun, leaving a trail of red and blue dust behind them. It was a fine afternoon with no hint of cloud. Coral felt the excitement mounting in her as they rose over the Rift Valley, higher and higher into the sky. This was different than flying in the balloon, even more powerful and exhilarating. She took in with disbelief the spectacular panorama of plains, snow-capped mountains, escarpment, lakes, and ridges that went on for miles, all thousands of feet below.

A multitude of animals now came into view: giraffes, zebras, impalas, and hartebeest stopped grazing and watched, bunched together, as the aircraft approached and flew over, startling them into sudden flight. In whatever direction the plane turned, creatures were to be seen in astonishing numbers and varieties.

"I've noticed how much you like your job," Rafe remarked as Coral started to take out her camera.

"Hmm… " She busied herself with one of the lenses. "The best way for me to express myself is through the camera. I've always liked beautiful things, and what can be more beautiful than the world around us? Every day, one comes across beauty, scenes that lift up one's spirit: a breath-taking sunset, a mother nursing her child, a tree standing alone in the wilderness, the expression on the weathered face of an old African wise man, the delight on the face of a child eating an ice-cream. With my photographs, I can hold and freeze the beauty of one moment forever." Coral fitted a new lens on the front of her camera and peered through it for a moment, testing the aperture. "Of course, there is also ugliness and unhappiness around us, and sometimes I'm able to capture that too, in the hope that it'll wake up a few numb consciences. I am presumptuous enough to assume that I may be able to make a difference." She let out a little self-deprecating laugh. "Can you understand that?"

"I understand perfectly," he answered.

"What about you? Where did you learn how to fly? I didn't know you were a skilled pilot."

Rafe grinned at her behind his pilot's goggles. "Ah, my dear, there are many skills of mine that you still ignore."

Coral brushed off his flippancy. "Really, where did you learn how to fly?"

He shrugged wearily. "Oh, here and there, I guess." Rafe was still eluding her questions.

"You're a hunter, aren't you? Someone mentioned that you conduct hunting safaris." Coral was facing away from him, busy taking shots of a mustering of storks that were gathering around a lake before beginning their long flight to Europe.

"I have hunted. I don't anymore." It was like drawing teeth.

"Why?"

"Hunting has deteriorated in the last few years. It's not a fair sport anymore. Too many Dales in the world, I'm afraid — bloodthirsty poachers who kill game for trophies, regardless of whether the animal is rare or not. There was one millionaire party that shot twelve lions in two days. They didn't walk, they raced over the plains in small trucks, and what they caught up with they shot. Stories like that make me sick. These sorts of people will be the ones to finally cause the extermination of the great herds that used to roam freely all through this continent."

"You didn't hunt for trophies?"

"No, not really, but sometimes I had to for clients I took out on safaris. It was part of the job description. You couldn't really object. These people came to Africa to hunt, and they intended to do so."

"Where was this, in Kenya?" Coral was determined to dig deeper.

Still, she had barely finished her question when Rafe cried out, pointing at what from afar appeared like a yellow patch on a mound on the edge of a clearing in the distance. "There they are! Your lions!" He sounded just as excited by the sighting as she was. "I'll bring you as close as possible so you can get some good shots."

As he spoke, the little plane began to plunge. He brought the aircraft down so low that they nearly touched the tops of the acacias. Coral had the distinct view of a pride of lions with their cubs, lying on a small rise in the clearing, sunning themselves under the heat of the early afternoon. As Rafe flew over them, the male got to his feet. He was a magnificent animal, powerful and strong. The huge beast casually looked upward, walked a few paces, and flopped down again in the shade of an acacia, his mane waving in the breeze. "I've got a good one of him," Coral said with a triumphant little laugh.

The next moment, Rafe was taking them back into the air, climbing higher into the brilliant sky, drawing a great big circle, and flying back down again over the pride. The lioness had been sprawled out a few paces away from her little ones. Now she was on her way to them, baring her fangs, back arched, and legs stiff. Coral could practically feel the hairs along the lioness's back bristling in alarm and hear the thunderous roar as she prowled gracefully, turning her head from left to right, trying to assess the danger.

"We've disturbed their peace. She obviously feels threatened," Rafe said. "I'm glad we're not down there; she doesn't seem at all pleased."

"I've taken shots of her too, and her cubs." Coral was thrilled. "Thank you, Rafe, I think I've taken enough photographs. You're a star."

"It's my pleasure." His mouth curled into a faint smile. "I've brought a picnic. It's been a long time since breakfast, and I'm starving. Nothing too grand, just a few sandwiches and a bottle of wine, if you fancy a glass, and a bottle of cordial. There's a valley not too far from here. Might I set us down there?" He glanced at her, laughter glinting in his eyes as if daring her to take up the challenge.

"Why not? I think that's a tremendous idea." Coral decided to join in with his game. She knew what she was in for, but the only effect that had was to spur her on and stimulate her senses. She felt a little reckless. Today she would live for the moment, and the moment was now. On and off all day, with Rafe so close to her, she'd had an almost uncontrollable urge to touch him. He was obviously in his element, doing what he was good at. From time to time, he would shoot her a glance, and his sensual mouth would break into a smile that melted her insides. Why worry about what might happen? Even if he did not care for her in the way she wanted, she was sure he yearned for her as much as she did for him. Theirs was a visceral, almost primal, attraction.

The plane was in the air for more than an hour. They flew over blue lakes, torrents, and streams that snaked through the vast plains, and long savannahs with dry river beds foaming, great gashes of red, yellow, and white in the earth. At last they came out on a glade. Coral could see a narrow brook and a darker fringe of immense acacias down at the bottom. Slopes of golden grass over six feet high lay on either side of the watercourse. Up behind came solid gray cliffs; their silvery peaks rose and vanished into the heavens, holding captive the sagging mist of the afternoon.

The plane touched down in a valley surrounded by snow-capped mountains, and though the scenery was dramatically beautiful, for some reason Coral felt uneasy.

"It's taken us a little longer than I thought," Rafe said as he pushed open the cockpit cabin roof door, braced his feet on the wing of the plane, and jumped to the ground, "but we've arrived." Coral wriggled out of her seat and gingerly stepped onto the wing, sitting on it for a moment as she scanned the surroundings. There was something eerie about the place, as though they were not alone — the uncomfortable sensation that they were being stared at by wild creatures — and she had a vague sense of foreboding. A shadow must have touched her face because Rafe frowned. "Is anything the matter? You seem troubled."

Coral smiled down at him, not wanting to spoil the moment. "It's very wild, very beautiful. You seem to have a predilection for enchanting, remote places."

"In fact, this place isn't as remote as you might think — it's on the edge of a Masai village. There's actually a road not far from here that runs straight to Narok, close to Lady Langley's plantation."

Rafe raised his arms to help her off the aircraft. He lifted her toward him, and she felt his strong torso against her breasts. She could sense a heart thumping uncontrollably; was it hers, or his, or both? She couldn't tell. As he set her down, she gazed up at him. "Oh, Coral, don't look at me with those eyes. I can't vouch for my reaction if you do," he said, his voice sensually low. He let go of her shoulders, gently pushing her away a little. Taking a hamper and a blanket out of the plane, he added, "Let's have a spot of lunch and a glass of wine."

Though the afternoon sunshine was beginning to fade, the air was still hot and heavy. Coral was struck by the awesome silence that surrounded them. Not a bird in sight, no shuffle in the undergrowth, even the insects were elusive. They climbed a little way up the escarpment over the plateau and found a spot that dominated the view of the whole glade. Rafe spread out the blanket under an acacia tree. They ate some chicken sandwiches and eggs and polished off the bottle of cordial. They chatted casually, like old friends, about unimportant mundane things, as though they were both trying to ward off the real issue, to stifle the burning embers that were smoldering dangerously in both their minds and their bodies.

All the while, Coral had been aware of the need blossoming inside her, clouding all reason with desire. She could tell that he was fighting his own battle. Why was he holding back? Was he waiting for her to make the first move? Rafe was laying on his side, propped up on his elbow, his head leaning on his hand, watching her through his long black lashes. The rhythm of his breathing was slightly faster, and she could detect a little pulse beating in the middle of his temple, both a suggestion of the turmoil inside him. Rafe put out a hand to touch her but seemed to change his mind and drew it away. Coral stared back at him, her eyes dark with yearning, searching his face.

The shutters came down. "Don't, Coral," Rafe whispered, "don't tease. There's a limit to the amount of resistance a man has."

"But Rafe… "

A flash of long blue lightning split the sky, closely followed by a crash of thunder. Coral instinctively threw herself into Rafe's arms, hiding her face against his broad chest. She had always had a strong phobia of thunderstorms. Now she knew why the place had seemed eerie, why there had been no bird song or insect tick-tocks, no scuffling and ruffling in the undergrowth. Even though the skies when they entered the valley had not foretold the electrical storm that was to come, just like with the animals, her instinct had told her that something was wrong. But she had been too distracted by the turbulence crackling between her and Rafe to pay attention to the changing sky.

Rafe, too, was shaken out of his daze and turned his head to see that the sun had dropped behind the mountain. Dense clouds had swept into the valley and were hanging overhead like a black mantle.

"Where did that come from? No storm was forecast for today." he muttered, jumping up.

There was another tremendous peal of thunder, lightning lit up the whole glade, and again another crash. Then the heavy drops of rain came hammering down against the treetops, pouring down through the foliage.

A wind was starting up. Without hesitation, Rafe folded the blanket into a small bundle and tucked it under his arm. He slung the hamper over his shoulder, and lifting Coral into his arms, he climbed his way up to the next level of the escarpment where a ledge of rock was jutting out and found the entrance to a cave where they could shelter. Coral was shivering. She tucked her face into his shoulder, her fingers tightly gripping his shirt. She was completely inert, paralyzed by fear. They were both drenched.

There was no way they would be able to get back to Narok tonight. Coral knew from her childhood that storms were always long in this part of the country, and through her panic she prayed that he wouldn't be piloting that little plane back in this howling gale. At least here they were protected from the storm. It was not yet completely dark. Rafe looked around, still holding her tightly against him. Coral couldn't stop herself as she sobbed uncontrollably.

"Shush, it's all right," he whispered softly in her ear. "It's only a storm. By tomorrow morning it'll all be over." He brushed her tears away as more fell. "I'm going to have to set you down for a moment, Coral. I need to light us a fire and get you out of those wet clothes."

Coral tightened her grip. "No, no, please don't leave me." Her voice sounded like a lost and terrified child.

Rafe pressed her slender frame against him. "I'm not going to leave you," he reassured her, "I'm just going to light us a fire. You'll soon feel warmer, and a fire always cheers up a place." He put her down gently and unfolded the blanket he had stuffed under his arm. He seemed relieved to find it was still fairly dry. Rafe wrapped the blanket around her before setting about looking for something to make a fire with. In a corner at the entry to the cave, he found a few twigs, some branches, and a heap of dry leaves that past storms had driven into the shelter of rock. At first, he had considerable difficulty creating a spark because most of the twigs he found were damp. He had to break up some of the branches and then stacked the wood in the shape of a pyramid. Upon putting his lighter to the dry tinder, he soon had a small flame going. It licked up strongly at the sticks, and within fifteen minutes a blaze was giving the cave a cheery glow.

Coral had stopped crying. Sitting on the floor of the cave, she was still shivering, but she was not afraid anymore. She felt safe now; Rafe seemed to have taken the situation in hand and knew what he was doing, which didn't surprise her. She was now deeply ashamed of her behavior. How could she have been so weak? Why was it that the less attractive features of her personality always came out in front of Rafe, when all she wanted was for him to admire her and love her?

Coral watched as he busied himself with the fire. He had taken off his damp clothes save for the scanty briefs that clung to him like a second skin. His body was slightly flushed, his wet hair smoothed back and glossy, and his eyes seemed over-bright in the reflection of the flames. She longed to reach out and stroke the contour of his muscles, touch and feel once more his hardness against her, but she dared not. Just before the storm had erupted, he had pulled away from her, even though he must know how much she wanted him, and she knew he felt the same.

He looked up and smiled. "Feeling better?" He rose to his feet and moved toward her.

"Yes, much better, thank you. I'm sorry I was no help to you earlier on. Ever since I was a child, I've been terrified of storms." Coral drew her knees up to her chest, still shivering despite the growing warmth of the fire. "One night when I was three years old, a storm broke out. My parents were out for the evening, and Aluna had been taken ill and was not in her bedroom when the storm woke me up. There was a big tree not far from my window that was struck by lightning. Some of its branches were set on fire, and it seemed like a great giant, swaying in the wind. I saw its limbs shrivel up and fall to the ground. When Aluna eventually came in, I was huddled under my bed crying and calling out for her. Apparently it took a while to bring me out of my hiding place. Ever since that night, I have been astraphobic." She gave a weak smile. "I'm much better than I used to be. I haven't had an attack for at least five years, but I think that being caught by surprise in the open just triggered it."

"It must have been a terrifying experience." Rafe's face was brooding, then his thoughts seemed to change. "Each person has his demons, and each person reacts to them in a different way. There is nothing wrong with that. You're still shivering — you'd better get out of those clothes. With this sort of blaze going, they'll be dry in no time." There was a crackling noise as a burning branch collapsed and a shower of sparks soared up. Rafe added more wood to the fire. "It's really not good to stay in wet clothes," he said to her again.

"I'm all right," she said, "truly."

"No, you're not. You'll catch your death. Don't worry; just pretend that I'm not here. I promise not to turn around." Rafe moved away to the entrance of the cave and faced outward into the night. The sky radiated with flashes of forked lightning, zigzagging from over the escarpment like golden wires. The dull roar of thunder rumbling in the distance told of more gusts of wind and torrential rain approaching through the trees and shaking the forest. Coral stripped off her clothes. She pulled the blanket around her, and then watched Rafe standing with his back to her, outlined by the inky night sky. Her body was recalling the pleasure, the melting feeling inside her when she had been in Rafe's arms by the lake, and as it did, her mind pushed aside the tiny voice telling her she was sailing toward disaster. Coral let the blanket fall to the ground. Casting aside inhibitions, she went toward Rafe. Leaves crackled under her feet, and he turned just as she was going to reach him. They were a few paces apart.

She stood with the flames behind her, offering herself willingly, longing to submit to him.

Rafe's face paled, and his eyes darkened. Coral could see the hollow at the base of his neck pulsing, the intensity of his desire obvious. "Oh, Coral, Coral," he murmured, his tone almost reproachful, but still he did not make any attempt to cross the space between them. Unspoken words and unfulfilled gestures trembled in the air. In the flickering light of the fire, his bronze skin glowed warmly. Rafe stood there very still, the muscles in his body tense. Coral knew he was waiting for her. She could feel the familiar ache, shattering the last of her control. Before she knew it, she was against him, her arms around his neck. She looked up at him, her lips parted, soft and moist.

Rafe gazed down at her and drew in a ragged breath. "You're so beautiful," he said, his voice hoarse.

"So are you, oh, so are you, Rafe," she breathed.

Rafe lowered his head and found her lips. There was nothing soft, nothing tender about his kiss. It was a savage, almost barbaric kiss, desperate and all-consuming. His head slid down her body as a hand cupped the fullness of one breast, his mouth nipping then licking the taut pink peak, sliding over to the other breast and claiming it with the same passion, his kisses hungry and bruising. Wild flames rushed through every inch of Coral's flesh, responding to his touch. She moaned as pain and pleasure alternated in her body, and she pressed herself against his arousal, aching to feel him inside her.

He lifted her up gently and laid her on the blanket that he carefully smoothed beneath her. His eyes locked onto hers as his hands traveled caressingly across her curves, exploring lovingly every corner of her body, the intensity of her rising passion fueling his own. His fingers found the core of her desire where she had never been touched, and she whispered his name as they brushed her most sensitive flesh, making her palpitate with tension under his contact. "I want you inside me," she moaned breathlessly, every nerve trembling with her need for him. Her hands searched and found his hardness, and she stroked and fondled the velvety tip, pressing him, showing him where she wanted him the most. Rafe touched his mouth to hers, and this time his kiss was soft and soothing. She knew he could sense her climax coming as his fingers moved with increasing urgency.

For a moment, he seemed to hesitate, as if battling with some inner turmoil of emotions. Coral yearned for him to slide into her, and she pushed her hips urgently against him. Rafe ignored her writhing and pinned her down gently. Leaving her lips, his head dipped slowly, and his mouth, brushing first against her tummy, moved lower and lower until he tasted the blossoming of pleasure inside her. Coral cried out his name as a series of electric shocks burst through her, and she moaned and whimpered as a million rainbows exploded in her mind. Only then did Rafe let himself go against her, his body convulsing into a fierce climax as he shuddered and groaned, his head coming up and nestling in the curve of her neck. They lay against each other, their hearts beating in unison, their bodies still quivering with the overwhelming feelings that had erupted and burst inside them.

An hour later, they were still silently lying together. Coral had cuddled up to Rafe, and with his arm around her, Rafe held on to her as though he never wanted to let go.

The storm had subsided, but it still rained outside. The fire had burned down to a heap of smoldering ashes. Rafe got up and placed a few branches on top of it. Rekindled, the fire leapt up with purple fervor. As she watched the flames throwing dancing shadows on the wall, Coral's eyes grew heavy.

From beneath her lashes, she watched as Rafe uncorked the bottle of wine and poured out a glass for himself. He lit a cigarette and sat next to the fire, leaning against the rock, watching the swirling smoke that rose above him. There was a strange look about him that seemed to mix excitement with sadness and made Coral wish that she could read his mind. He must have known so many women, she thought, perhaps even slept with many without discrimination. Whatever his past experiences, he appeared like a man who had probably hurt others but had himself been wounded too. He had made himself an island, and how she wished she could cross those waters to him and set him free. Coral lay there half-awake as Rafe sat silently ruminating by the fire, until finally she gave in to a deep and exhausted sleep.

When Coral awoke, the rain had stopped. As dawn broke, a pool of saffron light had crept into the entrance of the cave. Rafe was standing at the opening, looking out onto the valley. Coral watched him for a few minutes as the soft hues sent shadows on his body, and her heart swelled with floods of tenderness. She rolled herself into the blanket, silently came up behind him, and wrapped her arms around his waist, laying her cheek on his strong back. How good it was to be so close to him. He tensed at her touch and turned, smiling.

"Good morning, rosebud. Slept well?"

"Umm," she murmured languidly. A honey-gold halo hung round the tree-tops. As Coral stared into the distance, she could see the spire of Mount Kenya, hundreds of miles away, rising ice blue against the glow of sunrise. The picture was ephemeral. The horizon beside it broke into flames as the African sun burst forth into an incandescent sky. The vision of the glimmering peak melted away, and for a moment, Coral wondered if she had dreamed it. "The rain has stopped. Look, there's a rainbow," she cried out, pointing at the shimmering mirage that formed a broken arch over the glade. "Isn't it beautiful?"

"Yes, it is," he whispered, although a shadow clouded his face as if it held a meaning for him that he was reluctant to speak about. Coral was not apprehensive about such things as a rule, but she remembered an old African superstition that she had heard from Aluna and wondered if it had occurred to him too. A small broken bow, such as the one they were seeing, meant that enemies were on their way from that direction. But who would that be? *Oh*, she thought, *it's only mumbo jumbo*. Rafe shifted uneasily. "It's time we went," he said. "They must be fretting at the plantation."

"Rafe," she said as she watched him dress. "Can I ask you a question?"

"Go ahead." He smiled.

"Why didn't you make love to me as if I was a real woman? I mean… I wanted to feel you inside me." Coral could feel herself blush.

Rafe sighed, came to her, and cupping her face with his hand, he lifted it up and regarded her gravely. "I have robbed you enough of your innocence. But I am not totally without a conscience, and fortunately there are still many pleasures for you to discover. One day you will meet the person who will take you on that journey, but until then, my little rosebud, protect and cherish what you have, because once it's gone, it's gone forever."

"I want you to be the first one," she whispered. "I love you, Rafe. You think that I'm naïve and inexperienced, and yes, I may be that, but I also know the way I feel and have a pretty good idea of what I want. I'm not asking you to marry me; I'm just asking you to treat me like a woman and take me to bed."

He raked his hand through his hair and shook his head. "You are one hell of a stubborn woman, Coral," he said, holding her gently. "Believe me, it would be an honor for me to be your first. You are a beautiful, sensitive, and generous lover. But I'm not right for you, Coral, in so many ways… I'm more than ten years older than you."

"So what?" she protested. "What does age have to do with love?"

Rafe's hand dropped to his side. "It has everything to do with it. Can't you see that?" He turned his face and walked away from her.

Coral struggled to make out what was going through his head. One minute he surrendered to her, and the next he was wavering and pulling away. Surely the difference in their age was not the only thing troubling him? Was he secretly in love with Cybil after all, his heart divided between Coral and her stepmother? Were things more serious with Morgana than he'd let on?

Rafe broke into her thoughts. "You have your whole life ahead of you, whereas I have already lived enough for two people." His words began to tumble over each other as if he were grasping at reasons to push her away. Coral noticed his jaw harden resolutely, but she knew him well enough now to see the panic flicker in his eyes before he turned away. "Besides, I don't believe in everlasting love. I can hardly keep up with the number of times I've thought myself to be in love." Rafe laughed bitterly, and Coral saw that the drawbridge had finally come down. "Sorry to shatter your illusions, rosebud, but I live for the day, and my love for a woman may last a night, two nights, a week at the most, but never a lifetime. I'm afraid these are the hard facts about me. Is that what you want?"

"I'll make you love me; I know I can. You won't ever want another woman." Coral's voice echoed in the empty cave.

He whistled as he turned back to face her. "That's a dangerous ambition that you may never fulfill."

"I'm prepared to take the risk."

"You're just infatuated with me, on the rebound after Dale. But I tell you what," he said, looking directly at her, "you think seriously about this conversation and about other stormy ones that we've had. After that, if you still want to go ahead with this madness, it'll be my pleasure to oblige."

"Hold me close as you did last night," she said softly, wanting to draw him back from the cold fortress where he had retreated. A pale flush crept up her cheeks as she slipped her arms around his neck and lifted her face up to him, lips parted, her body arching in an obvious plea.

For a second, Rafe was as still as a statue. He encircled her waist, his hand holding it in a vice when she tried to come closer, almost as though he was keeping her from him. His head came down, and he placed his lips on hers in a fleeting, almost chaste kiss. Then, before she had time to protest, he dropped his hands, walked a few paces away from her, and picked up the hamper and blanket. "I'm afraid we really have to go, Coral," he said, his back turned to her. "They'll be sending a search party out for us if we're not back soon." Coral sensed that the moment to talk with him had passed, so she picked up her clothes from the floor, her emotions raw as she dressed quickly.

Dawn had gradually brightened into daylight. Beads of rain shone on the leaves of trees outside the cave, caught in the morning light. Rafe and Coral wound their way down the escarpment, climbing slowly over moss-covered rocks, cut ages ago on the face of the ruddy cliffs, now covered by broken tree trunks. The warm air was filled already with a symphony of birdsong and cicadas as bronze-winged butterflies and other flying insects fluttered under the sun, making hay after the overwhelming violence of yesterday's storm.

As the plane came into view at the end of the valley, they could see in the far distance that a group of native men and women were crowded around the aircraft. Rafe swore under his breath.

"It's probably just curiosity," Coral remarked.

"Yes, but it'll be difficult to get rid of them. The tribes can be awkward to deal with. We'll most likely need to pay them off with some sort of gift. Don't worry; I'll take care of it."

"What sort of gift?"

"I don't know yet, but I have an idea. We might have to pay our respects to their chief, which will delay us, but it could be inevitable. A couple of years ago his son was dying of typhoid. The witch doctor, or *mishiriki* as they call him, had not been able to cure him. To cut a long story short, one of the more educated men who work for me told me of the case. I managed to secure the right antibiotic, and he was saved."

"So he owes you big time!"

"I won't go as far as that. The tribal drink of the Masai is a mixture of cow's milk and blood. I was offered some by the chief after his son's recovery. To refuse it would have been an affront. So I had some, which was a seal of our friendship. I fear it might not be seen kindly if we flew off without paying him a courtesy visit."

"How did they know we were here?"

"These tribes have a way of finding out everything that happens in their vicinity. Every movement is followed in the jungle by invisible eyes and is related in their own telegraphic language."

"The tom-tom?"

"By the tom-tom or by other means. The Masai don't use the tom-tom, like other tribes. They use smoke, light, or fire."

So her eerie feeling that they were being secretly watched had been right. Coral shivered even though the sun was already hot.

They were now approaching the aircraft. The villagers were laughing and talking among themselves. As Rafe and Coral drew nearer, the tall, lean, and haughty men and women fell silent. The men wore red sarongs thrown over their shoulder in the

Roman way and wooden armlets. Some of them were armed with spears, assegais, and sticks. The women had their heads shaven and carried around their slender necks the most beautiful jewelry in intricate designs, made out of leather and beads in white, red, green, blue, and orange. Though she had read about them, Coral had never before come across members of the Masai tribe. Often during her strolls in the markets, she had watched out for them but to no avail. They were really very handsome with their oblique eyes and sharp features. She wished she could take some photographs for her article, but realized that this was neither the time nor the place.

Presently, an ebony-skinned young man emerged from the group, his face daubed with ochre paint. Coral noticed that he was splendidly built, taller than the others, and his bearing was nobler. A maroon cloth encircled his waist and fringes of long white fur hung round one of his knees. He wore a lion's mane headdress and a string of lion's teeth around his neck. She had read about this somewhere; it meant he had killed a lion with his bare hands and was therefore a warrior. He carried a tuft on his spear, which was longer than those of his fellow countrymen, apparently indicating his predominance and that he was on an errand of peace. The young warrior appeared very serious as he walked toward the couple. Then, as he reached them, his face broke into a broad smile. *"Jambo, bwana,"* he said. Then he continued, speaking to Rafe in slow but correct English while ignoring Coral's presence. "It has been a long time since we met. My father will be very happy to see you again. Perhaps you would like to visit our village and give a donation to help us build a school for our children? We are one of the first Masai *manyattas* to launch this venture."

"This is the chief's son who I saved from typhoid," Rafe murmured to Coral under his breath. "It looks like he has been through the Eunoto ceremony since I last saw him. His head is shaved," Rafe added, seeing the question on Coral's face. "That means he has recently graduated to the next level of warriorhood, so his father will want to show him off. I'm afraid his is an invitation we can't refuse."

They walked for half an hour through the open plains to the local village. Under the intense, reflective light of the morning, the flat countryside was vibrant with mirages, and the whiteness of the fields glistened like snow. Finally, they reached the Masai settlement.

The village was completely enclosed by a tall fence made of thorn-tree branches at least two meters high. Inside the fortified enclosure, a dozen huts built of branches, twigs, and cow dung stood in a circle. A cluster of children were chasing one another, and some women sat at the entrances of their houses, milking cows or threading beads. A group of Masai elders seemed to be having some sort of meeting under a baobab tree, while a few young men hummed and shouted while practicing their jumping, their thin long legs springing off the ground with a bounce as if they were on a trampoline. When Rafe and Coral made their appearance, all stopped what they were doing and watched the newcomers with staring eyes and open mouths. Coral could tell that they were not used to seeing many strangers in their village and seemed deeply distrusting of Rafe's and her presence.

"I will take you to my father," said the Masai warrior, talking to Rafe again as if Coral did not exist.

"Wait here. You'll be all right, don't worry," Rafe whispered to Coral before following the young man and disappearing into a hut that was slightly larger than the others.

Coral stood alone under the fierce sun. She looked around her, feeling a little awkward, and moved to the shade of an acacia nearby. Some of the villagers picked up their activities where they had left off before the foreigners' arrival; others just disappeared into their huts or stood staring at her. The group of elders had dispersed and gone their various ways, save for one solitary shriveled-up man who was still squatting under the baobab tree with a young boy at his feet. He seemed to be staring at Coral with insistence. Finally, he signaled to her to come forward. At first, she decided to ignore him and turned her attention to the youths that were still jumping and shouting, but she could feel a mysterious compulsion to glance back toward the old man. Suddenly, drained of all resistance, she felt her head moving and met the fixed and unwavering stare. The old man beckoned her again to come nearer to him, and this time she obeyed.

His eyes had a faraway look, as if scanning invisible horizons that held millions of secrets. "You *Bwana* Walter's daughter; he *Bwana* George's grandson. He want Mpingo. Bad, bad man. *Matokeo ya utafutaji kwa.*"

"What do you mean? How do you know my father's name?" Coral was shocked by the man's words. She felt chilled to the bone despite the heat, and a cold sweat ran down her spine. The sense that he was peering into her soul was almost physical. This man had to be their shaman. Fighting the fear that was creeping over her, she continued, "Who are you? Did you know my father?"

"*Matokeo ya utafutaji kwa. Matokeo ya utafutaji kwa,*" the shaman chanted, his eyes rolling, his head moving from side to side like an uncontrolled pendulum.

In the meantime, Rafe had come out of the hut, accompanied by the Masai chief and his son. Presently, they came up to Coral. Rafe introduced her to his friends, then, taking leave of the Masai, started off toward the entrance to the village. As they moved away, they heard the old man's rasping voice showering a torrent of incomprehensible words at their backs. They turned round, and he gave a cackling laugh that echoed, swelling and then slowly dimming until it sounded like the vibrating rolling of distant drums.

They walked quickly and in silence. Coral was shaking, still ill at ease and in the grip of vague fears. For once, she understood a little of what some people rather distastefully called the primitive black man's country. It was a world beyond range of the Western man's total comprehension.

"You're trembling. What was all that about?" Rafe asked when they had reached the outskirts of the village.

"I don't know," she said. "That man seemed to know you."

"Yes, he's the witch doctor I challenged some years ago because he was getting nowhere with curing the King's son from typhoid. The *mishiriki's* nose was put out of joint when my antibiotic proved more efficient than all his potions. The *mishiriki* is a highly respected spiritual figure with the tribe who is also supposed to be able to cure all illness with his various herbs, remedies, or rituals. I suppose it's a dangerous thing to get on the wrong side of someone like that, but I had no alternative. I couldn't have just left the boy to die."

"He seemed to also know who I am. He said something about your grandfather. Was your grandfather named George?"

Rafe seemed uncomfortable. "You mustn't let these people get to you. There's a whole array of customs, traditions, and beliefs that we can't hope to understand. We live in a way so unlike theirs and think in a completely different fashion. We don't really have a home among them, and we'll never be wholly accepted. The motto, if you want to survive in Africa, should be 'watch and listen, but stay detached.' Anyhow, I don't suppose you'll be around for much longer. You've got your documentary pretty much wrapped up, and it'll soon be time for you to go home. Africa is not a place for a beautiful, delicate rosebud."

"I don't know. I may want to make a life here in the future," she said.

"That would be unwise. The years to come belong to the Africans. The people you have seen and met here are part of the swiftly receding past."

Half an hour later, they made it back to the plane, and when they finally arrived at Narok, the plantation was in a state of upheaval. Lady Langley had informed the authorities that the aircraft was overdue, and a search was planned for the next morning if no news of the missing plane arrived.

Rafe had been silent all through the flight back and had withdrawn behind a very thick wall. Coral felt as though a vast schism had suddenly opened between them. It would have been easy to put it down to fatigue due to an eventful and exciting night. Tramping through the bush for the better part of the day could not have helped matters either. Still, in her heart of hearts, she knew that there was more to it than that; something had taken hold of him this morning in the cave, but she could not put her finger on it. Had she been too honest about the way she felt about him? Her mother had always warned her against that sort of thing. "It drives men away," she had told her. Still, she'd wanted Rafe to know that nothing in her life up until that day had felt as right as being in his arms. Despite his honorable rebuff, she knew their desire was mutual, and she was ready to give herself to him, even if that meant that she would lose him as a friend forever.

As Coral was preparing for bed, there was a knock at the door. Cybil popped her head into the room. "Can I come in?" she said, entering before Coral had time to answer. Seating herself in an armchair, her stepmother crossed her long, tanned legs. As usual, she was impeccably dressed and groomed, though Coral noticed that despite the skillful makeup, faint telltale lines on her skin this evening were beginning to betray her true age. "It's time you and I had a little talk, young lady," she said huskily as she lit a cigarette.

There was a short awkward silence during which Coral finished brushing her hair. She had no doubt what was to come and did not intend to let herself be intimidated by her stepmother. Deliberately taking her time, Coral went into the bathroom and tidied up her clothes. Then she came back into the room and sat back on her heels on the bed.

She raised questioning eyebrows. "I'm all ears," she said evenly, staring her stepmother right in the eye.

Cybil inhaled deeply and slowly expelled a gust of smoke. "I'll come straight to the point," she declared, managing a stilted smile. "As I have no doubt mentioned to you before, Rafe and I go back a long way. To put it bluntly, I have been his mistress for many years. Our relationship dates to the days of his marriage in Tanzania. We were lovers then, and we are lovers now. At the risk of shocking you, I'll admit that we were lovers even while I was married to Walter." Coral noticed that her stepmother's gaze didn't flinch at this revelation. "I loved your father, but Rafe and I share a very special bond that nothing could ever break. He is a compulsive womanizer; for him, running after a woman is a sport. I know that, and I've accepted it. He will never marry me or any other woman for that matter." Cybil's green eyes narrowed at Coral through twists of smoke. "His marriage was a living hell, and his wife's death was a blessing in disguise. When Faye drowned, he was finally released from the cage that imprisoned him. Rafe enjoys the chase in the same way huntsmen do, and more often than not, his prey falls victim to his charms. Sometimes it gets away unscathed, but most of the time he will toy with it for a while, amuse himself, gnaw at it, even mangle it if it suits him, with the same ferocity as a wild animal. And then, when he's had his fun, he walks away from it and moves on."

Having delivered her vitriolic message, Cybil leaned forward, stubbed her cigarette in the ashtray on the coffee table, and got up. High heels tick-tocked on the wooden floor. At the door, she turned. "I'm not telling you this because I'm afraid of you or even jealous. I know Rafe fancies you. How could he not? You're so young, so fresh." She gave Coral a bitter smile. "But I've been there before. I thought I'd better tell you the facts of life. I wouldn't like to see you hurt. After all, you are Walter's daughter, and as I told you earlier, I was deeply fond of him, despite everything. So don't say you weren't warned." On that note, she walked out of the room, closing the door behind her, leaving Coral dumbfounded.

These were serious revelations. Coral had always worried that Rafe and Cybil were carrying on an affair, despite Rafe claiming that her stepmother was just a friend. *Another lie?* No, it wasn't possible for him to be so loving and tender while hiding this from her… Was it? Cybil had put it plainly enough now. *When he's had his fun, he walks away.* Afterward, Rafe had drawn back from Coral — again. The seed of doubt pushed its sharp roots into her mind, and pain tore at Coral's insides as the full impact of her stepmother's words hit her. She pressed her hands to her heart as though to stop it from breaking. She felt empty and lost; worse still, she felt a fool. She leaned her head back onto the headboard and closed her eyes.

Rafe had left for the coast immediately after dinner, as usual with no word about where he was going or when he would be back, which meant that Coral might have to wait days before being able to confront him. But confront him with what? She had known from the very beginning that Rafe was a womanizer, and he had told her himself very plainly that he was not the marrying type. He had also admitted to being Morgana's lover, so whether he had one or ten mistresses should not make a difference. So why had he lied about Cybil? Only an hour ago, she had been determined to give herself to him without demanding anything in return. Only an hour ago, she had trusted him.

Rafe had deceived her. He had always given the impression that he had been a good friend to her father, and a good friend doesn't fornicate with his friend's wife. In her heart of hearts, Coral had never given much credence to all the gossip she had heard about him, but now countless questions sprang up in her mind. Aluna had often alluded to a mystery surrounding his wife's death, and according to her old yaha, Cybil and Rafe were somehow even the cause of her father's death, even if only by their adultery and sapping his will to live. If Rafe was lying about an affair with Cybil, what else was he hiding about his past? Like a moth to a flame, she had been compelled even more by the aura of mystery that surrounded him, and now she was getting burned.

His contradictions confounded her. He could have taken advantage of her the night before, but he had refrained. Only that morning had he not forcefully told her that she should think long and hard before giving herself to him? This was not the behavior of the cynical, heartless person Cybil had described. Was it a case of Dr. Jekyll and Mr. Hyde? Some kind of dual personality seemed a little far-fetched. She sensed there was a missing part to the puzzle yet to find.

**

As soon as Rafe reached the Kongoni estate, he packed a bag and left for Nairobi. His chest felt tight — his life seemed to have suddenly taken a new course these last few days. He could hardly believe the magnitude of what was happening between Coral and him. Thankfully, he was catching a plane for Paris the next day. True it was a business trip that had been planned a few weeks ago, but it suited him to be running away — he could not trust himself with Coral if he remained near her any longer. She loved him. And by now she must have realized how he felt about her.

On his way, he stopped off at the clinic and picked up Frank, whose car was at the garage having its brakes fixed. In the car, Rafe's face was pale and stern, his usually laughing eyes dark, and his mouth taut with tension. They had been driving without a word for fifteen minutes when Frank broke the silence.

"What's up? Any problems?" he probed gently.

Rafe shot his friend a fleeting glare. "Damn it, Frank, I nearly committed the irreparable last night."

The doctor smiled indulgently. "What are we talking about here? If you could put me in the picture a little more, I can tell you if you're once again blowing things out of proportion."

"Coral. We were stranded in a cave during yesterday's storm…" Rafe sighed.

"Ah, something finally happened between the two of you. Are you telling me you made love to her?"

"Well, yes and no, you know what I mean. We've been so often thrown together lately, and it's all getting a little out of hand."

"I've certainly noticed the charged atmosphere when you're both in the same room — the way you look at each other."

"Is it so obvious?"

"Yes. You must be aware that she's in love with you."

"I am. Of course I am. And I never intended for it to happen."

"And why is that?"

"You know that I'm not the man for her, Frank. How can I love her the way she ought to be loved if I don't even like myself? Coral needs a younger man without all the baggage I'm carrying. I can hardly cope with it myself, how can I expect her to put up with it? I love her too much for that."

"Nonsense! I've told you before, and I'm telling you again that you have amplified this whole business in your head. Stop blaming yourself. You have nothing to reproach yourself for. On the contrary, you've just been the victim of circumstance and gossip. You have always behaved honorably, and it's high time you threw away this stick you're beating yourself with and started to live."

Rafe gave a self-deprecating laugh. "You're given one life, Frank, and already I've lived mine."

"Don't be ridiculous. You're in your prime; you should be rebuilding your life. Don't you want to have children? I really don't understand this determination not to let go of the past."

Rafe shook his head. "It would be unfair to Coral."

"For heaven's sake, man, she's a grown woman. Just because there's a ten year gap between you, it doesn't make her too young to decide about her own life." Frank raised his hands in desperation.

"Okay, Coral may be twenty-five, but she's still pure, Frank."

"Rafe, she's immature and unworldly where men are concerned, perhaps, and certainly in comparison to the women with whom you've surrounded yourself for the past few years, but she's not that innocent."

"Even if I explained, she wouldn't understand." Rafe sighed, maneuvering the car round a dusty bend in the road. "She wouldn't believe me anyhow."

"I think you're selling her short. I've spoken to her. Coral is an intuitive and intelligent woman. She's inexperienced, so she might have some immature reactions sometimes, and she's as passionate as you are, but she's not a fool. In fact, the two of you are pretty alike in spirit."

Rafe gave a slight smile as he recalled some of their skirmishes. "Yes, Coral is a very passionate woman. She has a good brain too. Watching her work the other day was an eye opener. Everything you've said is true… but I can't help feeling guilty."

They drove silently for a while.

"D'you remember the witch doctor that I angered a few years ago when I saved that Masai boy?"

"Do you mean the King's son?"

"Yes."

"What about him?"

"Well, he popped up today as we were visiting the Masai camp."

"What Masai camp?"

"It's a long story, but in short, because of the storm, we were forced to leave my plane in a field. This morning when we went back to it, a few Masai from the neighboring village had surrounded it. The King's son was there and insisted we pay a visit to the village. Obviously, I couldn't refuse. The shaman was there and recognized me. I'm not sure what poison he served up to Coral while I was with the King, but she asked me all sorts of questions after we left."

"And what did you tell her?"

Rafe's expression darkened; he wasn't proud of himself. "Well, I fudged the answers as usual."

"You may be a shrewd businessman and usually a master in the affairs of the heart, but I must say that with Coral you're clueless." Frank shook his head.

Rafe smiled ruefully. "You're right, of course, but it's because I've never wanted a woman as much as Coral. When I'm around her, I can't think straight."

"You're looking at the problem from the wrong angle. You've been wrong about this from the start. The earlier you come clean, the better it will be for both of you. It's high time you faced reality and dealt with your past."

Rafe's face seemed to brighten up a little. Maybe Frank was right, maybe after all there was light at the end of the tunnel. Occasionally, he had let his imagination wander and dreamed about what life would be like if he married Coral.

"Y'know, Frank, I would give anything to spend the rest of my life with her."

"Well, then, what are you waiting for? As you said, we're given one life, and you seem determined to let yours pass without giving yourself any chances."

"I know she loves me... but what if she doesn't believe me?"

"Listen, Rafe. Knowing you as I do and having been part of this whole tragedy from the beginning, I think it's the only way forward. You may both be missing out on a very beautiful love story."

"D'you think she'll agree to marry me?"

"She may need time... you might both need time to adjust, but you'll never know if you don't ask her."

"Yes, I'll need to let her know my intentions are honorable... " Rafe's brows furrowed. "I need to step back and think about this before embarking on something we might both regret. Anyhow, I can't do anything immediately. I'm leaving for Paris on business in the morning, and by the look of it, I might be away for a while."

"That might be a good thing. It could be that you'll both cool off and that will be an end to the matter. But if not, this trip will still give you the opportunity to think things over and once and for all get rid of this misplaced guilt that has been smothering you for years."

Frank was right. It was time Rafe put some order in his life and stopped reliving the past. It was as if a load had been lifted off his shoulders.

"Thanks, Frank. You've always been a good friend to me."

"The problem with you, old chap, is that you analyze too much. But then you let your passion get in the way of your strong sense of right and wrong, which is not altogether a bad thing… It makes you human instead of a robot."

Rafe brought Frank to the garage in Nairobi and asked to use the office phone. "Sorry, *bwana*, the phone lines are down because of yesterday's storm, and it will be a while before they are fixed," the office manager explained with an apologetic smile.

Damn it! Rafe paced up and down, knowing he had to get a message to Coral. *But maybe this is for the best*, he thought. Once he got to Paris and had everything clear in his mind, he would send her a letter.

Chapter Ten

As soon as Coral returned to Mpingo, she went across to Whispering Palms. Cybil's words had shaken her deeply, but there were still gaping holes left in the tapestry her stepmother had so cleverly woven. She could not believe that Rafe was as black as he had been painted, but she needed to get the truth out of him. He had also become an obsession; every fiber of her being ached for Rafe, and the memories of that tempestuous night she had spent with him haunted her. Coral didn't know whether to love him or despise him. If she didn't put an end to this situation somehow, she would go mad.

When Coral arrived at Whispering Palms, the house was shuttered and closed. She walked through the garden and down to the plantation. Indian and African cutting laborers were tying up and girdling the sisal leaves before loading the bundles in light railway trucks to transport them to the decorticating factory. None of the workers were particularly talkative, busying themselves with their jobs. Finally, she managed to have a conversation with one of them and deduced that Rafe was still away, but no one knew when he would return.

She went back the way she had come, through the garden. As Coral reached the house, she noticed that one of the shutters was open. Her breath caught in her throat, and the rapid beating of her heart thundered in her ears. He was there. Quickening her step, she had just started to run up the stairs of the veranda when Morgana appeared on the threshold. She wore a saffron-yellow caftan that clung to her curves like a snake's slough, and the lush jet-black hair that cloaked her bare shoulders glistened in the sunlight. She wore no makeup save for a line of kohl around her large, dark eyes. She was beautiful and sexy — a female Rafe. Once again Coral had no difficulty imagining what they got up to in private, which was not the case when she looked at her cold stepmother.

"Good morning, Miss Sinclair," said the dancer, looking down at the newcomer. "Still pursuing him? Why don't you give up? Haven't you gotten the message yet?"

"I have nothing to say to you. I need to speak to Rafe," Coral said, doing her best to sound haughty.

"Bad luck again. He's not here."

"Where is he? Is he not back yet from Narok?"

Morgana ignored Coral's question. "There is a saying I am fond of which goes: 'It is dangerous to awaken a lion, and the tiger's tooth is sharp, but the most terrible of all terrors is the mania of man.' Don't try to awaken the wild beast in Rafe. Once unleashed, you will never be able to look back, and it will destroy you."

Morgana had come down the stairs slowly, and now she was only a foot away from her opponent. Coral could smell the heady scent that she wore, could clearly see the fervor silently burning her up; she seemed cool on the outside, but the air almost crackled with the storm that was raging through the Middle-Eastern woman. Coral mustered her courage and squared up to the fiery dancer.

"Not so long ago, you tried to convince me that Rafe was some sort of weak and soulless prisoner, trapped in his own nightmare world. The person you are suddenly now describing sounds like a totally different man, don't you think?" Coral said scornfully. "Neither is particularly flattering, and I'm sure that Rafe would be pretty offended by your views of him. Anyhow, why should I trust you? You're just defending your territory like the other witch I've got at home. I feel sorry for Rafe. Honestly, with friends like you, who needs enemies?"

Coral leaned forward and glared at Morgana. "Let me tell you something. I have gotten to know the man and, in some ways, this 'beast' you describe too. All of you can stand there spouting your theories and the stories you'd love me to believe about him. But don't bank on it! I'm not afraid of you. I love Rafe and will never give him up. And there is a good chance he loves me too," she taunted, lifting her head defiantly. "So put that in your hubble-bubble and smoke it!" Pushing past the dancer, she strode off.

"Suit yourself," Morgana shouted after her. "But remember that desire is something for which one always pays a high price."

When Coral got back to Mpingo, Aluna was waiting for her at the front door. The African woman looked as though the color had been drawn out of her face. "Where have you been all morning? You must never go out without telling me."

Coral sighed. "Oh, Aluna, when will you learn that I'm not your little *malaika* anymore? I'm a grown woman."

"Listen to me, child," the *yaha* went on, her voice turned down to a mere whisper. "There is evil around you. You must listen to me and believe what old Aluna tells you."

"What is it now, Aluna? I'm really not in the mood for your cloak and dagger stories."

"Great noises under the ground have been heard. The tribal leader from the *Mijikenda* tribe has summoned you." Aluna followed behind Coral as the younger woman went and threw herself down into a nearby chair on the veranda. "He has sent his messenger over to speak to you. The boy has something to show you. He will reveal to you the secret that will protect you from the evil one."

"What evil one are you talking about, Aluna? I really am tired of you seeing devils and evil ones behind every bush and in every shadow."

"Don't talk this way, dear child — you will anger the spirits. If they are angry they will cease to protect you. Please, just this once, speak to the messenger. It is important."

"All right, Aluna, just this once. Is that quite understood?"

"Yes, yes. Good child, good child."

"Where's the messenger?"

"He's in the garden. I will call him."

"No, I don't want him coming into the house. Take me to him."

They went into the garden. The messenger was standing next to a jacaranda tree. Coral recognized him as the young boy from the Masai village who had squatted next to the old shaman under the baobab tree. So, the old man was the tribe's *mishiriki*, their witch doctor. Had he sent the boy? As she approached the youth, he smiled shyly and nodded his greeting. He handed her an old newspaper cutting and said something to Aluna that Coral did not understand.

"He says if you want to learn more, you need to go to the *mishiriki's* hut, which is not far from here."

"How come?" Coral looked distrusting. "The Masai village is miles away."

"No, no, he doesn't live there. The *mishiriki* roams all over the bush. He is used to walking for miles," answered Aluna.

Coral was now tired and irritated at being ordered on such a wild goose chase. "Tell him he can keep his dirty newspaper cutting, and I'm not going with him to any huts or anywhere else." As she spoke, there was a small breeze, and the scrap of paper flew out of her hands. She ran after it and picked it up, muttering under her breath. Her gaze fell on the photograph of a couple and the headlines above it that read: *Mpingo Heiress Elopes with French Doctor*. The writing was faint, almost illegible. She had another look at the photograph. There was something familiar in the woman's smile, the curve of the eyebrows, the well-defined lips, but especially in the eyes. She broke into a cold sweat. Could they be? Yes, she was sure now: Rafe's father and mother were gazing at her from the picture. Dear God, what on earth was a witch doctor in Kenya doing with a newspaper cutting that was almost forty years old? And what did Mpingo have to do with it?

Coral hesitated for a few moments and then, making her mind up, she turned to Aluna. "Tell the boy I'll go with him. You'd better come with me to translate; though I have a feeling this *mishiriki* speaks our language well enough. Besides I'd rather not go alone."

They went by car up to the Ngomongo village outside Mombasa and left the vehicle at the edge of the forest. From there, the two women and the Masai boy carved their way on foot through long grass and bushes into a varied countryside, climbing through belts of bamboo and crossing stony ground where the rocks had been worn smooth by the passage of feet. The path began to slope steeply downward until they reached a cunningly concealed clearing in a hollow of the grassland where there stood a magnificent giant banyan tree. Coral had never come across a banyan tree before but had seen pictures of them. It had large prop roots growing laterally up out of the soil making them almost indistinguishable from the main trunk, while its branches grew downward into the ground. They looked like woody pillars forming strange galleries one could walk through.

This banyan was particularly grand, and Coral imagined what a wonderful photograph this would have made for her article. The young messenger patted the tree as he went past and said something in Swahili that Coral did not understand.

"Aluna, what did he just say?" Coral whispered.

"He was greeting the tree spirit. It is like a prayer for good luck. Each time a villager passes this sacred banyan, they say it so that the tree spirit will continue to give its medicine to the *mishiriki* and the village." Aluna was looking racked with anxiety, and she held tightly onto Coral's hand. The boy turned, smiling and nodding to them to follow him.

The *mishiriki's* hut stood a few paces away from the tree. It was squat, round, and quite wide, and was made of woven branches with only a hole for its entrance. Coral and Aluna crawled into it behind the messenger boy. It was dark inside save for a fire that blazed on a primitive hearth built with three large stones. The hut was surprisingly large, and they found they could stand upright as soon as they were inside. The curved wall was dressed with strange animal skins that appeared to be from red eagles, iguanas, great anteaters, and boas. The earth floor was strewn with chips of shells and debris of other marine creatures. Coral noticed with a shiver the skull that was suspended over the hearth by a few sprigs of sisal. She glanced at Aluna — the poor woman looked terrified. There was a vague smell of decay mingled with the balsamic odor of precious woods and resin that the witch doctor was burning. She was mad to have come here. This was a very isolated spot; nobody would ever find them. What had she been thinking?

The *mishiriki* was sitting on a seat that looked like a throne shaped from the bones of giant buffalos' heads, where the horns had been turned down to form supporting legs, surrounded on the floor by pebbles of many colors and sizes. The shaman looked even more haggard than he had at the Masai village, with lines of a long life written on his face, deep-set deadened eyes, and sunken cheeks. The skin stretched tight across his chest showed the outline of his ribs beneath, and his hair was painted red with clay. He signaled to the two women to sit, and then he spat in a large, iron pot that held a thick red liquid before placing it on the hearth. Scooping up some pebbles, the old man threw them into the pot together with a handful of powder. A loud, wild cry went up from him, and immediately the skull that hung from the ceiling started to rotate slowly.

The sorcerer then beckoned Coral to come closer and crouch beside him. Reluctantly she obeyed and found herself compelled as if by some strange power to look into his face. The dead pupils of the old man seemed to suddenly recover their sight as he started to chant an incantation with a strange, guttural murmur. The skull resumed its gyratory movement in reverse and finally stopped to face Coral.

Coral held her breath. What was going to become of her? She was conscious of a cold numbness in her body as a fear greater than she had ever experienced seized her. Her instinct was to run blindly out of the hut, but she was frozen to the spot. The old sorcerer drank some of the infusion he had concocted in the pot and gestured to her to open her mouth. As she did, she tried to force her terrified mind to think. Was he giving her poison? Mesmerized, she felt the question evaporate and watched as, with the help of a hollowed-out bone, he trickled some of the liquid onto her tongue.

The *mishiriki* got up from his throne and lay himself down on a lion's skin that the young boy had spread on the ground and appeared to drop off into a deep sleep. The boy covered him with a kind of white cloak and, crouching next to him, began to hum a sort of litany, punctuating this funereal chant with the hypnotic swaying of his body from side to side. Soon the movement accelerated. His chest streamed with sweat, and his turned-up eyes seemed lifeless. Coral began to feel strange as the room grew darker; the walls first faded into a blur and then disappeared altogether. She fell into a state of semi-consciousness.

Time went by. Suddenly the young boy ceased his chanting and gave a great cry as he uncovered the witch doctor. The *mishiriki* sat up, and Coral seemed to recover her senses all at once. The *mishiriki* turned toward her. "You have come to find out about the Frenchman," he said in perfect English. "This man has come to this land with hatred in his heart to take back by force what he feels is rightfully his."

222

Coral's mind was now alert. The numbness had subsided from her body, and she felt refreshed as if she had awoken from a long, deep sleep. "What do you mean?"

"The Frenchman's mother angered her father when she ran away with her French lover. The father owned Mpingo. He disinherited her and then sold Mpingo to the White Pirate, your father. The Frenchman came to this land to take back his inheritance. He had all of his wife's money after she died and then tried to buy Mpingo, but your father refused to sell to him. So the Frenchman wormed his way into your father's house like a jackal, and he took the White Pirate's wife as his woman. Now you have returned, and the Frenchman wants to enslave you using his black magic so you will surrender to him and he can take back Mpingo as his own. He is the devil! Run from him, run or he will destroy you, drown you as he did his wife, as he drags you down into the underworld from where you will never return."

A mighty roar vibrated through the hut, and in that second, Coral met the sorcerer's stare; she saw a rage and hate that filled her with horror. The corners of his mouth were turned down in an expression so savage it appeared inhuman and evil. Coral felt like she was staring into the eyes of a monster.

Taking the spear that the young boy was now handing him, the *mishiriki* lifted it and, holding his breath, flung it toward the suspended skull, landing it in the middle of the eye sockets and shattering the death head in two. As he did so, the ground seemed to tremble under them and the walls shook. The *mishiriki* then rose from his seat and, bobbing and bending, hobbled out of the hut without looking back. The young boy signaled to Coral that it was over and said something in Swahili to Aluna who had cowered as close to the hut's mouth as possible, totally petrified. Approaching Coral, the boy beckoned her to follow him.

Aluna babbled unintelligibly in the car all the way back to the house. "I warned you evil was coming, Missy Coral. You would not listen to old Aluna. The Frenchman, he is the devil in disguise. Now what is to happen to my little *malaika*? Yes, yes, run from him, yes, run from him!" The African woman hugged herself and swayed from side to side, muttering odd words of Swahili.

It was dark when they reached Mpingo. Coral went straight up to her room, sending Aluna off to her quarters. She realized it would take the poor woman a long time to recover from the terrifying experience. Coral felt guilty and sorry for the *yaha* who had loyally followed her little malaika on her unreasonable expedition. Still, she did not regret what she had done; the story she had been told was an extraordinary yarn, but at least she had some sort of answer to most of her questions, even if they did seem rather amazing. Coral wondered how the newspaper cutting had come into the *mishiriki's* possession in the first place, but then she remembered her mother had once told her. "These witch-doctors are no fools," she had said. "They are powerful and dangerous men if you get on the wrong side of them. They have spies and informers all over the place — it's how they keep their people under such control." Coral decided she would verify the *mishiriki's* words by visiting the *Mombasa Gazette* offices in the morning and checking their archives for old newspaper articles.

Back in her room, Coral went about in a daze. She hung up her clothes, had a hot bath, and got into bed. Only then did she react to the information she had just learned. Her body went icy cold and started to tremble as if she had fever. Pulling the sheet toward her, she lay curled up like a sick animal, hugging herself protectively as a tide of misery washed over her.

How could her intuition have been so wrong? The painful truth dawned: Rafe had fooled her utterly, every step of the way. He had used their physical attraction to lure her into loving him. She did not know who she hated more: Rafe, for being unscrupulous and Machiavellian, or herself, for being not only gullible but so wanton. *Desire is something for which one always pays a high price*, Morgana had said to her, and so very right she was. How Rafe must have laughed at her naiveté.

If only she could stop thinking about him… But no matter how hard she tried to drive his image from her thoughts, it was no use. She felt guilty and ashamed, but she could not deny it. Rafe had gotten under her skin; her love for him ran in her veins. But how could she love someone she held so much in contempt? Warm tears ran down her cheeks, and she sobbed in desperation as her soul shattered into a million shards.

***

Early the next day, Coral set off to verify the witch doctor's words at the *Mombasa Gazette*. The offices were in a drably colored midget skyscraper that many towns in Africa, despite the enormous open spaces around them, put up as an indispensable proof of their commitment to progress. The employees were kind and helpful. An old Indian man behind an imposing desk seemed to recall the incident.

"Yes, yes, I remember. I was still a lad," he said. "The story made a lot of noise at the time. The year escapes me now. Close to forty years ago, it must be. Her father was a well-known settler. She was a beautiful woman, not young, mind you, in her thirties, but still very beautiful. Very proper lady. No one would have imagined. It just goes to show, still waters run deep. I think it was a shock not only to her father but also for many people too." Having supplied the information, he waited and gave Coral a slanting look. "Why d'you want to know? Is she a relation?"

"Oh, no, no! I'm writing an article on society scandals in Kenya," Coral replied casually. "Would you keep articles of this kind in your archives?"

"We keep all articles, and we are very well organized," he answered proudly.

The clerk gave orders to two young *kikuyus* who came running to answer his request and brought over to them mounds of files and boxes. All morning, Coral plowed through the archives, painstakingly pouring over dusty, bound copies of newspapers, each year made up of three hundred and sixty issues. Finally, she found a series of articles and photographs that told the whole story. Indeed, Carol Stevenson Wells had been a beautiful woman, strong and charismatic. Obviously her son had not only inherited the deceptive side of her character, but also her looks. They both had that kind of devastating attraction that few of the opposite sex can resist, usually leaving disaster in its wake.

The *mishiriki* had not lied. George Stevenson Wells, Rafe's grandfather, had in fact disinherited Carol, his only daughter, for eloping with her lover Dr. Paul de Monfort, a scientist working for the Pasteur Institute in French Guinea. A harsh punishment,

225

Coral thought, but in those days, she supposed, codes of conduct were much stricter. However, a few years later, Carol's father sold Mpingo to a new English settler, Walter Sinclair, and had gone back to England immediately afterward, never to be heard from again. Rafe was thirty-six now, which meant Carol Stevenson Wells had been pregnant when she left Mpingo. Coral pitied Rafe. In some way, she could not blame him for wanting his inheritance back, but why the underhanded manipulation? Maybe if he had told her the truth, they could have come to some arrangement, she thought as she drove glumly back to the house.

The next morning, Coral awoke to the sound of voices outside her window. She had spent a fitful night and now felt the stinging lack of sleep. She climbed out of bed and went over to the window to see the postman handing her stepmother a letter. Rubbing her eyes, Coral slipped into her dressing gown. Perhaps there was a letter from her mother. Angela Ranleigh wrote to her daughter regularly, and usually her letters, though full of gossip about their Derbyshire village and people that Coral hardly knew, were often entertainingly indiscreet and read like an English soap opera. Today, Coral could do with something to cheer her up, and news from her family would make her feel less far from home.

While Coral was running down the stairs, she saw Cybil standing in the garden. She had torn open the letter and was engrossed in the contents, her face slightly pale.

"Anything for me?" Coral asked. Her stepmother's head shot up, and she hastily stuffed the letter into the pocket of her dress.

"No. Nothing for you. Just a letter for me from an old relative," replied Cybil. Her hand was on her throat, and she seemed to regard Coral almost with shock.

"Is there something the matter? Are they ill?" asked Coral, not exactly feeling sympathy for Cybil, but there was something very odd-looking about the expression on her stepmother's face, and she was gripping the letter tightly in her pocket.

"Yes. Yes, that's right. There's an illness in my family. An old aunt." Cybil was now distractedly fiddling with the tight bun of hair at the back of her head, and her gaze flitted away from Coral. "Inevitable, really." Her stepmother barely smiled as she walked past, leaving Coral to wonder what kind of dear old aunt could make a woman like Cybil look so upset.

The next few weeks went by at a snail's pace, with bitter-sweet thoughts of Rafe threading through Coral's brain. Her waking hours were a torture of days as her mind went to and fro, trying to understand conversations, rumors, and her own feelings. Her nights were just as painful, with periods of sleep broken by unpleasant and vivid dreams.

Where had he been all this time? She needed explanations from Rafe, and the waiting was driving her to distraction. As soon as he returned from his travels, she would insist on talking to him. Still, a voice inside told her that these were only excuses to see him again, feel his arms around her, the warmth of his body against her, the melting sensation that drenched her limbs whenever he was close… No, she must try to control these feelings; otherwise, they would destroy her.

Coral had to be inventive to keep herself busy. Her articles were mostly in their final stages. They needed brushing up, but it was difficult for her to concentrate when secretly her mind, her body, and her heart were always with Rafe. The Mpingo estate almost managed itself. Robin Danvers was doing a wonderful job and did not seem to need her input. She hardly saw Cybil nowadays. Her stepmother kept pretty much to herself, and when they did meet, they both made an effort to be civil to each other. She often wondered if Cybil had any news or any inkling of Rafe's whereabouts. She searched in her mind for some lame excuse to bring up the subject but still did not dare to ask, and anyhow, she was sure that her stepmother would not disclose any information even if she did know something. Coral spent a lot of time on the beach and taking solitary walks through the countryside. Once or twice, she found herself ambling in the direction of Whispering Palms in the hope that Rafe had returned, but she did not venture too close to the house in case she bumped into Morgana.

Time passed, and today, for the first time in weeks, Coral was less broody. She lazed in a hammock under a flame tree, listening to the cicadas' ziz and churr, and enjoying the cheerful glow the sun shed over the garden. The air was hot and still. Glimpses of calm, blue sky interlaced the topmost branches of the trees, and the heavy scent of ripe fruit from mango and papaya groves floated around her.

Most afternoons, Coral tried to take a nap, but she was unable to really sleep, just dozing and daydreaming or reading quietly on her bed. This afternoon, her room felt rather stuffy, so she set herself out on a reclining chair in the shade on the veranda. The heat was intense, and the garden was filled with a warm haze and the soothing drone of bees. She could hear the murmur of the palms and the sea surf in the distance, and they lulled her to sleep.

In her dream, she hurried along the path of an eerie garden, through avenues of palm trees like sleeping giants on either side, past clumps of flowering shrubs, the blooms drained of their color by the night. Waxen and phosphorescent in the moonlight, their scent impregnated the air. Where was she going in such haste, a night nymph, her flimsy white dress flowing behind her in the breeze? Suddenly, she knew she was running to Rafe. She could hear him calling her in the distance as he struggled to rid himself of his three captors. She saw him clearly now, surrounded by Cybil, Morgana, and the *mishiriki*. Rafe's arms stretched out toward her, but her legs seemed held to the ground, treading the same place, not moving forward. Her heart thumped hard against her ribs as she tried to quicken her step to reach him, but to no avail. Then the *mishiriki's* face grew larger and larger still, his devilish black eyes turning red, inches away from her own, as he gave his blood-curdling cry. A hellfire erupted around the small group, engulfing them all in its flames, while Rafe's voice resounded in her ears, calling her again and again. Coral screamed out his name. She could still hear her scream as she woke up, shaking, her hair clinging to the back of her neck, a heaviness pressing down on her chest like a big stone stopping her from breathing.

***

It was almost twilight when Coral awoke. She showered and walked down to the beach. The herbaceous borders in the garden were humming with multicolored hawk moths, hovering in front of the flowers, their wings fluttering so swiftly that they seemed invisible. Blue shadows climbed the walls, and cactus and gray-green spears of aloes shot out above them between the tall, sparsely growing palm stems.

The Indian Ocean was shining silver in the half light, spread out in front of her as she strolled lazily, barefooted on the beach, delighting in the feel of warm sand under her toes and the refreshing breeze on her face. Nothing except a handful of bathers disturbed the quietude of that hour, leaving the landscape at peace. At the edge of night, her arms wrapped around herself, she sat on the shore under the open sky and watched the sea in the dimming light as the waves lapped at her feet.

Coral's dream had deeply shaken her. Most of the time she did not remember her dreams, and when she did, they were rarely as vivid. But this time Coral had a feeling of foreboding. Where was Rafe? Was he in danger? Why had he been away for so long? Was she ever going to see him again? Did she want to?

The sun was just setting, staining the horizon with rose and deep gold. The ball of red fire dropped suddenly into the ocean; its reflection intensified and deepened before fading quietly away into the shadows of the evening. Soon the globe of the full moon took its place, as large as a balloon and as red as blood, an awe-inspiring spectacle that took Coral's breath away. She loved the red moons that rose some African nights.

The deepening dusk was charged with melancholy. After the long hot day, the soft night air was very pleasant, but she must be thinking of getting back soon. There were no bathers now — not a soul in sight. She was sorely tempted to stay on a little longer, even though she knew that it was not reasonable to be wandering alone at this hour on the deserted beach.

Suddenly, a few meters away, a thin pencil of light cut the gloom, startling her. It shone straight on her, and Coral stood up, raising her hands in front of her face. Turning off his torch, Rafe emerged from the darkness and stopped just twenty paces away. Lost in her thoughts, she had not heard him approaching. Coral's heart leapt; she inhaled deeply, feeling the blood quicken in her veins. Silent, they stared at each other in the moonlight.

Coral's body was riding a tidal wave of emotion, drowning out any rational thought except how much her body craved his touch, but she just stared at him.

"How did you find me?" she asked quietly.

"I rang the house. I know that you love the beach, particularly at this time of the evening." Rafe looked like he was holding his breath, gazing at her intently, still keeping a few feet away. "Did you get my letter?"

"No. What letter?"

He took a step toward her and suddenly looked anxious. "You didn't? From Paris… I wrote you a long letter a couple of weeks ago… I wanted to tell you… "

"Tell me what, Rafe? What did it say?" Now that he was standing in front of her, Coral felt a mixture of intense feelings burning her insides. Rafe stared at her, his features sliding into a serious expression, and she was struck by the marks of strain and tension that furrowed his face as he finally came close to her.

"My sweet Coral, you are the most desirable woman I've met, and I love you to distraction. It's been hell these last weeks, and I know now that life won't be worth living without you. All these years it's as though a part of me was missing, but since you came into my life, I've felt whole."

Oh, God, Coral thought, *he loves me*. An almost unbearably sweet pain pierced her heart. She wanted to believe what he was saying to her. At the same time, a nagging voice at the back of her mind would not be silent.

Rafe traced her cheek with his fingers, and then his arm was around her waist, his eyes still locked on hers as he slowly pulled her against him. For a moment, she resisted, but his arm drew her back with a gentle possessiveness, his expression pleading, and his mouth still moving toward hers. He kissed her with deliberate delay, stroking her bare skin, and her pulse quickened immediately at his touch. She had time to withdraw from his embrace if she wanted to, but this felt so good, so right. Warmth flooded her, and she remained.

"I want us to get married. I want you to be my wife," he whispered in her ear, his voice low and thick with passion.

His words struck her like ice cold water. The threatening specters of Cybil and Morgana swam into her head as her mind spun with confusion and shock. *He will destroy you, drown you like his wife.* The words of the *mishiriki* echoed in her head like screaming birds, and her heart was pounding like a drum in her chest. Now, so suddenly, his misgivings were gone? Now, when he thought he was safe, that she was so in love with him she would not hesitate to be his wife, he had reappeared out of nowhere and finally dropped his mask. She wrenched herself away from him.

"So it's true! Every word I have heard about you is true!" she said, anger sweeping through her veins. "You want to marry me, do you? Is this your latest scheme? Do you think I don't know you want to marry me to take back Mpingo? You don't love me — it was all pretense. You're a cold, calculating, and unscrupulous gold digger." Coral was sobbing now, frantically stumbling back in the sand. Words suddenly seemed useless. In her distress, she wanted to scratch his face. She went for him, hammering his chest with her clenched fists. "I hate you, I hate you, I hate you… "

He stood there staring at her wide-eyed. "Will you tell me what's going on? What all this is about?" He seemed almost paralyzed by this frenzied outpour. Coral welcomed the adrenaline that raced through her veins and felt fury rise up in her. Teeth clenched, she lashed out at him to hurt him as he was hurting her. "I see you clearly now," she hissed between sobs. "You've used our bodies as an instrument for your own ends. Even now as you asked me to marry you, you were trying to influence my answer by striking at my weakness and seducing me first."

He took a pace or two away from her, a dazed expression on his face, and passed his hand over his head like a man in a dream. "Honestly, Coral," he said numbly, "I don't know what you're talking about. I love you, and I thought you loved me too… "

"Yes, oh yes, I fell for you all right, like all your other women," she said with a sneer. "You acted your role beautifully. But I'm stronger than you think, and I will not let you destroy me as you did your wife — or my father! You never told me that you were the grandson of the settler who sold Mpingo to my father. You married your heiress, got rid of her, and inherited her estate. How much more vile can you get? Is that what you want to do to me? Well, I have news for you… "

He glared at her, smothering a profanity, his face drained of all color, his features distorted by anger but also by incredulity and pain. "Enough!" he bellowed. "Don't you dare drudge up this venomous filth. You know nothing of my past and nothing of me. Nothing! You're an unbalanced, hysterical, and spoiled child, and I don't give a damn if I never set eyes on you again."

His face burned with contempt as he wrenched a little box from his pocket and threw it at her. "Here, that's yours. I have no use for it anymore," he said before he turned his back on her and strode off.

Still trembling and crying, Coral watched his silhouette fade away slowly until it was swallowed up by the night. She waited for him to look back, but he did not. Throwing herself down on the cold sand, she crumpled up, weeping bitterly.

She had never seen Rafe lose control like that. What was he hiding? If what she said was so scandalously untrue, why did he not defend himself? Of course she knew nothing of his past. Maybe if he had been more forthcoming, she would have understood him better. Then the image of his face swam in front of her and the pained look that had overwhelmed him. She realized with horror that she had gone too far.

Did she hate him? It was said that hate was akin to love. Now she had lost him, she realized that she truly loved him. But however agonizing this realization was, she had done the right thing. She had listened to reason instead of her heart. He was not for her. She must be strong and pull herself together. She was young. With time she would get over him. Exhausted, Coral fell into a deep and dreamless sleep.

When Coral opened her eyes again, stars overhead were starting to wane as though the first chilly breath of dawn had reached them, dimming their brilliance. She sat up and hugged herself against the cold, wiping her face with the heel of her hand. How long had she been there? The beach was deserted and remote, the sudden hush before sunrise when dark patches would soon be tinted pink. Coral noticed the small, black box on the sand beside her. She reached out for it and opened it. The most beautiful diamond ring lay on its velvet cushion like a large, iridescent tear. She held the little box to her chest and wept, this time for her shattered dreams. "Oh, Rafe... Rafe," she sobbed, her face buried in her hands, her whole body shaking uncontrollably. Dear God, how this hurt. Why had he not explained himself before things had gone this far? She wanted to trust him; she would have gone to any lengths to erase from her mind all doubts and misgivings. Just a few words would have sufficed, but those words had remained unspoken and instead others had been said, causing irreparable damage.

She would leave Africa as soon as possible. She had written her articles, taken her photographs, and had made a good job of it. There was no need for her to remain here anymore. Suddenly her heart yearned for England. She missed the mellowness of its colors, the coolness of its air, the ethereal scents that floated in its gardens. Africa was too dazzling, too passionate, and too savage. Her life in Derbyshire was more uneventful, but at least there she could be at peace with herself and with the world.

***

Rafe had walked all night, smoking and thinking of Coral. Loving her was tearing him apart. The fury had drained out of him. He replayed in his mind over and over again Coral's senseless outburst, wondering what could have brought on such terrible accusations. He was aware of the gossip and poisonous aspersions that surrounded him. His father-in-law used to tell him to ignore it. "The more they talk about you, my boy, the more venom they spread, so the more jealous of you they are. It only means that you are successful." Rafe had taken his advice and disregarded malevolent tongues. At the beginning, it was hard. With time, he had learned to accept rumors as a fact of life. Until this day, they had never really harmed him.

Today, the evil of this gossip had finally caught up with him, destroying the loveliest thing he had ever known. Just as he had thought he would never find his heart's desire, Coral had waltzed into his life. She had roused him, and despite his misgivings, he had fallen in love with her. For the first time in his life, he had known what it was like to feel safe, loved, and fulfilled. He was so close to holding his dream, and now it was being snatched from his hands.

It was his own fault. He had been so excited to see her that he had not explained everything to her first, and instead had foolishly stunned her with a marriage proposal. *Why didn't you defend yourself?* The voice at the back of his mind kept reprimanding him. *There's still time. Go to her, find her, and tell her everything.* But pride had set in. She shouldn't have lent an ear to such slander; she should have given him the benefit of the doubt. During these last weeks in Paris, he had finally determined to tell Coral how he felt. He had asked her to be his wife, and she had thrown it back in his face.

Obviously she did not love him. *I'm not asking you to marry me; I'm just asking you to treat me like a woman and take me to bed.* Weren't those her words to him that night of the storm? As he had feared, her feelings for him were simple infatuation, a physical attraction that he admitted freely he had encouraged. But wasn't the Coral he knew incapable of passion without emotion? Not like the other women he had been with who just wanted him for mindless physical pleasure. That had suited him well enough until he had met Coral and had discovered the beautiful fusion of body and soul in her arms. And yet now it was unbearable that her faith in him, her love for him, was not enough for her to take him as her husband.

She had shaken the very foundations of his world, and now he must rebuild them. After all, he thought, perhaps it's for the best. He was too old for her, she would have eventually tired of him, and sooner or later he would have lost her. At least this way, fate or circumstances had taken the decision out of his hands, and he would not try to alter the situation, however much he suffered. He had fought fiercely against his demons… but it was no use; he should have known that it was a losing battle from the start. It had been madness to think that it could have been otherwise.

Dawn was breaking when he got back to Whispering Palms. Morgana awaited him, sitting on the stairs, and he smiled ruefully as he saw her. Poor, kind, loyal Morgana — how she loved him. Somehow he wished he loved her too, a straightforward, uncomplicated love where passion had no place, but peace was king.

Presently, she came up to him and laid her hand on his arm. "You look tired," she said, eyeing him with concern. "Come, I will prepare you a hot bath. It will relax and soothe you." Rafe knew this was her way of asking him if he needed to vent his physical frustration in her arms. He shook his head. "No, my sweet." He brushed her cheek with the back of his hand. "This time, at least, it's no use and not fair to you. I think I'll shower and go straight to bed."

Rafe went to his room and stood on the veranda, his features set and remote, waiting to meet the new day. Darkness paled, and he watched the lightening of the sky as the streaks of color seeped through from the east. It was all so gentle, the fading away of blackness, the opening of the day's gates, so much in contrast with the turmoil that inhabited his soul. Coral's wounding words went round in his mind like a whirlwind. In all his black despair, he felt no hate for her. His love was still there, bruised perhaps, but still there, tugging at the root of his being, whole and frightening in its strength.

The sun finally rose. He must rest; he had a long day in front of him. He had so much wanted her to be a part of this new life ahead of him, but now he would be facing it alone. Preparations had to be made. But without Coral, he now found the prospect tiresome and almost pointless. There were so many things about Africa that he would miss... eating by a campfire under a full moon to the sound of the animals' cries, sleeping out in the bush beneath the blazing stars, listening to the sudden volley of tom-tom beats, the warmth and the vivid colors in the hills, and the eternal chirping of cicadas. Now, without Coral, civilization and all its obligations seemed monotonous and unbearable. Rafe resigned himself to a sentence of solitude in the jungle. He was alone again, as he had always been.

Chapter Eleven

It had been a fortnight since Coral's quarrel with Rafe on the beach. How long ago that all seemed now. Lying in her hammock among the frangipane trees, Coral was feeling resigned. After dawn had broken, she'd sat there, miserably reflecting on the past months and the immediate future. It had been mid-morning when she had finally brought herself to go back to Mpingo.

Aluna had not tired of telling Coral how worried she had been by her disappearance that night. When the young woman had not shown up at nightfall, Aluna had gone searching for her on the beach and had found her in a crumpled, exhausted heap in the sand. Aluna had pleaded for her to come home, but Coral had remained, secretly hoping that Rafe would return. Though Coral would not speak to her over the following days, the older woman repeated endlessly that "the devil Frenchman" was responsible somehow for her little *malaika's* distress.

Since then, time had drifted on as golden, luminous days turned into sapphire moonlit nights. But to Coral, life was like being suspended in a sort of twilight. She half expected the telephone to ring at any moment, but it had stayed mute. Of course he would not call — why would he following her crushing words? She had debated whether to go to him, but pride, guilt, and mortification kept her from making the first move. After what she had said, how could she face him?

In the cold light of day, things now appeared differently to Coral; she could find no concrete evidence for her recriminations. In retrospect, most of them were based on hearsay and the rest could have been her false deductions mixed with pure imagination. Even if they had been true, why had she reacted with such a volcanic eruption? Could she not have controlled herself and been less wounding, at least giving him a chance to defend himself? Once again her willful temperament had got the better of her. She had been immature and even unjust, but most of all she had turned what they had shared so deeply, their beautiful love-making, into something vulgar and vile. There was no reason for him to forgive her this time. Their brief and fiery relationship was over.

Soon she would be back in England, a little earlier than planned, but that was a good thing. She would be busy with the new documentary, and life would become more down-to-earth again. At some point she would need to go into Mombasa to buy a plane ticket, but for the moment she just wanted to take advantage of the sun, the sea, and the beach.

A few days later, Coral decided to head down to the beach. Opening the front door, she found Morgana standing on the threshold. The dancer looked tired and pale, giving her a sallow appearance. Her cheekbones seemed overly prominent. Big, dark shadows under her eyes gave her a mask-like expression, and she had lost a noticeable amount of weight. Gone were the luscious curves along with the haughty demeanor that had both made Coral feel small. Nevertheless, she was still beautiful, with a new vulnerability that somehow made her less bewitching but more feminine.

The dancer smiled. "I'm sorry. You are going out. It'll not take long, but I need to speak to you."

"Please come in," said Coral, a little puzzled, before leading Morgana to the living room. "Can I offer you some refreshment? It's a hot day."

"You're very kind. There's no need for that, thank you."

They sat down. A few moments passed in silence. Morgana tilted her head a little. "It's about Rafe. He is very ill and he needs you. Please, Miss Sinclair; he will die if you don't come." Morgana passed a trembling hand through her hair.

Coral did not react immediately. What was Morgana up to now? Was she playing some sort of sick game? She surely did not look well herself, but Coral did not trust her. "If you're fishing about our relationship, I think you should know that Rafe and I have nothing more to say to each other. He's all yours, my dear," she said, pleased that she managed to sound cool and detached.

Morgana shook her head. "You don't understand." There was a faint tremor in her voice. "Rafe has caught some sort of fever. Dr. Giles says it's likely to be one of his bouts of malaria. He has had it often before, but this time he's not fighting it and is letting himself go."

Coral shrugged in feigned indifference. "I don't see what that has to do with me."

"Miss Sinclair, this isn't easy for me. I have come to you because I love Rafe more than life itself." The dancer seemed to be trying to remain calm, but there was an audible catch in her voice. "Unfortunately, he doesn't love me. Well, anyhow, not in the same way. It is you he's calling out for in his delirium, you he wants, you he needs at this time next to him, or I am afraid he will let himself die."

"Surely you're exaggerating." Coral was still not convinced but was beginning to feel unnerved.

"Before Allah I'm telling you the pure truth and I'm not exaggerating," she said, wringing her hands, her voice starting to sound shrill. "Would you like Dr. Giles to talk to you? He hasn't left Rafe's side for a week — that is how serious the situation is."

Coral leaped up from the sofa, trembling and a little unsteady as she went to the door. There was no use trying to fight him with her mind when her heart urged her to run to him. "I'll get my bag. I'm coming with you. Do you have a car?"

"No, I came walking."

"Then we'll drive."

"Thank you," Morgana said, welling up with tears of relief. "Thank you, and I'm sorry if I have caused you grief in the past. I have always known that Rafe loved you, and I was jealous. Since he met you, he has slipped away from me." She suddenly looked humbled. "I only hope my words were not the reason that brought about your split."

Coral smiled at her. Coming back toward the other woman, she laid a friendly hand on her arm. "No, Morgana. You can put your mind at rest. You played a very small part in all this," she said. "I'm young and inexperienced, I suppose. I've never met anyone like Rafe. He is my first true love. I didn't understand him, and I'm afraid I'm a lot to blame."

She went up to her room, her head buzzing, hoping that Morgana had been exaggerating. In this part of the world, people tended to make a mountain out of a mole hill. Her mother called it "their drama in everyday life." Still, Coral needed to see for herself. If there was any truth in what she had heard, then she must be at Rafe's side. Her hands were suddenly cold and clammy, her heart heavy. *Dear God, make him all right.* She would never be able to live with herself if something happened to him.

***

When they arrived at Whispering Palms, Frank Giles was in the kitchen, making tea. He looked like he hadn't had much sleep lately.

"Hello, Coral," he said, coming out of the kitchen carrying a tray. "Nice to see you again. You're just in time for some tea."

"How is Rafe?"

"Not so good, I'm afraid," he said, shaking his head. "Rafe first caught malaria in Tanganyika, and relying on time and his experience of treating it with quinine, developed a system of immunity to it that stood him in good stead for many years, although it failed him this time when his morale was low. Silly man, he seems to have lost the will to fight." He smiled sadly at Coral. "Still, we'll soon get him back on his feet, won't we?" He grinned at both of the women standing in front of him. "He doesn't know just how lucky he is to have two such beautiful ladies looking after him." Frank was trying to sound cheerful, but Coral could easily sense the anxiety in his voice. "I'll take you to him. He has some spells of awareness, but most of the time he's asleep or unconscious."

Rafe was lying listless on his bed, his thin waxy face half-covered under the blanket, beads of sweat on his forehead. Coral looked at the still face, avidly scanning familiar features. The man she loved with all her soul was lying there between life and death, and she was powerless to save him. She had read about these tropical fevers that took over the body and killed without mercy. Controlling her anguish, she reached for the damask towel that lay in a bowl of water and vinegar on a small table next to the bed, and wiped his brow with a fleeting caress, while Rafe mumbled something in his sleep. He seemed so vulnerable, so helpless and lonely; she wanted to take him in her arms and sooth the pain away, protect him from the troubles that appeared to surround him.

"It's good for him to sleep," Frank said. "Soon the shivers will recur and the fever will go up. He will perspire and then feel better for a while. Malaria is a nasty disease that can be kept under control nowadays, although it's the wicked plague of Africa that has killed many people over the years and unfortunately still does. Come, let's sit down and drink our cup of tea." He flashed her a reassuring grin. Coral was not duped. She knew he was trying to conceal his concern behind a façade of cheerfulness.

Morgana had quietly retired, and Frank and Coral were left alone with Rafe in the room. "Is he going to pull through?" The expression on her face left no doubt about her feelings for Rafe.

"He's a strong man," Frank said, regarding her kindly. "There's no reason why he shouldn't. He has a lot to live for." He gave her hand a gentle squeeze.

"We had a fight. I was horrid. I said some dreadful things to him," Coral said, happy to be able to unburden herself at last. "I've been very childish, I'm afraid, and I've spoiled everything. I listened to gossip and never gave him the benefit of the doubt or a chance to defend himself."

"Malevolent tongues have always pursued Rafe, unfortunately. When his wife died, people were only too pleased to spread evil rumors about him that were totally untrue."

"Would it be overly inquisitive of me to ask what those rumors were and why they happened?"

"I'm really not in a position to tell you everything. The family did not want her to see a psychiatrist. Suffice it to say that I was the physician who treated Rafe's wife, and I am bound by professional secrecy. But you can take my word for it: Rafe was the perfect husband, and he nearly lost his life in trying to save hers."

"Was he not carrying on an affair with my stepmother at the time?"

Frank shook his head and gave a little laugh. "Rafe has a very strong sense of right and wrong. Only after Faye's death did he give in to Cybil. She pursued him from the first day she came to Tanganyika, but he remained faithful until he was widowed. They had a very brief affair. Cybil tried every trick in the book to make him marry her, but she eventually gave up and came to Kenya, no doubt to try her luck with another unsuspecting man. It is pure coincidence that they should have met again here, and contrary to the local gossip, he did not take up with her where he had left off, despite all your stepmother's attempts. She is very persistent." He sighed.

"But Cybil told me that she and Rafe are still lovers and they have been all along."

"That is pure wishful thinking on her part, I can assure you. Rafe is fond of her. She did help him through a difficult patch after Faye's death, and he is grateful to her, but in no way does he love her, nor has he had any contact with her other than as a friend since she left Tanganyika. She is a wicked woman if she told you otherwise, but then that does not surprise me."

Coral hesitated before asking her next question, wondering if Frank knew about Rafe's claim on Mpingo. "Why did he leave Tanganyika and come to Kenya?"

"That is a long story that Rafe will have to tell you himself. In all fairness, the only thing I can say is that he was a good friend to your father despite the nasty rumors that were spread at the time — " Frank raised an eyebrow " — and to which, I'm sure, your stepmother contributed, knowing her, as she did after Faye's death to drive Rafe into her arms. Rafe gives the impression of being a cynical playboy from time to time, but he is far from it. After Faye's death, I thought he would never come back from that dark place. He did, but not as the same man. He withdrew into himself with misplaced guilt, and that's why he has learned to wear a mask, to protect himself."

As she listened to Frank, Coral thought back over everything she and Rafe had been through, and suddenly the pieces started to fit together. She could also imagine how Rafe and her father had become friends, and how Walter Sinclair came to regard Rafe as a son.

"Did you know my father?"

"I met him socially a few times, but I was not closely acquainted with him. He was a character though. Very charismatic but maybe a little too easy to influence, particularly where women were concerned."

Rafe stirred. A tremor shook him, and then the uncontrollable shivers came, raking his body with terrible spasms, waking him from his stupor. Frank and Coral rushed to his side. Rafe dragged his gaze from Frank Giles's face to Coral's. She smiled at him and touched his burning brow. "I'm here, Rafe," she whispered, trying to hold back her tears, "I'm here, and I'll never leave you again."

Rafe winced as if the light was hurting his eyes. He tried to open them and look at Coral, and momentarily his face lit up as he reached out his hand. But then his features contorted with pain and his eyes shut again.

"I'm afraid it'll be too much for him to speak," Frank said close to Coral's ear.

"It's all right, my love," she replied, stroking his feverish forehead lovingly, "you'll be back on your feet in no time. But hang on in there; you're very precious." She could not repress her tears anymore, and they spilled freely down her cheeks.

Frank placed a comforting hand on her shoulder. "You must keep your nerve and your strength, my dear," he said gravely. "Rafe needs you to be strong."

***

The light hurt him; an intolerable ache raged through his head that rattled with startling explosions as though a rifle were being fired against his ears. Coral… Coral was there; his angel was back. Was he dreaming? He wanted to look at her, drink in the beloved features, but the pain was unbearable. His lids were heavy; they shut down over his burning pupils.

Rafe's temperature was rising. During the brief moments of consciousness, he was aware of Coral at his side, of her cool, soft touch as she caressed his face gently with one hand while with the other she held his. He could hear her sweet voice murmuring loving words that tugged at his heart strings, infusing him with her strength and love, willing him to fight this vicious fever and hold on. He wished he had the energy to explain everything to her now, to tell her about all the things he had bottled up inside him for so long because it hurt to let them out, but the strain of thinking was too much for him. He felt weak and tired, and the pain was so great.

At night he woke up many times. He tossed and turned restlessly, screaming her name, reaching out for her blindly as his mind struggled through the hallucinations of delirium. He plunged in and out of dark abysses, his brain hammering inside his head while he gasped for air, finding it difficult to breathe with pains in his chest. In the first hours of the morning, after Frank had given him an injection, he finally fell into a deep sleep, holding onto Coral's hand.

***

Rafe slept all day with Coral sitting next to him, helping him up, holding him against her when bouts of recurrent chills shook him, or gently pushing his shoulders back into the pillows when the fever agitated him. From time to time, she would urge upon him spoons of hot tea or press a water-soaked cotton cloth to his parched lips to refresh him.

In the evening, Coral rang Aluna and told her that she would be staying with some friends for a couple of days and would come over in the morning to take a change of clothes. Morgana reappeared briefly to ask if they needed anything and if Coral wanted to have a rest while she took her place at Rafe's side. Coral thanked her but said that she would remain. She would sleep on the couch that she had pulled next to his bed.

Instead, Coral spent most of the night watching Rafe and trying to get a grip on her anxiety. She had never encountered this kind of sickness before, and the fact that the man she loved was now fighting so desperately devastated her.

At six in the morning, Frank insisted that Morgana relieve Coral. "You must rest. It will be a long haul to convalescence, and you don't want to fall sick yourself. Rafe needs you, so be reasonable." His tone was kind but firm.

"What if he wakes up and doesn't find me?"

"Don't worry; he'll sleep for another four hours at least. His pulse is regular, which it hasn't been for the past weeks. The sedative I've administered is strong, and he seems to have reacted favorably to it."

"Will you call me if he wakes up?"

"Yes, I promise you. Have a lie down. You can get at least four hours' sleep before he awakens. Morgana will show you to the spare bedroom."

"Then I think I'll go home and have a shower. I need a change of clothes. I'll be back within the next hour, and then I promise to have a snooze."

Back at Mpingo, Coral was confronted by Aluna, who followed her up to her bedroom, questioning her suspiciously about where she had been.

"You were not with your friends, I'm sure. You were with that Frenchman, weren't you?" Aluna was cross, and it was no use being evasive or lying to someone who knew her too well. Reluctantly, Coral explained what had happened.

"This is the work of the *mishiriki*." Aluna warned. "You must not interfere or the spell will reverse itself onto you."

"Look here, Aluna, I've had enough of all your ignorant rubbish," Coral said irritably as she packed a small suitcase, throwing pell-mell into it some clothes and other essentials. "Listen, I'm very fond of you, but all this talk about sorcerers and wizards doesn't have any effect on me because I don't believe in it, and you shouldn't either."

"You saw it for yourself."

"What I saw was the very elaborate stage setting for a theatrical performance, arranged by an evil and clever man to manipulate naïve and ignorant people. I was upset and confused at the time, and it clouded my judgment. Everything is much clearer now."

"Your father was not an ignorant man, and he believed in it."

"Yes, and I'm afraid it might have been his undoing."

Aluna suddenly left the room for a minute and returned, holding a small battered leather-bound book. "Here, he kept this next to his bed. Read it and maybe you'll understand what I mean."

"I really have no time for this nonsense, Aluna. I'm in a hurry."

"Take it, child, and read it at your leisure."

"All right, all right." Coral shoved the book into her bag.

"When will you be back?"

"I haven't the faintest idea. Don't worry about me. I've told you before, I'm old enough to take care of myself. Will you please tell Robin to send a telegram to my mother saying that I've postponed my journey to England? I'll let her know as soon as I've got a new date for my return." She closed the case and ran down the stairs. On her way out, she crossed Cybil on the staircase.

"Where are you going in such a rush and with such a large case?" her stepmother asked as Coral breezed past her.

"Out — now!" came the concise answer. Cybil was the last person she wanted to see or talk to at the moment.

The older woman ran after her and caught her arm. "You're going to Rafe, aren't you? He's ill. I've been there, but they wouldn't let me see him. That belly dancer woman and Frank are guarding him like Dobermans," she burst out.

Coral flinched. "Let me go," she rasped as she wrenched her arm out of her stepmother's grip. She hurried down to the car.

"You hate me, don't you?" Cybil went on as she ran after her. She caught up with Coral in two strides. "It's I who should hate you. Rafe loved me before you came on the scene." Her hands were clenched at her sides, and her green eyes glittered dangerously. She took a step closer, leaning over Coral. "Yours is just a youthful infatuation — you'll outgrow him. He's everything to me, and he loves me even if he's distracted at the moment." Her voice rose harshly. "No one knows him as I do… You'll be the end of him! You'll destroy him! Leave us in peace… *Go back to England and never come back!*" She shouted out the last phrase as Coral pushed her aside and got into the car.

Coral turned on the engine and wound down the window, trying to keep calm in the face of such malevolence. "I think you really believe that, Cybil. I don't hate you, my dear. I pity you," she said coolly and drove off.

Rafe was still asleep when Coral reached Whispering Palms. Morgana took her to the guest room. "I hope you'll be comfortable," she said to Coral as she placed some clean towels on the bed. "The bathroom is next door. The cupboards are empty; you can keep your belongings there if you like. Should you need anything, I am in the guest house." Morgana gave a wan smile. "I moved out from here some months ago," she explained and quickly departed.

Coral felt sorry for the young woman. Morgana obviously loved Rafe very deeply. She recalled her argument with Rafe that evening as they were coming back from the lake. He had said that Morgana was kind and loyal. Coral couldn't understand it at the time, but he was right, and mortification overcame her as she remembered how she had accused the dancer of being vulgar and calculating. Coral was learning the hard way, and quickly.

After she had unpacked, Coral showered and stretched out on the bed. She breathed in the fresh sea air coming through the window and listened to the breeze whispering through the palm trees in the garden. A sense of release swept over her. She took out the book that Aluna had given her — her father's bible, she assumed. It was in French. The title was *L'Exteriorisation de la Sensibilité, une Étude Experimentale et Historique*, and Coral flicked open to the contents page and read the first four entries: Psychology Esoteric, Hypnotism, Reincarnation, and Occult. She smiled. It was just like her father to have such a book next to his bed. He had been a great believer in the occult and black magic. It used to drive her mother crazy. She wondered if these strange beliefs had finally gotten the better of Walter Sinclair and had eventually affected his health — that and the excessive drinking which could not have helped. Since her unnerving experience at the hands of the *mishiriki*, Coral had picked up some books on auto-suggestion and the paramount influence it had in affecting health or disease, happiness or unhappiness. Acts of black magic could apparently be lethal provided the elements of belief — fear, a feeling of wretchedness, and auto-suggestion — were already combined in a person. Where her father was concerned, had these things been present in his mind at the time of his death? If he truly imagined that Rafe and Cybil wanted to do away with him and had used a witch doctor for that purpose, could he have conjured up all sorts of imaginary signs and contributed to his own death? She read a couple of pages of the book that had so obsessed Walter Sinclair and soon drifted off to sleep.

Coral woke up three hours later, feeling much better but anxious to see Rafe. As she was dressing, she noticed a silver frame on the dressing table and picked it up. It was a color photograph of two men on the beach, holding a shark between them, broad grins lighting up their features: her father and Rafe. Coral stared at the photograph. They looked happy, and the great affection between them was obvious. A lump rose in her throat. How she had misjudged Rafe! Would he ever forgive her?

Rafe was still sleeping when she joined Morgana and Dr. Giles in the sick room. Rafe had suffered a couple of spells of nausea, but he'd also had a few good hours of uninterrupted sleep, they told her. The effect of the sedative had worn off, so he would be waking up any time now.

"I'll take care of him now, Dr. Giles," said Coral, taking her place on the chair next to the bed.

"Call me Frank."

"All right, Frank." She laughed shyly.

"He will need to be rubbed down," Morgana said. "I will do that. I know how to do it." She spoke calmly but firmly.

Before Coral had time to say anything, Frank agreed with her, "Yes, my dear, I have watched you. You're good. You should be a nurse."

Immediately Coral tensed, finding the idea of any other woman touching him unbearable, let alone Morgana, who had been his mistress. Coral was on the verge of arguing when she met Frank Giles's kindly gaze which held hers for a few seconds, silently commanding her to acquiesce without discussion. "Rafe is at a most vulnerable stage," he explained. "He must not catch cold and must also remain calm." Coral got the message.

Rafe stirred. Coral went over to the bed, and he smiled weakly. "Coral," he whispered. She bent down and kissed his feverish lips tenderly. The red patches on his cheeks were standing out like daubs of paint on the deathly pallor of his skin. Coral's heart ached, realizing he was a long way from being well. Still, she smiled at him and squeezed his hand.

Frank approached the bed and took his pulse. "How are you today, old chap? You slept better than you have for two weeks. I think we're on the way to recovery."

"Really?" Rafe's voice was faint, almost inaudible. He sounded like a sad little boy, and Coral turned her head so he would not notice her tears, but he caught her hand. "Why are you crying, rosebud?"

"I'm not, I'm not." Coral dashed the back of her hand across her face.

"There's nothing to cry about," Frank said. "Come now, we decided there'd be no emotions, no excitement." He took Coral's arm, his steady hand directing her firmly to the door. "We'll leave Morgana to look after him."

"Can't I stay?"

"No, not today, my dear. Not today. Let's go to the kitchen and heat up some soup. I'm sure Rafe will welcome it after his wash."

Coral swallowed hard as she felt her throat constrict. A wash? Morgana would be propping up Rafe to wash him, she would be holding him, he would feel her against him, and she would run her hands all over his skin... The color rushed to her face. She felt guilty and ashamed as her imagination conjured up pictures of the two of them together and forced them away. This obsessive jealousy must stop. Rafe was fighting for his life, and all she could do was make up stories in her head that would be no help to anyone.

When Coral returned to his room twenty minutes later with a cup of steaming beef tea, Rafe was alone, sitting up against cushions and smiling. She seated herself next to him. "You definitely look better. Obviously Morgana's hands accomplish miracles," she said, hating herself for being so transparent even as she said the words.

Was it the light, or did she detect the old gleam of irony glittering faintly in his tired eyes? "Jealous?" he asked.

"Yes, very." They both laughed.

"Haven't I told you before that you've got nothing to worry about?"

"Yes, you have." Coral caressed his face tenderly. "I'm a very possessive woman, Rafe. I can't bear anybody else touching you, particularly when it's someone you've been intimate with."

He lifted her hand to his lips, turned it over, and kissed her palm. "Everything else in my life now is in the past. For years, I've lived for the moment. I had sex for sex's sake, for the thrill alone. I was reckless with my life. Now I want more; I want to live with the woman I love. I want you, Coral. I need you. I'll never leave you," he said, huskily.

He was agitated and breathless. Coral could see the beads of sweat reappearing on his forehead, and his skin felt damp. It was all her fault. She should not have encouraged this sort of conversation, and she again felt as if she had failed him in some way. Panic bubbled up inside her. What if he did not make it? What if she lost him forever?

"Shush, my love," she said, trying to master the small quiver in her voice. "I know… I know all this. It's just me. I'm incorrigible; don't take any notice. Now you must try to sleep and not think. It's bad for you to tire yourself." As she spoke, she took away the pillows that propped him up, helping him back into a lying position and smoothing his hair back. She pulled the covers up and gave him a small hug, feeling him tense and shiver at their closeness, wondering anxiously whether this was the effect of the fever or whether his body was responding to her embrace. If it were the latter, she hoped that this was a sign that he was on the way to recovery.

Weeks of nausea, fever, and the dreaded shivers passed. Some days were better than others, but Coral never left Rafe's side or lost hope. She had resolutely put aside ill feelings of Morgana, whose only concern was to nurse Rafe back to health. Frank Giles returned to his clinic in Narok, confident that the two women would work together to help Rafe pull through, but he visited twice a week to monitor his patient's progress.

And progress there was. Rafe was a good patient. His urge to get better showed, and Frank had been adamant from the start that it was an important factor for a cure — half the battle won. Coral noticed Rafe's senses seemed to sharpen every day as he submitted to his daily shot, drank his beef tea, ate all he was given, and slept a great deal. After a while, the danger subsided; Rafe had turned the corner. From then on his condition improved markedly, and Coral watched with hope and relief as he gained strength day after day.

At last, convalescence was at hand. Coral and Rafe started off by sitting together on the veranda of Whispering Palms when it was cool, then gradually took short strolls in the garden until they were able to have an hour's walk in the early evening. Tacitly avoiding all stressful conversations, they did not indulge in anything that would interfere physically or mentally with Rafe's total recovery. Morgana appeared rarely now. She had taken up her dancing again at the Golden Fish and slept late in the morning, keeping largely to the guest house, and quietly disappearing for the remainder of the day. Coral silently admired the woman's selfless love and devotion to Rafe. The dancer had nobly accepted that the happiness of the man she loved was not to be found with her and had proudly subsided into the shadows.

One beautiful sunny day, Coral was lying in a hammock in an especially lovely spot in the garden while Rafe was sitting restlessly on a seat opposite her under a bower of white gardenias. Coral was aware of him watching her and was afraid that the magnetic stirring that welled up within her whenever he was near might be too overwhelming, so she was trying to keep a prudent distance between them. Frank Giles had given strict instructions: no emotion, and no mental or physical strain until Rafe's recovery was complete.

They were chatting casually and laughing; it was so easy to laugh in the sunshine when they were together. Suddenly there was a loud twittering over their heads, disturbing the lovers from their dream world. Startled, Coral sat up abruptly, still a bit jumpy and protective around Rafe since her malevolent experience of the *mishiriki*.

"What's that?" she exclaimed, leaping out of the hammock and instinctively moving over to Rafe and nestling in his arms.

He hugged her, obviously trying to ignore the rush of emotion suddenly assailing him at her contact, and laughed. "Nothing to worry about my love," he said. "It's only a honey-guide bird. Come, let's follow him. He may lead us to a beehive on the estate that I wasn't aware of." At the perplexed look on her face, he explained further. "I agree it's a most peculiar phenomenon, and I must admit I've never come across it myself, but I've read about it. The bird will screech and twitter over your head until you follow him. You see, it feeds on beeswax, larvae, and wax worms in bee colonies. Consequently, it needs someone to open up the hive, and it knows that humans are fond of honey. Legend has it that it gets very annoyed if you don't share the honey with it and, if cheated of his share, will seek revenge and lead you to a snake or some other dreadful and dangerous creature."

"How horrible." Coral frowned. "It's such a pretty thing." She watched as the little, gray-winged creature emerged from the leaves above, flicking its white tail feathers and showing off the vibrant yellow streaks in its plumage.

They followed the honey-guide for about twenty minutes and finally arrived at a very old and impressively large acacia tree. "It must be here," Rafe said as they approached the tree, surrounded by a lot of buzzing bees. "You stay here. I'll investigate."

"Be careful. You've not come prepared for this. Bees can be vicious when protecting their property."

"No, quite the reverse, I think. I read somewhere that they are actually very docile." He moved nearer to the spot where it seemed the bees were coming from.

To their surprise, Rafe did find the beehive nestled in the huge trunk of the acacia tree; it was honeycombed from the outside, and loads of bees swarmed inside it. "There is definitely a colony of very happy bees living here," he said cheerfully. "This hive is about fifteen inches tall and deep." As he moved closer to examine it, he got bumped a little by the insects, but to the young woman's amazement they did not hurt him. "Fancy us never suspecting its existence," he chuckled, coming back to where Coral was standing. "It may just be a temporary hive. I'm sure we would have noticed it if it had been there long. I will have one of the workmen open it."

At twilight that day, Rafe and Coral sat on the patio where a couple of months earlier Rafe had served her dinner, the last evening they had spent together before her journey to Narok. The rays of the sun had begun to slant among the palms. The saw-like noise of cicadas that had sounded ceaselessly all day had stopped, and the shrill piping of frogs living among the ferns by the little pools of water in the garden had picked up the strain. Coral loved this patio. She and Rafe often came here to relax after their daily walk or in the evenings, like today, to have dinner. Now their private little place seemed to dream in the moonlight. It was peaceful and still, and the flowers, most of which were asleep, gave off their sweet scents as they intermingled with the brine of the sea air. After dinner, Rafe leaned forward and lit the candles on the table. She saw the gleam of his eyes and the dazzling quality of his smile. Coral thought how well he looked, and her heart filled with joy, not only for his sake but for her own. He had been through hell. Please, God, let her give him all the happiness he deserved.

She looked up, noticing Anatole France's saying on the fountain. Rafe followed her gaze and gave the familiar smile she knew so well. "We chase dreams and embrace shadows," he murmured.

They had talked a lot during the last few weeks, but there were still so many unanswered questions between them, and though Coral would have liked to press for some answers, she was afraid to do so.

"A penny for your thoughts," he asked as his stare glided back to her.

Coral felt the warmth abruptly rush up her cheeks. She shook her head but knew he was aware of her thoughts; he had always been able to read her so well. When Rafe cocked his head, she noticed a muscle tensed at his temple. His expression tonight was devoid of sarcasm but tinted with sadness instead. "The time has come for me to answer all your questions, isn't that so?"

"Rafe… " she whispered, not knowing what to say or even what she wanted to say.

"I know. Sooner or later I'm going to have to rummage among those painful old memories."

Coral continued to stare at him, and he took her hand, covering it with his own. "I'm not going to be able to run away forever… Since we're going to be sharing the rest of our lives together, it is only fair that I should level with you, tell you things as they were… as they are, and clear up all your doubts about me."

"Rafe, I love you. I'm not interested in — " she started, but he pressed two fingers to her lips, his face grave. His sudden contact made her dizzy. They hadn't touched intimately for so long.

"Shush, my love," he said. "Sooner or later I will have to face up to it all again." His laugh was hollow. "Frank says that it's the only way I'll truly rid myself of my ghosts." He took a sip of scotch, his expression bleak.

It shocked Coral to see him so troubled. She was afraid to say anything at all; the last thing she wanted was to press him and make him relive whatever haunted him so much. Still, she needed to know. If she did not, his past would always be a barrier between them; in time, it would create resentment. She gave him a small, encouraging smile.

Rafe's face relaxed a bit, and he reached out for her hand again. "We'll go very slowly, if you don't mind," he said with a disarming smile that made him look very young. He rubbed his shadowed jaw. "Let's start with Anatole France's wise words that puzzle you so much... *We chase dreams and embrace shadows*." He cleared his throat. "When I met Faye, I was very young: twenty-two and at medical school in Paris. That year, unusually, I went back home to Conakry in French Guinea for the Easter holidays. She was there with her father, Stanley Bradshaw, a rich English settler in Tanganyika and a philanthropist who had invested on a large scale in various Pasteur Institutes and other non-profit foundations around Africa." He took another sip of scotch. In the flickering candlelight, his face had taken on a dreamy, faraway look.

"At the time, I thought she was the most bewitching creature I had ever seen. She was very tall and willowy. She had a perfect oval face, features like a Madonna with magnolia-pale skin, jet black hair, and eyes as dark and treacherous as night. She was beautiful and spoiled to the core. I was young, impulsive, and blind. I fell hopelessly in love, but that was only the beginning."

He had spoken with a husky edge in his voice. Coral paled and instinctively turned her face away from him as the burning stab of blind jealousy pierced her heart like a hot poker. How could she be jealous of a dead woman? Nevertheless, a dead woman who had left a scar so vivid he still trembled when he spoke of her. Now, not only did she have to put up with sexy women running after him, but she had to compete with a beautiful dead wife with whom he had been hopelessly in love. None of it made sense.

Rafe's observant eye had not missed the young woman's reaction. "Look at me," he said, gruffly. His tone softened as he read the distress in her eyes. "Oh, Coral, don't misunderstand me.

All this happened a very long time ago. I was young and didn't know better. If I'm upsetting you, then maybe we should stop this conversation right now, but I do owe it to you to be open and frank about everything that happened. I love you, Coral, truly I do. I love you with the experience of a man who's been burned by life, but only singed. Then you came along, with your innocence and your pure and giving love. You made me have a second look at my life, at who I was, at what I was becoming. I realized the mess I was making of it all. You gave me hope, a reason to want to be a real human being again."

As usual, that look of his that touched her caressingly, and now so passionately, drove all doubts and fears from her mind. "I'm all right, really I am," she reassured him. "It's just my jealous and possessive nature, I suppose." She smiled at him.

"You have nothing to worry about. I've told you that before. But you'll learn to trust me. I will make you trust me."

"Is Faye the reason why you gave up medical school?"

Rafe winced at that thought. "Yes... yes," he said. "She wanted me to spend all my time with her, and I was in too deep to want anything else at the time. I had a big fight with my father about it at the end of the holidays. He saw through the whole set-up. He was a doctor, you see. I should have known there was something wrong, but I would not listen to reason. I was chasing my dream. Besides, Stanley Bradshaw, who subsequently became my father-in-law, was very supportive of us and made it all very easy. I suppose he was desperate for Faye to settle down... "

Coral looked quizzically at Rafe. "I'm sorry, I don't understand. Was there something wrong with Faye?"

Rafe paused for a moment, looking intently at Coral with a sadness she had never seen before. He took a deep breath and continued.

"We got married in Tanganyika. It was a huge wedding, of which I remember practically nothing. I was in a daze all through the ceremony and for most of the luxurious honeymoon Stanley arranged for us in Hawaii, which made the awakening so much more brutal and cruel. It was not long before I realized that Faye was depressive — the term used by Frank was manic depression. She had certainly been highly strung since childhood but as she grew up, things became worse. That's how I first met Frank. He had been the family doctor and had been treating her for a few years, keeping her moods under control with medication. To begin with, it wasn't too bad. As time went by, it transpired that Faye would never have children.

"That is when the drinking started… " He hesitated, and then his voice dropped. "The drinking and the promiscuity." He gulped the rest of his scotch down in one go, poured himself another large one, and stood up. Leaning against a trellis, he continued. "I threw myself into my work. Stanley owned the biggest tour company in Dar es Salaam and had a substantial sisal farm. He'd come to love me like a son and obviously felt guilty about the way things had turned out. He taught me how to hunt and fly and showed me all the ropes of the trade, loading onto me as much work as I could handle. I was often traveling. I suppose I was running away. Looking back on it, I admit I was not much of a support to Faye. I was angry and hurt… all the time. You have no idea what that does to someone."

"So you had many affairs," Coral stated plainly.

Rafe did not answer immediately. "Coral, how quick you are to jump to conclusions and judge." His tone was harsh, and though his eyes were hidden in shadow, she knew they were dark and brooding. "Funny enough, affairs, no. A few one-night stands, yes. But they meant nothing — they were just a way of releasing pressure and frustration… and forgetting the pain."

"Surely your relationship with Cybil was more than a one-night stand," she argued.

"I went with Cybil only after Faye's death," he corrected, "and the affair ended when she left Tanganyika. We never resumed it, and you must believe me about that." He shifted his position and took another sip of his scotch.

"On the day of the accident, Faye and I had a big quarrel. I did not want her to go on that hunting expedition. She was in one of her electric, frenzied moods, and those were the worst because they made her reckless. Besides, she had started an affair with a despicable creature who I knew to be after her money. He was going to be a member of the party, and I did not relish the thought of witnessing her make a fool of herself. I nearly didn't go, and that would have been so much better. But at the last minute, Stanley had to attend to some problem on the farm, and he asked me to accompany her." He sighed, shifted his position again, then came back to the table and sat down. He drained his glass.

"I have never spoken about this to anyone. Frank was there that day, but we have never talked about it." His voice faltered as he tried to gauge her reaction. There was pain, hope, guilt, love, and so many other emotions in his expression Coral was unable to decipher. His face was pale, the hollows of his face shadowed with hurt. She knew he was reliving that whole ghastly episode of his life, and the wound was still raw. She wanted to put her arms around him, to relieve him from the pain with her caresses and her love, but she had to let him finish. Frank had been right: for Rafe, exorcising his demons was the only way to heal the hurt and move forward.

"Faye drank all through the morning and lunch. Her spirits were at their highest. I'd never known her to be so elated. I tried to calm her down, to stop her from drinking anymore, but she abused me in front of everybody, saying I was useless as a husband and as a man, that I only thought of money, and so on and so forth. In the afternoon, we were walking along the bank of a tributary that feeds Lake Tanganyika — the rapids there are well known to be treacherous and dangerous. Faye got it into her head to show her friends how bold she was. I tried to stop her again, but she started to rant and shout, so in the end I let her be and detached myself from the little group. She leaped from rock to rock, singing and laughing, a bottle of champagne in her hand.

"Finally she slipped and fell into the water." Rafe paused, and his voice trembled a little as he continued. "The water carried her away. She managed to catch hold of some reeds. I heard the scream and jumped into the water, making my way between the rocks to reach her. I seized her hand, fighting the current, trying to drag her out, but she wouldn't help herself. I kept telling her to hang on, that we'd make it. I struggled for a while, and we were nearing the bank, but suddenly she looked at me and consciously, deliberately, I know it, let go of my hand. I tried again to reach her, but the fast-flowing rapids swept her away, and she disappeared into the canyon far below." He buried his face in his hands, as if to blot out the horrific memory. "It was all my fault," he whispered, hoarsely. Then the heart-wrenching sobs began.

Coral let him cry for a long time as he let go of his anger and the guilt that had been crushing him. She understood so many things now. Of course he had it all wrong. She could imagine how it might have seemed to an onlooker when Faye drifted away, and someone like Cybil could easily have played on that for her own ends, fueling the rumors. Rafe had nursed his pain for so long that he had completely twisted the facts. He should have sought out help immediately; Frank should have seen to that. Her heart squeezed painfully as she thought of the hell he must have been going through all these years. She had not helped, of course, but she would make it up to him.

When Rafe finally looked up, his lids were swollen and red; he seemed ill. Coral felt a pang of guilt. She shouldn't have let him talk. He was not yet up to it; he was still convalescing. She was silent for a few seconds, debating what she should say. Then, reaching out, she took his hand and kissed it in the same way he had done so many times to hers. "I love you, Rafe," she whispered. "I will always love you."

He caught her other hand across the table, his long fingers sliding gently and curling round her wrist. He stood up, came toward her, and pulled her up against him, burying his face in her hair. His proximity was making her dizzy, but she let him hold her tightly for a moment, drinking in his touch as he caressed her head with his cheek. Then at once his body was in flames of desire; she could feel the torment of his arousal. He was breathing heavily, his eyes shining, his hands roaming all over her body. He was not yet well enough; the doctor had warned her against such indulgences. She turned her head so he would not read the fierce need that was making her ache and gently pushed him away.

"Why, Coral, why are you rejecting me?"

"I'm not rejecting you, my love," she said, panting a little as she took two steps along the patio to escape him. "I'm protecting you. You've had enough emotion today, don't you think? We must be reasonable."

"Is that all that's keeping you?" he asked, his eyes gleaming mischievously, the old fire burning in them as strong as ever. He moved toward her.

"Don't, please don't, Rafe," she begged in a small voice. "I won't be able to resist you."

That was enough. In one stride, he crossed the space that separated them, and she was in his arms. He hugged her to him, and his hands found her contours again, palms wandering over her, seeking, finding, and then caressing her with a hunger and a passion that made her tremble, waves of pleasure rippling through her body. The more she shuddered, the more she yielded, and the more he touched and excited her, fueling his own arousal.

"Coral, I love you. I want you so badly," he whispered against her mouth, kissing her ever so slowly and then cupping her chin with both hands as his kisses became more urgent and more demanding. "Can you feel the things you're doing to me?" He slid his hands under her thin blouse and peeled off her strapless bra. The shirt came off too, and Coral surrendered longingly to his caresses, her breasts swollen with desire. His tongue found her nipple, and his teeth started to tease it.

His warm breath and the cool evening breeze were tantalizing her. Excitement raced through her; she was desperately aroused now, and he must have known it by the thundering of her heart and the quickening of her breathing. He dipped his hand gently into her shorts. Instinctively, she parted her legs a little, but he was being cruel — his touch was designed to increase her desire, making her wait, making her want him more. Without conscious thought, her hands slid down below his waist. She unzipped his jeans and discovered his warm and satiny arousal. She heard his intake of breath as she clasped him gently, applying pressure, stroking up and down. She felt his fingertip locate her most sensitive spot, brushing at first lightly and then rubbing a little harder and faster as she moved with him, until they both tipped over the edge of a high cliff, soaring, gliding, and floating down to earth again in the throes of unbridled pleasure.

Chapter Twelve

That night, they slept in each other's arms in his large bed. Rafe was the first to drift off to sleep while Coral lay there, snuggled against his warm body, listening to the even rhythm of his breathing and looking out through the open window at the moonlit darkness. She fell asleep, her heart and mind full of Rafe.

When she awoke next morning, Coral was astonished to find him washed, shaved, and dressed, propped up on his side on the bed next to her, his gaze caressing her adoringly.

"Good morning, rosebud," he said as he placed a butterfly kiss first on the tip of her nose then on her parted lips. "Your skin has the translucence of fine china, so fresh, so unblemished. Such perfection is almost sinful." He grinned and brushed back a lock of blond hair from her forehead. Still full of sleep, Coral gave him an indolent smile and stretched herself lazily. Rafe pulled her against him, into the shelter of his embrace, and she felt how well her body fitted with his. For a moment, Coral could feel him struggling with his desire to take her there and then, but he reluctantly pulled back and leaped off the bed. "We've got a lot to do today," he said. "I'm going to paint you in the garden. I know exactly where. I was thinking about it as I watched you sleep."

He laid out breakfast on the veranda while Coral showered and dressed: champagne, freshly squeezed pineapple juice, the fruit salad he knew she liked so much, scrambled ostrich eggs and caviar, hot toast, delicious exotic jams, eucalyptus honey, and his very special coffee from the Kongoni estate.

After breakfast, he took her to a remote part of the garden that she had not seen before. "This is my studio," he said as they reached a rectangular outbuilding painted in terracotta, with a thatched makuti roof, and surrounded by coral-pink kapok trees and a few acacias. He pushed the front door and the shutters open, and the white walls of the room were suddenly bathed in sunshine. There was both exuberance and a serenity about Rafe's mood as if a big load had been lifted off his mind. "Will you sit for me outside, or will it be too hot?" He took a white linen coat off a peg and put it on.

259

"I shall be delighted to sit for you wherever you choose." She laughed, her face shining with happiness, as they went back into the garden. Rafe had recovered. Not only that, he was a changed man. She had always known him to be energetic and alert, but there was something different this morning. At first she could not put her finger on it, and then slowly it came to her: the sadness she had so often perceived at the back of his eyes had vanished.

Coral's hair was pulled back into a loose bun, and rebellious tendrils framed her face. She wore a white cotton dress edged with lace; nearly transparent and charmingly feminine in its simplicity, it made her look ephemeral. Rafe stared at her.

"What is it?" She felt almost shy under his intense gaze.

"Nothing, rosebud. It's just that you remind me of the nymphs in my favorite ballet, *Les Sylphides*."

Rafe sat her on a stone bench beneath a climbing white rose tree. Close by, a lonely lizard stretched motionless on an old wall covered in lichen while quarrelsome birds hopped and fluttered in the kapok trees, each trying to drive the other away. It was a dreamy sort of morning, untroubled by any thoughts of the outside world.

He put a canvas on an easel, picked up some brushes, and quickly began to mix some paints on his palette, as though fearing that his inspiration would flee.

"Where did you learn how to paint?" Coral asked as his skillful artist's fingers started to sketch.

He shrugged. "It came naturally, I suppose. When I was a child, my mother painted. She used to take me to the beach, and we'd spend days playing at being artists together. We would bring our canvases back home, and in the evening my father, my nanny, the cook, and sometimes one of our neighbors would be the judges, and the winning painter would receive a prize, usually a bar of coconut covered in chocolate, which I remember enjoying immensely." A wry smile hovered on his face, and his eyes were dreamy.

"Where was that, in French Guinea?"

"Yes, in French Guinea. All that stopped when I was eleven and my mother died." A muscle twitched briefly in his jaw at the painful memory. "Then I was sent to France, to my father's parents in the Luberon where they lived. I was put into a Jesuit school as a boarder. I hated it and ran away twice. Once a year, during the summer holidays, I returned home to Conakry to visit my father. I spent the Christmas and Easter holidays with my grandparents. They were very kind but old, and there were no children in the neighborhood I could play with. I had the run of the *manoir* and its grounds. The gardener's sons used to come over from time to time, and that was fun. Still, I was very lonely. Every year I waited impatiently for what they call in France *les grandes vacances*, so I could go back to the sun and the sea and the wide spaces of Africa."

"So it wasn't a happy childhood?" Coral was beginning to understand what lay behind Rafe's complexity.

"It wasn't an unhappy one but as I said, I hated boarding school. Besides, I missed my mother terribly. She was a lovely lady — very affectionate, passionate, and in some ways flamboyant. She wasn't a beauty, but people always said she had charm and charisma, and she was kind, very kind. I think that is the quality my father fell in love with. I only learned about their love story after my father died and I found my mother's diary. Until then I knew nothing about my mother's side of the family. I'd been told that they were all dead, that the only family she had was my father and me. I never thought to ask, and consequently I had no idea she had eloped from Kenya with my father and been disowned by her own family. Up until then I had no idea about Mpingo either. When I came to Kenya years later, I didn't even know whether Mpingo was still in existence. I was intrigued to find it, but not for any financial reason — I already had money. Stanley Bradshaw was a decent and generous man. When I married Faye, he had given me a share in his company."

"Probably out of guilt," Coral was quick to point out.

"Maybe. Nevertheless it was very generous of him — some people wouldn't have cared about their son-in-law. I think he was genuinely fond of me. After Faye's death, I stayed on in Tanganyika to help him with the business — mainly out of inertia — but I was very unhappy. There were too many bad memories there, and the gossip about the accident never ceased. When I learned about my mother's past and about Mpingo, it gave me a reason to start my life afresh. My father-in-law kindly bought my share out. It was worth a lot and would be amply sufficient to set me up without me having to touch the modest inheritance that came from my father after my grandparents died. Somehow I was never very interested in all that. Besides, it only really amounted to the manoir, big though it is. Lawyers in Paris were taking care of affairs, so I never really thought of it being mine. But Mpingo was different. It had belonged to my mother, and I wanted to somehow reclaim the part of her — and my own roots — that had been lost when she was disowned by her family. I admit that I came to Kenya with a view to buy my inheritance back. I even offered your father a great deal of money for it. But once he had explained to me that it was not for sale and he was keeping it for his wonderful daughter" — he eyed her with a smile — "I put it out of my mind."

Rafe had worked while talking, without respite, and now stepped back to view the effect of his creation.

"Can I have a look?"

Rafe held out his sketchbook. The image of a beautiful young woman with huge sapphire eyes gazed out of the page, with a fire in her look and slightly parted lips — features that were absent from any other picture he had painted of her beforehand. He had read her thoughts while sketching: it was provocative and sensual — the way he made her feel when he was close to her. Her eyes were soft and luminous. She looked like a woman in love, drawn by someone who was so profoundly in love himself that he could conjure the intimate essence and perceive the inner-most secrets of the person he loved. Once again Rafe had captured her soul.

"It's beautiful," she murmured, "but you make me feel naked. You read me so well. How do you know?"

"I love you, and I let my heart guide me."

He came to her and took her in his arms. In doing so, he brushed against a branch of roses and brought down a mass of fully bloomed rose petals. They fell in a cascade of snow on Coral's hair. She gave a clear, crystal laugh. Rafe gasped at the sight of her and stepped back, clearly stunned by the image in front of him.

262

"Wait!" he said, seating her back onto the bench. "Stay where you are. Don't move." He disappeared into his studio and returned with a large blue velvet box. Lowering himself to one knee, he took her slim hand in his with infinite tenderness. "Coral, my darling, as long as the sun rises and the night falls, I promise that from this day forward I will love you with my whole heart. I will shield you and comfort you till my last breath, remain faithful, and prize you above all for the rest of our lives. Will you be my wife?"

Coral could hear the emotion in his trembling voice and see the intensity of his love written all over his face. She remained silent for a minute, hardly able to believe what she was hearing, before throwing her arms around him.

"Oh, Rafe! Yes, yes, yes," she said with a sigh of relief. "After the way I behaved, I thought you'd never ask me again." Her voice broke. "I love you, worship you with all my heart, my body, my mind, with every breath of life in me, and I will until my dying day. I think I loved you from the moment you first spoke to me, before I even met you." She tightened her arms around his neck, trying to convey to him all her adoration.

Rafe tipped up her chin and kissed her very gently, then sat next to her on the bench. "Life would never be the same again if you'd have said no." Coral looked at him and saw the mischievous look. "This has traveled a very long way to come to you," he said, laying the velvet box on her knees.

"But, Rafe, you've already given me the most beautiful ring," she protested. "It's up at Mpingo in the safe. I don't need — "

He pressed two fingers to her lips with one hand and carried her hand to his mouth with the other. "Shush, my sweet. That was long ago, in another life… "

Coral lifted the lid, and her breath caught in her throat, "Oh, Rafe," she breathed as she uncovered the sapphire choker set with diamonds, a bracelet, a ring, and matching earrings, all resting on a velvet cushion. "These are fabulous." She reached out a hand and held up a teardrop earring; it caught the sunshine and glittered with an explosion of rainbow colors. Coral was silent. "It's too much," she whispered. "I don't deserve this, not after the way I — "

263

"My sweet little rosebud, these belonged to my great-grandmother, and after her to my grandmother. In different circumstances, they would have been handed down to my mother, as my father had no sisters, but I doubt she ever saw them. She had made a new life in Africa, and they have been locked away in the solicitor's safe in Paris until they arrived by courier this morning." Rafe ran a finger gently down Coral's cheek. "I dearly want you to have them. One day you will give them to our eldest son's wife. That is how heirlooms work, at least in the de Monfort family."

"Thank you," she murmured. She gazed up at him. "I feel we are already part of each other. I don't want to ever be separated from you again." She snuggled against him and put her head on his shoulder.

"Then we'll have to make preparations for a wedding soon." He chuckled softly, bending his head, his lips ardent on hers. He tightened his arms around her.

"Where will it be?" she said with excitement.

"Wherever you want it to be, my love. It is your day." His hands now cradled her face.

"My family and friends are in England."

"Then it will be in England, if that is what you wish."

"No, I want it to be at Mpingo, here in Africa, where we met and where we fell in love. My mother and my friends, at least the ones who are worth it, will be only too pleased to visit Kenya. Anyhow, I don't want a big wedding. I want something small and intimate and romantic." She stopped suddenly, realizing that maybe she was being selfish, laying down the law like this without a thought to how he felt. She colored. "I'm sorry, perhaps you would like it to take place somewhere else? Where are your friends?"

"I have a few friends here, but I don't need anybody if I've got you, my sweet." He turned her in his arms to face him and drew her more deeply into his embrace, pressing his lips to her mouth, her temples, her cheeks, and her throat with infinite tenderness, almost reverently. "To me, you are the most precious jewel in the universe," he whispered. "I will treasure you all my life. Now that I've found you, I will never let you go. Nothing else on earth counts."

"Will we live at Whispering Palms?"

"I thought we might live at the Manoir de Monfort," he said hesitantly. "No one has lived there since my grandparents passed away ten years ago. It is the family home, and it is dying of neglect. It is my heritage, and it will be our children's one day. We owe it to them to keep it in good condition. Will you help me give it a new lease of life?"

"What will happen to Whispering Palms and to Mpingo?" Her voice was tinged with regret. "I thought you loved Africa."

He shook his head, and a shadow passed briefly over his face. "The Africa I know is slowly disappearing, but we will come back every year if you wish, and we'll spend time at Whispering Palms and at Mpingo. Besides, in France your career would have a greater opportunity to prosper. We can come over here for long, lazy holidays, two or three months at a time. That way we'll have the best of both worlds." A smile lit his features. "Does that suit my romantic rosebud?"

She smiled her confirmation. "Yes, that sounds reasonable." Hand in hand, they strolled back to the house.

***

The marriage was to take place in August at Mpingo. Though they knew it would be hard, Coral and Rafe had mutually agreed to stay apart and have no communication for a month before the big day. He had business to attend in Paris, and she was fully engaged in the wedding preparations. Coral's mother and Uncle Edward had flown out from England to help with the organization. The twins, who were to be flower girl and page, were to follow closer to the set date with their nanny. In a month's time, the wedding bans had been published, guest lists had been drawn up, invitations had been sent, the dinner menu, music, and flowers chosen, and the grounds of Mpingo, as well as the house itself, had been brought up to scratch.

The ceremony was due to take place in the afternoon in a secluded place in the garden, which could easily seat the two hundred or so family and friends, some local and others who had flown from various parts of the world to celebrate the special event. Though a few of the guests would be staying at Mpingo and Whispering Palms, hotel rooms had been reserved and coaches booked to accommodate the remainder.

Lady Ranleigh was the epitome of English reserve, but even she could not help reveling in her daughter's wedding preparations, and Coral had been delighted when her mother had produced her own mother's wedding gown, which she herself had worn on her day. "I hope that when the time comes you will in turn give this to your daughter," she said as she handed over the original Worth box in which the delicate dress lay between sheets of tissue paper, together with the cap veil, the dainty high-heeled shoes, and the satin casket that contained the matching jewelry.

As Aluna diligently finished buttoning the fifty-seventh minute pearl button that ran up the back of her gown, Coral surveyed herself critically in the cheval mirror that stood in the corner of the room. The long dress was an ethereal work of art that suited Coral so much, it looked like it had been created especially for her. Combining dreamy ecru chiffon with matching silk lace inserts, the skirt had an intricate cut and molded to her hips before falling with fluid grace in full folds to the ground. The silk lace motifs embellished with pearls and ton sur ton crystal beads depicted leaves, tendrils, and flowers in full bloom — a design of the utmost feminine allure.

"I hope he is a patient man," muttered the old *yaha*, shaking her head. "These buttons will be hell to undo."

At first, Aluna, ever protective and set in her ways, had still tried to put Coral off marrying the Frenchman, despite now knowing that Rafe was not the devil she had supposed. But as time went by and the preparations for the wedding were well on their way, the African woman had mellowed somewhat and warmed to the idea in the face of all the happiness and jollification around her, finally giving her blessing to her little *malaika*.

"Put this around your wrist. It will keep the evil spirits away," she said gruffly, trying to hide her emotions as she handed Coral a white velvet ribbon to which was attached a small blue bead.

"You make such a handsome couple that no doubt you will be inviting envy and jealousy."

"Oh, Aluna, dear Aluna, thank you!" Coral's voice choked as she fondly hugged her old yaha. "Something old, something new, something borrowed, something blue. That completes the set. You've assured me a life of perfect happiness."

"Do not hope for a life of perfect happiness, my child," Aluna said gravely. "Live the happy moment fully by all means, but remember that happiness has its storms."

"You are a born pessimist, Aluna. There you are lecturing me again, even on my wedding day," Coral said with a laugh.

She twisted and turned, trying to examine the dress from every possible angle. The silk slip that lay next to her skin caressed her body with every movement. It made her yearn for Rafe's touch, profoundly aware of the yawning emptiness inside her at his absence. Even though the month had passed in a flash, her thoughts had been full of him. She often wondered how he had been feeling while they were apart. Coral looked at the diamond ring he had given her, glittering with a thousand rainbow colors. Just one demonstration of his love: this morning on her breakfast tray, a love letter had been laid next to a rosebud. She had read the missive until she knew parts of it by heart. In a couple of hours, they would be reunited, and by tonight that union would be forever. Coral felt her insides melt. Her heart was singing.

"Miss Coral, would you please stand still for a while," Aluna remonstrated as her dexterous fingers busied themselves with the young woman's hair, hanging in spirals down her back. "I will not be able to string these pearls through your hair if you keep moving your head like a weather vane!"

Just then, Thomas and Lavinia burst into the room, laughing and pushing each other. The twins were also dressed in ecru silk clothes and looked like two little blond cherubs with their dimpled chubby faces and large blue eyes.

"Quiet, you two," Aluna said, putting on her severe face. "Go and sit down there, on the sofa, like well-behaved children."

Still giggling, the twins rushed out of the room as suddenly as they had come in.

Aluna turned her attention to the headdress. The hugging cloche cap was sophisticated and sleek. It was made of lace and had a slim band of pearl blossoms around the edge. The dramatic ten-foot-long veil was made of very delicate lace, designed to be held in place by little bouquets at each corner under the ears.

"Lavinia and Thomas need to hold this train up to keep it from dragging on the ground. It will get ruined in the garden," the servant muttered. "Huh! Fancy giving that sort of responsibility to five-year-olds."

Sandy, who was the only bridesmaid, came in just as Aluna was affixing the headpiece to Coral's head. "Oh, Coral," she gasped, "you look absolutely stunning! How exquisitely feminine." Sandy circled Coral and chuckled. "Poor Rafe will have a job keeping his hands off you until tonight."

Coral felt herself blushing. Rafe's hands! She really did not want to think about Rafe's hands just now. It was important that she remain cool and poised; recalling his palms roaming over her body was certainly not the sensible way forward. "You look wonderfully glamorous yourself," she told her friend as she took in the bridesmaid's raw ecru silk dress modeled on her own, with a bodice embellished with satin ribbon and a sculptured skirt broken above the hipline by bias-cut lace ruffles. "So very nineteen-twenties!"

"I've got your bouquet," Sandy said, laying it gently on the table. It was the most beautiful waterfall bouquet of alabaster anthuriums with white orchids cascading down, their stems trailing with green foliage. Coral had chosen native exotic flowers in lieu of the more traditional roses and carnations, giving the last touch of romantic mystery to her outfit. "Don't forget to throw it in my direction when the time comes — I want to be the next bride." Sandy laughed. "Looking at the gardens downstairs and all the magnificent preparations has really made me broody."

Lady Ranleigh came in with the casket of jewelry. "Oh, darling, let me look at you," she said. "All brides are beautiful on their wedding day, but I think you look heavenly. I only hope Rafe realizes what a lucky man he is."

"I'm very fortunate too, Mummy," Coral reminded her, smiling sweetly. Her mother and Uncle Edward had met Rafe very briefly, only a few days before his departure to Paris. Though nothing was said directly to her, Coral had overheard her stepfather referring to him as a dark horse, and she sensed that they were both slightly worried about this union.

Lady Ranleigh took out the jewelry from the casket. First the long rope of pearls, which Coral wrapped several times around her neck, then the matching bracelet, and finally an exquisite pair of stud diamond earrings from which dangled a tear-shaped baroque pearl. Coral slipped on the matching dainty stilettos, adding a few inches to her height, and stared at herself in the mirror for the last time before going down for the ceremony. She had never thought herself glamorous, but today she was sparkling. She glanced at the dial on the diamond watch her mother had lent to her for this occasion; she was already twenty minutes late. She must not let Rafe wait any longer.

It was an ideal afternoon for a wedding. The sun had been hot and penetrating all day, but at this hour the August sky had deepened in blue as the air grew more fresh and cool.

The ceremony was to take place in Mpingo's secret garden. Surrounded by a high wall of hedges, a narrow wooden gate marked its entrance and the beginning of the scented walk into the center of the enclosure. The dappled tunnel of classic arches, overgrown with white honeysuckle and delicate pink trumpet vines, led to the Roman-inspired pavilion at the center where the altar had been set up. Artifact containers were dotted around the enclosure, spilling over with a profusion of sweet-smelling white flowers and greenery, adding lush fragrance to the surroundings. Rows of chairs were placed for family and friends on either side of the arches in the temperate and peaceful shade of acacia trees. An organ had been borrowed from a second-hand shop in Mombasa and had been fittingly tuned for the occasion.

Coral stood at the gate for a few seconds with Uncle Edward while Sandy helped the twins as they tried to cope with the yards of delicate lace that made up the train of her veil. The signal was given, and the first rich notes of the wedding march rose in the silent air. Heads turned. On her stepfather's arm, Coral started the slow walk down the bowered aisle on a carpet of rose petals, bathed in mottled light. An audible gasp resounded as the full cortege floated gently along the pathway. Coral was aware of the many smiling faces of her friends and family as she passed by. She was deeply moved by how many of them had traveled such a long way to wish her well.

At the end of the bowered walkway she could see Rafe, a tall lean figure, and his best man Frank Giles standing beside him halfway up the steps of the pavilion. Rafe was groomed to perfection in his tailored morning suit with a starched white shirt and a white tie. His hair had been trimmed, and his powerful bronzed features seemed even more striking than those etched on her memory. The breath caught in her throat as his ardent gaze scorched her with its golden appraisal. Even at this distance she was aware of the overwhelming physical magnetism between them. Her legs suddenly felt weak and wobbly, and her heart hammered so hard she gripped her stepfather's arm to steady herself. Both Rafe and Frank beamed an encouraging smile her way.

At last she was there, at his side. Coral glanced up at him adoringly, echoing his own fervor as he feasted his eyes on his bride. For a few seconds, nothing seemed to count — people, place, or time — as they slipped into that world where it was just the two of them. He turned with that easy grace that so characterized him and took Coral's arm.

"You look incredible. I'm so proud to become your husband, my darling." His voice was a velvety murmur as they moved up the steps of the altar.

"Dear friends, we are gathered here today… "

The rest of the ceremony went by as in a dream. The vows and rings exchanged, the priest hesitated a few seconds before adding with a smile, "You may kiss the bride."

Rafe turned, his dark head bent solemnly toward his bride's uplifted face. "I love you," he whispered as his lips moved slowly over hers, provoking an instinctive response. Their kiss deepened, and everything else fell into oblivion. The priest cleared his throat, and as the first few notes of the organ sounded, the couple sprang apart, slightly dazed and a little embarrassed. A loud cheer went up among the congregation as they turned toward their guests, arms linked together, and started back down the walk in the declining afternoon haze.

Rafe leaned in to whisper in Coral's ear, and she felt him breathe in her scent like a man thirsting in the desert who had finally found water. "I can't tell you how happy you have made me, rosebud. I've dreamed of you night and day for the past month. Every part of my mind, every nerve in my body has missed you and ached for you, my darling. I can't wait to be alone with you tonight."

Coral thought she would melt as a hot rush of anticipation coursed through her, and she tried to steady herself to control her blushes.

Across the garden, the sun was setting, and the late August sky glowed gold and pink over Mpingo. As gray turned to an indigo twilight overhead, simultaneously the grounds around the house lit up with rainbow-colored lights, twinkling and glowing in the trees. People began to drift inside as music wafted from the house to welcome the wedding party, and the silky smooth voice of Andy Williams sang "Moon River" as waiters glided around with trays of champagne and canapés.

Hand in hand, Rafe and Coral moved among their guests. Everybody wanted to greet them, hug them, and wish them well. The reception flashed past in a whirlwind of laughter, hugs, congratulations, kisses, and toasts. They hardly tasted the splendid dinner as chilled champagne and speeches flowed, the cake was cut, and the bridal bouquet was flung. Soon there was the dancing. One of the Kenyan bands from the Golden Fish began to play a heady offering of Taarab music, the beautiful mixture of African, Arabic, and Indian harmonies blending together as the lute-like strains of the udj instrument bubbled along with tambourines and accordions to a wild and joyful drumbeat. Then everyone cheered as the musicians struck up a traditional Kenyan wedding song, "Leave Your Friends, Forget the Dances!" The singers whooped and hollered each line:

"Raphaël, you are now married. You should know,
you are now an elder.
Coral! Coral is married. Know that you are now a wife.
The community has grown. Mambwa has slept.
The community of unmarried women is now one less."

271

The music whirled, and the congregation all spun around the dance floor in a happy blur of smiles and laughter. Coral took it in turns to dance with Rafe, Uncle Edward, and Frank, and watched happily as her dazzling new husband danced with his mother-in-law and Lady Langley.

While they were dancing, Coral, who had removed her cumbersome veil for the reception, suggested that she would change into something more casual before leaving the house. Rafe's mouth twisted into a mischievous smile, "No one's going to have the privilege of lifting you out of this dress except your loving husband," he said huskily, drawing her closer into his embrace.

"Those buttons are a nightmare to deal with." Coral smiled as she remembered Aluna's words earlier that afternoon while she was dressing.

"Then it will be my pleasure to slowly turn the nightmare into a wondrous dream," he parried, his golden eyes creasing into a wicked smile.

It was close to midnight when they were able to tear themselves away from the celebrations under a luminous shower of petals. As they left, fireworks split the sky with dazzling colors. Kaleidoscopic bursts and sparks darted sideways and across the grounds as well as into the air.

Finally they made it to the awaiting car. Rafe's Alpha Romeo, decorated with white ribbon and flowers, slid smoothly on the road in darkness, the brilliant beam of its headlights a unique glow in the pitch black night. "Where are we going?" Coral asked for the umpteenth time since they had left Mpingo.

Rafe gave her one of his slow smiles and lightly squeezed her hand. "Patience, woman! 'Let your thoughts travel to a faraway land,'" he whispered. "'A place of your dreams where you long to be. Relax, let your soul fly away and climb to the clouds and you'll live as never before.'"

"That's beautiful. Is that your own?"

"I wish. It's a quote from a little-known philosopher, Gilbert de Villier."

The car turned onto a mud road and bumped its way down the soft ground. Through the open window, Coral could hear and smell the sea. There was no sign of habitation; the landscape was surrounded by arid loneliness. Suddenly the road curled between high cliffs. There, on the white sandy beach, nestled in splendid isolation among dunes and serenely facing the Indian Ocean, lay the white-washed cabin, glistening like a solid mass of pearl under the silver light of a full moon. Coral sucked in her breath. "Oh, Rafe, how did you discover such a jewel?" she whispered as he brought the vehicle to a smooth stop.

"It's Frank's hideaway. He's kept it very dark all these years," he said with a chuckle. "Even I didn't know about its existence until recently. This is where he goes to escape when work gets on top of him." He slipped out of the car and came round to help her out. Then, lifting her up into his powerful arms, he carried her all the way to the front door.

The cabin was made up of two charming rooms, large and whitewashed, along with a bathroom and small kitchen. A wide veranda along the entire front of the house jutted over the beach with a miraculous view of the ocean, which tonight was profoundly dark, gleaming almost surreally in the moonlight. The power and magic of the landscape created an extraordinary sense of stillness and peace that enwrapped the lovers like an enchantment. Husband and wife, they were finally alone. A cold dinner of lobster salad and champagne was waiting for them, but they had no need for food, only hungry for each other.

"You can't imagine how many times I've dreamt of this moment," Rafe said huskily, cupping Coral's face in his hands. "I've yearned for you for so long. I never thought you could be mine one day. I still feel a bit of a seducer. You're so beautiful and so innocent, my love."

"Maybe not so innocent." Coral smiled as she pressed herself against him, every inch of her body telling him what he wanted to know.

"Oh, my darling..." Rafe scooped her up and carried her across into the bedroom. He set her down gently next to the king-size bed. "Stay where you are. Don't move," he said as he did away with his clothes in double quick time. "I want to make love to you."

Coral removed her jewelry, her gaze fixed on her husband's muscular body: a beautiful bronze statue of an archaic god. It was her wedding night, and she was a virgin. She should have been shocked by his blatant virility, a little afraid of his promising possession; instead she felt flames of desire licking up her body. She wanted to touch him, to feel his skin brush against hers. As she lifted her arms to start unbuttoning her dress, he anticipated her gesture and was beside her, drawing her back into the warmth of his embrace. "Patience is a virtue," he whispered, gently nibbling her ear.

Rafe moved behind her and set about undoing the first button in the long track down her dress. With each disconnected button he paused to kiss her, flooding her with the exquisite torment of anticipation. Rafe's expert lips and practiced hands moved knowingly, erotically over her cheek, her neck, and through her hair. Now as he reached her waist, he freed her shoulders and her back from her dress. Coral could feel his warm breath, his burning mouth, and the cool tip of his tongue on her skin as his kisses moved from the nape of her neck to her shoulder blades, down every bump on the length of her spine, making her quiver and moan helplessly.

Soon the dress slid to the ground. He unfastened her bra with a flick of his finger and peeled off her skimpy panties. Then, lifting her up again, he cradled her in his arms and set her down gently onto the bed. She lay on the white sheet, her hair fanned out on the pillow, shafts of moonlight bathing her trembling body. She gazed up at him, ignited by the fiery expression in his eyes and his obvious desire. Breathless, she pleaded for release as she felt her pulse leaping against her skin and the ache building up more and more within her. She lifted her arms toward him. "Now. Love me now, Rafe… "

Rafe knelt on the bed and stretched himself out to his full length next to her. Coral turned a little and brushed against his muscled thigh. She felt him shudder as her hand found the satiny tip of his arousal. He groaned as her fingers encircled it.

As if about to lose control of himself, Rafe carefully moved her hand away. When she resisted, he buried his face in the warmth of her neck as he fought the passion that seemed ready to explode.

"Not yet, my darling, not yet," he breathed. "This is our wedding night. First let me pleasure you slowly; otherwise I won't be able to stop myself, the way you're stirring me up right now."

She heard the urgent tremor in his voice, and recognized the willpower he was using to hold back. She closed her eyes and gave herself up to him without restraint.

Rafe's mouth claimed her hungry lips, and his hand slid over her smooth skin, stroking and teasing her breasts, her tummy, then her thighs. His touch was altogether wild, yet gentle and possessive, making her gasp and shudder and cry out his name. Coral let herself go, enthralled by the magic of his hands on her, moaning her pleasure. She writhed insatiably, and the more she yielded, the more he gratified her, seeming to revel in her desire for him. Several times he carried her to the brink of pleasure, only to bring her back and raise her up again to new heights. There was not an inch of her body that his fingers, his mouth, his tongue had not intimately explored with loving art and skill.

Finally, when all the muscles in their bodies tightened, when the ache of her need was overwhelming, he moved onto her, keeping his weight slightly off her body. Instinctively she parted her thighs for him, inviting him into her warmth, knowing that the moment she had been longing for all these months had come. His palm under her bottom lifted her up, she arched her back to meet him, and with one smooth, slow stroke, he slid inside her.

Coral's muscles tensed as he entered her, and she smothered a small cry as a burning sensation darted through the length of her body. And then she opened up her body to take him in deeper and deeper, moving with him, crying out his name again and again as they took the final plunge together into space, swept away by the violent storm of their passion, to a world of ecstasy. There they remained clasped, a perfect fusion into one body, locked up in their voluptuous dream, where emotion and sensation merged into one and transgressed the bounds of their senses.

Completely spent, drunk with love, and satiated passion, they finally fell asleep in the hammock on the veranda under the stars, lulled by a warm summer breeze and the sound of the sea. It was dawn when they woke up. Just as it had attended the birth of their love months ago aboard the deck of a ship, today it was the dawn again that was witnessing the prelude to their life together, this time in a wooden cabin on an isolated beach.

"I love you," he whispered.

"I love you more," she said.

They lay there, huddled against each other, their heads touching, their arms intertwined, the burning embers of their love glowing as they watched the long, spindly streaks of morning light seeping glorious colors into the sky, heralding the onset of a fresh new day. And mutually, silently, they vowed never to let go.

About the Author

Q and A With Hannah Fielding

African Adventure

What is it about Africa that inspired you to write *Burning Embers*?

Burning Embers began not as a story, but as a vivid landscape in my mind. The seed of the ideas was sown many years ago when, as a schoolgirl, I studied the works of Leconte de Lisle, a French Romantic poet of the nineteenth century. His poems are wonderfully descriptive and vivid — about wild animals, magnificent dawns and sunsets, exotic settings and colourful vistas. Then later on, I went on holiday to Kenya with my parents and I met our family friend, Mr Chiumbo Wangai, who often used to visit us. He was a great raconteur and told me extensively about his beautiful country, its tribes, its traditions and its customs. I was enthralled. What a beautiful, wild, colourful, passionate country in which to set a love story!

The specific idea for *Burning Embers* came to me one night at my home in France. I couldn't sleep and I was sitting up in my bed gazing out at the Mediterranean, watching the silver full moon shimmering on the sea. Then an ocean liner, all lit up, glided past. It was such a romantic sight that I found myself wondering about the lives of the people on board that ship. Who were they? Where were they going? And into my head walked the heroine of *Burning Embers* — Coral, a beautiful, naïve young woman returning home to the land of her birth. I grabbed the notebook beside my bed and began to write, and the skeleton outline of the first chapter took shape… Coral, alone on the deck of a ship grieving for her father and a love that was destroyed, and the appearance of an enigmatic man, the alluring Rafe, who offers her the classic comfort of strangers.

What did you most want to convey in Coral and Rafe's characters?

Coral is interesting in that at twenty-five, she is still emotionally immature, despite the sexual social revolution that took place while she was growing up. I deliberately wanted to write a rites-of-passage love story with a naïve heroine who was nevertheless a product of her time in terms of her independence and ambition; and it's essentially this combination of innocence and sophistication that attracts Rafe to her and holds his attention. She's intelligent and sensitive enough to realise when it is time for her to grow up and put aside her childish ways. Her love for Rafe teaches her to control her fiery impulsive nature, to start giving, and to trust.

I wanted Rafe's vulnerability and compassion to be instinctively perceived by Coral, despite his notorious reputation, making their chemistry all the more powerful. He's a passionate man with a strong sense of right and wrong. Although he is very much in love with Coral and desires her more than anything, he nevertheless fights to keep his feelings in check; and when she offers herself to him, he finds a way of giving her pleasure without totally robbing her of her innocence. It's just this combination of strength and vulnerability that is irresistible and goes straight to a woman's heart.

Who is your favourite character in *Burning Embers*?

It would be too easy for me to choose Rafe, my Alpha man hero, who in my eyes represents the perfect man *par excellence*. But I also feel a strong pull to a secondary character, Morgana, the dusky Middle-Eastern dancer and Rafe's former mistress. A beautiful and passionate woman, she guards her love for Rafe with the fire of a lioness defending her cubs. As long as she thinks there is hope, and a chance to keep her man, she will fight for her love, all claws out. Morgana is sensitive and proud, and as soon as she realises that Rafe's happiness lies with another woman, she discreetly relinquishes her place and melts away into the background. That's what I call selfless love!

Do you believe in magic?

When I was a child, my governess told me fairy stories. These tales, full of wonderful and dreamy magic, were my first induction into 'the other'. I knew them for what they were — legends imparting moral meanings — but I enjoyed fantasising that such enchantment was real. Then when our family friend, Mr Chiumbo Wangai, visited, he opened my eyes to the darker side of magic with his stories of the witch doctors and voodoo ceremonies of his native Kenya. Did I believe in those stories? I tried not to, because doing so would give me nightmares!

Years later, when I started writing my own romantic stories, I found that I needed to revisit those magical stories of my childhood, deciding not only what I believed now, as an adult, but also what views I would put forward in my books. I realised that neither glowing angels nor wicked evil spells resonates with me; but instead I find it interesting that somewhere just on the edge of 'the other' is a realm of light and darkness. Like Hamlet, I believe there are more things in heaven and earth than are dreamt of in our philosophy. Exactly what, though, I'll never know! In that sense, Coral in *Burning Embers* is like me — bewitched, bothered and bewildered by black magic. But, ultimately, she has faith. Because if you don't believe in just a little magic — light and dark — how can you ever fall in love?

Wanderlust

Where does your love of travel come from?

When I was a little girl my parents took my sister and me on trips to Europe, which were magical and inspirational for a romantic like me. But after the 1956 war in Egypt, almost everyone was stopped from travelling. Throughout my teens, the desire to travel boiled up in me and I don't think I ever recovered. Two or three times a year I reach for my passport and set off. As St Augustine said: 'The world is a book and those who do not travel read only one page.'

Do you have a special place you like to stay?

The Old Cataract Hotel in Aswan. It's an opulent *belle époque* style villa built on the banks of the Nile, and many famous people have stayed there, including Sir Winston Churchill, King Farouk, the Aga Khan and Czar Nicholas II. The views from the luxurious bedrooms are mind-blowing: the sweeping vistas of the Nile, the picturesque surrounding countryside and the lush garden of Elephantine Island. In this captivating and mystery-laden atmosphere dwells much of the romance of a past, exotic age, yet with all the comforts of modern times.

What's your most impressive phrase in a foreign language?

When my English husband and I visit Egyptian markets, the local people talk freely about us because they assume that I'm a foreigner and that I don't understand what they're saying! I love to see their expressions change when I tell them, '*Ana masriya zayak wa batklam araby zayak*': 'I'm Egyptian like you and I speak Arabic as you do.'

Writer's Notes

When you're writing, who's in control, you or the characters?

Definitely me. I am extremely disciplined in the planning of my plot. I have a rigid routine which has served me well. Having researched my facts thoroughly, I plan my novel down to the smallest detail. Each character is set and will react according to the plot and the plan I have decided upon. I have found that planning ahead makes the writing so much easier and therefore so much more enjoyable. I use my plan as a map. I never set out on a long journey by car without a map, and the same applies to my writing.

Do you need silence or do you play music?

All through my research and planning I listen to music, usually in the language of the country in which the plot is set. While writing *Burning Embers*, I often listened to a wonderful African

Sixties pop song called 'Pata Pata', made famous by the South African artist Miriam Makeba, otherwise known as the 'Empress of African Song'. It has joyfully infectious African rhythms mixed with a Sixties sound. Apart from that, I loved listening to old classics, in particlar by Nat King Cole, the Beach Boys, Abba and Boney M.

Do you have any writing rituals?

My ritual is really straightforward. I get up in the morning, and after I've bathed, dressed, drunk a cup of decaffeinated coffee and finished any chores of the day, I sit down at my desk and write. I don't leave my desk until I have finished the work I've set out for myself.

How do you spend your free time? Do you have a favourite place to go and unwind?

I read: I love reading romantic novels — the thicker the book, the better.

I cook: I love cooking, using the various produce of our vegetable garden. Jams, chutneys, stuffed vine leaves (*dolmades*), stuffed savoury and sweet filo pastry cushions that I serve as nibbles when I entertain, stewed fruit for winter crumbles. All for the freezer. The list could go on for ever.

I entertain: I find nothing more satisfying that having friends over; and as I often travel, it's great to catch up with all their news.

I travel: To research my books. I find it exciting and exhilarating. Discovering new places, new people, new traditions and new cuisines.

I collect antiques: Chinese porcelain, Japanese sculptures and French and Italian glass, so you will often find me rummaging in flea markets and dark second-hand shops in the hope of discovering a treasure.

I go for long walks: I love the countryside in England and the seafront in France especially. There are many places I go for inspiration or when I have writer's block.

Find out more at www.hannahfielding.net